The Opposite of Me by Sarah Pekkanen is "fresh and funny and satisfying" (Jennifer Weiner).

TWENTY-NINE-YEAR-OLD LINDSEY ROSE HAS, for as long as she can remember, lived in the shadow of her ravishingly beautiful fraternal twin sister, Alex. Determined to get noticed, Lindsey is finally on the cusp of being named VP creative director of an elite New York advertising agency, after years of eighty-plus-hour weeks, migraines, and profound loneliness. But during the course of one devastating night, Lindsey's carefully constructed life implodes.

Humiliated, she flees the glitter of Manhattan and retreats to the time warp of her parents' Maryland home. As her sister plans her lavish wedding to her Prince Charming, Lindsey struggles to maintain her identity as the smart, responsible twin while she furtively tries to piece her career back together. But things get more complicated when a long-held family secret is unleashed that forces both sisters to reconsider who they are and who they are meant to be.

The

Opposite

of

Me

The
Opposite

of

a novel

SARAH PEKKANEN

WASHINGTON SQUARE PRESS

New York   London   Toronto   Sydney

Washington Square Press
A Division of Simon & Schuster, Inc.
1230 Avenue of the Americas
New York, NY 10020

First Washington Square Press trade paperback edition March 2010

WASHINGTON SQUARE PRESS and colophon are registered trademarks of Simon & Schuster, Inc.

For information about special discounts for bulk purchases, please contact Simon & Schuster Special Sales at 1-866-506-1949 or business@simonandschuster.com.

The Simon & Schuster Speakers Bureau can bring authors to your live event. For more information or to book an event contact the Simon & Schuster Speakers Bureau at 1-866-248-3049 or visit our website at www.simonspeakers.com.

Designed by Jill Putorti

Manufactured in the United States of America

10 9 8 7 6 5 4 3 2 1

Library of Congress Cataloging-in-Publication Data

Pekkanen, Sarah.
 The opposite of me: a novel / by Sarah Pekkanen.—1st Washington Square Press trade pbk. ed.
  p. cm.
1. Sisters—Fiction. 2. Twins—Fiction. I. Title.
PS3616.E358O77 2010
813'.6—dc22

                                      2009018250

ISBN 978-1-4391-2198-6
ISBN 978-1-4391-3475-7 (ebook)

For Glenn and our boys—Jackson, Will, and Dylan

Part One

Success

One

AS I PULLED OPEN the heavy glass door of Richards, Dunne & Krantz and walked down the long hallway toward the executive offices, I noticed a light was on up ahead.

Lights were never on this early. I quickened my step.

The light was on in *my* office, I realized as I drew closer. I'd gone home around 4:00 A.M. to snatch a catnap and a shower, but I'd locked my office door. I'd checked it twice. Now someone was in there.

I broke into a run, my mind spinning in panic: Had I left my storyboard out in plain view? Could someone be sabotaging the advertising campaign I'd spent weeks agonizing over, the campaign my entire future hinged on?

I burst into my office just as the intruder reached for something on my desk.

"Lindsey! You scared me half out of my wits!" my assistant, Donna, scolded as she paused in the act of putting a steaming container of coffee on my desk.

"God, I'm sorry," I said, mentally smacking myself. If I ever ended up computer dating—which, truth be told, it was probably going to come down to one of these days—I'd have to check the ever-popular "paranoid freak" box when I listed my personality traits. I'd better buy a barricade to hold back the bachelors of New York.

"I didn't expect anyone else in this early," I told Donna as my breathing slowed to normal. Note to self: Must remember to join a gym if a twenty-yard dash leaves me winded. Best not to think about how often I'll actually *use* the gym if I've been reminding myself to join one for the past two years.

"It's a big day," Donna said, handing me the coffee.

"You're amazing." I closed my gritty eyes as I took a sip and felt the liquid miracle flood my veins. "I really needed this. I didn't get much sleep."

"You didn't eat breakfast either, did you?" Donna asked, hands on her hips. She stood there, all of five feet tall, looking like a rosy-cheeked, doily-knitting grandma. One who wouldn't hesitate to get up off her rocking chair and reach for her sawed-off shotgun if someone crossed her.

"I'll have a big lunch," I hedged, avoiding Donna's eyes.

Even after five years, I still hadn't gotten used to having an assistant, let alone one who was three decades older than me but earned a third of my salary. Donna and I both knew she wore the pants in our relationship, but the secret to our happiness was that we pretended otherwise. Kind of like my parents— Mom always deferred to Dad's authority, after she mercilessly browbeat him into taking her point of view.

"I'm going to check in with the caterers now," Donna said. "Should I hold your calls this morning?"

"Please," I said. "Unless it's an emergency. Or Walt from Creative—he's freaking out about the font size on the dummy ad and I need to calm him down. Or Matt. I want to do another run-through with him this morning. And let's see, who else, who else . . . Oh, anyone from Gloss Cosmetics, of course.

"Oh, God, they're going to be here in"—I looked at my watch and the breath froze in my lungs—"two hours."

"Hold on just a minute, missy," Donna ordered in a voice that could only be described as trouser-wearing. She bustled to her desk and returned with a blueberry muffin in a little paper bag and two Advil.

"I knew you wouldn't eat, so I got extra. And you're getting a headache again, aren't you?" she asked.

"It's not so bad," I lied, holding out my hand for the Advil and hoping Donna wouldn't notice I'd bitten off all my fingernails. Again.

When Donna finally shut my door, I sank into my big leather chair and took another long, grateful sip of coffee. The early-morning sunlight streamed in through the windows behind me, glinting off the golden Clio Award on my desk. I ran a finger over it for luck, just like I did on every presentation day.

Then I stroked it a second time. Because this wasn't an ordinary presentation day. So much more was riding on today than winning another multimillion-dollar account. If I nailed my pitch and added Gloss Cosmetics to our roster of clients . . . I squeezed my eyes shut. I couldn't finish the thought; I didn't want to jinx myself.

I leapt up and walked across the room to look at my pictures of my babies, another one of my superstitious rituals on big days. One of my walls was covered with simple but expensive black frames, each showcasing a different magazine ad: a dad in a red apron barbecuing hot dogs; a preppy couple sinking their bare toes into their new carpet; a young executive reclining in her first-class airline seat. *Blissfully* reclining.

I smiled, remembering that campaign. It had taken me two weeks and three focus groups to decide on the word *blissful* instead of *peaceful*. Yet my whole campaign was almost torpedoed at the last minute because the model I'd chosen had the exact same hairstyle as the airline owner's ex-wife, who'd convinced him that true love didn't require a prenup. If I hadn't spotted a five-dollar tub of hair gel in the makeup artist's case and begged the client for thirty more seconds, our agency would've lost a $2 million account on account of a chin-length bob. Clients were notoriously fickle, and the rule of thumb was, the richer the client, the crazier.

The one I was meeting today owned half of Manhattan.

I grabbed the mock-up of the magazine ad my creative team had put together for Gloss and scanned it for the millionth time, searching for nonexistent flaws. I'd spent three solid weeks agonizing over every detail of this campaign, which I'd get maybe ten minutes to present in our conference room in— I looked at my watch and my heart skipped a beat.

Unlike other ad shops, it was the culture of my agency to blur the division between the creative work and the business side of our accounts. If you wanted to succeed at Richards, Dunne & Krantz, you had to be able to do both. Of course, that also meant all the responsibility for this presentation was mine alone.

The worst part, the part that gnawed at my stomach and jolted me awake at 3:00 A.M. on nights when I managed to fall asleep, was that all my work, all those marathon stale-pizza weekend sessions and midnight conference calls, might be for nothing. If the owner of Gloss rejected my ads—if something as simple as the perfume I was wearing or a splashy adjective in my copy rubbed him the wrong way—hundreds of thousands of dollars in commission for our agency would slip through my fingers like smoke. Once a Japanese tycoon who owned a chain of luxury hotels sat through a brilliant, two-months-in-the-making campaign presentation our agency's president had personally overseen—I'm talking about the kind of creative vision that would've won awards, the kinds of commercials everyone would've buzzed about—and dismissed it with a grunt, which his assistant cheerfully translated as "He doesn't like blue." That was it; no chance to tweak the color of the ad copy, just a group of stunned advertising execs with the now-useless skill of saying, *"Konnichi-wa!"* being herded like sheep to the exit.

I gulped another Advil from the secret stash inside my desk drawer, the one Donna didn't know about, and massaged the knot in my neck with one hand while I stared at the mock-up ad my team had created for Gloss.

After Gloss Cosmetics had approached our agency last month, hinting that they might jump from their current agency, our agency's president—a forty-two-year-old marketing genius named Mason, who always wore red Converse sneakers, even with his tuxedo—called our top five creative teams into his office.

"Gloss wants to kick some Cover Girl ass," Mason had said, swigging from a bottle of Lipton iced tea (they were a client) and tapping his Bic pen (ditto) against the top of his oak conference table. Mason was so loyal to our clients that he once walked out of a four-star restaurant because the chef wouldn't substitute Kraft ranch for champagne-truffle dressing.

"Gloss's strategy is accessible glamour," Mason had continued. "Forget the Park Avenue princesses; we're going after school-teachers and factory girls and receptionists." His eyes had roved around the table so he could impale each of us with his stare, and I swear he hadn't blinked for close to two minutes. Mason reminded me of an alien, with his bald, lightbulb-shaped head and hooded eyes, and when he went into his blinkless trances I was convinced he was downloading data from his mother ship. My assistant, Donna, was certain he just needed a little more vitamin C; she kept badgering him to go after the Minute Maid account.

"What was the recall score of Gloss's last commercial?" someone at the other end of the table had asked. It was Slutty Cheryl, boobs spilling out of her tight white shirt as she stretched to reach a Lipton from the stack in the middle of the conference table.

"Can I get that for you?" Matt, our assistant art director, had offered in a voice that sounded innocent if you didn't know him well.

Matt was my best friend at the office. My only real friend, actually; this place made a sadists' convention seem cozy and nurturing.

"I can reach it," Cheryl had said bravely, tossing back her long chestnut hair and straining away as Matt shot me a wink. You'd think that after a few hundred meetings she'd have figured out an easier way to wet her whistle, but there she was, week after week, doing her best imitation of a Hooters girl angling for a tip. By the purest of coincidences, she always got thirsty right when she asked a question, so all eyes were on her.

"Cover Girl's last commercial, the one with Queen Latifah, hit a thirty recall, and Gloss's latest scored a twelve," Mason had said without consulting any notes. He had a photographic memory, which was one reason why our clients put up with the sneakers.

I could see why Gloss was testing the waters at other agencies. Twelve wasn't good.

The recall score is one of the most effective tools in advertising's arsenal. It basically tells what percentage of people who watched your commercial actually remembered it. Cheryl, who's a creative director like me, once oversaw a dog food commercial that scored a forty-one. She ordered dozens of balloons emblazoned with "Forty-One" and blanketed the office with them. Subtlety, like loose-fitting turtlenecks, isn't in her repertoire. And I swear I'm not just saying that because I've never scored higher than a forty (but just for the record, I've hit that number three times. It's an agency record).

"I want five creative teams on this," Mason had said. "Have the campaigns ready for me three weeks from today. The best two will present to Gloss."

As everyone stood up to leave, Mason had walked over to me while Cheryl took her time gathering her things and pretended not to eavesdrop.

"I need this account," he'd said, his pale blue eyes latching onto mine.

"Is the budget that big?" I'd asked.

"No, they're cheap fucks," he'd said cheerfully. "Name the last three clients we signed."

"Home health care plans, orthopedic mattresses, and adult protection pads," I'd rattled off.

"Diapers," he'd corrected. "Ugly trend. We're becoming the incontinent old farts' agency. We need the eighteen to thirty-five demographic. Get me this account, Lindsey." His voice had dropped, and Cheryl had stopped shuffling papers. She and I had both leaned in closer to Mason.

"I don't have to tell you what it would do for you," Mason had said. "Think about the timing. We're presenting to Gloss right around the time of the vote. You bring in this one on top of everything else you've done . . ." His voice had trailed off.

I knew what Mason was implying. It wasn't a secret that our agency was about to decide on a new VP creative director. The VP title meant a salary hike and all the sweet side dishes that went along with it: a six-figure bonus, a fat 401(k) plan, and car service to the airport. It meant I'd be able to buy my sunny little one-bedroom apartment on the Upper West Side, which was about to go co-op. It meant first-class flights and obscene expense accounts.

It meant success, the only thing that had really ever mattered to me.

"I'm on it," I'd said, scurrying out of the office and diving into the world of Gloss Cosmetics.

Now I was surfacing for the first time in three weeks.

I gulped more coffee and finished scanning my ad. Something as simple as a typo could mean professional death for me, but our ad was clean. This ad was my 3:00 A.M. baby, born from the unholy alliance of too much caffeine, an entire bag of potato chips (but eaten in small handfuls, with the bag primly sealed up and put back in my pantry between handfuls), and my old reliable bedmate insomnia. Gloss wanted to steal a chunk of Cover Girl's market, but they didn't want to pay for celebrity models like Halle Berry and Keri Russell. I was giving them the best of both worlds.

Mason loved it; now I just needed to perfect my pitch to the owner and CEO of Gloss. I glanced at my watch again. Ninety-six minutes until their limo was due to pull up in front of our building. I'd be downstairs in seventy-six, waiting to greet them.

I pressed the intercom button. "Donna? Have the caterers arrived yet?"

"Don't you think I would've told you if they hadn't?" she snapped. She hates it when I second-guess her. "They bought red Concord grapes, though."

"Shit!" I leapt up so quickly I knocked my coffee to the floor. I grabbed a handful of napkins from my top drawer and swabbed it up. "I'll run out to the deli right now—"

"Relax," Donna said. "I already did. Green seedless grapes are in our freezer. They'll be ready in plenty of time."

Red grapes instead of green. It's the simple things that can annihilate a career.

"Thank you," I breathed as my heart slowed its violent thudding. I reached for one more Advil and promised myself with all the sincerity of a street junkie that it would be my last hit. At least until lunchtime.

I couldn't be too prepared. Cheryl and I had won the two

chances to present our Gloss campaigns, and she was a wild
card. Many of her campaigns were uninspired, but when she
nailed it, she was spectacular. I was dying to sneak a peek at her
storyboard, but I knew she was guarding it like a hostage. As I
was mine.

Cheryl was thirty-three, four years older than me, and she
worked hard. But I worked harder. I lived, breathed, and slept
my job. Seriously; if I weren't so chastened by Donna's disapproving huffs when she noticed the imprint of my head on my
couch cushion, I'd barely have any reason to go home at night.
Even though I'd lived in New York for seven years—ever since
Richards, Dunne & Krantz came recruiting at my grad school
at Northwestern and made me an offer—I'd only made one real
friend in the city: Matt. My job didn't leave time for anyone or
anything else.

"Lindsey?" Donna's head poked into my office. "It's your mom
on the phone. She said she's at the hospital."

I snatched up the phone. Could something have happened
to Dad? I knew retiring from the federal government wouldn't
be good for him; he'd immediately begun waging a vicious gar-
dening war with our next-door neighbor, Mr. Simpson. When I
was home for Thanksgiving—two years ago; last year I'd missed
the holiday because I had to throw together a last-minute campaign for a resort in Saint Lucia that was suffering a reservations
lull—I'd had to physically stop Dad from climbing a ladder and
sawing off all the branches of Simpson's trees at the exact point
where they crossed over our property line.

"Oh, honey, you'll never believe it." Mom sighed deeply. "I
bought a subscription to *O* magazine last month, remember?"

"Ye-es," I lied, wondering how this story could possibly end
in a mad rush to the hospital to reattach Dad's forearm.

"So I bought the November issue and filled out the subscription
card that comes inside," Mom said, settling in for a cozy chat. "You

know those little cards that are always falling out of magazines and making a mess on the floor? I don't know why they have to put so many of them in. I guess they think if you see enough of them you'll just go ahead and subscribe to the magazine."

She paused thoughtfully. "But that's exactly what I did, though, so who am I to cast stones?"

"Mom." I cradled the phone between my shoulder and ear and massaged my temples. "Is everything okay?"

Mom sighed. "I just got my first issue of *O* magazine today, and it's the November issue! Which, of course, I've already read." Her voice dropped to a conspiratorial whisper: "And so has your father, but you didn't hear it from me. That means I get only eleven issues and I've paid for twelve."

"Lindsey?" It was Donna again. "Matt's here. Should I send him in?"

"Please," I said, covering the mouthpiece.

Mom was still talking. ". . . almost like they're trying to trick you because they say 'Save fourteen dollars off the cover price' but if you end up with two of the same issue and you paid for them both, you're really only saving ten forty-five with tax— Dad sat right down with a paper and pencil and did the math— and—"

"Mom," I cut in. "Are you at the hospital?"

"Yes," Mom said.

Pause.

"Um, Mom?" I said. "*Why* are you at the hospital?"

"I'm visiting Mrs. Magruder. Remember, she had a hip replacement? She won't be able to manage stairs for six weeks. Last time I was here I noticed the waiting room only had copies of *Golf Magazine* and *Highlights* and I thought, No sense in me having two copies of *O* magazine. Maybe someone else can enjoy it. And there's a recipe for low-fat cheesecake with whipped cream—the secret is applesauce, of all things—"

"Mom, I'll take care of it." I cut her off just before the pressure in my head began boiling and shrieking like a teapot. "I'll call Oprah's office directly."

Matt stepped into my office, one eyebrow raised. He was wearing a black blazer, which looked good with his curly dark hair. I'd have to tell him black was his color, I thought absently.

"Thank you, honey," Mom said, sounding the tiniest bit disappointed that she couldn't milk it a bit longer. "It's so nice to have a daughter who knows the right people."

"Tell Stedman we should go fly-fishing again sometime," Matt stage-whispered as I made a gun out of my thumb and index finger and shot him in the chest.

"By the way, did you hear about Alex?" Mom asked.

I should've known it would be impossible for us to end our conversation without a mention of my twin sister. If she compliments me, Mom has to say something nice about Alex. Sometimes I wonder if Alex and I are as competitive as we are because Mom is so scrupulously fair in the way she treats us. Probably, I thought, feeling comforted that I could reliably blame my personal failings on my parents.

I sighed and squinted at my watch: fifty-eight minutes.

"Oprah," Matt croaked, rolling around on my office floor and clutching his chest. "Rally your angel network. I'm seeing . . . a . . . white . . . light."

"The TV station is expanding Alex's segments!" Mom said. "Now she'll be on Wednesdays and Fridays instead of just Fridays. Isn't that wonderful?"

When people learn I have a twin, the first thing they ask is whether we're identical. Unless, of course, they see Alex and me together, in which case their brows furrow and their eyes squint and you can almost see their brains clog with confusion as they stutter, "Twins? But . . . but . . . you look *nothing* alike."

Alex and I are about as unidentical as it's possible to be. I've always thought I look like a child's drawing of a person: straight brown lines for the hair and eyebrows, eyes and nose and mouth and ears generally in the right places and in the right numbers. Nothing special; just something to pin on the refrigerator door before it's covered by grocery lists and report cards and forgotten. Whereas Alex . . . Well, there's no other word for it: she's flat-out gorgeous. Stunning. Breathtaking. Dazzling. Apparently there are a few other words for it after all.

She started modeling in high school after a talent scout approached her at a mall, and though she never made it big in New York because she's only five foot six, she gets a steady stream of jobs in our hometown of Bethesda, in suburban Washington, D.C. A few years ago, she got a part-time job for the NBC affiliate covering celebrity gossip (or "entertainment," as she loftily calls it). For three minutes a week—six now that her appearances are being doubled—she's on camera, bantering with the movie review guys and interviewing stars who are shooting the latest political thriller film in D.C.

I know, I know, I hear you asking what she looks like. Everyone wants to know what she looks like. Alex is a redhead, but not one of those Ronald McDonald–haired ones with freckles that look splattered on by Jackson Pollock. Her long hair is a glossy, dark red, and depending on the light, it has hints of gold and caramel and chocolate. She can never walk a city block without some woman begging her for the name of her colorist. It's natural, of course. Her skin defies the redhead's law of pigmentation by tanning smoothly and easily, her almond-shaped eyes are a shade precisely between blue and green, and her nose is straight and unremarkable, the way all good, obedient little noses should be. My father can still fit into the pants he wore in high school; Alex got his metabolism. My mother hails from a long line of sturdy midwestern corn farmers; I got hers. But no bitterness here.

"I'll call Alex later and congratulate her," I told Mom.

"Oh, and she booked the photographer for the wedding," Mom said, winding up for another lengthy tangential chat. Alex's upcoming wedding could keep our phone lines humming for hours.

"I've got to run," I cut her off. "Big morning. I'm going after a new account and the clients are flying in from Aspen this morning."

"Aspen?" Mom said. "Are they skiers?"

"The really rich people don't go to Aspen to ski," I told her. "They go to hang out with other rich people. My clients have the mansion next door to Tom Cruise's."

"Are they movie stars?" Mom squealed. The woman does love her *People* magazine. And so does Dad, though he'd never admit it.

"Even better," I said. "They're billionaires."

I hung up and took a bite of blueberry muffin, but it tasted like dust in my mouth. It wasn't the muffin's fault; it was the unpleasant thought tugging at me like an itch. I'd told Mom about my presentation so the message would get back to Alex: *You're prettier, but don't ever forget that I'm more successful.* Don't get me wrong; I love my sister—she can be generous and outspoken and funny—but no one can push my buttons like Alex. Around her, I light up like a skyscraper's elevator control panel at rush hour. We're complete opposites, always have been. It's like our DNA held a meeting in the womb and divvied up the goods: I'll trade you my sex appeal strands for a double dose of organizational skills, my genes must've said. Deal, Alex's genes answered, and if you'll just sign this form relinquishing any claim to long legs, you can have my work ethic, too.

If Alex and I weren't related, we'd have absolutely nothing in common. The thing about Alex is that she doesn't just grab the spotlight, she wrestles it to the ground and straddles it and pins its hands to the floor so it has no chance of escaping. And it isn't even her fault; the spotlight *wants* to be dominated by her. The spotlight screams "Uncle!" the second it sees her. People are dazzled by Alex. Men send her so many drinks it's a wonder she isn't in AA; women give her quick appraising looks and memorize her outfit, vowing to buy it because if it looks even half as good on them . . . ; even cranky babies stop crying and give her gummy smiles when they see her behind them in the grocery store line.

If Alex weren't my sister, I probably wouldn't be nearly so driven. But I learned long ago that it's easy to get lost and over-looked when someone like Alex is around. In a way, she has made me who I am today.

I pushed away my muffin and glanced over at Matt. He was sprawled on my couch, one leg hooked over the armrest, half-asleep. How he always managed to stay calm amid the chaos and frenzy of our agency was a mystery. I'd have to ask him for his secret. When I had time, which I didn't right now, since I was due downstairs in forty-four minutes. Mason was letting me greet the clients, since I was presenting first, and Cheryl would get to walk them to their car afterward.

"Can we do one more run-through?" I begged.

"We did twelve yesterday," Matt reminded me, yawning. He opened one sleepy-looking brown eye and peered up at me.

"You're right, you're right," I said, lining up the pencils on my desk at a perfect right angle to my stapler. "I don't want to sound overrehearsed."

"Knock it off, OCD girl," Matt said, pulling himself up off the couch and stealing a bite of my muffin. "Mmm. How can you not be eating this?"

"I had a bowl of Advil for breakfast," I told him. "High in fiber."

"You're beyond help," he said. "What time is the party to-night?"

"Seven-thirty," I said. "Is Pam coming?"

Pam was Matt's new girlfriend. I hadn't met her yet, but I was dying to.

"Yep," he said.

Tonight was our office holiday party.

Tonight was also the night the name of the new VP creative director would be announced.

"Nervous?" Matt asked me.

"Of course not," I lied.

"Step away from the Advil," Matt ordered me, slapping my hand as it instinctively went for my desk drawer. "Let's get your storyboards into the conference room. You know you're gonna kick ass, Madam Vice President."

And just like that, the cold knot of anxiety in my stomach loosened the tiniest bit. Like I said, Matt was my only real friend at the office.

Two

WHEN THE STRETCH LIMOUSINE glided to a stop outside our building forty minutes late, I hurried to the curb and pasted on a welcoming smile. I hoped I looked okay. I'd gone for a professional, no-nonsense vibe, which was lucky, since those were the only kinds of clothes my closet was capable of coughing up. I was wearing a classic black Armani pantsuit with an ivory silk shell and black sling-backs. My hair was pulled up into its usual twist, and my earrings were pearls encircled by tiny diamonds—a gift to myself for my twenty-ninth birthday last month. Boring, yes, but safe, too. I wanted my clients to be dazzled by my work, not me.

"Mr. Fenstermaker? So nice to meet you." I greeted the head of the Gloss empire like he was Prince William as he grunted and heaved his squatty body out of the limo.

"And this must be Mrs. Fenstermaker?"

As if I hadn't read a half dozen magazine profiles about the Fenstermakers and studied their pictures so carefully that I could ID them out of a lineup of thousands. He looked more like a meat butcher from Brooklyn than a multimillionaire purveyor of glamour, but his wife—make that his third wife—more than made up for it. She could double for a Bond villainess, the icy blond kind who could open a man's jugular with a single swipe of a nail. He shook my outstretched hand, and she swept by me with a nod, oversize Prada sunglasses firmly in place.

"I hope you didn't encounter much traffic on the drive in from the airport," I said as we entered the building, crossed the gleaming marble floors, and stepped into the elevator. He grunted again, and she didn't deign to answer. I hate awkward elevator silences, but apparently the Fenstermakers didn't share my bias, which meant elevator silence was my new bosom buddy.

"I'll be presenting our first campaign," I said as we stepped off the elevator. "We'll be joined by Mason Graham, our agency's president, whom you already know. But first, let me offer you a drink."

I led the Fenstermakers into our oval-shaped conference room, which has glass walls showcasing a gorgeous view of the city. Even though I've seen it countless times, it still takes my breath away. Directly below us were yellow cabs duking it out for lane space and globs of people buying hot, salty pretzels from street vendors and shouting into cell phones and ignoring traffic signals as they swarmed across the streets. Middle fingers were flying and tourists were snapping photos and pigeons were squawking and a crowd was gathered around two guys dressed in togas who were banging on overturned plastic buckets that substituted for drums. I'd heard them before; they were really good. If you squinted and looked farther north, you could just make out the green oasis of Central Park, filled with walking paths and dog parks and fountains and playgrounds and the best outdoor theater in the world. All of New York—the messy, pulsing, glorious city of possibilities—was at our feet. But the Fenstermakers didn't even look at the view. They'd probably had a better one on the way in from their private plane, the one

I'd read was equipped with a massage table, a selection of rare single-malt scotches, and his-and-hers glass showers, each with six showerheads. Mrs. Fenstermaker had wanted a Jacuzzi, but the FAA told her the weight would endanger the plane. Apparently she'd reacted about as well as an overtired two-year-old to hearing the word *no*.

My storyboard and sample ad were still propped up on easels and covered with drape cloths, I was happy to see. I wouldn't have put it past Cheryl to steal my presentation props. Seriously; they'd gone missing a few years ago and I'd unearthed them in a Dumpster fifteen minutes before my presentation began. Cheryl blamed the maintenance man, but she'd smelled suspiciously like old eggs and wet newspapers. (Maybe I wouldn't have to check the "paranoid freak" personality box, after all. I could probably upgrade to the "anal-retentive, neurotic-celibate-workaholic" box. I'd better hire a bodyguard to ward off the men.)

"Espresso?" Mr. Fenstermaker grunted as he sat down.

I'd read that he was as miserly with his words as he was with his money, at least when it came to things other than his personal toys.

"Of course," I said, mentally thanking last year's *New York* magazine profile for mentioning that he mainlined espresso.

I poured some from a silver thermos into a tiny china cup and added a twist of lemon peel on the side. I turned to Mrs. Fenstermaker, who was glaring at her blood-red lipstick in her compact mirror as if it had just insulted her.

"Is room-temperature Pellegrino still your preference?" I asked.

She snapped shut her compact and took in the gleaming wood buffet I'd stocked with their favorites treats—bagels with Nova Scotia lox and chive cream cheese for him, frozen organic grapes for her. Green grapes, by God. I'd also ordered croissants, muffins, exotic sliced fruits, and fresh-squeezed juices from one of the city's best bakeries, just in case Mr. Fenster-maker's assistant had steered me wrong when I'd called about his culinary preferences. And Donna was standing by, ready to race out and fulfill any other requests.

My smiling lips were slicked with a fresh coat of Cherry-bomb, and Gloss's signature perfume, Heat, filled the room. A crystal vase overflowing with purple orchids imported from Thailand—Mrs. Fenstermaker's flower of choice, according to her personal secretary—sat squarely in the middle of the conference table.

Mrs. Fenstermaker looked at me for the first time. At least I thought she did; she'd put on her sunglasses again after she checked her lipstick, but her face was turned in the right general direction.

"Are you always this thorough?" she asked, sounding more bored than curious.

Mason strode into the conference room just then, his Converse sneakers squeaking against the wood floor.

"I can promise you she is," he said. "Lindsey's one of our best. You'll be in good hands with her, and you're going to love what she's got in store for you. I know you're busy people, so let's get right to it."

He turned to me. "Ready?"

I nodded and stepped to the head of the conference table. The sun had just broken through a cloud, and the room was flooded with light. It seemed like a good omen. My throbbing head, the knot in my neck, my nails, which were bitten so close to the quick that they hurt, my body that cried out for sleep—it all evaporated as the eyes of three powerful people turned toward me. Everyone was waiting to hear what I had to say, waiting for me to dazzle them with my skill and smarts and preparation. The bad taste in my mouth from the muffin disappeared. Now the only thing I could taste was the vice presidency.

*   *   *

Three minutes into my presentation, things were going better than I'd hoped. I'd just pulled the drape cloth off my dummy magazine ad, revealing a blown-up photograph of Angelina Jolie smoldering at the camera. Her lush lips pouted ever so slightly, and her famous mane blew back from her face, courtesy of two standing fans I'd spent a half hour adjusting during the shoot, which had stretched until 2:00 A.M. last Saturday night.

Except it wasn't really Angelina. The people at Gloss were cheap bastards, remember? I'd found an Angelina clone at the Elite model agency, a fourteen-year-old schoolgirl from Russia who didn't speak a word of English and whose scowling father accompanied her everywhere, on the lookout for the cocaine-wielding photographers he'd heard roamed freely in America. The poor makeup artist was still recovering from offering him a Tic Tac.

The copy underneath the ad was simple and boldface. "Isn't that . . . ?"

Then beneath, in smaller type: "Nope, but you can have her red carpet lips. Just slick on Gloss Cherrybomb and wait for the double takes. Brad Pitt clone not included."

The corners of Mr. Fenstermaker's mouth twitched when he read my copy. Mrs. Fenstermaker's sunglasses were still turned in my direction, which I sensed was a major triumph.

"We'll unveil our print ads and thirty-second television spots simultaneously," I said, my voice ringing with confidence, my posture ramrod straight. "I recommend an initial saturation in midwestern cities: Chicago, Indianapolis, St. Louis. We'll focus-group to test the appeal of different celebrities in each market and tweak each campaign before we take it national. If Jennifer Garner tests well in Iowa, this is the ad we'll run in Des Moines."

I unveiled my storyboard for a thirty-second TV spot. It featured an ordinary girl (you'd be surprised by how shockingly ordinary most models look without makeup) taking a swipe at Cover Girl: "Of course actresses look gorgeous; they're paid to have flawless skin. But what about the rest of us?"

A quick cut to her makeup bag—filled with Gloss products in their trademark black and silver tubes and bottles—and voilà! Our ordinary girl is transformed through the miracle of modern mascara into a Jennifer look-alike as the voice-over announces our tagline: "Gloss: Gorgeous for Every Day."

"When we spread to the coasts," I continued, "we can look at television tie-ins. Drew Barrymore is producing a new HBO series about colleagues at a fashion magazine. It's going to be this decade's *Sex and the City*. We'll want to look at a product placement deal."

"How much is this going to cost me?" Fenstermaker grunted.

Probably less than the Jacuzzi you had to scrap, I thought.

"Eight million for the initial phase," I said, making sure my voice didn't contain a hint of an apology.

"Can you guarantee I'll earn it back?" he asked.

"I think our track record speaks for itself," I said. "We can't make you more money unless we spend some first."

Fenstermaker grunted again. There was a bit of cream cheese on the tip of his bulbous nose.

"I could swear this is Angelina," he said, almost to himself, as he looked at my dummy ad again. "Just met her last week. She wanted me to donate to some orphanage."

He batted around his hand, as though the orphanage was a pesky fly he was trying to swat away.

"Every second our targets spend looking at that ad and trying to figure out if it's really her means that much more time for the Gloss name to brand itself into their subconscious," I said. "We'll make the fine print as fine as our legal department allows."

I was moving into my finale. I walked over to a row of three easels and whipped off the drape cloths, revealing three photographs.

"Surveys of plastic surgeons show that women want Angelina's mouth and Keira Knightley's eyes and Cameron Diaz's cheekbones," I said, gesturing to enlarged photos of each celebrity. "On the back of every package of Gloss cosmetic, we'll have a diagram showing women how to replicate the look of their favorite celebrity. For instance, Keira wears black mascara and eye shadows in the peachy-brown family for most of her red carpet events. Those colors are already all in the Gloss arsenal, meaning we don't need any new R and D, which we all know is the real money drain. What we'll do is shake up the packaging and marketing."

I stepped back to the front of the table and looked directly at Mr. Fenstermaker. I knew he was the decision maker; he'd dropped out of college during his junior year and built his empire from scratch. Behind his bulldog exterior was a whip-smart brain.

"We're not just selling lipstick," I said, lowering my voice and speaking slowly. This was it; I was rounding third base and running for home with everything I had. "We're making the childhood dreams of every woman in America come true. They're all going to become movie stars."

Fenstermaker nodded and swallowed a second bagel without appearing to chew.

"Any questions?" I asked. "No? It's been a pleasure."

This time Fenstermaker reached out to shake my hand first. It was a subtle detail, but I felt Mason notice it. I nodded and smiled at Mrs. Fenstermaker and headed for the door.

"Nice job, Lindsey," Mason said under his breath as I passed him.

As soon as I stepped out of the conference room, I lost it. Stage fright never hits me when I'm giving a speech or presenting to a client, but the second I'm done, I start trembling and my mouth goes dry.

"How'd it go?" Matt said as I stumbled into his office, which was directly across from the conference room.

I collapsed into a chair and put my head between my knees.

"That good?" he asked, putting down the photographer's proofs of turkeys—Matt was on the Butterball campaign—that he was studying with a little magnifying glass called a loupe. "Usually you just turn white. You must've done really well if you're about to puke."

"Give me a second," I croaked, waiting for some blood to rush to my head. "He kind of smiled at the end of it. That's good, isn't it? And she nodded twice. Her expression never changed, but I think it's because of the Botox."

"Better than pelting you with frozen grapes," Matt agreed.

"Helpful," I said, lifting up my head to look at him and grinning for the first time that day. Really grinning; my client smiles didn't come from the heart. "Supportive and positive. I think I got everything in. Focus group response, magazine ad placement, budget increases tied to performance targets—"

"It's in the bag," Matt interrupted. "I overheard Mason on the phone saying your campaign blows Cheryl's out of the water."

"He said that?" I asked eagerly.

"Not in so many words," Matt said. "I was just trying to get you to stop babbling."

"You're such a liar," I said, twisting my head around so I could peek into the hallway and see if Cheryl was approaching the conference room. "How can I trust you when you're such a liar? God, I hope I nailed it—"

"Look, can I ask you something?" Matt interrupted again, his fingers fiddling with the yellow grease pencil he'd been using to circle the photos he liked the best. "Why do you want the vice presidency?"

I stared at him.

"Seriously, think about it," he said. "Tell me why you want it so badly."

"Why did I become friends with someone who was a psychology minor?" I moaned. "I hate it when you do this."

"Classic case of avoidance." Matt pretended to scribble something in a notebook. "Look, you're making plenty of money. You're working hard. All a promotion would mean is more money and more work. Is that what you really want in life?"

"Lots more money," I pointed out.

"Okay, lots more money," Matt said, leaning back and putting his feet up on his desk. "But you make a ton already. And can I be brutally honest? You're not looking so good these days."

"Hey," I said, wounded. Maybe I wouldn't tell him black was his color after all. Maybe I'd say it was fuchsia. Unless he thought I was getting alarmingly thinner, in which case, all was forgiven.

"Do you even sleep?" Matt asked. "I got an email from you at two A.M. last week."

"Psychology minors with detective skills," I joked. "Lethal combination."

"Linds," Matt said, using his serious voice, the one he'd probably trot out when he was a dad and his kids had covered the dog with Crisco. "I've been wanting to talk to you about this for a while, but you're always too busy. I'm worried about you."

"Matt, that's sweet," I said. "But I'm fine."

I swiveled my head around again to check for Cheryl.

"See? You're not even listening to me," Matt complained. "You know you've got a lock on being VP. Even if Cheryl gets this account, which she won't because you're better than she is, you've still brought in tons more business than her. Everyone knows you're getting it. Donna even sent around a card for people to sign for you. So can you just listen to me for two seconds?"

"Do people really think I'm getting it?" I asked excitedly. "Who did you talk to?"

Matt exhaled loudly, like I was trying his patience.

"You need a vacation," he said. "When was the last time you took a vacation? And you need to start dating. You need to have something in your life other than work."

"I do date," I said indignantly.

"Two dates in the past six months," Matt said, "doesn't count."

I couldn't argue with that: One of my dates was with a marathoner who carbo-loaded his way through three bread baskets and spent ninety minutes talking about his training regimen—in a nutshell, it entailed putting one foot in front of the other. Scintillating stuff. I'd also gone out with a veterinarian, but since I'm allergic to cats and he hadn't changed his shirt after work, I spent the whole night dabbing at my watery eyes as I sat beside him on a barstool. A table full of middle-aged women who'd clearly been around the block a time or two thought he was breaking up with me.

"He's probably got a chippie on the side," one of them hissed as they shot him dirty looks. All in all, a bit lacking in the ambience department.

"I just really want to be VP," I told Matt. I picked up the tiny rake in the Zen garden I'd gotten him last year as a joke and smoothed new patterns in the sand (I'd written on the card: "This garden seems stressed. Can you help it?").

I really didn't want to have this conversation, not now, and it wasn't fair of Matt to bring it up. I didn't just crave the promotion, I needed it. If I didn't get it now, it would be years before I had another shot. Vice-presidency slots were as rare as solar eclipses. And next time around, I wouldn't be the agency's golden girl. By then someone else, someone younger and fresher, would be nipping at my heels. If I slipped and lost my momentum now, I'd never regain it, no matter how hard I scrabbled for a new handhold up the corporate ladder. I might even have to go to another advertising agency and prove myself all over again, to avoid the stigma of having been passed over for a promotion. How could I explain to Matt that working hard didn't scare me, it was failing that terrified me?

"Are you sure?" Matt asked. "Think about what it'll mean for your life. You'll be locked so tight into this place that you'll never get out. Can you imagine still being here twenty years from now?"

"I haven't thought that far ahead," I lied. Twenty years from now I wanted my name on this building. I wanted a house in Aspen and one in the Berkshires. I wanted a car and driver to take me to work every day, and to be waiting outside when I finished.

"Don't you ever feel like you're missing out?" Matt said, more gently this time. "Is this what you want?"

I dropped my eyes from his. So that one stung a bit. It was impossible not to notice that more and more of my friends were getting engaged. My old college roommate had just had a baby. They were expanding their lives, while mine shot like an arrow up its quick, straight path. But Matt knew how hard I'd worked for this. Why was he picking on me today of all days?

"I—" I began, but for some reason, my lower lip quivered. I cleared my throat and was about to start again. Then I saw something out of the corner of my eye. I never finished my sentence.

Cheryl was strutting down the hallway toward the conference room. Apparently she'd been a bit absentminded this morning, because she'd forgotten to put on her shirt. Sort of thing that could happen to anyone.

"Holy shit," Matt whispered in the hushed, intense way men do when they see their favorite athlete making an impossible play and saving the game. His feet fell off his desk and hit the floor with a thump.

Okay, maybe "forgotten" was an overstatement. Her shirt was there all right. All six inches of clingy, silky, backless black fabric. As she came closer, it became all too obvious that it was her bra she'd forgotten.

She looked fantastic, in an I'm-the-entertainment-at-a-bachelor-party kind of way. Her long hair was loose and wild, and her lips were so full I knew she'd had more collagen shots. Her heels were as high as skyscrapers, and she seemed like she was about to tip over, but that also could've been because of the front-loading. Was it possible she'd gotten more collagen shots in unorthodox places?

"What the hell is she doing?" I said.

"She's playing dirty," Matt said. "Don't worry, it just makes her look desperate."

"Really?" I asked eagerly.

He didn't answer.

"Matt!" I hissed.

"Huh? Oh, sorry," he said.

He moved his seat over a few inches for a better view. "I can see into the conference room from this angle. Do you want a play-by-play?"

"Yes," I said, chewing on my only fingernail that had a little life left. "No. I don't know." I leapt up from the chair, sat back down, ran my hand across my forehead. "Does she actually think flashing her boobs is going to win her the account?"

"No, but putting her hand on Fenstermaker's knee might," Matt said.

"What?" I shrieked.

"It's off the knee now," Matt said. "She's done with her greetings, now she's launching into her presentation. Her story-board's up."

"Why not just give him a blow job under the table?" I muttered.

"I think she's saving that for the grand finale," Matt said.

"Is he smiling?" I asked. "Does he look like he likes her? Is his wife pissed?"

"The wife's on the other side of the table," Matt said. "She can't see what's going on under the table. Plus, she's looking into her hand mirror."

"Oh, shit," I said. I covered my eyes with my hand and sank deeper into my chair. "Fenstermaker's wife is doing their pilot; I read about it on 'Page Six' when I was researching them. It was supposed to be a blind item, but it was obvious. Fuckity, fuckity, fuckity."

"Fuckity?" Matt said. "Seriously?"

I leapt up again and started to pace while I shot questions at Matt like he was on the witness stand.

"How does Fenstermaker look?" I asked.

"He doesn't look unhappy, let's put it like that," Matt said diplomatically.

"What's the wife doing now?"

"Eating a grape," Matt said. "*One* grape. Actually she hasn't eaten it yet. She's examining it like it's a diamond."

"*Look up from the grape!*" I willed Mrs. Fenstermaker the message.

Matt snorted, and I glared at him.

"Sorry," he said.

"This is so unprofessional," I hissed. "So . . . so . . ."

"So Cheryl," Matt finished for me.

My headache was back with a vengeance; I should've known Cheryl would've fought dirty. A few years after I came to Richards, Dunne & Krantz, when she and I were competing for a dishwashing liquid account, we went to Kentucky to do focus groups with stay-at-home moms. My campaign focused on speed—moms were too busy these days to scrub pots and pans, so our soap would get the job done in half the time. Cheryl went for a "same great product, new look" approach by redesigning the bottle. We sat there together, chatting up four different groups of moms, writing down their comments and thoughts and recommendations, and it was clear my campaign was the winner. Except when we got back to New York, hers was the one the client chose. I chalked it up to bad luck. Maybe the client had a thing for phallic-shaped bottles. Maybe he liked the new bigger, firmer bottle because of something missing in his own life (again, no bitterness).

Then, six months after the campaign aired, I learned Cheryl had switched the group's comments before submitting them to the client. It wasn't anything I could prove, just a whispered accusation from Cheryl's assistant as she left for a new job.

"She's bending over in front of Fenstermaker," Matt said. "I think she's pretending to drop something."

"What's Fenstermaker doing?" I asked.

"Watching her pick it up," Matt said. "Either that or putting a dollar in her G-string."

"She's so pathetic," I sputtered. "She's actually a very smart woman. She does good work. Why does she always pull this crap?"

"Because she's Cheryl," Matt said. "Hey, she must be wrapping up. Mason just stood up."

"What's Fenstermaker doing?" I asked.

"He's getting up, too," Mason said. "Whoops—he's following Cheryl into the bathroom for a quickie."

"What?" I squealed.

"Kidding," Matt said. "He just shook Mason's hand and they're all heading for the elevator. Hang on a sec. I'll go take a walk past them and eavesdrop."

Matt stepped out of his office while I let out all the air in my lungs with a whoosh and dropped back into my seat. I felt as weak and dizzy as if I'd run a marathon. Had I eaten dinner last night? No, I remembered, unless you counted the frozen burrito I'd microwaved when I finally stumbled home. It had tasted like the cardboard tray it came with so I'd tossed it in the trash after one bite and gobbled down enough Cherry Garcia to hit the food pyramid's recommended fruit allowance for the day. I needed to pick up some vitamins. Maalox, too; my stomach felt like someone was twisting it in knots and setting it on fire. It was probably the ulcers my doctor had warned me were in my future. By now it felt like I had a family of ulcers living in my stomach, who were all biting *their* nails.

What the hell could be going on in the hallway, anyway? Had Fenstermaker made a decision yet? I twisted around and peered out Matt's door just as he walked back in.

"No verdict," Matt reported. "But I heard Fenstermaker tell Mason he'd call soon."

"Soon?" I demanded. "In an hour? Next week? Next month? What the hell does *soon* mean?"

"Lindsey, knock it off," Matt said. "I told you, no matter what happens today, it's in the bag."

"You're just saying that because you're my shrink," I said, but I couldn't help smiling.

I stood up from my chair slowly, every bone in my body suddenly aching. It had to be postpresentation letdown; I couldn't be getting sick. At 6:00 A.M. tomorrow I was flying to Seattle to lead focus groups for a brand of sneakers whose sales were inexplicably lagging in the West. I needed to identify the problem and restructure the campaign quickly, before we blew any more money on our old ads. From there I was flying directly to Tokyo for thirty-six hours to oversee the shooting of a cologne commercial featuring a B-list celebrity. It was going to be a nightmare; like most washed-up former sitcom actors, he gobbled Ativan like popcorn, so I'd have to babysit him during the entire shoot. In between all this, assuming I won the Gloss account, I'd need to finalize details for our TV and magazine shoots and buy ad space and oversee the production.

"I've got a ton of work," I told Matt. "I'd better get back to my office."

"Hey, Linds?" Matt said.

I turned around.

"You never answered my question."

"Can we talk about it later?" I said, massaging my neck again.

By now I couldn't even remember what Matt's question was. There was so much to do before tonight, which was good. I needed the distraction so I didn't go crazy worrying about the announcement. Dozens of emails were waiting for me to sift through on my computer, plus I needed to review the point-of-sale displays and store promotion samples my team had put together for a new line of wine coolers and make sure we were on the same page as the client, who made Donald Trump look calm and humble.

I'd already proposed five different campaigns, all of which the wine cooler mogul had impatiently shaken his head at while he shouted into the cell phone that was permanently affixed to the side of his face, "I don't give a shit how expensive it is to harvest grapes! Tell him if he raises the price again I'll harvest his fucking nuts!"

I needed to light a fire under my team so we'd come up with something spectacular to appease him. I also had to ask Donna to book my flights. I made a mental note to remind her not to put me on a red-eye; the flight attendants always turned off the lights, and it was impossible to get anything done. Didn't they realize the cocoon of an airplane was the best place for uninterrupted work? Oh, plus I had to shake some sense into Oprah, stat.

I'd wanted so much to seal up the Gloss account before to-night's announcement, but I had to be patient. No matter what Matt and everyone else said, I wouldn't feel confident I'd won the promotion until I heard Mason announce my name. Not knowing whether I'd won was a loose end.

Loose ends made me nervous.

Three

BELIEVE IT OR NOT, I used to be the pretty sister.

I've even got proof: an old sepia-colored photograph of Alex and me as babies, being wheeled down the street by Mom as we sat side by side in our double stroller. My thick brown hair was tied up in crowd-pleasing pigtails with pink bows, and my arms and legs were soft and plump—the only time in my life when people have complimented me on that particular trait. I was a happy, easygoing baby who smiled a lot, even when the Greek grandma down the street pinched my rosy cheeks and turned them redder. Alex, on the other hand, was as scrawny and bald as a plucked chicken for the first twelve months of her life. She also had a bad case of baby acne, she was colicky and fearful of strangers, and her crying, as Dad says, still shuddering at the memory, "could drive bats insane."

I have no memory of what it felt like to have people's eyes drawn to me during that first year of my life, to have them coo and exclaim over my big eyes and pretty smile, to soak up their compliments while Alex wailed and spit up her breakfast. Because right around the time of our first birthday, our family photo album began telling a different story.

Alex outgrew her colic and acne and shyness, and though our eyes were a matching navy blue when we were born, mine darkened into a muddy brown while hers grew lighter and lighter, until they were the shade of a Caribbean sea with sunlight filtering through. She put on some much-needed weight, though she remained small-boned and delicate, and her hair began growing faster than Rapunzel's, coming out in long fiery-gold spirals.

No matter where we went—the playground, the beach, the first day of preschool—one sentence always surrounded us, like the background music of our lives: "Ooh, that hair!"

People would smile at me, too, and maybe even say something nice, after they'd finished gushing over Alex and telling Mom she should be in commercials. At least the kind people did. I remember once when I was about five or six years old and my family was eating lunch at our neighborhood deli. Alex and I were sharing an order of French fries—the good, greasy, crinkle-cut kind—as a reward for going to the pediatrician's office and enduring an immunization shot. Mom was just starting to divide up the fries on our plates, with Alex and me both watching to make sure the other one didn't make off with a single extra fry, not even the charred brown one that had gone a few extra rounds in the deep fryer, when an old lady tottered by. She was so arthritic and bent over that she was almost at my eye level, and I couldn't help staring because she looked just like the witch in my Snow White book. She was even dressed all in black. She didn't smile or say hello; she just reached out with a hand that looked like a claw and touched my head, while I sat there, frozen in fear.

"Too bad this one doesn't look like her sister," she said in a raspy voice.

Mom tried to distract me by talking loudly about something else, but I could still feel the touch of that blue-veined hand,

and I could tell Mom knew. Then, when Alex wasn't looking, Mom slipped me a few extra fries. That was what did it; that's what caused a lump to form in my throat that made it hard for me to breathe. It was like Mom was trying to make up for me not being as special as Alex. Like she was conceding the point, too. I hadn't cried at the doctor's office, not even when the nurse jabbed a needle into the soft flesh of my upper arm, but as I sat there looking at the French fries I was no longer hungry for, it took all I had to hold back the tears from rolling down my cheeks.

Don't get me wrong—my parents did the best they could. They tried for ten long years to have kids before Alex and I came along. On the day we were born, Mom, still woozy and weepy and holding a pink-wrapped bundle in each arm, asked the doctor for advice on raising twins.

He thought about it for a minute, then said, "They're individuals. Treat them that way. Don't dress them alike."

Mom took his words to heart: Those pink hospital blankets were the last things Alex and I ever wore that matched. We had our own rooms and our own clothes and our own friends. We never had to take the same ballet class or get the same haircut. But Mom needn't have worried. Left to our own devices, Alex and I would've carved out completely different paths all by ourselves. I can't imagine my life without Alex, but not because she's the only one who truly understands me, or because we have a psychic connection from the womb. It's because I've spent my entire life pushing away from Alex, like a swimmer using the force of a concrete wall to do a flip turn and kick away in the opposite direction.

I learned early on that if I embraced the same things Alex did, like popularity and flirting and fun, I'd always come in such a distant second that everyone would've lost interest and gone home by the time I reached the finish line. Alex was chosen for the homecoming court during our freshman *and* senior years of high school; she got to skip school to model in junior fashion shows for Saks Fifth Avenue and Macy's; she dumped the captain of the football team at the end of football season and started dating the captain of the basketball team just in time for their first game. As she flitted through the halls of our high school in the cheerleader's skirt that swished around her long legs, it was obvious from the stares following her that every girl wanted to be her, and every guy was secretly in love with her.

So unless I wanted to go through life being invisible, I had to figure out another way to get noticed, one that didn't require a perfect smile or long eyelashes or a size-four body. I learned that if I studied hard and brought home straight A's, the principal would call me up onto the stage at the end of the year to give me a certificate while my parents beamed in the audience. I learned that if I crammed four years of college into three and made the dean's list every semester, employers would come recruiting me. I learned that if I took a job in New York and made six figures and worked until my head felt like it was about to explode and my body felt like it belonged to a woman twice my age, I could fill out the questionnaires for my high school reunions with updates about my life that were sure to impress my former classmates.

Sometimes when I lay awake in the middle of the night, thinking about everything I needed to get done the next day, my mind would race so quickly that I'd feel dizzy and panicky. I'd toss and turn, my silk sheets twisting around me like snakes. Nothing could soothe me—not a comedy on my wide-screen plasma TV or the softness of my cashmere throw pillows or the vivid colors of the original abstract painting I'd bought at a Soho gallery with my very first bonus.

During those dark, endless hours, as lists flew through my

mind and my heart pounded, I sometimes thought about what would have happened to me if I hadn't had to fight so hard to carve out my own identity, one that would keep me from fading into a shadow when my twin sister was around. Would I be this driven, this fixated on success, if I'd been born into another family?

During those long, lonely nights when my body cried out for sleep but my mind refused to allow it, I sometimes wondered: If Alex wasn't my sister, would I be a completely different person?

"Are you sleeping?"

Matt's incredulous voice cut through my dream, a sweaty, fearful one in which I raced through an airport, trying to catch a plane that was about to take off, desperately running faster and faster even though I could see the gate agent close the door to the Jetway and stand in front of it with her arms crossed, shaking her head at me.

I lifted my head up off my desk and blinked groggily. Matt was standing in my office doorway, his preschool-teacher girlfriend by his side. A sheet of paper was stuck to my cheek, probably affixed with drool. A good first impression at all costs—that's my motto.

"I thought you never slept," Matt said.

"I was just resting for a second," I said. God, I sounded exactly like my father. I pulled the sheet of paper off my cheek and prayed my lipstick wasn't smeared across my face.

"Hi," I said to Matt's girlfriend. "I'm Lindsey, and I swear I'm usually more alert than this."

"I'm Pammy," she said, smiling sweetly. Pammy? I could forgive her for it, I decided. She was tiny and blond and looked perfect for Matt; his last girlfriend had been a moody vegetarian who always made scenes in restaurants by grilling the waiter about ingredients in various dishes.

"You're going to be late," Matt said. "You've got five minutes to change. We'll wait for you downstairs."

It was like he'd thrown a bucket of ice water over me. I leapt up from my chair and snatched the hanging bag off the hook on the back of my door. How could I have forgotten what night it was? I looked at my watch: It was five-thirty, and I'd been asleep for two whole hours. This was impossible; I never napped. Why hadn't my phones woken me up? Why hadn't anyone come into my office? The answer came to me in a rush: Donna. Sure enough, the sheet of paper that had been stuck to my cheek was covered in her spidery scrawl: "I'm holding your calls and telling everyone you're in a meeting. You need to rest or you're going to make yourself sick."

For the love of God, why couldn't I be the boss in anything but name around here?

I had five minutes to get ready, five measly minutes to make myself look presentable for the announcement that could change my entire future. I could do this, though; I was used to pulling rabbits out of hats around here. I unzipped my garment bag and pulled out the black silk dress a personal shopper had picked for me at Saks. It was simple and conservative, but elegant, too, I hoped. I raced to the bathroom, changed, and slipped into the shoes the shopper had tucked in the bottom of the garment bag. They fit perfectly, the heels weren't too high, and their style was classic. I made a mental note to use this shopper again; she could actually follow instructions, unlike the last one, who'd added holiday-themed sweaters to the clothes she sent over. I may not be a fashionista, but I know it's a hanging offense to wear anything featuring Rudolph's blinking red nose.

I rinsed out my mouth with cold water, splashed some

more on my cheeks, and spritzed on a little perfume. Then I leaned toward the mirror and studied my reflection. My hair was still twisted up and looked okay, but I really needed some concealer for the dark circles under my eyes and eye drops to get out the redness. The only makeup in my purse, however, was my Cherrybomb lipstick. I'd never liked makeup, probably because Alex kept telling me how much better I'd look with it. I slicked on a light coat of lipstick, just to give my face some color. Matt was right; I did look kind of pale, even with all that sleep.

I told myself I'd look better in the dim light of the party, especially because by then the crease marks on my face from sleeping on a wrinkled piece of paper would have faded. I popped a piece of cinnamon gum in my mouth and raced for the elevator.

"It's a Christmas miracle," Matt said as I stepped into the lobby. "C'mon, I've got a cab waiting."

We hurried to the curb and smushed ourselves into the backseat of the taxi, with Matt in the middle. I moved my leg as far away from his as possible so Pammy wouldn't feel jealous. The hairy-armpit vegetarian had hated me because she knew how close Matt and I were and it threatened her (my new suede purse hadn't helped matters, either—but I swear I only got it because it was on sale). But she never had any reason to feel threatened; Matt was just a friend. My best friend, really. There was no way we'd ever get involved.

Sure, the thought had entered my mind, but I'd given it a swift kick in the rear so it didn't get any funny ideas about my brain being a nice place to settle down in. Two years ago, Matt and I had both worked late one Saturday night, then caught dinner at this little Italian place with the best gnocchi ever. Two bottles of Chianti later, we'd ended up at Matt's apartment watching *Casablanca* (yes, we'd covered every possible romantic stereotype that night). As we sat side by side on his love seat (see!), I realized just how easy it would be to snuggle closer to him, to send a signal and see if he'd scoop it up and run with it. I could lean my head to the right and rest it on his shoulder. Six inches of space was the only thing that prevented me from forever changing the tenor of our relationship. The three glasses of wine I'd consumed made it all seem so simple.

I turned to look at him, and discovered he was staring at me instead of the movie. Our faces were so close I could see tiny flecks of green in his brown eyes. I'd never felt any wild attraction for Matt before. He's got a roundish face, curly dark hair, and he's about five eight—he's a teddy bear of a man, not a Harlequin hero who makes panties spontaneously combust. But in that moment, as I looked into his kind eyes with the smile creases at the corners, he was irresistible. So I leapt up and raced around his apartment, looking for my shoes and babbling about how tired I was. In retrospect, given that I was jumping around like someone who was repeatedly being mildly electrocuted, it probably wasn't the most believable excuse. But I was terrified.

What if Matt and I did get together, then broke up? What if my perfectionist tendencies—fine, neuroses—drove him insane and I couldn't live with his habit of leaving his toenail clippings in neat little piles in the bathroom? (I'm not sure why this is the hypothetical deal breaker I came up with, but it's probably best not to dwell on what it says about my psyche.)

But in those frozen seconds as Matt and I stared at each other, I'd fast-forwarded through our relationship and leapt smack into the middle of our breakup, and I'd glimpsed what my future would look like without him. It was like looking into a dark, lonely abyss. If he and I ended up not liking each other, I'd have no one in New York who truly cared about me. I wouldn't have a single real friend. Matt was the only person

I could complain to about work, the only person I knew who loved black-olive-and-mushroom late-night pizzas as much as I did, the only person who still liked me when I was tired and anal and insecure. I couldn't risk losing him—the abyss was too scary to contemplate—so I fled his apartment and hurried to the safety of my own. We hadn't been alone in his apartment since; I'd made sure of it.

"Turn right at the next corner," Matt instructed the driver as we neared the club.

"You ready for this?" he asked me.

"Absolutely," I lied. My heart was pounding again, and I felt light-headed, probably from skipping lunch. You'd think missing all those meals would be great for my waistline, but I heroically managed to make up the calorie deficit when I got home at night. Now, though, it was more than an empty stomach that was making me feel like I was about to pass out.

"It's going to be fun," Pammy chirped. I smiled at her and tried to shake off my anxiety. She really was adorable; all sunny and petite and friendly. And did I mention petite? I'd work really hard at overlooking the fact that both of her thighs could fit into one of my pants legs.

"You can let us off here," Matt said, and he paid the driver while Pammy slid out.

"She's cute," I whispered.

"You think so?" Matt asked me while the driver painstakingly counted out change. It's my theory that most cabdrivers take their time giving change in the hope that hyperactive New Yorkers will shout, "Oh, for Christ's sake, just keep it!" and race away.

We slid out of the car, Matt took Pammy's witty-bitty little hand in his, and a bouncer stepped aside and pulled opened the door to Night Fever. A blast of music hit me and almost propelled me back a few feet. Ah, now the name of the club made sense. A Bee Gee was wailing in what could've been misery but just as easily could've been ecstasy, a waitress with Farrah Fawcett hair and love beads passed by with steaming red-and-green-colored drinks on a tray, and even Mason was wearing bell-bottoms. Welcome to the seventies, because apparently we didn't get enough of them the first time around.

"Matt, great to see you!" Mason shouted, detaching himself from a knot of people and walking over to us. "Lindsey, can I borrow you for a second?"

Without waiting for my answer, he pulled me past a giant TV screen that was suspended from the ceiling. It was airing our top commercials of the year in a continuous loop. Every two feet or so, a waiter wearing John Lennon glasses or platform shoes was passing around a fresh tray of drinks, which meant new and inventive combinations of colleagues would hook up tonight and spend the next year suffering violent coughing fits and looking at the floor whenever they bumped into each other in the office hallways. In the weeks after our holiday parties, it always sounded as though our office had been hit with a record number of cases of bronchitis.

Mason motioned toward a corner, where oversize beanbag chairs were clustered in a semicircle under a disco light.

"Any word from Fenstermaker?" I blurted, eyeing a chair and deciding that, if I sat down, I'd never be able to get enough traction to stand back up again.

"Not yet," he said. "It may take him a few days to decide. Look, there's nothing to be nervous about. I wanted to tell you that you've done a great job for us this year. A great job."

Mason was slurring his words ever so slightly; those holiday-colored drinks must have been potent. I made a mental note to order a seltzer with lime that could masquerade as a gin and tonic.

"Thanks," I said. "That means a lot."

He leaned closer and whispered, "I shouldn't tell you this, but we voted this afternoon."

Time shuddered to a stop. I could feel each individual hair on my arms stand up.

"What?" I croaked.

"You're the new VP creative director," Mason said.

I closed my eyes as relief crashed over me, making my legs weak and unsteady. I'd done it; I was the youngest ever vice president creative director of Richards, Dunne & Krantz. All the vacations I never took, the movies I'd missed seeing, the weekend mornings when I got up to work while everyone else slept in or curled up with the *Times* or went hiking in the sunshine— they had all culminated in this glorious moment. Now I could buy my apartment. I could celebrate by splurging on any restaurant in the city, and even take a car service there instead of a cab. Maybe I'd make a grand gesture at Christmas and hand my parents plane tickets to Europe. I'd get a bigger office, one with an amazing view. I'd get my own monogrammed company stationery! I couldn't wait to get to a phone and call my parents and Alex. Inside I was exploding in joy, but I kept my face calm and professional.

Mason grabbed a passing waiter. "Get this lady a glass of champagne."

"I can't thank you enough," I started to say, but Mason interrupted me.

"You earned it," he said simply, smiling at me. How could I ever have thought Mason was an alien? He was the warmest, kindest man alive. A beautiful, beautiful specimen of a man. He should be an exhibit in MoMA.

"I'll announce it in about an hour," he said. "I want you to say a few words, too."

"Absolutely," I said, a giddy grin spreading across my face.

I took a gulp of champagne to hide the fact that I was blinking back tears of joy. It was sweet and delicious against my parched throat. God, I loved champagne. Why didn't I drink it more often? I should drink it every day. I should *bathe* in it.

"Enjoy," Mason said. "I'll signal you when it's time."

He walked away, and I hurried over to Matt and Pam, who were watching a copywriter attempt the hustle on the orange-and-avocado shag carpet.

"I'm declaring a new law for company holiday parties," Matt announced. "No one should ever see their coworkers dance or wear bathing suits."

"Oh, God, that's funny!" I said, laughing hysterically.

Matt took a closer look at me as I wiped the giddy tears from the corners of my eyes. "Are you pregnant?" he asked.

"Mattie!" Pammy chastised him. But she cast a discreet glance at my stomach as I instinctively sucked in. "You should never ask a woman that!"

"Either you're pregnant or you just got named VP," Matt said. "Because you're glowing brighter than those Lava lamps."

I couldn't help the huge grin from spreading across my face.

"You did it, didn't you?" Matt said, tapping his glass against mine. "Like it's a surprise."

"Congratulations!" Pammy squealed. "You're a vice president?"

"Keep it a secret," I begged them both. "Mason's not going to announce it for another hour."

"You look really happy," Matt said. "Good for you."

"It's kind of overwhelming," I said. "But I am happy. Really happy."

"Happy about what?" Someone stuck his face so close to mine that I could smell his lime-scented aftershave. I twisted to the right and found myself staring at Doug, one of the copywriters on my team.

Doug's gorgeous, if you like your men big, rawboned, and

as subtle as sledgehammers. Every woman in the office has a secret crush on him, and he seems intent on fulfilling all of their fantasies, one at a time. Or two at a time, if you believe the stories of what went on after last year's holiday party.

"And who's this?" Doug asked, turning to Pammy with a smile. Matt put an arm around her and pulled her closer.

"Pammy," Matt said tightly. "My girlfriend."

Doug held up his hands as if to say: *No harm, no foul, man— plenty more where that one came from.*

"Why so happy?" Doug asked me. "Are you the new VP yet?"

Matt saved me: "No, we were just talking about Lava lamps. Lindsey loves them."

"Seriously?" Doug said. "That's cool. So can I get you a drink, Lindsey? Pammy?"

"I'm good," Pammy said.

"Why not?" I said. Forget the seltzer; what harm could there be in downing a couple of glasses of champagne on the best night of my life?

"Hey now," Doug said, his head whiplashing toward the front door. Cheryl was making her grand entrance. She was still wearing the nonshirt she'd had on at her pitch for Gloss. The shirt hadn't gotten any bigger; if anything, it had caught the flu and lost a few pounds.

Doug was off like a shot to greet her.

"You may have to wait awhile for that drink," Matt told me.

"You think?" I said sarcastically. By now three other guys were vying for airtime with Cheryl.

"I should go on over and wish her luck on the Gloss account," I said. It was customary for competing creative teams to wish each other the best, much like boxers tapping mitts before beating each other to a pulp.

"I'll get the drinks," Matt said, and he waved down a waiter as I headed toward Cheryl. God, this was turning out to be an amazing day. My exhaustion was gone. Now I felt like I could stay up all night.

I was only a few steps away from Cheryl when my BlackBerry vibrated in my jacket pocket. I pulled it out and looked at the message:

You'll never believe where I am and who I'm with. Call me.

I smiled. The message was from my old buddy Bradley Church. I hadn't talked to Bradley in weeks, maybe even a couple of months. I'd call him later tonight, I promised myself. Getting his message made me realize how much I'd missed him. Bradley and I had officially become friends in the second grade when the class bully tripped Megan Scully in our school lunchroom, making her fall splat on top of her tray of mystery loaf. As she sat there groping for her glasses and crying, Bradley had quietly uncapped the bottle of ketchup on our table and dumped some into the bully's glass of orange juice. The bully went to swig his juice and ended up spitting it all over his white shirt.

When the bully started clenching his fists and looking around for the culprit, I tiptoed over and slid into the seat next to Bradley's and pretended we'd been chatting the whole time. We'd stayed pals ever since that moment, even going to our senior prom together as friends, but we didn't see each other much these days. Bradley still lived in our old neighborhood and worked as a photographer for *The Washington Post*. His portrait of a nine-year-old girl sleeping on her living room floor with the fireplace lit up for warmth while her mother stared at a stack of unpaid bills had just won an award.

Bradley was still sticking up for the underdog, I thought, smiling fondly as I visualized his face.

I'd call him right after I phoned my parents and Alex, I decided as I approached Cheryl and fought my way through the crowd of guys jockeying for position around her.

"Cheryl? Just wanted to wish you luck," I said, putting out my hand.

She looked down at it for a long moment before shaking it.

"Thanks," she said. She dimpled up as one of the account executives handed her a red drink that exactly matched her lip color.

"I doubt we'll hear anything for a few days, so I guess we can relax," I said. Now that I was going to be VP, I'd have to try to make peace with Cheryl. She'd be working for me, after all.

"Oh, I think we'll hear a lot sooner than that," she said, taking a sip of her drink and holding our eye contact above the rim of her glass.

Something about the gleam in her eyes sent a shiver down my spine.

"Really?" I asked, trying to affect a careless giggle that somehow came out like a Woody Woodpecker laugh (men *love* this, I'm told—it probably accounts for my runaway success in dating).

"What makes you say that?" I asked Cheryl. "Mason said Fenstermaker hadn't decided yet."

Cheryl stared at me for another beat and licked her shiny red lips as I forced myself to hold her gaze. It was a power play; that's all it was, I told myself. She was trying to throw me. Even that predatory lip-licking thing was probably a move she'd seen on Animal Planet and rehearsed in front of the mirror.

"Oh, just call it a feeling," she said and turned away from me.

I stared after her, trying to shake the sense of unease creeping over me. I felt like a deer in the woods who has just caught the scent of a hunter. Something was wrong.

Cheryl knew I had the promotion lined up; she was just playing her usual games, I told myself. I had nothing to worry about.

But . . . why the hell did she look so confident? She should be kissing up to me.

I started to walk slowly back across the bar to Matt and Pammy. Trust Cheryl to try to put a damper on the best day of my life. She was just jealous. I needed to forget about her and start planning my speech. I glanced at my watch for the umpteenth time: Mason should be making his announcement soon. I'd keep my comments short and sweet, I decided.

"Here's your drink," Matt said when I reached him.

He handed me a fresh glass of champagne, and I took a gulp. It didn't taste quite as good as it had a few minutes ago. When I looked up at Matt, he was frowning. He wasn't looking at me, though; something across the room had caught his eye. I followed his gaze.

He was staring at Mason.

"What's up?" I asked.

Matt didn't answer.

I turned to get a better look at Mason. He was pacing in a corner, jabbing buttons on his cell phone. He ran his free hand over and over his bald head, like he was trying to soothe a jittery dog by stroking it. Gone was his happy, tipsy vibe. He looked like a man in a panic. His big eyes were roaming the room, but when they met mine, they dropped to the floor.

As if he couldn't bear to look at me.

"Matt?" I said, feeling the floor shift under my feet. My voice came out kind of strangled.

Now Mason was shouting something into the phone, but the music was so loud I didn't have a chance of hearing him.

"Everything's fine," Matt said, putting a warm hand on my shoulder. I hadn't realized how cold I was. "He's probably just talking to an insane client."

"Ooh, looks like the food is ready," Pammy said. "Yummy, pigs in a blanket. Should we go get a plate?"

"Let's hang out another second," Matt said, his eyes never leaving Mason. Now one of our agency's founders, Mr. Dunne, was hurrying across the room to Mason's side. The two of them huddled together, gesturing frantically, and at the exact same moment, they both turned to look at me.

"What's going on?" I whispered. Nausea rose in my throat.

"It's going to be okay," Matt said in a low voice, and I tried desperately to believe him. I felt like I was watching a horror movie and the heroine was about to descend a rickety staircase into an unlit basement. Cheryl was being too cocky. Mason looked too upset. Now Mason was passing the cell phone to Mr. Dunne, and he was talking into it. Something bad was going to happen; the killer was in the basement.

Oh, God, why were they walking over to Cheryl?

Mr. Dunne was shaking Cheryl's hand, and she was smiling. Something about her smile . . .

"I need to—" I couldn't get out the rest of the words. My stomach was bucking. I raced to the bathroom and flung open the stall door just in time. I hadn't eaten much of anything all day, so the only thing that splashed into the toilet was champagne.

"Lindsey?" Pammy had followed me in. "Oh, no. You're not really pregnant, are you?"

"I think I just ate some bad sushi for lunch," I lied, flushing the toilet and closing the lid. I sat down on top of it. My legs were shaking so bad I didn't trust them to hold me up.

"Can I get you some water?" she asked. "Maybe a few crackers?"

"That would be great," I said hoarsely. I couldn't imagine eating a thing, but it would get Pammy out of here and let me be alone so I could fight through my panic. I needed to stay calm; I was good at staying calm. I was good at fixing things, too. I could fix this, whatever it was.

What was happening?

Logically I knew there could be a million explanations. Maybe Matt was right; maybe a big client was being difficult.

Maybe Mason and Dunne had turned to look at me because they were thinking of handing him off to me but decided to give him to Cheryl. It was probably that. I was sure it had to be that.

It wasn't that.

I knew it with a staggering, rock-solid certainty. Something big was about to happen, something awful. What had Cheryl done? My mind raced as I considered the possibilities. She couldn't have messed with the agency vote; Mason had already told me I'd won the VP title. I had the job locked up.

Didn't I?

"Lindsey, here's your water," Pammy said, entering the bathroom again. "That bald guy was looking for you, but I told him you were in the ladies' room. I didn't tell him you were throwing up, though. He's making some speech right now, so he said he'll talk to you afterward."

I unlocked the stall door and stepped out, a giddy, hysterical hope rising inside me like a balloon. Could I have been wrong? Could the champagne have made me paranoid? Mason was giving his announcement; everything was proceeding on schedule. And he was looking for me. That had to be a good sign, right? I rinsed out my mouth and smoothed my hair.

"Thanks, Pammy," I said, accepting the water and crackers she handed me.

I could hear Mason talking, but the bathroom walls distorted his words.

"Should we go out?" she asked.

"Give me one more second," I said. I reached into my purse and put on a layer of Cherrybomb. I took a deep breath and stared at my reflection for a moment, marshaling my strength until I was ready.

"Hey!" Matt was standing just outside the door. He motioned us over. Mason was up in the DJ's booth, speaking into a microphone while everyone crowded together on the floor beneath him. Cheryl was near the front of the pack, a broad smile stretched across her face. Matt was standing a few feet to the side of everyone, so he had a view of both Mason and the crowd.

"What did I miss?" I whispered.

"Nothing yet," Matt said.

Mason continued talking. ". . . really a tough decision for us, one of the toughest we've ever had to make . . ."

God, just get to it, I silently begged him.

". . . exceptional work this year and every year since she joined our agency . . ."

"Did Mason say why he was looking for me?" I asked Matt.

He shook his head.

"How did he look?" I whispered.

Matt inhaled slowly and met my eyes. "I'm not sure," he said. "Something seems . . . off."

I shut my eyes and prayed a simple, fervent prayer: *Please.* The tension was unbearable. My stomach started to roil again.

". . . she put the cherry on top today. Not only did Cheryl win the Gloss account, but she so impressed Stuart Fenstermaker that he phoned a little while ago and announced he is entrusting all of his advertising to Richards, Dunne, and Krantz. Not just for Gloss but for all seven of his companies. Cheryl brought in a fifty-million-dollar account this morning while everyone else was getting a latte. Not bad for a day's work."

No.

". . . pleased to announce Cheryl Davis is our new vice president. Cheryl, will you come up here . . ."

Matt was standing beside me. His hand was back on my

shoulder: "Deep breath," he whispered into my ear. "Inhale slowly."

I followed his directions like a robot. This was a bad dream. In a minute I'd wake up and I'd lift my head from my desk and see Donna's note.

Heads were swiveling around. Were they looking for me, to see how I'd react? I instinctively took a step back, behind Matt.

Cheryl accepted the microphone from Mason and stood there beaming while applause rained down like confetti all around her. The disco lights shot tiny rainbows of color on her bare, golden shoulders and upturned face. She'd never looked more beautiful.

"Mason's heading this way," Matt said. He spoke slowly and gently, like you do to someone who's been in a car accident: *Do you know your name? Do you know who you are?*

"Do you want me to get you a drink?" Matt asked.

"Thank you so much," Cheryl began.

"Don't leave me," I begged Matt.

"I'm right here," he said.

"Cheryl's the vice president?" Pammy said, wrinkling her nose. Her voice was too loud, and it reverberated inside my head. "Are you both vice presidents?"

My mind slowed down like a mechanical toy whose battery was running out. I could barely understand what everyone was saying. Their mouths were moving, but their words made no sense.

"Lindsey."

It was Mason. He stood in front of me, still running his hand over his head.

"God, I'm so sorry. Can we just move over here and talk for a second?" he said. I nodded mutely. It took every ounce of my concentration to lift up my feet one at a time and follow him to a corner. It was the same corner where he'd told me I'd won the vice presidency. The same beanbag chairs. The same Lava lamps. How could it all be the same, as if the world hadn't folded in on itself and flipped everything upside down?

"Fenstermaker called fifteen minutes ago," Mason said. He was looking at my left shoulder instead of into my eyes. "He offered us all his business. Cheryl must've really done a number on him. Then Cheryl threatened to jump to another agency and take his accounts with her if she didn't get the vice presidency. She forced our hand, so we had to have an emergency vote. She beat you out by one vote."

I nodded again, like it all made sense.

"You deserved this," Mason said. "You still had my vote."

He was trying to make me feel better. He was throwing me a few extra fries.

"You still have a good future with us," Mason said. "A great future. A few years down the line, who knows?"

I tried to croak out a word, and couldn't. My throat had closed up.

"I need to get back up there," Mason said. "Will you be okay? Can I get you anything?"

I shook my head. I was fine; I was just so cold.

"We'll talk more later," Mason said. "Let's go out for lunch tomorrow. We'll figure something out."

He stepped away, and that's when I saw it: The faces of my colleagues were turning toward me, just a few at first, then more and more joining in, like fans at a stadium doing the wave. Cheryl had finished talking, and Mason was still walking toward the stage. His motion had attracted everyone's attention. I was as exposed as if I'd been standing there stark naked. Everyone was staring at me, curiosity and pity on their faces. Everyone knew I'd failed, that I wasn't good enough.

I looked around wildly and saw a red exit sign. I'm not even sure how I got there, but I must've run, because suddenly I was bursting through the door, out onto the sidewalk, where a panhandler sat on an overturned milk crate rattling coins in a plastic cup, and people lined up in the doorway of a restaurant, and a car skidded through an intersection just as the light turned red. Where life went on as usual, even though mine had just exploded into a million jagged shards.

Four

MY NEW SHOES RUBBED raw patches into my heels and the cold night air cut through the thin material of my dress, but I kept walking. I'd left my purse and coat at the bar—I vaguely remembered my purse slipping off my shoulder and scattering its contents across the floor as I ran toward the exit—but that didn't matter. How could things like my wallet and cell phone and my business cards, the ones I'd carried in a silver monogrammed case my parents had given me for Christmas, matter anymore? The only thing that mattered, the single most important thing in the world, was that I focus every ounce of my concentration on walking. If my body kept moving, maybe my mind wouldn't.

I no longer felt nauseated or scared or devastated, but I knew those emotions were lurking close by, like animals in a cage, coiling their strength until the lock turned and they could unleash themselves. I had to keep walking; I had to keep the animals at bay. Besides, I had nowhere to go. I couldn't bear to go back to the bar and face everyone. I couldn't go home without my keys. I couldn't go to a hotel without a credit card. The only thing left for me to do was to keep turning aimlessly down streets and up boulevards, crisscrossing the city as evening commuters with their overcoats and briefcases were replaced by couples heading out on dates and rowdy groups of people going to bars and tourists on their way to the theater.

"Hey, baby!"

I'd been walking for what felt like hours when a thin, blond guy lurched toward me, holding up his hand like it was a stop sign.

I stared at him as if he was speaking Sanskrit. He was wearing a suit, but its collar was badly frayed and his right dress shoe was missing its laces.

"Want to get a drink?" he asked. His yellow teeth seemed like they belonged to a different man, a much older one. When he smiled, I noticed his incisors were pointed like tiny little fangs.

"Or do you want something else?" He sneered, his expression flipping from friendliness to anger like a coin. I looked around. I didn't know this neighborhood. A thin dog sniffed at a Dumpster, and the storefronts were shielded by black accordion gates that were covered with graffiti. I didn't feel fear or anger; I didn't feel anything except the bone-numbing cold. I didn't know if I ever would again.

I stepped around the drunk like he was no more substantial than air. He shouted insults in my wake as I kept walking. I wanted to walk forever. I wanted to be like Forrest Gump, reaching one end of the country and turning around and heading for the other coast. I passed by a twenty-four-hour liquor store and a deli with red flowers clustered in buckets out front. I stepped over the chalk outline of a child's hopscotch game and the broken amber glass of beer bottles. I keep walking, my shoes tapping a steady rhythm against the sidewalk of the city I'd loved so much.

Some time later—maybe an hour, maybe three—I passed a street I recognized. I stood on the corner, staring up at the street sign. Somehow, I'd looped around and now I was only ten blocks away from my office. The temperature had dropped fifteen degrees, and the wind was picking up. A storm was coming. My teeth chattered, and I could no longer feel my feet.

A thought wormed its way through the numbness of my brain. I had an extra set of keys to my apartment and twenty dollars in my desk drawer for emergencies.

No one would be at the office now; they'd all still be partying. I could slip into the building, then I could go home and swallow a sleeping pill and escape into oblivion.

I turned right, toward my office, and kept walking.

"Want me to turn on a light for you?" the security guard asked. I'd knocked on the glass window outside his station, and he'd put down his fork and Tupperware container of spaghetti and let me into the building. He used his passkey to open the door to my office after I mumbled a story about leaving my purse in a cab.

"I'll get the lights," I said, my voice coming out all husky, as if I'd been screaming for hours. "Thank you, John."

"Don't work too late now." He tipped his head at me and headed for the elevator, whistling a song I didn't recognize.

I sat down in the leather chair behind my desk and reached for the drawer with my money and keys, but before I could open it, I noticed something amiss on my desk. My pencils and Clio Award and stapler had been moved to one side, to make room for the magnum of champagne someone had put in the center. There was a silver card attached to the bottle. I reached for the card and laughed a mirthless laugh when I read it.

"Congratulations to our newest—and youngest ever—VP creative director!" the card said. It was from the board of directors of our agency.

I picked up the heavy bottle and turned it around and around in my hands. Dom. Nice to know that even though they'd stabbed me in the back, they hadn't skimped on me.

Suddenly I was desperately thirsty. I must've walked for miles, inhaling black exhaust fumes from buses and cabs, and my throat felt so sore I could barely swallow. I pulled off the foil and wire twisted around the neck of the bottle and used my thumbs to pop the cork. I ignored the foam that cascaded over my hands and took a greedy gulp from the bottle.

When the phone on my desk shrilled, I nearly dropped the heavy bottle on my toe.

Who could be calling me at the office at—I squinted at the clock on the wall—nine-thirty on a Friday night? It was probably Matt, or maybe Mason. They could leave a message; there wasn't anyone in the world I wanted to talk to right now.

I finally glanced at the caller ID on the third ring. It was Bradley Church.

Bradley, who always made me feel good. Bradley, who'd had a not-so-secret crush on me since the second grade. Bradley, whose red felt heart printed with the words "Be My Valentine" had been tucked in the secret compartment of my old jewelry box since the third grade. He was the one guy in the world who'd always made me feel like I was pretty. Like I was special. His deep voice would be a balm to my soul.

"Hey, you!" Bradley shouted. His voice was happy, excited. "I've been trying to reach you all night, but you didn't answer your cell or at home. I can't believe you're still at the office!"

"Yeah," I said. "Got tied up in a meeting. How are you?"

"Great," he said. "Really great."

I closed my eyes and pictured Bradley. His brown hair was always rumpled, he was on the skinny side, and his hands and feet seemed too big for his body, like a puppy's. His eyes were earnest behind his big wire-rimmed glasses, and he always carried a pen and notebook in his back pocket like a wallet, and at least two cameras slung around his neck. Bradley was the kind of guy people considered a geek in high school, at least the people who weren't able to see how kind and good and honorable he was. Suddenly I missed him terribly.

"You won't believe what happened to me tonight," Bradley said.

Bet it can't top my night, I thought, grimly swigging another gulp.

"I got stuck in an elevator for three hours," he said. "You know that parking garage in downtown Bethesda? I was going to pick up a book at Barnes & Noble, and on the way back to my car, I got stuck between the third and fourth floors. It took forever for the firemen to get us out."

"What a pain," I said, covering a yawn.

It had been a mistake to answer the phone. I couldn't do casual chitchat tonight, even with Bradley. Exhaustion was starting to crash over me in thick, heavy waves, and I desperately wanted to succumb to it. I ached to collapse into my bed under my fluffy down comforter, to put my pillow over my head and curl up in the darkness.

"Well, at least you had something to read," I said, cradling the phone between my ear and shoulder and opening my drawer with my free hand, the one that wasn't clutching the champagne in a death grip. I found my keys exactly where I'd left them, a twenty-dollar bill pinned to the key chain with a paper clip. And they say anal-retentiveness is a character flaw.

"So there I was, stuck in the elevator," Bradley said. I heard a woman giggling nearby. God, I hoped he'd wrap this up quickly. I needed to get off the phone.

"And guess who I ran into in the elevator?" he said.

I so didn't want to play this game.

"No idea," I said briskly. I didn't want to be rude, but Bradley was too happy and chatty and I really needed to go home.

"I'll give you a hint," he said. "She's a redhead."

"A natural one!" a familiar voice shouted. "You've seen the proof, Bradley Church!"

This time I did drop the champagne bottle: "Shit!"

"Lindsey? Are you okay?" Bradley asked.

I snatched up the bottle before too much spilled.

"Alex?" I asked tentatively.

"None other." She giggled. She must have been perched by Bradley's side. Their faces must have been close together with the cell phone in between so they could both hear. Their cheeks were probably in that electric space just before skin touches skin.

"What a coincidence," I said. The numbness was draining from my body; anxiety was evicting it and staking a claim.

"We're starving to death after our ordeal," Bradley said.

"Our heroic ordeal," Alex added.

"Heroic," Bradley agreed.

"Well, *you* were heroic," Alex said. "Bradley gave me his bottle of water."

"But you insisted I drink half," Bradley said. "So you were noble."

What the—what the—what the *fuck*? Why were they finishing each other's sentences like an old married couple?

"Anyway," Bradley said, "we're about to grab dinner at that Thai place. Remember? It's where you and I went the last time you were in town."

We'd shared chicken satay with peanut sauce and crispy spring rolls and talked for hours. The restaurant was on the dark side, I suddenly remembered. With soft background music. And votive candles at every table.

"So this is really funny," I said. I took another long gulp of champagne. "And natural redhead? What are you talking about, Alex?"

"I showed him the proof," she said.

I closed my eyes. Alex was using her husky, there's-an-attractive-man-in-the-house voice. Something close to hatred gripped my stomach like a fist.

"She showed me her forearm hair," Bradley said quickly. "Trust me, we had a lot to talk about during those three hours."

"Great!" I said too heartily.

"Why didn't you tell me how handsome Bradley has gotten?" Alex said, laughing.

I could see her now, putting a hand on Bradley's thin shoulder, brushing a crumb off his chest, leaning in to take a bite of his food off his fork. Alex could no sooner stop flirting than breathing.

My insides clenched up like a giant hand was grabbing them and mercilessly squeezing.

"Where's Gary tonight?" I asked casually. Gary was Alex's fiancé.

"Working," Alex said, stretching out the word and making it sound like bo-ring. "As usual. Just like you. What are you doing at the office now?"

"I think our spring rolls are coming," Bradley said.

"I'd love another glass of wine," I heard Alex tell the waitress. "Bradley?"

"Sure," he said. "We deserve it."

Alex laughed, an intimate, knowing laugh that reverberated in my mind like a villain's cackle. "Are you sure? You told me you get tipsy after one glass. I might have to drive you home."

I leapt up from my chair, feeling a scream rise in my throat. That was my private joke with Bradley, the fact that the two of us couldn't have more than a single drink without feeling giddy.

That was *our* restaurant. Were they sitting at our table, too? Was Bradley going to send her a freaking valentine?

"Call me later, Sis," Alex said, and the phone went dead.

I gulped champagne so quickly it burned as it slid down my throat. My mind was raging. Damn it, Alex had a fiancé, a rich, gorgeous guy. So why did she need to prove how irresistible she was? Why did she always need to have a pack of guys panting in her wake? It didn't matter that she hadn't known about Bradley's crush on me. I'd never told her about it, but she knew Bradley and I were friends. She knew how close we were. Couldn't she have left alone the only guy in the world who actually thought *I* was the special sister?

I paced my office, hot tears flooding my eyes.

I'd killed myself for a promotion that Cheryl won because she was sexier.

The guy who'd had a crush on me for twenty years spent a couple of hours with Alex and forgot all about me.

The moral was obvious: The pretty girls always won. No matter how smart I was, no matter hard I worked, it didn't matter. I'd never be good enough. And what did I have to show for all my hard work? A one-bedroom apartment that I'd have to demolish my savings account to afford to buy, the account I'd spent seven years building up. A golden award on my desk. The beginnings of carpal tunnel and a body that was falling apart and a headache that never seemed to quit. I was twenty-nine years old, and the only thing in this world I had was a job that had betrayed me after I'd given it absolutely everything.

I wanted to leap out of my own skin. I wanted to run screaming down the streets of New York. I wanted to curl up under my desk and cry.

I wanted to be anyone but me.

Without being fully aware of what I was doing, I yanked

open the door to my office and stalked down the shadowy halls to the conference room. Cheryl's storyboard was still up on the easel. I pulled off the drape cloth and stared at her campaign.

I took a step backward. Unbelievable. I'd spent a lot of time imagining her campaign, but I'd never expected anything like this.

She'd gone for a slice-of-life commercial. It was grade-schoolish in its lack of sophistication: Two pretty twenty-some-thing women stood side by side in front of a bathroom mirror talking about their lipstick. One girl couldn't believe Gloss could make her thin lips look plump and pretty, but she was won over when her friend made her try some.

This had won Cheryl $50 million in new business? The tired, trite, naysayer-turned-true-believer slice-of-life ad?

But of course it hadn't won Cheryl the account, I remembered, narrowing my eyes. Her face and body and sultry voice had won it. Cheryl had done her research, too, I had no doubt. But a different kind of research. Instead of figuring out Fenstermaker's favorite drink or which type of bagel he preferred, she'd analyzed his ego for a weak spot and zeroed in. What middle-aged man wouldn't be flattered by the gentle scrape of long nails against his knee, by the gaze that told him he was irresistible, by the deliberate flash of cleavage, especially when his marriage had dried up and his wife was sleeping with a thirty-year-old pilot? I had no doubt that Cheryl would follow up her flirtation with action. She'd probably already spent the afternoon in a hotel room with Fenstermaker; she'd probably known he was about to call so she could hold Mason's feet to the fire.

Suddenly something clicked into place; Cheryl had made an abrupt mystery trip last week. Not even her assistant knew where she'd gone. Had she flown to Aspen and engineered a meeting with Fenstermaker? Had their relationship started then?

Oh my God, I thought, staring at her storyboard. She'd had the winning strategy all along. She was smarter than me after all.

I raised my champagne bottle in a mock salute: Nice going, Cheryl. You've single-handedly set women's lib back fifty years. I closed my eyes and tilted the bottle to my lips. I nearly toppled over and had to grab the back of a chair for balance. The champagne was hitting me at last, mercifully dulling the edges of my anger and pain.

"Don't think for one second I'm going to call you boss," I muttered, waving my champagne bottle at Cheryl's ad. Probably not the most effective workplace threat ever, but I was going with what I had.

I was turning to leave, to finally go to the blessed sanctuary of my bed, when I heard footsteps in the hallway. Better not be a burglar, I thought grimly. Actually, I half-hoped it would be. It would feel good to smash the champagne bottle over his head, to unleash some of the rage and hurt I was carrying inside. I looked down at the bottle. It would be a shame to waste it, though. Maybe I could just finish it before I knocked out the burglar. I tilted up the bottle and drank as quietly as I could, which ended up being at about the same decibel level as a marching band, since I lost my grip on the chair, fumbled for Cheryl's storyboard, and brought it crashing down on top of me as I fell, thumping my head on the floor for a grand finale. This was not shaping up to be my day.

"Lindsey? Is that you?"

In an instant Doug was beside me, pulling the stupid storyboard off my head and helping me to my feet.

"Are you okay?" he asked.

"Fine," I said, squinting at him with one eye closed. And I would be, if he'd just stop swaying back and forth.

"I'm glad," Doug said softly. He kept hold of my hands as he rubbed his thumbs along my palms. Doug made Bill Clinton look like a nun wearing a chastity belt at a Victorian tea party. "I didn't expect to see you here."

"I was just leaving," I said, but I didn't move. "What are you doing here?"

"Forgot my cell phone in my office," he said. "I didn't want to leave it here all weekend."

I nodded.

"Rough night, huh?" Doug said. His chocolate brown eyes seemed sweet and sincere, and his voice was low.

"Yeah," I said glumly. What was the point in pretending?

"Everyone thought you should've been named VP," he said, still holding my hands.

"Thanks," I said, swallowing hard. I'd be having this same conversation with every single person I worked with for the next month. Some people would be genuinely sorry; others would be happy to see me fail. I didn't know which would make me feel worse.

I couldn't bear to see the pity in Doug's eyes, so I turned my head and stared out through the conference room's glass walls. The streets below were as busy now as they had been at eight-thirty this morning. The bucket-thumping guys had been replaced by an old man wearing clothes that were so faded and worn he looked like a ghost blending into the gray building behind him, but his saxophone shone like spun gold. A new shift of cabs took up the battle for lane space, and people clogged the sidewalks, heading to restaurants and bars and jazz clubs, ignoring the guy in a giant hot-dog costume trying to hand out flyers. At the corner a man and woman stood arm in arm, waiting for the light to change. As I watched, he reached out and tilted up her chin for a kiss. But he didn't kiss her lips. He rained slow kisses on her forehead and cheeks and on the tip of her nose. The gesture was so tender and intimate it made me ache with longing.

No one had ever loved me that way.

Right now Bradley and Alex were leaning close together, talking and laughing. The candlelight would play across her high cheekbones and pick up the gold glints in her hair. People at the restaurant would recognize her, like they always did, and Alex would smile graciously and pose for a picture and crack a joke that would make everyone laugh, because Alex could be kind and funny as well as self-centered. Bradley would be dazzled by her; I was certain of it.

Would my friendship with him ever be the same? I wondered. Sure, we'd still be buddies, just like back in tenth grade, when we'd spent hours passing back and forth a bowl of popcorn and the answers to trigonometry problems. Back then Bradley and Alex had moved in different social orbits; she'd been as real to him as a pinup poster. And, if I were being brutally honest, that was by my design. I'd encouraged them to remain strangers.

How many times had I suggested to Bradley we study at his house instead of mine? How careful had I been to invite him over only when Alex was at cheerleading practice or out on a date? Even on prom night, I'd made sure he picked me up after Alex had already left. I didn't want him to see me standing next to her in her long golden dress, the one that clung to every curve of her body.

Now Alex knew how funny and smart and good Bradley was. Now they'd connected. They'd probably talked more tonight than Bradley and I had in the past two years. The next time I went home and saw him, would he ask about Alex? Would he oh so casually suggest we invite her along? Would he look at me . . . and wish he were with her instead?

Or would she and Bradley stay in touch after tonight? Would

she discover that Bradley liked honey on his popcorn instead of butter, which sounded disgusting but tasted unbelievably good? Would he—this was the thought that sent an arrow stabbing through my core—would he look at her the same way he used to look at me?

"You okay?" I'd almost forgotten Doug was still there. I nodded.

"Then what's this?" He released one of my hands and reached out with a fingertip to wipe away the tear rolling down my cheek.

"Nothing," I said. "It's just been a really long night."

Doug was still holding my other hand, I suddenly noticed. Now would've been a perfect time to announce I had to leave and march briskly out.

"Beautiful view," Doug said. I turned to him and saw he was starting straight at me. Oh, God, I silently groaned.

But I looked back at him. I kept looking back.

"Your hair is coming down," Doug said. "I don't think I've ever seen your hair down."

He reached up and unclipped it, letting it fall around my shoulders, then he slowly smoothed it back from my face with his big hands. I closed my eyes so I didn't have to look at him. This was awful; this was sleazy, cheesy Doug. Well, sleazy, cheesy, gorgeous Doug. Still, I had to stop this, immediately.

Or at least in the next two to five minutes. Because his fingers were rough but his touch was so exquisitely gentle, and the combination was intoxicating.

"You look pretty like this," he said, his hand lingering on my cheek.

I opened my eyes. The room was dark, but moonlight flooded in through the glass walls.

"I do?" I whispered.

You know how in that moment before something momentous happens—like when a solemn-faced doctor tells you to sit down, or when you're waiting to see if a pink line shows up on a pregnancy test, or when a car comes skidding toward you on an ice-slicked road—time seems to sputter to a stop? That's what happened as my fingers encircled Doug's wrist. Everything around us seemed to fade, leaving just me and Doug in a spotlight of color in a world that had suddenly gone black and white. He was so close I could hear the faint noise he made when he swallowed. I could see the patch on his chin he'd missed when he shaved. For several heartbeats we stood close together.

"You're beautiful," he breathed, staring at me with those melted chocolate eyes.

That's when I grabbed him, hard, and kissed him.

He tasted delicious, like cinnamon and red wine, and his broad back felt strong under my roving hands. All my pent-up feelings from the day washed away as waves of pure lust crashed over me. Now the only thing I could think about was how quickly I could tear off Doug's shirt and run my hands over his chest.

"Lindsey," he breathed. "I never thought—"

"Don't say anything," I begged. If he came up with one of his recycled lines, the moment would be ruined, and I wanted so desperately to lose myself in it, to let the delicious sensations overtake me and crowd away my pain.

Doug's lips were soft and warm, and when the stubble along his jawline scraped the sensitive skin of my neck, shivers rippled through my belly. He kissed me until I was almost delirious, while his fingertips slipped under the neckline of my dress and drew gentle, tantalizing circles around my shoulders. I leaned against the conference table, my head thrown back and my eyes closed, as his fingers moved lower and lower.

"Beautiful," he whispered again as he reached behind me and

unzipped my dress. I reached back and unhooked my bra and impatiently tossed it aside, then pulled Doug close to me so I could feel his skin against mine. Sensations bombarded me: the warmth of his skin, the nearly unbearably exciting feel of his lips biting my earlobe, the electric touch of his fingers as he slid my dress down to my hips. I wanted this. I wanted this so badly it made me weak.

Doug's fingers froze.

"What's that?" he whispered.

Oh, God; had he discovered my granny panties?

"Did you hear that?" he whispered.

I shook my head, my arms still wound around his neck, feeling groggy and disoriented. Why'd he stop? I didn't want him to stop, not ever.

"Shit," Doug muttered, and he let go of me so abruptly that I almost fell over again. He bent down and grabbed his shirt off the floor just as footsteps approached the conference room.

"My storyboard should still be in here," someone—*Cheryl*—was saying.

"Can't wait to see it," a man responded. "The fifty-million-dollar storyboard. I want it framed."

The light flicked on, and I squinted as its sharp brightness jabbed at my eyes.

Cheryl was standing in the doorway, staring straight at me. And next to her was Mr. Dunne. A beat too late, I crossed my arms over my chest. The lust drained from me as quickly as if someone had pulled a plug.

Cheryl found her voice first.

"Lindsey?"

I stared at her dumbly.

"Well, I've never seen this side of you," she said snidely, looking pointedly at my chest.

"It's—it's not what it looks like," Doug stuttered. He'd never been able to think on his feet; I'd even put words to that effect in one of his performance reviews.

I turned my back and pulled up my dress with trembling fingers.

"I can explain," I said over my shoulder.

"I'd like to hear it," said Mr. Dunne. "In my office. Two minutes."

Then he turned on his heel and walked away.

Five

MR. DUNNE SAT BEHIND his mahogany desk in his enormous corner office, the one with a full dining room and a
private bathroom outfitted in cool blue granite and stainless
steel. It was the office I'd had my eye on; I'd always figured in
another ten or fifteen years, when Mr. Dunne retired, I'd be in
line to get it.

Mr. Dunne was the nicest of our three agency founders. He
looked a bit like Santa Claus, with his shock of white hair and
full belly, and he even played the part on Christmas Eve, when
he walked through the office handing out goodies to everyone
who was still working. Last year he'd given me a candy cane
and an orange, and when I'd said, "Thanks, Mr. Dunne," he'd
laughed and said, "Who's Mr. Dunne? I'm Saint Nick!" It was
kind of sweet, in a clueless-grandfather sort of way.

But right now his mouth was a tight, disapproving line.

"Sit down," he said, gesturing to a chair in front of his desk.
I quickly obeyed. This was going to be awful. I'd never felt so
humiliated and ashamed. I was desperate to get this over with
as quickly as possible.

"I want to tell you how very sorry I am," I began. I could

hardly look him in the eye. I'd flashed Saint Nick, and I knew I'd think of it every single time I saw him.

"Nothing like this has ever happened before and I assure you it will never—"

"Lindsey," he cut in, his voice a whip. "Doug is your employee."

I blinked in surprise. Where was he going with this?

"Well, technically, yes," I said. "But he doesn't report directly to me."

"I don't care who the hell he reports to. He works on your team," Mr. Dunne said. "What were you thinking?"

"It was a mistake," I said, dropping my head in shame. "A terrible, terrible mistake. One I'll never—"

"I know you're disappointed tonight, but that's no excuse," Mr. Dunne said. "You've left me with no choice."

Anxiety exploded inside of me, cutting off my airways and making me gulp shallow breaths. Suddenly I knew what he was about to say, and I had to stop him; I had to change Mr. Dunne's mind.

"Doug started it," I babbled. "Ask him; he'll tell you. Of course that doesn't excuse what I did, I'm not saying that at all—"

"I have to let you go," Mr. Dunne said.

His words hit me with the force of a thunderclap ripping apart the sky. I opened my mouth, but no words came out. My entire body started to shake.

Mr. Dunne exhaled. "Lindsey, I like you. You do good work. But aside from the fact that you've violated basic standards of decency in the office, you've left this agency open to a major sexual harassment lawsuit. You know we have a policy in place to prevent this sort of thing."

"Doug won't sue!" I said, my voice rising to a hysterical shriek. "Let me talk to him; I swear he won't sue."

"No, you will not talk to him!" Mr. Dunne thundered. Now he was really angry; spots of red appeared high on his cheeks.

"Do you want him to say you asked him to keep quiet? Do you want him to say you threatened him? Do you want to drag the name of this agency—the agency I built from scratch—through the mud of a lawsuit?"

"No, no, no, I didn't mean that," I said, unconsciously clasping my hands, as though in prayer. God, how could I possibly be making this worse? I had to think clearly now; everything depended on it. I had to sell myself like I'd never sold anything before.

"Please, just give me another chance," I begged. I would've gotten down on my knees if it would've helped. I would've kissed his feet and brought him coffee every day. I would've done anything to keep my job. How could this be happening to me?

If I'd been anxious before, waiting for Mason's announcement, it was nothing compared to this. Panic spread through my body like wildfire. I was shaking so hard that even Mr. Dunne noticed, and his expression softened slightly.

"I'll work harder. I'll do better. I swear I'll never do anything like this again." My voice was a shriek.

"I believe you," Mr. Dunne said. "But it's too late. The damage is done. You knew about our policy. You understood the consequences. I'm sorry."

"No, no, no," I said. "You can't mean that. You can't. Please."

"Lindsey, I'll give you a reference," he said. "That's all I can do."

"But—" I started to say.

"You need to leave now," Mr. Dunne cut me off. "Please pack your things immediately. This isn't easy for me, either."

I stared at him, my mind reeling. I had to fix this, I could still fix this, I could—

But Mr. Dunne was standing up, and walking over to his door, and holding it open for me to leave.

And just like that, in the snap of a finger, my life was over.

Six

I STAYED IN BED for three days straight. My insomnia was cured; now I had the reverse affliction. All I wanted to do was sink into a deep, dreamless sleep. I drew my shades so darkness and silence wrapped themselves around me. I turned off my phone and let my mail pile up in a heap in my hallway and slept for hours and hours, waking only to pull another quilt out of my closet and add it to the pile on top of me, or to sip from the glass of water on my nightstand. Like a severely injured patient who is put into a medically induced coma to speed healing, my body was self-medicating, taking me away from the reality of my pain and into the blessed reprieve of sleep.

Once I heard someone pounding on my door, but I put my pillow over my head, and eventually they went away. I dove into sleep again, the hours passing like seconds, my exhausted body soaking in rest.

On the fourth day, I made it all the way from my bed to the bathtub, taking small, careful steps. I kept the lights low and filled my tub with almost unbearably hot water and added an entire bottle of Molton Brown bubble bath. I brought a cup of chamomile tea with honey into the tub and soaked for an hour, my mind still numb. Just making the tea and filling the bath had exhausted me all over again.

I lay in the tub, not thinking about anything but the patterns my fingers were aimlessly tracing in the bubbles. I felt insulated from everything, like a fragile china cup rolled up in layers of newspaper and tucked between sheets of Bubble Wrap. Nothing could hurt me in my little apartment; I was safe and protected and warm. When my fingers turned soft and raisiny, I pulled the plug, put on an old T-shirt, and toddled back to bed, my movements as slow as an old woman's.

Hours later, I awoke to hear the door of my apartment opening.

I didn't have the energy to move. If it was a burglar, he could take everything, as long as he left my bed. I wanted to stay in it forever, hugging my soft blue cashmere pillow, my mind in a fuzzy place where reality couldn't intrude.

"Miss Rose?"

It was the superintendent of my apartment building.

"Are you in here?"

Most supers were Queens through and through, with the requisite gold chains and generously unbuttoned shirts. Mine was a struggling poet who weighed less than I did and had squealed like a Catholic schoolgirl when a resident discovered a baby mouse in the laundry room.

"I'm coming in, is that okay?"

I closed my eyes again. Maybe when he saw that I was sleeping, he'd go away.

"Lindsey?"

This time it was a different voice. Matt's.

I should get up and offer them some tea, I thought vaguely. But my arms and legs were too leaden to move. Maybe they'd go ahead and make it for themselves.

"God, if she did something to herself—" Matt was saying.

"Hand me that frying pan," the super said.

"Why?" Matt asked.

"If it's foul play, the perp may still be here," the super said knowingly.

"For Christ's sake," Matt said. "Move out of the way."

My bedroom door squeaked open. I should ask the super to fix that squeak; how convenient that he was here. It was like fate, or kismet. Was there a difference between fate and kismet? I wondered vaguely. If so, it was a question for greater minds than mine.

"Miss Rose?" the super yelled into my face. "Can you hear me?"

I dragged my eyes open.

"Lindsey?" Matt shoved the super, nearly knocking him down, and appeared at my bedside.

"Hey," he said softly, peering down at me. He put my purse on the bed. "I brought you this."

I lifted a hand and gave a little wave. A wave was so pretty, I thought, watching my hand gently flap back and forth. If you did it slowly enough and spread your fingers, it looked like a fan. People should really wave more.

"Do you feel all right?" Matt asked. He was wearing a suit. He must've come right from— *No.* My mind recoiled, like a hand jerking back from a hot stove. I wasn't going to think about that.

"Good," I tried to say, but my voice was a croak. I cleared my throat and tried again.

"Good," I said. "Sleepy."

I closed my eyes again and started to drift off.

"She might've overdosed," the super said. "We should probably put her under a cold shower."

I opened an eye and tried to muster up a glare.

"Linds?" Matt said. He leaned closer to me. He had a red spot on his tie. It looked like spaghetti sauce.

"Remember the gnocchi?" I asked him.

"The what?" he asked, a furrow forming between his brows.

"I think she said Nokia," the super stage-whispered to Matt. "She wants her cell phone. She might want to say her good-byes. Call her friends and whatnot."

The super leaned closer to me. He was trying, with minimal success, to grow a goatee, I noticed. "Who—do—you—want—to—call?" he said, exaggerating the pronunciation of every word like an English as a second language teacher speaking to a particularly dim-witted student.

"Lindsey, did you take anything?" Matt asked.

"Hmmm?" I said,

Matt yanked open my nightstand drawer and rifled through it, then he dropped to the floor in a push-up position and peeked under my bed.

"You didn't take any pills, did you?" Matt called from my bathroom. I hoped he wouldn't notice I hadn't wiped down the tub after my bath. There wasn't anything worse than a bathtub ring.

"Check her pupils," the super advised, pulling a minuscule flashlight out of his pocket—he was the only super in town who refused to wear a work belt—and shining it into my face.

God, that little man was annoying. I put the pillow over my head again, hoping they'd take the hint and leave.

"Lindsey," Matt said. "Can you tell me what day it is?"

I took off the pillow and made an effort to smile reassuringly at him.

"Look," I said, speaking as politely as I could. "Thank you both for coming by. But I really must rest now."

That should do it. I closed my eyes again.

I heard the two of them muttering in the corner. It was kind of comforting, actually, as though someone had turned the tele-vision on low to a soap opera.

". . . just sleeping pills, but only one was missing . . ."

". . . check for alcohol?"

My refrigerator door opened and shut, then I heard some-one rummaging through my cabinets. Maybe they were fixing something to eat. I should be hungry, but I wasn't, which was lovely, because it meant I'd never have to get up again.

". . . breakdown. My aunt had one . . . same symptoms . . ."

". . . hospital?"

". . . call someone?"

I snuggled deeper under my comforter, curling up my body so I was as small and cozy as possible, like a little squirrel snug in its nest. I'd nearly fallen asleep again when one sentence sliced through the thick fog in my mind, as clear and frighten-ing as an air-raid siren.

"I found her address book," Matt said. "I'm going to call her parents and sister."

I sat up in bed and threw back the covers and shrieked at the top of my lungs, "Nooooo!"

Two hours later, I was sitting on my couch, wrapped in a warm bathrobe, a half-empty bowl of chicken noodle soup on my lap. Matt had found a can in my pantry—it was just about the only thing in my pantry—and heated it up, then watched me eat every spoonful. Even though the smell made me feel ill, I'd managed to choke down enough to satisfy him. He'd also made me take a shower, and he'd opened the blinds. It had snowed while I was sleeping; the streets were clear, but the treetops still wore little white lacy caps. The cold, bright sunlight told me it was midday. It had taken me a while to figure out which day. Tuesday.

"I'm okay," I said for the hundredth time. "I was just tired."

And I was still exhausted, but I knew I couldn't go back

to bed. I had to start dealing with my life, or what remained of it. My answering machine was blinking with sixteen new messages. Most of those were from Matt, but my parents had probably called, too. They might be getting worried; I was the responsible daughter, the one who always called back on the same day.

"I thought you'd done something stupid," Matt said. "I would've killed you if you had."

"Your timing has always been a bit off," I said.

Matt stared at me for a second, then he smiled. I'd always loved his smile, which was the tiniest bit too big for his face. Suddenly a bone-deep sadness settled inside me. I was only twenty-nine, but I felt so much older. My skin felt as tight and dry as a husk, and my eyes ached, like I'd been reading for far too long in a dim light. I felt worn-out, like I'd used up my life and now it was ending. And in a way, it was; at least life as I knew it was ending.

"So what are you going to do?" Matt asked. I put my bowl of soup on my coffee table and leaned back with a sigh.

"I can't stay here," I said. "I can't afford it."

"Don't you have some savings?" Matt said.

"It's going co-op," I said. "I was going to buy it, but . . ."

My voice trailed off as I looked around my apartment. I loved every single thing about it. My couch and oversize chair were a winter white chenille, and my coffee table was made from the knobby door of an old barn in upstate New York. My bedroom held nothing but my queen-size bed with its snow-white sheets and comforter and a simple wooden nightstand and a leafy green plant in one corner. It was as uncluttered and peaceful as a monk's room. In my closet, my clothes were arranged from darkest to lightest hues, with the wooden hangers all pointing in the same direction. Everything shone with cleanliness. Everything was neat and organized and perfect.

I took a deep breath and started again.

"I need to look for another job," I said. "But not in New York."

I'd come to this realization in the shower, and I'd turned my face into the spray of water so Matt wouldn't hear me cry. I'd thought the sobs would tear themselves out of my chest with awful wrenching sounds, but only a single tear made its way down my cheek and mingled with the water swirling into the drain. I was too numb to cry.

"But you said Dunne was going to give you a reference," Matt protested. "You don't have to leave. You could get a job any-where."

"I know," I said. "That's why I'm going to move home."

"To Maryland?" Matt asked incredulously.

"Look, I know Cheryl already told everyone what happened between me and Doug," I said. I'd shielded myself for three days; now I needed to step up like a big girl and take my hits. "Didn't she?"

Matt's eyes ducked away from mine. "Screw Cheryl," he said. "Everyone knows she's a bitch."

"And everyone knows I got fired Which means every other agency in town is going to know it, too. You know how fast gossip spreads. People aren't just going to call Dunne for a ref-erence; they're going to check in with everyone they know at our agency. Someone's going to talk. They're going to find out what I did."

Matt sighed. "So what? You made one mistake. One mistake in seven freaking years."

"A mistake," I said. I choked out a strangled little laugh that sounded more like a cough. "I destroyed my career, and there's no way to fix it. I can't fix this, Matt. So I've got to start over. There are some good agencies in D.C. I can stay at my parents' house for a while and commute into the city until I get every-thing sorted out."

Matt shook his head. "I don't think it's a good idea. I think you should stay and fight. This is going to blow over in a month. Take a vacation, then come back and look for a job. You don't have to move."

I looked down at my lap and thought about it. Could Matt be right? I imagined going to work at a new agency, settling into a different office, greeting my colleagues and seeing them hold back smirks and whisper to each other— *No.* I couldn't bear it.

Suddenly I was transported back to the ninth grade, to my first month of high school. I'd been delivering a note from my honors chemistry teacher to the principal, and I was taking a shortcut through a hallway where all the seniors had lockers. I still remember the metallic clang of those locker doors shutting, the scuffed orange-brown linoleum under my feet, the yeasty smell of old socks that permeated the air. I marched through the hallway wearing new Levi's with creases down the front and a pink flowered shirt and the training bra I wouldn't need for another six months, feeling proud my teacher had chosen me out of all the students in the class.

"Hey, who's this?"

A guy spun away from his cluster of buddies and blocked my path. He was wearing a white T-shirt and jeans, and he looked kind of like James Dean, only with a meaner face.

I stared at him, my eyes begging him to let me pass.

"She can't talk," his friend said.

"Dumb, isn't that what they call them?" the first guy said, leaning closer to me and snapping his fingers in my face. "Hey, dummy."

"I can talk," I said. "Please let me pass."

"Please let me pass," he mocked. "See, dummy, I can't do that. This is the seniors' hall. And you're not a senior. You're trespassing."

"Citizen's arrest!" one of his friends hooted.

"If you'll just put your arms behind you, no one will get hurt, dummy," he said.

"Use my belt as handcuffs," another guys said, pulling it through the loops of his jeans, while his friends laughed and crowded closer to us.

My heart started to pound as my eyes darted around, searching for an escape. I felt like a trapped animal. Even though they were laughing, these guys weren't just joking; the ringleader had a real cruelty in his narrowed eyes. By now a dozen people were encircling us, watching but not saying anything. Where were all the teachers? Why wasn't someone helping me?

My lower lip started to tremble. God, don't let me cry, I silently prayed. Somehow I knew that would only make things worse. Much worse.

"Arms behind you, please," the James Dean guy said. "This is your last warning."

"I've got a holding cell," his friend said, opening his locker.

I've always been a little bit claustrophobic. I looked into that dark, coffinlike space and imagined myself crammed in there, yelling and screaming and crying. The bell was about to ring for the next class; the teachers would have their doors shut. No one would hear me. I'd be trapped. I wouldn't be able to see or breathe or move.

"Please don't," I said, desperation making my voice soft.

The James Dean guy looked at me.

"She seems sorry," he said to his friends. "Do you promise never to do it again?"

I nodded vigorously. My nose was running, and I wiped it with the back of my hand.

He looked at me and shook his head. "Nope, not good enough. Into the holding cell."

His friends laughed as he reached out and grabbed me, and

suddenly I was fighting as hard as I could, flailing my arms and kicking out with my legs. But he was so much stronger than I was that he easily pinned my arms behind me and lifted me up and carried me toward the locker.

Then a voice cut through the crowd.

"What the hell are you doing, Ralph?"

Ralph turned around, turning me with him, and I saw Alex. She was wearing her cheerleader's outfit with some guy's letterman jacket draped over it. People were moving aside to give her room, and staring at her, the way they always did. Even at age fourteen, Alex had that kind of power.

"Hey, babe," Ralph said, then he announced: "Now that's the only freshman who's allowed up here."

"Amen," another guy said reverently.

"Let go of her," Alex ordered, and suddenly I was released. I collapsed on the floor and scrabbled away from Ralph like a crab.

I could feel the energy of the crowd shift. The guys were focused on Alex now. Their alpha dog had been replaced.

"Just having a little fun," Ralph said, crossing his arms and putting his fists under his biceps so they looked bigger. "Why do you even care?"

But the bluster was gone from his voice. He wanted Alex's approval. He wanted her to like him.

"She's my twin sister," Alex said. "C'mon, Lindsey."

I got up and hurried over to her, and as we walked away, I could hear the mutters:

"Twin sister?"

"No fucking way."

"Are they sure it's really a sister and not the family dog?" one of the guys said, and the sounds of slapping hands and laughter reverberated in the hallway.

Alex tensed up beside me and stopped walking. I could see

her wrestling with the instinct to tell the guys to fuck off. To defend me.

I stood beside her, still shaking with fear and rage, my insides churning, hoping she'd do it. I wanted them to feel a little of my pain, to know what it was like to be humiliated in front of a crowd. Alex was good at quick comebacks; it would be so easy for her to lash out and make them wish they'd never messed with me. Then Ralph would be the one everyone would laugh at.

But Alex kept walking. She kept walking.

In that awful moment, I knew she'd done the math and decided risking her own popularity wasn't worth sticking up for me. The cost was too high. She'd defend me to a certain point, but that was as far as she'd go.

I hated her for not defending me.

But not as much as I despised myself for needing her to.

"Are you okay?" Alex asked when we were out of earshot.

"Fine," I said angrily, wrapping my arms tightly around my body.

"Those guys can be jerks," she said. "Especially Ralph."

How did she know their names? How did they all know *her*? I was still getting lost in our school's endless hallways, while Alex had half the senior class wrapped around her pinkie. The male half. High school was going to be just like junior high, and elementary school, and summers at the swimming pool, and every camp and dentist appointment and birthday party we'd ever attended: Alex was the star, and I wasn't even in her orbit. How could I have been stupid enough to think it would be any different? How could I have hoped that at a school this big I'd find my own niche, my own friends, my own place to shine?

This was Alex's fault; *everything* was Alex's fault. It was only by comparison to her that I looked ugly. I knew in my heart that I wasn't what anyone would call beautiful, but I wasn't homely, either. I was just . . . unremarkable. Maybe I could lose ten pounds, but even so, I was closer to pretty than ugly. But next to Alex, I was nothing but a huge disappointment. A terrible surprise. A genetic punch line.

"I'm fine," I said, swiping my nose again. "Leave me alone."

"Leave you alone?" Alex said. "I just saved your ass."

"Thanks for all the help," I said sarcastically and stormed away, leaving her staring after me.

It was fifteen years ago, and I still remember the way Ralph's upper lip curled into a sneer just before he grabbed me, the way one chubby guy watched us with a mixture of disgust and excitement, and the sound of the crowd's laughter when someone called me the family dog.

I hadn't walked down that hallway again for the rest of the year.

In some ways, the world of New York advertising was like high school. Sure, the gossip traveled via BlackBerry or over martinis at Velvet or Sugar instead of by folded-up notes, but the grapevine was alive and thriving. If I stayed, everyone in the business would know how spectacularly I'd screwed up. It would be a permanent footnote to my résumé: Lindsey Rose, the woman who holds one-on-one meetings with her male employees after hours. Clothing optional. I'd never get past it, never stop seeing the gleam of recognition in my colleagues' eyes when they heard my name for the first time.

Would my future bosses be watching me whenever I was around male subordinates? Would a simple touch or a glowing review spark the gossip all over again?

I'd spent my entire life transforming myself into someone who was admired and respected. I couldn't bear to lose that. So I couldn't stay in New York.

Matt was still sitting next to me on the couch, watching me.

"I don't think I can start over again in New York," I finally said. "I need to go somewhere else. I need to go home."

And with those words, deep within me, I could feel the faintest flickering of my old determination.

Home, where everyone still thought I was successful. Home, where my parents depended on me to negotiate the best deal when they were buying a new car and pick the right stocks for their retirement plans, and where the neighbors always asked about my latest business trips and promotions. Home, where Bradley used to love me and might again still.

I wasn't going to curl up in bed forever. I'd never been a failure, and I wasn't going to start now, damn it.

I'd figure out a way to explain my return, and I'd put my life back together. Maybe I wouldn't be a vice president anytime soon, but I'd get a good job. I'd work my way up again. I'd still have everything I'd ever dreamed of, everything I'd ever wanted. No matter what it took.

Seven

IN THE END, ALL it took to erase any sign that I'd lived in New York was a rental truck, a trip to an upscale consignment store, another one to Goodwill, and a half day on the phone canceling utilities and negotiating an early end to my lease and arranging for my painting and plasma TV to be put in storage.

And suddenly I was standing in my bare apartment with dust motes floating in the sunlight and two suitcases at my feet. Just the way I'd begun my life here seven years ago.

"I can't believe you don't have more stuff," Matt said, picking up one of my suitcases. I was spending tonight, my last night in the city, on the couch in his apartment before catching the 9:00 A.M. train home to Maryland tomorrow. I hadn't asked how Pammy felt about this.

"Aren't girls supposed to have more stuff?" Matt asked.

"I've got stuff," I protested. "I took a truckload to Goodwill."

"A quarter truckload," Matt corrected me. "Where are all your scrunchies? Where are all your clothes? Where are your stacks of magazines that tell you how to drive your man wild with an ice cube and Saran Wrap?"

"First of all, I stopped reading *Penthouse* when I was ten," I said. "And scrunchies? Do you know how disturbing it is that you even know that word?"

"We're talking about *your* inadequacies, not mine," Matt said.

God, it felt good to banter with him again, to act like everything was normal, even if underneath the surface I felt like brittle glass, ready to splinter under the slightest tap.

"So what's the plan for tonight?" I asked. "Mexican and a movie?"

"Hell, no," Matt said. "It's your last night in New York. We're going out."

He picked up my other suitcase and I locked my door and we walked to the elevator. I didn't look back, not even once. I had to keep my eyes forward. I had to keep moving.

When we got to the lobby, I walked up to the perpetually smiling doorman and handed over my keys. Don't think about it, I instructed myself. Just do it. Put the keys in his outstretched hand. Now let go of the keys. That's it, baby steps.

"Here you go, Hector," I said.

I reached into my purse for the little envelope containing his early Christmas tip. Hector was in his late forties, one of the steady, stalwart people New York couldn't run without. He shows up every day wearing a crisp white shirt and the same blue suit, and he keeps a vigil on the door so he can jump up and open it every time someone approaches. I was about to say something else—to thank him for the times he'd kept my deliveries behind his desk, or hailed cabs for me in the rain—but a young couple I vaguely recognized from the floor below me burst out of the elevator and rushed over.

Suddenly the three of them were tossing around words like *chemo* and *daughter* and *prayers,* and Hector was unashamedly wiping a tear from his eye as he said, "Remission. Yes, the doctor said it is a remission."

Then they were hugging him, first the wife and then the

husband, who initially stuck out his hand but at the last second changed his mind and pulled Hector in for a big, back-thumping hug. Hector was smiling and bowing his head and saying, "Thank you, God bless you," over and over again.

"Does his kid have cancer?" Matt whispered to me.

"I guess so," I said slowly.

I looked down at my plain white business-size envelope while Hector thanked the couple for the lasagna they'd cooked for him while his daughter was in the hospital. Inside my envelope was a hundred dollars. I hadn't included a card. I hadn't baked him lasagna. I hadn't even known his daughter was ill. All I'd done was smile at Hector as I rushed by on my way to work, and absently thank him for opening the door as I zoomed in again at night, my arms laden with my briefcase and take-out Chinese, my mind full of taglines and dialogue and storyboards. Hector had been as much a part of the background to me as the fake tree in the corner of the lobby. Now I wondered: How old was his daughter? What was her name? Was the cancer going to come back? How had he come to work every day and smiled and opened the door for me like it was the best thing he'd get to do all day, while his whole world was shaking and crumbling around him?

"Ready?" Matt said.

"Sure," I said.

But first I reached into my wallet, grabbed all the twenties in it, and stuffed them in the envelope. I left it on Hector's desk and slipped away while he was still talking to the young couple.

I'm sorry, I whispered as the door closed behind me, so softly no one could hear.

"What's the plan?" I asked Matt once we were settled in a yellow cab.

"First we're dropping your insane amounts of stuff at my

apartment," he said. "I hope we can squeeze in all the scrunchies. Then—"

"I have a request," I interrupted. "I want to see the Naked Cowboy."

Matt looked at me out of the corner of his eye.

"Seriously?" he said.

I nodded vigorously.

"And I want to buy a knockoff Prada bag on Canal Street," I blurted, the words tumbling out of me faster and faster. "I want to take a horse-drawn carriage ride in Central Park. I want to see a celebrity, a real one, not the B-listers we usually get stuck working with. I want to window-shop in Soho. I want to eat sushi at Ruby Foo's and get a drink at Tavern on the Green."

"Good God," Matt said in mock horror. "You're a . . . a tourist."

"I've never done any of those things," I said, feeling a twinge of sadness.

And it was true: I'd lived in New York for more than half a decade, but I might as well have been standing behind a glass wall the entire time, watching other people get kissed on street corners and dance to bucket-thumping drummers and head out to bars with rowdy groups of friends. I'd lived in New York, but I hadn't really *lived* in it.

And to Matt's eternal credit, he didn't laugh at me or threaten to kick me out of the cab. He just leaned forward and told the cabbie to step on it, because we had a lot to do that day.

Ten hours later, every single one of my wishes had been granted, as if a fairy godmother had waved a magic wand over my head. Trust me to get the fairy godmother with the world's worst timing. I could've used her that night in the conference room; instead, she'd shown up a few weeks late, shaking the wrinkles out of her gown and straightening her tiara and muttering about traffic and broken alarm clocks and the dog eating her schedule. Still, at least she'd given me today.

"You'd never guess it was a knockoff, would you?" I said for the tenth time, admiring my Prada bag while we sat in a corner booth at Ruby Foo's.

"I swear on my mother's life that, if you put it next to a real Prada bag, I couldn't tell the difference," Matt said solemnly, putting a hand over his heart.

"Oh, shut up," I said. "You're just jealous."

"That's definitely it," he agreed.

"Is the stitching crooked?" I wondered, peering more closely at my bag.

"You got it for twenty dollars," Matt said. "You're lucky it has stitching instead of superglue."

"I was good at haggling, wasn't I?" I asked smugly.

"Brilliant," Matt said. "You wore him down."

"He wanted twenty-five," I reminded Matt.

"You broke him," Matt said. "He's a broken, bitter man. Now can we get something to eat?"

"I want a California roll," I said. "And a tuna roll. Ooh, and scallion pancakes and shrimp dumplings."

"Perfect," Matt said as the waitress scribbled down our order. "I'll have the same."

Matt leaned forward and looked at me closely.

"So, I know this has got to be hard for you—" he began, his teddy bear–brown eyes all soft and sympathetic.

"Reese Witherspoon is even prettier in person," I interrupted. "And I've got her lip gloss!"

"You mean you stole her lip gloss," Matt said.

"Finders keepers," I said, gulping my dainty little cup of sake. It was hot and vaguely medicinal and exactly what I needed.

"That was a brilliant idea, though, to stand outside Letterman's studio right before the taping," I said, tilting my cup at Matt. "And an added bonus that she dropped her purse! That woman next to me only got one of her dirty pennies."

"You got the better end of that deal," Matt said. "I think the penny was there all along. Anyway, I was going to say it must be really tough for you—"

"Do you think the Naked Cowboy stuffs his underpants with a sock?" I cut him off. "I mean, nothing else about him is natural. He stands there in Times Square in boots and underwear and a spray-on tan, strumming that guitar and posing for pictures. God, the girls love him, though. I thought that blonde was going to punch me when he put his arm around me for a picture."

"Definitely a sock," Matt agreed, a bit too eagerly. I didn't blame him; the Naked Cowboy could make any man feel inadequate.

"I really love this lip gloss," I said, pulling it out of my purse. "Isn't the color perfect? I like it almost as much as my bag."

"Okay," Matt said, leaning closer to me. "What's going on?"

"What do you mean?" I asked.

"You're being relentlessly cheerful," he said.

"I had a good day," I protested.

Matt gave me one of his dog-covered-with-Crisco looks.

"I'm glad you had fun," he said slowly. "So did I."

"So let's not ruin it by getting all serious," I begged him.

I opened the menu again. "Look, they have tutti-frutti ice cream!"

"Lindsey," Matt said, then he sighed. "Look, I've gotta say it. Sometimes I worry that you don't deal with stuff all that well. You're so busy and gung-ho and frantic all the time that you don't ever sit back and think about what you really want and how you feel. I mean, you've got to be upset, but you're babbling on about your bag and lip gloss like they're the most important things in the world. You're not dealing with your emotions."

"I hate it when you hang out your shingle," I said, punching his arm lightly. "You're just like Lucy from *Peanuts*."

"I get it," Matt said tightly. "You don't want to talk about it. Fine. But tell me this: What are you going to do in D.C.?"

"Get a job," I said. Wasn't it obvious? "Start working again."

"And in another six months, it'll be like nothing ever happened," Matt said.

I blinked in surprise.

"Are you kidding?" I said. "There's no way I'll be that high up in another six months. It's going to take three years."

"And that's what you want?" Matt said. He leaned closer to me and put his hand on the table between us. His hands were like the rest of him—comfortable and warm and solid. "That's all you want?"

His voice was low and gentle. Somehow that frightened me more than if he'd shouted.

"That's exactly what I want," I said.

"Fine," Matt said, sounding like it was anything but.

"Fine," I echoed, feeling vaguely pissed off but not sure why.

He folded his arms across his chest and looked down at his napkin. I twirled my lip gloss around in my fingers like it was the world's smallest baton. This was just what I needed, for Matt to turn all serious and grumpy. What did he want, for me to curl up again and sob about the disaster my life had become? I'd done that, and it still terrified me to think about how fuzzy and distant those lost three days had felt. I couldn't go to that place again, not ever.

Didn't Matt see that the only way I knew how to survive this was by putting everything behind me, starting right now? I was moving on, and I'd have to do it at warp speed to accomplish everything I wanted to accomplish. I didn't have time for regrets and psychoanalysis and Bikram Yoga or whatever he thought I needed. Didn't Matt know me well enough to know the only way I could get through this was to keep moving and working and *not* thinking?

I glared up at him and discovered he was glaring down at me. I couldn't help it; I smiled. I've never been able to stay mad at him.

"You've got Reese Witherspoon's lip gloss on your tooth," Matt said. Then he smiled, too.

"Share a tutti-frutti for dessert?" I asked. It was the closest I could come to an apology. An apology for what, I wasn't sure.

"Sure," Matt said, and he unfolded his arms.

"We'll definitely need another bottle of sake, please," he told the waitress when she came over with our platters of food.

I looked up and met Matt's brown eyes.

"Thanks," I mouthed.

Matt stood on the platform, his hands in his pockets, watching as my train rumbled out of Penn Station. People bustled past him, nearly swallowing him up in their mad morning rush, but he stood his ground in his jeans and red fleece jacket. I'd argued that I could take a cab on my own to the station, but he'd insisted on seeing me off.

He'd put a note in my hand as I'd boarded the train. I looked down at it now.

"Psychiatric help, five cents," he'd written next to a sketch of himself in Lucy's booth. In the sketch he was wearing a beret and smoking a cigarillo.

"Call anytime," he'd written. "I'm going to miss you, kiddo."

I'm not going to cry, I told myself fiercely. I took a last look back at Matt. He looked smaller now that there was distance between us. I wished he'd smile. His face looked so sad without that big smile of his.

A year from now, I'd come back to visit Matt, I vowed. Or maybe I'd invite him to visit me. By then I'd be back to my old self. I'd show him around my office and my new apartment—because I definitely wouldn't be living with my parents then—and he'd see how quickly I'd put my life back together.

One year, I promised myself. Twelve months. Three hundred and sixty-five days. I'd fill every second with work, and I'd be too busy to miss Matt and my old life.

A year wasn't so long to wait, was it?

Part Two

Home

Eight

I HADN'T BEEN HOME in more than a year and a half, and I felt like Alice right after she shot through the rabbit hole to Wonderland. I could swear my parents had gotten smaller—either that, or I'd gotten bigger, which was a distinct and troubling possibility I refused to dwell on. I'd nearly walked right by Mom and Dad at Union Station, partly because I didn't recognize them beneath the matching puffy down jackets that engulfed them from chin to knee.

"Fifty percent off at the Lands' End outlet!" Mom crowed triumphantly, before she even hugged me hello. It was like being assaulted by an overly amorous marshmallow.

Dad, clad in the more manly brown version of the coat, was clutching a luggage cart in a death grip and shooting "Go ahead, make my day" looks at anyone who dared to venture within ten feet of it.

"Good to see you," he said to me.

He reluctantly released one hand from the cart, but only after shooting a warning glance at a thieving granny who'd tottered dangerously close to it. Dad and I embraced in our usual tender way, with him patting my back as vigorously as if I were choking and he was trying to dislodge a chunk of bread from my windpipe.

"You look wonderful," Mom said, peering at my face once Dad had released me from his Heimlich and I'd gulped some air. "Tired, but wonderful. Are those circles under your eyes?"

"Got a luggage cart," Dad announced. "I'll load up your bags."

"You must be hungry," Mom said. "Is that coat warm enough?" She shivered theatrically. "Ooh, it's so chilly out. Aren't you chilled?"

"Did you have a good trip?" Dad asked. "Any delays?"

"I'm a little tired, not too hungry," I said. Amazing how quickly I adapted to the parental volley of questions. It was like leaping aboard a bicycle after years at sea and taking off down the street without a wobble. Some things you never forget.

"My coat's definitely warm enough," I continued. "No delays. The trip was wonderful." If your idea of a rollicking good time was trying in vain to read the latest journalistic investigation by the good folks at *People* magazine ("Are Hers Real? Stars Inflate Their Top Lines!"), then browsing the food car three times, half-finishing a crossword puzzle, and finally just staring out the window at the scenery rushing by, wishing you could jump out of the train and race along with it. I'd never been good at sitting still, and today it had been harder than usual.

"It's so good to see you," I said, interrupting a fresh assault of questioning.

"You too, honey," Mom said, reaching out to tuck my hair behind my ears, like she's been doing ever since I was three years old. I instinctively shook my hair back out, just like I've been doing ever since I was three years old. Dad, always more comfortable with action than words, made a production out of loading up the luggage cart.

"Knew this would come in handy," he said, thumping the cart like it was a melon and puffing out his thin chest. I didn't have the heart to tell him the three of us could easily manage my two medium-size suitcases.

"You've got to be starving after that trip," Mom fretted, brushing imaginary lint from my shoulder.

"It was only three hours," I protested. "And I had Chee-tos." Plus, um, a tiny little chocolate-chip cookie. Hardly worth mentioning, really. And the only reason I ate a second one was because they came two to a package. I had no choice in the matter; I was a prisoner of Amtrak packaging.

"Still," Mom said as we headed for the car. "We're thinking of Antonio's for lunch. Of course, they don't always wash their silverware as well as they should."

"Once," Dad said, rolling his eyes toward heaven, which was presumably full of men who could sympathize with his plight. "You found a speck of dried spaghetti on your fork once. A *speck*. Better than that Indian place with the druggie hostess."

"Just because she has blue hair doesn't mean she's an addict," Mom said. "She could be expressing herself. She could be an artist. Someday she'll be famous and you'll be sorry you weren't nicer to her. And it was more than a speck. It was easily a quarter strand."

"That druggie hostess always makes me spell my name three times," Dad grumbled. "Marijuana. It kills brain cells."

"Well, you know we can't go to Pines of Italy," Mom said. "It gives you gas."

"Only the garlic bread," Dad protested, heaving my suitcases into the trunk of our old station wagon, the one with all the dents in the sides. Mom and parking garage columns don't always play nice.

"But you can't stay away from that garlic bread," Mom said. "If you'd just have a piece or two instead of the whole basket—"

"Antonio's sounds perfect," I said. Mom and Dad both started, then looked back over their shoulders at me, like they'd forgotten I was there.

So, I might as well get this confession over with. Here's the thing: I'd told my parents I was coming to Bethesda to open a new branch of Richards, Dunne & Krantz. In twenty-nine years, this was the only real lie I'd ever told my parents, notwithstanding one or two "Alex ate the last cookie," garden-variety, arguably developmentally necessary childhood fibs. I'd hated doing it. It had felt all wrong, like wearing an itchy wool sweater to a picnic on a sweltering July afternoon.

But when I'd phoned to tell my parents I was moving back home, Mom had asked, "Moving home? But you're doing so well in New York."

Then her voice had grown the slightest bit shrill: "Aren't you?"

And when Dad had jumped in on the other receiver and said, "Is everything okay, Lindsey?" instead of leaving any potentially emotional discussions to Mom and fleeing the room like a tornado was incoming, as he usually does, I'd frozen up. As their worried voices pelted me with questions, I'd thought about my last visit home. Dad had insisted on cleaning the gutters against all reason. The facts that it was raining, that the trees still had plenty of leaves left to shed, and that he'd just cleaned the gutters two months earlier were trifling, inconsequential details. Dad was gripped in the throes of a gutter-cleaning frenzy. So I steadied the ladder for him—someone had to do it, or he'd probably break both legs—and I found myself at eye-level with his ankles. Suddenly I was struck by how bony they were. The skin around them was loose and dotted with brown age spots I'd never noticed before.

At dinner that night, I'd looked at my parents—*really* looked at them—and I saw the changes that had come on so gradually they'd been nearly imperceptible. The reading glasses and hesitation on the stairs, the gray overtaking Dad's brown hair, the slight tremor in Mom's hand when she lifted up a scoop of mashed potatoes—that night I saw it all too clearly. My parents were getting older. They wouldn't be around forever. It wasn't just Mom's lumpy mashed potatoes that made me swallow extra hard.

My parents were so proud of me. Because I was successful, they considered themselves successes as parents. Their identity was knotted up in my own. How many times had I overheard Mom on the phone, satisfaction ringing through her voice as she talked about my perfect report cards or my acceptance to a half dozen colleges? I couldn't become a disappointment to them, not now, not during what should be their golden years.

"Everything's fine," I'd finally said into the phone. I'd closed my eyes, then blurted out: "It's actually good news."

"Oh," Mom had breathed. "I was worried for a minute there. But of course, I shouldn't have been. When have you ever given us reason to worry? So what is it? Another promotion?"

"I tell you, we did something right with Lindsey," Dad had said proudly. "She makes more money than I ever did, that's for sure."

And that's how we ended up all heading to Antonio's, the site of the great unwashed fork, for my triumphant return to Maryland.

"Tell me more about your promotion, honey," Mom said as we settled into the station wagon, with me on the hump in the backseat, feeling like I was twelve again.

"It's not technically a promotion," I said.

"Modest," Mom said to Dad, who grunted in agreement.

I cleared my throat and started again. "It's really not that big a deal. The firm is thinking about opening a D.C. branch, so

I'm here to scout everything out. You know, start scoping out clients and stuff."

"How much office space do you need?" Dad asked.

"Not sure yet," I said, fidgeting with a lock of my hair. "We'll, um, look into it once we figure out how many staff we'll need to meet the business demand."

"I still can't believe it," Mom said. "Both of our daughters living in the same city with us! You know Alex is sorry she couldn't make it for lunch. She's doing a shoot today for *Capitol File* magazine."

"Yeah, I've heard," I said. Mom had only mentioned it three times. Secretly I was thrilled; Alex wouldn't ask me much about my job if we were alone—she didn't find it all that interesting—but if she saw me squirm my way through my parents' questioning, her bullshit detector would kick in.

"And it's so nice you'll be home for Alex's engagement party tomorrow night," Mom said. "The timing couldn't be better!"

"Wouldn't miss it for the world," I said. Hey, imagine that! This lying thing got easier and easier. You'd think Alex might've let me in on that years ago.

"Now where did I put that parking ticket?" Mom wondered as we pulled up to the attendant's booth. She opened up her purse and rummaged through it. "I swear it was right here."

"There's a car waiting behind us," I said, twisting around and giving an apologetic wave.

"Give me a second," Mom said, pulling out a slip of paper. "No, that's a coupon for Antonio's."

"At least we can use it at lunch," I said.

Mom studied it: "It expired last year."

Dad rolled down his window.

"Just looking for the ticket," he told the attendant. "Nice afternoon, isn't it?"

"It's the darndest thing," Mom said. "I just had it in my hand."

The car behind us honked.

"Want me to look?" I offered.

"I usually put it in the outside pocket of my purse," Mom said. "Why wouldn't I have done that today?"

"I'm really good at finding things," I said anxiously. "I'm a good finder." Was it just me, or did I sound exactly like Rain Man?

I looked back: Now there were three cars waiting, practically revving their engines. In New York we'd have been shot by now. Any judge in the city would've ruled it justifiable homicide.

"Did you check your pocket?" Dad suggested.

"There's an idea," Mom said cheerily. "Nope, not there."

"Maybe it's in your other pocket," Dad said.

"Not there, either," Mom said.

More honking, and a shout from behind us that sounded something like "Brother Tucker!" I was pretty sure it wasn't someone shouting an enthusiastic greeting to a passing monk.

"People need to learn patience," Dad opined. "It's a lost art."

"Here it is!" Mom said triumphantly. "Oh, wait, that's my grocery list. I sure could've used that yesterday. I forgot the lettuce."

She scrutinized the list more closely: "And the strawberry Pop-Tarts."

"I wasn't going to say," Dad said. "But I did notice this morning."

"What's that under the sun visor?" I asked desperately.

"Aha!" Mom said triumphantly. "See, I knew we'd find it."

I slumped against the backseat, feeling slightly sweaty. Technically, I'd been living at home for a grand total of sixteen minutes, and I'd just remembered something. I loved my parents, but every time I spent a few hours with them, I came away with a desperate need for a few Advil and a Yanni CD.

A quick word on my parents' home. Remember my clean, uncluttered, monklike apartment? Matt would probably say it was my way of rebelling.

My apartment was the antithesis of my childhood home, where Dad usually sits in the den, blaring the television louder and louder, while Mom stomps around and hollers, "Get a hearing aid!" and blasts her soap operas in retaliation. Their living room is like a graveyard for Sony, because that's where Dad stores the broken electronics he hasn't gotten around to fixing. It's also where Mom piles the laundry she hasn't gotten around to folding, and the mail that hasn't been sorted. Every week or so Mom makes a big production out of gathering trash bags, a dust mop, and the vacuum cleaner. Then she stands in the doorway to the living room, grimly surveying the disaster, until she gets completely overwhelmed and has to retreat to the kitchen in exhaustion and pile a plate high with comforting chocolate croissants.

Serenity Lodge it isn't.

Oh—about those electronics crammed into the living room? My parents ignore the directions booklets that accompany devices in favor of pressing buttons as frantically as possible, preferably all at once. "Try the blue button!" my mother hollers. "No, the other blue one! Did you press it hard enough? Try the red one!"

Before they go on vacation, I have to email them explicit directions for retrieving their answering machine messages, which they invariably lose before they get to the airport. Plus Mom is constantly deleting all the photos on her digital camera, and Dad is terrified of the cell phone we got him last Christmas.

He leaps a foot into the air every time it rings and barks "Rose here!" into it so loudly that he singes the eardrum of anyone unlucky enough to be on the other end. Once, just to be cruel, Alex put it on vibrate and called him repeatedly. He was twitchy for days.

At least my childhood bedroom was still neat, with the books organized alphabetically by author, just as I'd left them. In fact, everything in my room looked the same, yet somehow different. Or maybe it was me who was different. The last time I'd lived in this room was after my sophomore year of college, and then for only two weeks before I'd headed to New York for an internship. Back then, I'd been so filled with energy and hope and ambition that I'd had trouble falling asleep at night. This room was just a pit stop, a place to idle and refuel before the race toward real life began. All the necessities in life—sleeping, eating, doing laundry—had seemed like a huge waste of time, interferences I could barely tolerate, given everything I wanted to accomplish.

I had to find my way to that frenzied, hungry place again. I had to find my way back to *myself*. I didn't even know the person who'd fooled around with a coworker on a conference room table at work, but I knew she wasn't me.

I kept walking around my old room, soaking in the memories. My wooden desk was still covered with stacks of dog-eared books and my *It's Academic* trophy, which was probably the cleanest thing in the house, given how frequently Mom polished it. My framed certificates—National Merit semifinalist, senior class salutatorian—hung on the wall over my desk. I still remembered how Mom and Dad had leapt to their feet, a two-person wave, yelling, "Go, Lindsey!" when I'd strode across the stage to collect that award.

And on the other side of the room, on top of the wooden dresser that matched my desk, was my old jewelry box. I walked over and reached for it. The pink velvet was so faded it was nearly white, and the ballerina inside was mortally injured, but a few rusty notes of *Swan Lake* still played when I creaked open the lid. Bradley's valentine was inside, just where I'd left it, along with a rose from my senior prom. By now the petals were so fragile that I knew they'd crumble at the slightest touch.

Bradley had surprised me with a wrist corsage of red roses and baby's breath, even though we'd gone to the prom as friends, I remembered, smiling. I hadn't thought about the prom in years, but now the images came back to me, like a film unspooling on a reel. Bradley had worn a rented tuxedo that barely covered his knobby wrists because his arms were so long and gangly, and I'd worn a white silk dress with gold braided rope criss-crossing the waist. I'd saved up months of babysitting money to buy it. I'd also worn my first ever pair of heels, and my skin was flushed because I'd spent the afternoon sunbathing. When Bradley came to pick me up and I'd opened the door, the smile had slid away from his face as cleanly as if someone had taken an eraser and wiped it off. Somehow I knew that was a good thing.

He'd handed me a small white florist's box, and then he'd said—

"Want a Snapple?" Mom hollered from outside my door. "I have Eggos, too. Homestyle ones. I know they're your favorite."

"Didn't we just eat lunch?" I reminded her. "Like an hour ago?"

"You look pale," Mom said. "Are you sure you're not getting sick? I'm going to the grocery store. Can I get you anything?"

"Just some yogurt," I said.

"Now, honey, you're not dieting, are you?" Mom said. "Because you don't need to lose a pound."

"I could definitely lose a pound or ten," I said, pinching

an inch—whatever, three inches—around my belly button to prove it.

"You know, most men prefer women with a little meat on them," Mom said. "It's only women who judge other women so harshly."

"Forget the yogurt," I said. I felt grimy from the train ride, and all I really wanted was a hot shower, not a Hallmark after-school-special talk.

"But I have to get you something you'd like," Mom fretted. "You need to eat or you'll waste away."

"Mom." I exhaled slowly. "You can get me whatever you want. It's fine."

"But what is it that *you* want? That's all I asked in the first place," Mom pointed out.

"Long, streaming hair," I muttered, trying to conjure up a visual of Yanni. "White robe." I reminded myself this situation was just temporary.

"Did you say you wanted white toast?" Mom asked.

"It would be great if you'd stock up on Snapples and Eggos," I told her.

"I knew you loved them," she said with satisfaction.

I rolled my eyes, then put my suitcases on top of my bed and unzipped them. I pulled out my tissue-wrapped pieces of black, cream, and navy-colored suits, blouses, and skirts one by one. Each piece of clothing probably cost more than all my bedroom furniture combined. I believed in buying classic, high-quality outfits that would last for years. Even back when I'd been a copywriter, I'd still dressed the part of a vice president. My hands hesitated as I unfolded my black Armani suit, the one I'd worn the day of my Gloss presentation.

No looking back, I reminded myself, briskly shaking out the suit and laying it on my bed. It would be ridiculous to toss out Armani just because of the bad memories associated with it.

I hung my clothes in my closet, automatically sorting them from darkest to lightest colors, as I mentally reviewed my plans. It was Friday, so I'd take the weekend to get organized, then I'd start blanketing businesses with my résumé on Monday morning. I'd have half a dozen interviews lined up within a week, I decided. I'd give myself a month to land a job—not just any job, but the right job, one with plenty of room for advancement—and a month beyond that to find an apartment. I'd want something close to downtown. Maybe in Adams Morgan, near the streets lined with shops and restaurants so it would feel a bit like New York.

I finished unpacking and neatly stacked my suitcases in my closet, then I sat on my bed, suddenly exhausted even though I'd done nothing all day but sit on a train and eat lunch. It was just so much harder making a fresh start at age twenty-nine than it had been at twenty-one. I lay back on my bed and stared up at the ceiling. Directly above my head was an old water stain. "You know it looks exactly like a scrotum," Alex had told me once when she and I were thirteen. "No, it *doesn't*," I'd said authoritatively. I still wasn't sure which worried me more: that she was right, or that it took me six more years to find out that she was right.

Alex.

I'd see her tomorrow night at her engagement party for the first time in eighteen months. It was the longest we'd ever gone without seeing each other. Hard to imagine that Mom used to touch her stomach and wonder if it was Alex's foot or mine that was kicking her back. Now our lives were as separate and distinct as cars on parallel highways, heading to destinations on opposite sides of the country.

Unlike my life, Alex's was settling into place perfectly. I'd only met her fiancé, Gary, once, back when they were first dating and Alex had come to New York with him on business.

We'd had a late dinner at Daniel on East Sixty-fifth Street, where you couldn't get an entrée for less than the cost of some people's monthly mortgages. Gary had picked the restaurant. He was exactly what I'd expected: tall and successful and gorgeous. I wrinkled my nose, trying to remember what exactly it was that Gary did. Real estate investing, that was it. On the night I'd met him, he'd spent the first half hour talking into a cell phone, trying to keep a deal from falling apart, then, just when I'd decided he was an ass, he'd ordered a three-hundred-dollar bottle of wine and turned to me with those electric blue eyes. "You must think I'm an ass," he'd said, before proceeding to charm the hell out of me. He was perfect for Alex.

Since she'd been with Gary, Alex and I had talked less and less often. Our phone calls—never all that frequent—had dwindled to maybe once a month. Alex had been busy, and so had I. She and Gary had moved in together six months ago, and they'd gotten engaged four months later, on a chartered sailboat as they toured the Amalfi coast. She'd sent me a photo of them clinking champagne glasses at sunset. Even in that moment of spontaneous joy, Alex's pose for the camera was calculated and model-perfect. Her hips were twisted slightly, her shoulders were thrown back, and her chin was tilted up. I'd stuck the photo in the back of an album instead of a frame.

I'd see them both tomorrow night at their engagement party. All of our neighbors would be there, too. So would my parents' friends, and some of my and Alex's high school classmates. I rubbed my temples; the headaches that had plagued me for years were starting up again. I pulled off my jeans and sweater and T-shirt, then changed into the pajamas I'd left folded on my pillow. I climbed under my old blue comforter, wondering if I could squeeze in a catnap before dinner. Maybe I was coming down with something after all. I never took naps.

But the thought of tomorrow night was exhausting. I'd have to spin lie after lie, like a circus performer struggling to keep plates spinning on a pole, and act as though I was living the life I'd always wanted, the life everyone always expected of me. I'd do it, though, and I'd do it with a smile on my face. After all, what alternative did I have?

Nine

HAWKINS COUNTRY CLUB LOOKED like a fairy-tale cas-
tle. A winding macadam driveway lined with graceful topiary
bushes and gas torchlights led to the imposing main building, which was surrounded by acres and acres of lush, green
lawn. The evening was crisp and clear, and the country club's
roof seemed to stretch forever into the sky. Tonight, in honor
of Alex and Gary's engagement party, dozens of white silk
bows wreathed the stair railings and a white carpet was rolled
out over the stairs, making me cringe to think about the dry-
cleaning bill. It was the most beautiful place I'd ever seen.
Gary was a member here, and Alex would be, too, now, I
supposed.

"Classy," Dad noted as we pulled up. Unfortunately, he drove
over the curb with an awful scraping sound. He backed up and
tried again, with even less success. A gloved bellman sprang
forward to open our station wagon's doors.

"Tip him," Mom hissed.

"I'm not going to tip him," Dad bellowed while the bellman
stood by with an expressionless face. "He only opened my door.
I could've done it myself if he'd have just given me a second."

Mom rummaged around in her purse, came up with a crumpled dollar bill, and pressed it into the bellman's hand.

"Thank you, sir," she said loftily.

I climbed out of the backseat with as much dignity as I could muster (it could fit in a thimble with ample room left over for a thumb) while Dad wrestled with the car key, struggling to remove it from his key chain.

"Never give them the whole ring," he stage-whispered to me. "That's giving strangers keys to your home. While we're at the party, they could be cleaning out our house."

Just making a graceful entrance, Rose family—style. The bellman remained impassive, but I was pretty sure he was going to funnel sugar into our gas tank.

We stepped inside the club, and my breath caught in my throat. The foyer ceiling stretched up imposingly, and the walls were lined with beautiful arched windows. At the end of the hallway was an enormous stone fireplace with leather couches cozily clustered around it. I'd been inside some pretty nice places before, but this club could compete with the best of them.

A slim, middle-aged woman in a winter white suit approached us, a welcoming smile on her face.

"You must be the bride's family," she said. I wondered what could possibly have given us away as not being distinguished patrons of the club.

"I'm Diana Delana, and I'm coordinating Alex and Gary's engagement party."

Within minutes, Diana had relieved us of our coats (she seemed a touch eager to ferry Mom's and Dad's matching marshmallows away to the checkroom), given us a quick tour of the club's main rooms, and gone over the evening's schedule. The other guests wouldn't be arriving for an hour, but Alex had wanted us here early for family pictures.

"Alex is with the photographer now," Diana said. "I'll take you to her immediately."

"May I use the ladies' room first?" Mom asked.

"Could stand a pit stop myself," Dad announced.

"Certainly," Diana murmured, her face a mask of discretion.

That impassive look must be a requirement for working here. They probably made employees go through a rigorous training course, and those who couldn't keep a straight face when confronted with a gassy father of the bride or a toothpick-chomping, shotgun-toting, country cousin named Hoss were washed out of the prospective employment pool.

"I'll take you to the restrooms first," Diana said. "Please follow me."

"I'll go ahead and find Alex," I said.

"Sure you don't want to wait so we can all go together, honey?" Mom asked.

I'd navigated dozens of foreign cities on my own, stood up to bully millionaire businesspeople, and elbowed my way through feisty crowds of New Yorkers to hail a cab during thunderstorms. Now my parents thought I needed them by my side to traverse a suburban country club?

"I think I can manage," I said, smiling at Diana as if to say, "Parents."

She smiled back understandingly.

"Just take the elevator to the second floor and walk straight ahead into the Chevalier Room," Diana told me. "You won't be able to miss Alex."

Story of my life, I thought wryly.

I walked down the endless hallway toward the elevator. This place really was outrageously delicious. Every possible surface was covered with crystal bowls full of perfect white tulips, and *whoa*—was that an actual Monet hanging on the wall, just above the original Chippendale table? Probably; I'd heard the initiation fee for this club was close to six figures.

Another white-gloved employee was waiting to press the elevator button for me so I wouldn't sully my index finger. As I rode up to the second floor, I checked my reflection in the mirrored elevator walls. I wore a long navy blue dress and simple diamond earring studs. My hair was a bit longer than I usually liked it, but I'd pinned it up in my usual twist. All things considered, I didn't look too bad for an unemployed twenty-nine-year-old who lived with her parents, although I suspected the competition wasn't all that fierce.

The elevator doors opened, and I saw ornate lettering spelling out "Chevalier Room" on the door of a room directly ahead, just as Diana had said. I crossed the hall, my heels sinking soundlessly into the lush Oriental carpet, and opened the door.

"Beautiful!" someone was saying.

Yep, Alex had to be here.

"Stay just like that," a man's voice said so quietly I had to strain to hear. "Don't move."

I eased the heavy door closed behind me as I stood there, taking in the room. Alex was partly hidden from me because I hadn't ventured out of the small entrance area, but from my angle I could just see her leaning up against an open window on a far wall. I moved a step farther into the room, making sure I didn't make any noise so I wouldn't interrupt the photographer's concentration.

I immediately saw why he'd posed her against the floor-to-ceiling windows. The windows opened in the middle, like French doors, and both sides were thrown back to reveal the background of the evening sky. Alex wore a shimmery silver dress that shone as brilliantly as the stars behind her. I stayed tucked away in my hiding place, staring at her for a full minute as the camera flashed. Her hair was loose and wavy, and she'd gotten even thinner. Her waist seemed impossibly small in that dress, like Cinderella's. But as always, it was her face that captured my attention. Its structure had always been classic, but those extra few missing pounds made her cheekbones even more pronounced and her blue-green eyes seem bigger. She looked more hauntingly beautiful than I'd ever seen her.

"Should I toss my head back?" Alex asked.

"No," the photographer said, so softly I had to strain to hear him. "I don't want you to pose."

Something about his voice was tugging at my mind. It sounded so familiar.

"Posing is what I do for a living," Alex said, her voice playful. "Want me to look sultry? Blissfully happy? Or should I pout? Let's have a little direction here, Bradley."

"I want you to look like you," Bradley said gently.

Bradley?

I shrank back against the entranceway wall, my mind swirling in confusion. Bradley was here? He was taking pictures of Alex? What was going on?

"I've got enough from this angle," Bradley said.

Now would be the perfect time for me to clear my throat and step forward. But I couldn't move. Since when was Bradley doing the photos for Alex's engagement party? No one had told me about this. I felt blindsided, like a wife opening her husband's office door and catching him feeling up his secretary. Jealousy roared through me, weakening my knees and roiling my stomach. Bradley was staring at Alex through his camera lens, capturing her perfect face again and again. *My* Bradley. He didn't even know I was in the room!

"Can we try something different?" Bradley asked.

"Sure," Alex said. "What do you have in mind?"

Why was it everything she said sounded like a double entendre?

"Sit down," Bradley said.

"On the carpet? I'll ruin my dress," Alex said, but she sat on the floor anyway. Her dress pooled around her like spilled mercury.

"Take off your shoes," Bradley said.

"You're a kinky one, Bradley Church." Alex laughed. She slipped off her delicate silver sandals and wiggled her toes. "Oh, that feels so good. Those heels were killing me."

Bradley's camera flashed.

"Hey!" Alex cried. "You didn't tell me you were shooting me like this."

"Relax," Bradley said. "It's just us here. You don't have to pose."

He moved closer to her.

"I don't?" Alex said. She leaned her head back against the wall, and I could see her shoulders relax. Her collarbones were as delicate and fine as a bird's wings. Why did every single part of her have to be so perfect?

I craned my neck and strained to see exactly how close Bradley was to her. Two feet, maybe. Too close. Much too close.

"Nope," Bradley said. "I don't want you to look perfect."

"You're the first photographer who has ever said that to me," Alex said. "Trust me, they've said everything else."

The teasing note was gone from her voice. She crossed her arms over her bent knees and leaned her head forward, resting it in the cradle of her own arms.

"Are you tired?" Bradley asked.

Alex nodded, then she lifted her head and looked worried. "Do I look tired?"

"No," Bradley said.

He didn't say anything else—didn't tell her that she was breathtaking or gorgeous or flawless—but that simple word seemed to reassure her like nothing else could. She took a deep breath and closed her eyes. Bradley slowly raised the camera to his face and snapped another picture.

My heart was thudding so loudly I was surprised they hadn't heard it. I couldn't see Bradley's face from this angle. Was he frowning, like he usually did when he was concentrating? Even when he frowned, Bradley never looked fierce. His face was too gentle for that. I studied his back, which was all I could really see from my vantage point. His hair had gotten longer and it curled a bit around his neck, and he was wearing a suit, but I'd bet he wasn't wearing a tie. Bradley hated ties; they made him feel like he was suffocating. Did Alex know that? She couldn't know that.

She didn't know Bradley nearly as well as I did, I thought, my eyes swimming with angry tears. She didn't know that, in the fifth grade, he ate Wheaties for a solid year for breakfast because he desperately wanted to win the hundred-yard dash at our school's field day, and that he'd come in a crushing fourth place. She didn't know that Bradley had memorized the words to dozens of Beatles songs. She didn't know that he'd given the eulogy at his mother's funeral after she'd died of breast cancer when he was only seventeen, and that I was the one who listened to him the night before the service while he practiced. His voice had broken when he'd spoken about how she'd spent an hour reading to him every night at bed-time long after he learned to read for himself, but after he'd rehearsed three times, he was finally able to get through his speech without crying.

Alex didn't know *anything* about him.

Why hadn't Bradley sensed I was in the room yet?

"Okay," Alex said. "Do you know what I really want to do?"

"Tell me," Bradley said.

"I want to stick my head outside that window and breathe," Alex said. "I've been running around all day, and it took the hairdresser an hour to make my hair look like I just rolled out of bed, and my head is killing me because she kept yanking at my hair with her brush. I think a redhead must've stolen away her first husband and she was taking it out on me. And I'm going to have to talk to people all night and I'm horrible at remembering people's names so I'll probably offend half the guests."

She grinned wickedly. "Which means they won't give me nearly as expensive wedding gifts as they should."

Bradley laughed.

"Do it, then," he said.

His camera clicked as Alex slowly stood up. She left her shoes off. She leaned out the window, moving slowly, like she wanted to savor every second of the experience.

"It's beautiful out, isn't it?" she said quietly.

Bradley stood to one side, capturing her profile with a flurry of quick shots, then he moved behind her and snapped another set of pictures. It was an unusual angle; most photographers wouldn't have captured the bride from the back. But Bradley's photographs had always discovered beauty in the unexpected.

As Alex stood there—arms outstretched, barefoot, her hair cascading down her slim back—I could see what Bradley saw. That was what scared me.

I desperately wanted to do something—to knock against a table and send a vase crashing to the floor, or open the door and let it slam loudly—to break apart the moment. But I couldn't; I had to watch it unfold. I had to see what was going on between Alex and Bradley.

After a minute, Alex turned around and smiled at Bradley. A real smile, one that stretched across her entire face. It would've been a perfect picture, but Bradley lowered his camera.

For a frozen moment, they stood there, looking at each other. Just looking.

I eased back toward the door, feeling blindly behind me for the knob. I had to leave. In a minute or two I'd come into the room again and pretend I'd never witnessed this intimacy between them. Acknowledging it would somehow make it worse—would make it real. Bradley probably treated all his subjects like this, I told myself, even as fresh tears filled my eyes and my vision blurred. It was why he was such a good photographer. His job was to connect with people and get them to let down their guard. Alex wasn't special to him; she couldn't be. He acted like this with everyone. And to her, Bradley was just another guy to charm. He meant nothing to her, absolutely nothing. She was getting married in six months, for God's sake. She was marrying the grown-up version of a Ken doll. She should be ashamed of flirting with a sweet guy like Bradley.

But the worst part was, I knew Alex well enough to know she wasn't just flirting. She wasn't being nice to Bradley so he'd take a good picture of her.

She genuinely liked him.

As I opened the door and slipped into the hallway, I could hear Alex whispering, "Bradley? Thanks."

Somehow, I got through the rest of the night. When Mom and Dad and Diana came upstairs a few minutes later, I pretended I'd been lingering in the hallway the whole time, studying the artwork on the walls. By the time the three of us entered the room, Bradley was busy adjusting one of his lights and Alex's shoes were back on. I could almost pretend the intense, charged moment between them had never happened.

"Lindsey!" Bradley carefully set down his light and walked over to me. He held out his arms, and I stepped into his familiar embrace. Bradley always gave real hugs, not one-armed, stiff embraces like most guys. I inhaled his familiar smell—woodsy and fresh, but in a way that hinted of soap, not expensive cologne—and relaxed just the tiniest bit.

I moved back and snuck another, longer look at Bradley out of the corners of my eyes. His hair was turning the slightest bit gray at the temples. It suited him, as did the new length. He'd replaced his old glasses, too, and this pair didn't take up half his face. He was still thin, but you definitely wouldn't call him skinny any longer. After all these years, Bradley had finally grown into his looks, I realized with a jolt. He was certifiably hot. I could see why Alex had flirted with him.

"What a great surprise!" I said, smiling. I reached out and gave Alex a hug, being careful not to mess up her hair and makeup, as Bradley greeted my parents. See? I don't hold grudges. Kind, reasonable Lindsey, who looks like she can hold her own in a pie-eating contest—what guy wouldn't choose her over her supermodel sister?

"Nice dress, Sis," Alex whispered in my ear. "But what's the point in having boobs like yours if you don't show them off?"

"You do it enough for both of us," I whispered back, smiling to show that I was joking, of course.

"So, Bradley, I had no idea you were coming tonight!" I gushed. Meryl Streep had nothing on me.

"Kind of a long story," Bradley said, shooting a look at Alex.

Nonononono. Uh-uh. The two of them weren't going to have any private stories around me.

"I'd love to hear it." I laughed gaily. Oh, what fun we were all having reminiscing together!

"Oh, our old photographer flaked out—I'm pretty sure he ditched us to cover some Hilton sister wedding in Vegas—and I thought of Bradley," Alex said.

See? Not such a long story, after all. A very brief story. Barely even a story at all. Hardly an anecdote. More like a caption.

"Diana, do you know if Gary's downstairs?" Alex asked.

Diana murmured something into her lapel, like a Secret Service agent, then nodded.

"He just arrived," she said. "He's on his way up."

"Why don't we do a few photos of just you and Gary, then we'll get the whole family together," Bradley suggested, just as the door to the room opened and Gary strode in.

Gary wore a black suit that looked custom-tailored and a brilliant blue dress shirt that had to be pure silk. It made his eyes leap out from his strong-featured face. His overcoat was cashmere, and his watch was a Rolex. Forget woodsy bar soap—Gary reeked of pure, undiluted success.

"Hank, great to see you," Gary said, crossing the room in long, purposeful strides—the kind of walk they taught in rich executive school—to shake my father's hand. He leaned over to kiss Mom next.

"You look beautiful, as always," he said. "Be careful or you're going to steal away all the attention at the wedding."

"Oh, go on," Mom said, giggling like a schoolgirl and swatting him on the arm.

"I'm serious," Gary said, mock sternly. "Hank, you should fill up your wife's dance card early or you might not see her the whole night."

Mom tittered and all but curtsied. I've never actually heard someone titter before, but she managed admirably.

"Lindsey, it's wonderful to see you again," Gary said, kissing my cheek softly. "I hope we get to spend a lot more time together now that you're back in town."

I had to choke back a titter myself. No politician has ever worked the room more smoothly; when Gary's attention was on you, you felt like the only person in the room. Hell, in the universe.

"Gary, you remember Bradley," Alex said. The two men shook hands. Gary was a full three or four inches taller than Bradley, and probably had twenty pounds of muscle on him. I wondered if there was some way I could subtly point this out to Alex, just in case her observational skills weren't as finely honed as usual.

"So, what's the plan?" Gary asked, wrapping his big arm around Alex and giving her neck a quick nuzzle. I silently cheered him on.

"I'd like to get a few photos of just you and Alex, then some of the whole family," Bradley said. He surveyed the room quickly. "How about you two stand over by that bouquet of flowers?"

Gary and Alex complied, and the rest of us stared at them while Bradley snapped away. They looked custom-made for each other. Even though she wore three-inch heels, the top of Alex's head just barely came to rest underneath Gary's jaw, and she seemed more delicate than ever in his arms. They looked like an ad for a support group for Beautiful People Anonymous ("Hi, I'm Alex, and the first time I realized I was beautiful—sob—I was only six." Shocked murmurs from the support group: "Only six.").

"I got some really good ones," Bradley said after a few minutes, clicking through the shots on his digital camera. "Of course, it isn't hard with subjects like you two. I was just thinking we'd go for some candid shots next before we do the family photo. Why don't you two just act natural? Forget I'm here."

Gary looked at Alex and broke into a grin, then he pulled something out of his breast pocket.

"For me?" Alex asked. "What is it?"

"Just a little engagement present," Gary said.

"You already got me one," she protested. No, not protested. *Protested* would mean she didn't want the gift, and she was already snapping open the box and shrieking. Inside were dangling earrings that glittered with green stones. Emeralds,

I guessed, though I wasn't close enough to see for sure. But somehow I sensed Gary wasn't a cubic zirconia kind of guy.

Alex threw her arms around Gary, who swept her up like she weighed no more than a child and spun her around in a circle. Alex was laughing and tossing back her head, and Gary was staring at her in pure adoration. Bradley moved around them, trying out different angles as he snapped dozens of shots.

Mom and Dad and Diana and I stood back and watched. This was my sister in her element; this was the Alex I knew. The woman who'd curled up on the floor and admitted to being tired and stressed was a stranger. Now the vulnerability I'd glimpsed was long gone; Alex was the center of attention, as usual, and she was loving every moment of it.

Gary whispered something in her ear, then kissed her on the tender spot just below her ear, and she laughed again. I couldn't imagine sharing such an intimate moment in front of a crowd, but Alex seemed to revel in it.

Then Bradley lowered his camera and looked over at me and smiled.

He looked at *me*! How many times had Bradley looked at me through the years? Hundreds? Thousands? Funny how it suddenly made my heart take a little leap. I smiled back and walked over to him, unconsciously reaching up a hand to check my hair.

"They look great together, don't they?" he asked me, gesturing to Alex.

"They really do," I said.

But enough about Alex. "Have you shot a lot of engagement portraits?" I asked Bradley.

"First one," he said. "But I couldn't turn down a friend."

A friend. That's all Alex was. And I'd been Bradley's friend much longer, I reminded myself.

"I can't wait to catch up. Want to grab a movie this week?"

I asked, feeling inexplicably nervous. "I'll even sneak in some honey for the popcorn."

"Love to," Bradley said. "I really want to hear about what's up with your job."

I kept smiling. "Same old stuff, just a new location. But it's good to be back home."

"I'm glad you're back, too," Bradley said.

His clear blue eyes, a much gentler shade than Gary's, remained fixed on mine. I'd almost forgotten how Bradley did that; he'd keep his eyes on you the whole time you were talking, soaking in what you were saying, instead of scanning the room or impatiently waiting to interject his own thoughts. And he had this lovely habit of pausing for a moment when someone was done speaking, as though making sure they were truly finished, before he responded.

"Maybe we could hit the Thai place for a drink, too," I said casually.

Suddenly I urgently wanted to go back there with Bradley; to smooth over any memories he'd created with Alex at the restaurant, like a wave erasing footprints in the sand. I wanted to replace them with memories of me.

"Great," Bradley said.

I realized I'd been holding my breath, and I let it out slowly. Bradley still cared for me. He might've been momentarily dazzled by Alex, but he was a smart guy. He'd be able to see through her. She'd forgotten all about Bradley once Gary and his emerald earrings were in the room.

Maybe I didn't look anything like Alex in my plain navy dress, but when the glitz was gone and the magic had lifted, who would Bradley rather be with? Someone who flirted with him and forgot him, or someone who'd always cared about him?

"I'll call you this week," Bradley said. He smiled. "Can you believe I still have your number memorized?"

And in that moment, I began to believe that moving home might not have been such a terrible thing, after all.

All in all, it wasn't such a bad night. Not nearly as bad as I'd feared, anyway. After we took our family photo, things happened quickly. Diana ushered us into the grand ballroom for the party, and soon the room filled with close to two hundred people, who toasted Alex and Gary with champagne and nibbled on a giant raw bar's offerings of caviar and oysters and sushi. Waiters passed by with trays of Kobe beef on garlic crostini and vegetable tempura and dozens of other appetizers that were as beautifully presented as they were mouthwatering.

"Must've set Gary back a pretty penny," Dad said at one point, hitching up his trousers and surveying the room with an appraising eye. "We offered to pay, but he wouldn't hear of it."

"Generous of you," I said, giving Dad a gentle pat on the back. Score one for Gary: I wasn't sure Dad would ever recover from the shock if he glimpsed the real bill.

All through the night, Alex was flitting everywhere, her slim silver dress catching the light as she hugged guests and danced with Gary and made everyone laugh. She and Gary moved in a special kind of magnetic space, where the very air around them seemed charged with excitement. People watched them out of the corners of their eyes, and when Alex and Gary joined a group, the laughter became louder and the gestures more animated. I had to hand it to Alex, I thought as I watched Gary tell a story and the crowd around him hang on his every word: She'd found the perfect male counterpart, one of the few guys who could hold his own with her.

As they worked the crowd, Bradley followed close behind them, his camera clicking constantly. I mostly stayed on the fringes of the party, dodging questions from my parents' friends about my job and making sure the quality control remained constant for the chocolate-covered strawberries. It was an important job, and one I undertook with grave seriousness.

But Bradley came over to talk to me not once, or twice, but three times. And every time he did, I felt a giddy, rising sensation in my chest. I found myself watching him as he worked, admiring the way he took the time to put people at ease before snapping their photos. He was even careful to stay out of the way of the dozens of waiters and waitresses ferrying around trays of champagne.

As the night wore on, I began to relax. People weren't looking at me and instantly realizing I was a fraud. No one grabbed a microphone away from the bandleader and pointed at me and yelled, "She was fired! *And* she mounted a subordinate on a conference room table!"

Maybe things were going to work out for me after all, I thought as I turned down a waiter's offer of a glass of champagne and stuck to my seltzer. I doubted I'd ever be able to look champagne in the eye again. But at least Mr. Dunne had promised me a reference, and my résumé was stellar. I'd have a new job within a month, just like I'd vowed. And Bradley and Alex were friendly, but it was obvious to everyone she and Gary belonged together.

Plus Bradley had said he would call me soon.

I hugged that secret knowledge all night long like it was a pillow. Seeing Bradley had awoken all sorts of feelings in me, feelings I hadn't known had been lying dormant for so long.

Why hadn't I ever felt attracted to Bradley before? I wondered as I watched him drop to his knees to take a photo of Gary's four-year-old niece, who would be the flower girl at the wedding. At first she was shy and hid under her mother's long skirt. But then Bradley started joking around, saying to the mother, "Ma'am, I hate to have to tell you this, but you've grown two more feet! Look down!" And the little girl started giggling and eventually came out.

Was it possible I'd known Bradley too well? I wondered as he turned around and caught my eye and smiled his familiar, shy smile. Had I seen him as more of a brother, and just needed a bit of distance to recognize how desirable he really was?

Bradley had had a crush on me for years. Maybe he'd known something I'd been too busy or blind to see. Maybe he'd known all along we were meant to be together, that we were each other's destiny, and he'd been biding his time until I realized it, too.

Ten

"I SHOULDN'T BE TELLING you this," the president of Givens & Associates said, reaching out with slim fingers to realign the stack of papers on her desk. I sat ramrod-straight in the hard wooden chair across from her desk, barely daring to breathe. She gave me one last appraising look. I was glad I'd worn my charcoal Prada suit today, even though the last thing I'd expected when I got dressed this morning was that I'd need its professional mojo. I silently thanked my trusty anal gene for making sure I was always prepared; I'd have to reward it with a new day-by-day organizer.

"I think you'd fit in very, very well here," Ms. Givens said slowly, nodding her head slightly, as if to second her own opinion. She had one of those powerfully soft voices that made me strain to hear her every word.

"Thank you," I said. I smiled back in a way that I hoped was modest but confident, but my heart was smashing against my chest. I could hardly believe this was happening. It was Wednesday, just three days after Alex's engagement party, and my life was clicking into place so quickly it seemed unreal. I'd come by this office—the biggest ad agency in D.C.—just planning to drop off my résumé. The personal touch was important, and I thought that, by handing it to the receptionist, I might have a slight edge over other candidates for the open account director position. Maybe the receptionist would put my résumé on the top of the pile, or tell her boss I hadn't looked like a mass murderer. Who knew that Cynthia Givens herself would be hurrying across the lobby toward the elevator at the exact moment I stepped inside, and that when I put out my arm to keep the door from closing on her, she'd look at me and say, "Thank you. You wouldn't believe how many people don't bother to do that."

Her hair was shorter now and she was wearing glasses, but I'd done my homework and I instantly recognized her from the photo on her website. She was the founder of D.C.'s top ad agency, the agency that was number one on my list of places I wanted to work.

By the time the elevator reached the sixteenth floor, Ms. Givens was scanning a copy of my résumé and I was desperately trying to remember nuggets from her bio, which I'd read last night on the website. She'd founded the agency eighteen years ago with five thousand dollars and a single employee. Her agency had produced four Super Bowl commercials, and its clients included Sprite and Snickers. She spoke three languages fluently, had opened up offices in Hong Kong and London, and was recently profiled in a glowing front-page article in *Advertising Age*.

As I sat across from her, I snuck quick looks around her office, trying to glean any tidbit of personal information I could use to help me make a good impression. If she'd had one of those lumpy clay paperweights kids made in preschool, or a bunch of flowers in a vase I could compliment her on, or a framed photo . . . But no. Her office was bereft of knickknacks and personal touches. Her bio hadn't mentioned anything about a spouse or children, and she wasn't wearing a wedding ring.

Ms. Givens herself—somehow I couldn't see myself calling

her Cynthia—sat in her chair with the erect posture of a balle-rina. She wore a black suit, and her only pieces of jewelry were a delicate gold-and-diamond necklace and a Chopard watch. Her makeup was minimal and tasteful, and her movements were careful and deliberate. Everything about her screamed, "Money! Success! Power!" Or maybe whispered it in a cultured, boarding-school-bred voice.

"I mean, this work on the airline campaign . . . ," Ms. Givens said, letting her words trail off as she picked up the ad from my portfolio and studied it more closely.

"Business increased by fourteen percent within two weeks of that ad's launch," I said quickly, pulling a page filled with the relevant statistics out of my briefcase and handing it across the desk to her.

She nodded again.

"Do you have any questions for me?" she asked, steepling her fingers.

Just one: How do I get your life? I thought.

Everything in her enormous corner office shone. Her leather couch looked like it had never suffered the indignity of meeting a behind, and her desk held only a computer so thin it would make a supermodel jealous and the stack of aforementioned perfectly aligned papers. Even the trade magazines arced across the coffee table with a businesslike precision.

Before I could answer—I had to have a question, otherwise I'd look too eager—someone knocked on her open door.

"I apologize for the interruption."

It was a heavyset woman in her mid-forties—about the same age as Ms. Givens—and she really did look sorry, and also the tiniest bit scared. She glanced at me, and Ms. Givens nodded sharply at her. "Go on."

"Kaitlin hasn't come in yet," she said, speaking in a hushed voice. "I don't think she's coming in today."

Ms. Givens didn't betray any emotion, except a slight tightening around her eyes.

"Call the temp office immediately and have them send a replacement," she said. "Let them know if this one doesn't work out we'll be withdrawing our business permanently."

The woman eased out of the room as Ms. Givens leaned forward and picked up her phone: "Jocelyn, please forward all my calls to the front desk and go cover it while we deal with this mess. And I'll need you to book me through to Hong Kong after my speech in San Francisco tomorrow; then I'll stop in at our London office on the way home. Unannounced—do not tell them I'm coming."

Ms. Givens didn't wait for a response before she hung up the phone. She exhaled and refocused her attention on me.

"This isn't how I enjoy starting off my day," she said, briefly rubbing her temples. I wondered why she was handling such low-level personnel issues. Wasn't that what her assistant was for? Maybe her assistant didn't have initiative, in which case Kaitlin probably wasn't the only one who would be pounding the streets in search of a new job.

"Personnel issues are always complicated," I said sympathetically. "I oversaw twenty people at Richards, Dunne and Krantz, and I know how important it is to have employees who are conscientious."

"Why did you leave?" Ms. Givens asked.

I'd prepared for this one.

"A family member is ill"—my temporary insanity counted as mental illness—"and I want to be closer to home. But be assured my work has never suffered and would never suffer because of personal issues." So it was only half a lie, really. A lie-light. They could sell it in the diet aisle, and women could check its calories against fibs and white lies.

Ms. Givens nodded, then stood up abruptly and stuck out her hand.

"Thank you," she said. "I'll be out of town for a few days. Can you come in a week from Monday at two? I'd like to talk to you again, and I'd like our agency president to meet you."

A week from Monday would also give Ms. Givens time to check my reference, but Mr. Dunne had promised me. He'd *promised*.

I couldn't look too eager; Ms. Givens had to think other companies wanted me, too. I paused a moment, mentally shuffling around my imaginary schedule to create a hole, then I smiled.

"A week from Monday it is," I said. "I'll look forward to it."

Her phone rang. She glanced at it, and I quickly said, "I'll show myself out."

By the time I was halfway to her door, she was already chatting with a client, setting up a dinner meeting for that night. I stepped into the hallway as a huge smile erupted across my face. I was going to get this job; I was certain of it. Ms. Givens wasn't the type to waste time. She wouldn't have asked me back for a second interview unless she was dead serious about me.

I walked down the hallway, toward my lucky elevator, barely containing the impulse to kick up my heels. As soon as I left this building I was going straight to the nicest restaurant I could find and buying an extra-large cappuccino and chocolate croissant to celebrate. I'd still call a headhunter this afternoon like I planned—one could never be too careful—but I knew in my bones this was a done deal. I *felt* it.

I was meant to work here; everything I knew about this agency fit in with my life plan: the overseas offices; the select, impressive client list; the prime space in a building on K Street, in the hub of the nation's capital. I'd start on the creative team, and within six months, Ms. Givens would wonder how her agency had survived this long without me. They thought I worked hard in New York? They hadn't seen anything yet. I was being given a second chance, and I knew how rare those were.

This one wouldn't slip through my fingers; I'd hold on to it too tightly to ever let it go.

Just before I got to the reception area, I passed a door to the ladies' room. Blame it on nerves; suddenly I really had to go. I stepped into the bathroom and checked my reflection in a mirror—excellent, there hadn't been a piece of Pop-Tart between my front teeth during my interview—then I ducked into a stall. Even the bathroom stalls were nice here; they were enclosed from floor to ceiling, and the walls were tiled in what looked like hand-painted Italian porcelain. Oh, yes, I could slip back into this kind of life again very quickly.

I was still smiling when I heard the door swing open.

"She isn't following us, is she?" a woman said.

"I don't think so," another woman said. "But if we're in here longer than a minute, she'll probably unleash the bloodhounds."

That voice—I'd just heard it. It was Ms. Givens's assistant, the woman with no initiative. Inside the stall, I froze.

"She'll be gone tomorrow," another woman said. "Then we won't have to hide out in the bathroom."

"Only for a few days," the assistant moaned. "She's spending four hours in San Francisco. She'll probably call me every hour. Then she's going to Hong Kong for two days. Who goes to Hong Kong for two days? Doesn't it take two days just to get there and back?"

"I know how you can torture her," the colleague said. "Knock one of her magazines out of alignment."

The two women burst into laughter.

"Just because she doesn't have a life, she resents it if anyone else does," the assistant said. "Can you believe I had to beg to get time off for my kid's school play? She made me stay late Friday night to make up for it."

"Is she gay?" the colleague asked. "I've always wondered."

"Who knows?" the assistant said. "She never gets any personal phone calls, and she works late every night. I think she's asexual. Who would want to sleep with her anyway?"

"Especially because she probably pencils it into her day planner: Foreplay from oh-nine-hundred hours until nine-oh-five. Penetration from nine-oh-six until nine-twelve." The colleague giggled.

"And too bad if the guy isn't done by then," the assistant said. "She'd probably write a performance review and tell him he needs to work on his efficiency. Hey, want to grab lunch tomorrow? I might actually be able to eat it this time."

"I think I have an opening from twelve-oh-four until twelve-sixteen." The colleague laughed as the door shut behind them.

I stayed put, still not daring to move. I hadn't been aware that I'd been holding my breath, and when I let it out, it echoed off the tiled walls of my little stall.

Okay, so they hated Ms. Givens. What employees didn't gripe about their boss? So Ms. Givens was a control freak. And a workaholic. How else would she have risen to the top of her field? They were probably just jealous of her corner office and posh lifestyle.

So what if Ms. Givens was a demanding boss? I could deal with a demanding boss; that didn't frighten me. She wouldn't be able to find much of anything to criticize in me anyway. I didn't take off time for personal issues, and I never balked at staying late or working on weekends. Hell, I did it voluntarily. In New York, my first boss had actually told me I should use more of my vacation time instead of always cashing it in.

My palms felt sweaty, and my hand slipped off the lock when I tried to open the door to the stall. I fumbled for the lock again as the walls of the stall started swaying and buckling in on me. Suddenly a powerful attack of claustrophobia was upon me. *Get out,* my brain screamed. I tried to suck in air as I pushed my shoulder against the door. I finally realized I had to pull it open. I burst out of the stall, my legs so unsteady they could barely hold me up.

I had to get a grip, quickly, before someone else came in here and saw me all wild-eyed and shaky. I walked over to the sink, ran cold water on a paper towel, and patted it on my forehead and cheeks. I took slow breaths, forcing my body to calm itself.

My claustrophobia had been sparked by residual nervousness from the interview, I told myself, turning on the water again to wash my shaking hands. There wasn't any reason to read anything else into it, to analyze the situation and jump to conclusions, like Matt would've been itching to do.

Yes, I wanted to be in Ms. Givens's position in ten years. But that didn't mean I'd be anything like her. I didn't want that kind of a sterile, lonely life. And I wouldn't have it, I assured myself, lifting my trembling chin a notch higher. There were plenty of women who juggled work and families, and did it well. Plenty of successful women who had rich, fulfilling personal lives. I pushed away the nagging little voice that wondered how I'd even find time to have a baby, to have a family, when I couldn't get away from the office for a weekend.

I'd just about convinced myself everything would be fine when I looked down at my hands. They were still compulsively washing each other.

Eleven

MY CELL PHONE VIBRATED in my pocket as I lifted my cup of cappuccino to my lips for my first sip. The buzz jolted me, and I sloshed some foam down the front of my suit jacket. The cute guy sitting three tables over hid a grin behind his newspaper.

It was Alex, of course.

"Can I ask a favor?" she asked.

"Sure," I said, dabbing at my jacket with a napkin as the waitress deposited a huge chocolate croissant on my table. Memo to cute guy: I'm a glutton *and* sloppy—sure you don't want to hit on me?

"Will you come over and look at my wedding dress?" Alex asked. "I need an honest opinion."

I glanced at my watch. I had a lot to accomplish today, now that the nonsense in the ladies' room was over. I wanted to fully research Givens & Associates, plus I needed to make contact with that headhunter. If I could line up another interview or two fast, word might get around to Ms. Givens. Being in demand couldn't hurt when it came time to negotiate my compensation package.

"Today?" I hedged.

"No, I was thinking in July, after the wedding," she said. "C'mon. Even you can take off for lunch. And we barely got to talk the other night at my party."

"Fine," I said, mentally reshuffling my day. Alex and Gary's house was in Georgetown. I could hit a cybercafe afterward and work there the rest of the afternoon, instead of going back home. I'd probably get more done anyway, considering Mom and Dad's dueling televisions were pitting soap operas against *SportsCenter.* Dad had had the volume up louder when I'd left the house, but those daytime divas were giving the Redskins a run for their money.

"I'll order in some sushi for lunch," Alex said.

I snapped my phone shut, surprised. Why did Alex want me to see her wedding dress? She made no secret of the fact that she thought I dressed way too conservatively. I wouldn't have thought my opinion mattered to her. And the whole thing about us not having a chance to talk . . . I mean, come on. It's not like we were the kind of sisters who talked every day. I knew there were some who traded confidences and hung out on weekends and called each other with every breaking detail of their lives, but Alex and I had never had that kind of relationship. We weren't even close enough to have rip-roaring fights, like other sisters I knew. I was happy with that arrangement, and thought she was, too. So why did she want to see me now?

Maybe she was reaching out.

I rolled the unfamiliar idea around in my mind, testing it. Alex and I would never be best friends—we were too different—but if she was trying, I supposed I could meet her halfway. We were grown-ups, and living in the same city for the first time since high school. Now that my life was veering back on track, it wouldn't kill me to take more of an interest in Alex's. I could start with her wedding, I supposed.

Besides, I could spare the time, I thought with satisfaction. I'd had a hugely successful morning, plus I'd spent the previous weekend whipping my parents' house into shape. I'd even tackled their refrigerator, scrubbing down the shelves and tossing out a petrified, clove-studded orange I recognized from a few Christmases ago.

I leisurely finished my cappuccino, then called the headhunter and managed to catch him at his desk. We chatted awhile and he asked me to email him my résumé, then promised he'd be back in touch within a day or so to talk about job prospects. Right after I hung up, my phone buzzed with an incoming text message from Matt:

Breaking news . . . Cheryl's implants exploded when she was on Fenstermaker's plane and it depressurized . . . funeral details to follow. (Separate services are being held for her implants; donations to the Silicone Society are suggested in lieu of flowers)

I grinned and paid the bill the waitress had dropped on the table, leaving a good tip to make up for camping out for so long. Fifteen minutes later, I was getting out of a cab in front of Alex's place.

From the outside, it looked deceptively small, since the houses on the narrow Georgetown streets were all packed in tightly together, like subway commuters at rush hour. But once Alex opened the door, I realized the façade of the house was an optical illusion. Inside it was high-ceilinged and roomy, with glass doors leading to the green oasis of a big backyard terrace. Toward the back of the house, I could see a cleaning woman in a white uniform mopping the wooden floors.

Alex had told me Gary'd hired a top interior designer when he bought the house, which made sense, because the French country–inspired decor was far too elegant and immaculate to have been conceived by Alex. When we were growing up, her bedroom was a complete pit, with open bottles of nail polish hardening on her dresser and so many clothes tossed over her bed it was a wonder she didn't get buried alive at night. Someday soon I'd have a house like this, too, instead of my scrotum-ceiling bedroom, I vowed, looking around.

"Nice place," I said.

"I hate my dress," Alex announced. Her hair was swept up in a ponytail, and she was wearing a pink bathrobe.

"It is a little informal for an evening wedding," I agreed.

"Shut up," she said. "Come on. It's upstairs."

I followed her up the graceful spiral staircase, into her dressing room, which was roughly the size of Mom and Dad's living room. Now this room looked like Alex. Dozens of pairs of shoes were scattered across the floor with the heels pointing up like lethal little spikes, a hidden speaker played Amy Winehouse, and an entire wall was covered with a giant mirror. A table in front of the mirror held more makeup than a Clinique counter. Alex still left off the tops of her bottles of nail polish, I noticed, but now she wouldn't have to beg Dad for extra allowance or go shoplift new bottles when her old ones dried up. From the looks of this place, Gary could buy Sally Hansen herself.

"I want you to be brutally honest," Alex said.

She shrugged off her bathrobe unself-consciously, and I averted my eyes. But not before I'd glimpsed what seemed like acres of smooth, glowing skin and a pale lavender thong. Who wore a thong around the house with a cozy bathrobe? It would be like putting a thumbtack in your bedroom slippers.

"The wedding planner talked me into this dress," Alex said, her voice muffled as she pulled it over her head.

"Alex!" I scolded, hurrying over to help her. "Jesus, don't tug on it like that. You're going to rip it."

"It's just a sample," Alex said. "They still haven't fit the real one on me."

I smoothed down the layers of her dress, then stood back.

"So?" she said. "What? Why are you looking at me like that? Do you hate it, too?"

I shook my head.

"You really like it?" Alex asked.

I nodded.

"But isn't it too . . . poufy? I always said I'd never wear a poufy dress. But Toothy Tori the wedding planner kept saying, 'It's the one time in your life when you can wear a poufy dress without looking ridiculous.' Toothy made me try on a hundred of them, and by the end of it I was so exhausted I just gave in. That's how they do it, you know. They show you millions of hideous dresses, then they pull out one that isn't half bad and you jump on it because your perspective is completely screwed."

"Alex," I said, finally finding my voice. "Shut up. It's perfect."

And it was.

I'd expected Alex to go for something sleek and sexy, maybe a thin silk gown with a big slit up the thigh. I'd thought she'd want to show off her body in something form-fitting. But the dress she'd chosen was a winter white silk with three-quarter-length lace sleeves, a scoop neck, and a tightly nipped waist. It reached the floor, but it didn't have a train. It was simple yet classic, elegant without being frumpy. Even with her hair in a ponytail and her feet bare, she took my breath away.

"I don't know," Alex said, frowning. She twisted around me to see herself in the mirror. "Really?"

"C'mon, Alex, you know you look great," I said, growing impatient. Was this all a game called "Let's reassure Alex she's as gorgeous as ever"? Because if it was, I didn't want to play.

"Now I have to figure out how to wear my hair," Alex said. "How do you think it would look up?"

If she expected me to stand around, oohing and aahing while she experimented with it, then that ponytail was too tight and it was cutting off circulation to her brain. It was one thing to talk to Alex about her wedding, entirely another to try out for the job of president of her fan club.

Alex hadn't asked me anything about my job yet. She hadn't asked me how it felt to leave New York. She only wanted to talk about herself. Or, more specifically, she wanted our conversation to revolve around her looks.

Why had I thought today would be any different? Why had I thought our relationship could ever be any different than it had been when we were growing up?

"Don't you have six months to decide about your hair?" I asked, plopping down on a leather ottoman and picking up *The Washingtonian* magazine from the floor. I skimmed the cover lines before noticing Alex was on the cover in a blue bikini. I let the magazine fall to the floor.

"Yeah, I guess," Alex said. "There's just so much to do. It's kind of overwhelming."

"You've got a wedding planner," I pointed out. "Isn't she supposed to do the work for you?"

Alex thought she had a lot to do? It was noon and she was still in her bathrobe while a maid mopped her floors and a deliveryman brought her sushi. She probably had nothing lined up for this afternoon but a facial and a session with Sven the personal trainer.

Okay, maybe that was a tiny bit unfair. Her personal trainer was probably named Mike. Fine, fine, so Alex did work, and her job required her to look good. She even got to write off those facials. Still, my annoyance flared. This is why Alex and I couldn't spend two minutes together. She'd always been a bit spoiled—too much attention will do that to you—and for some reason, her self-absorption chafed me more than usual today.

"So what's it like, living with Mom and Dad?" she asked, nudging me with her foot. I shifted over on the ottoman, and she sat down next to me.

I rolled my eyes at her question, then sighed and shook my head.

"It's exactly what you'd think," I said. "Mom stands outside my bedroom door yelling questions at me, but she thinks because she doesn't come barging in she's giving me plenty of space. She even called me on my cell phone yesterday. From *one room over.*"

Then a memory came to me and I smiled.

"What?" Alex demanded.

"The other day at lunch the three of us all ordered glasses of wine," I said. "So Dad pulls a pencil out of his pocket and starts scribbling on the tablecloth, trying to figure out if it was cheaper to get it by the glass or carafe."

"The druggie hostess place?" Alex asked.

"Unwashed fork," I said.

"Ah," Alex said. "Antonio's. When Gary first met them, we went there, too. They got out of their car and stood on the side walk arguing for five minutes about whether Dad had remembered to lock the car door."

"So much simpler to walk back and check," I said.

"But then they couldn't argue about it," Alex said.

"Of course," I said.

There was another pause, but it didn't feel quite as awkward this time.

"Oh, and Dad keeps talking about Mr. Simpson like they're mortal enemies. Remember how they used to be buddies?"

"The day after Dad retired, Mr. Simpson cut three inches off the hedge between their yards," Alex said, grinning at the memory. "Dad went ballistic."

"Transference," I said. "Dad had to channel his energy somewhere."

"Don't throw your fancy SAT words at me," Alex joked.

"It's a psych term," I said. Matt had taught it to me. I smiled again, thinking of the drawing he'd pressed into my hand when I'd gotten on the train. I'd call him this weekend and tell him all about my new job.

"What?" Alex demanded.

"I was just thinking of a friend," I said. "Someone in New York."

A gleam came into Alex's eyes: "A *special* friend?"

"Shut up," I said. "You sound like a preschool teacher."

"Now that—"

Her phone rang, interrupting whatever she'd been about to say.

"It's probably the sushi guy," she said, standing up.

"Hello?" Her voice ratcheted up in warmth about thirty degrees. "Hey, you! I was going to call you later today."

She reached up and absently released her hair from her ponytail, letting it cascade around her shoulders as she wove her fingers through it.

"Tonight?"

I picked up the magazine again and flipped through it. For a few minutes, Alex and I had been having an actual conversation. But when we finished analyzing our parents, would we have anything else to talk about? Did we have anything in common but our gene pool?

"I'd love to," Alex was saying. "Gary's in New York, but I can meet you after I film my show . . ."

I tuned out the rest of her conversation as I began reading an article about a personal organizer who'd transformed a woman's paper clutter. Yup, yup, that was one of my favorite tricks— open mail directly over the trash can so you can toss the junk before it has a chance to accumulate on a kitchen counter. Oh, but I didn't know this tip about keeping appliance receipts stapled to the insides of the instruction books so they'd be handy if you ever needed a refund.

"Sorry," Alex said, hanging up the phone. "That was Bradley. I should've asked if he wanted to say hi to you, but I didn't think of it."

Something that felt like an electric current charged through me.

"That was Bradley calling?" I asked. My voice sounded rusty. I cleared my throat and pretended to cough.

"Uh-huh," Alex said, looking at herself in the floor-to-ceiling mirror.

From my vantage point on the ottoman, I was trapped between her and her reflection. Everywhere I looked, all I could see were masses of red-gold hair and white silk. Alex was in front of me and behind me and even smiling up at me from the magazine in my hands. I couldn't escape her blinding, overpowering beauty.

"What did he want?" I asked.

"We're going to grab a drink tonight so he can show me the proofs from the engagement party," she said. She slipped out of her dress again and tossed it on the ottoman next to me.

Why had Bradley called Alex and not me?

"Gary's not coming?" I asked. God, were Alex's thighs ever sculpted. I could see the slim cords of muscle running down the middles of them.

"Doesn't Gary want to see the proofs, too?" I asked.

"I don't think he cares which ones I pick," she said, dotting a peachy lipstick on her full lips. "It's more of a girl thing."

An Alex thing, you mean, I thought bitterly. What could be better than to spend a night looking at pictures of yourself with the guy I liked, the guy who might like me again, too, if only my sister would stay the hell out of the way? Maybe Alex didn't know how I felt about Bradley, but it didn't matter. He was *mine*. Why couldn't she leave him alone?

I leapt up and grabbed my purse. But it was the wrong purse;

Alex had a dozen littering the floor. I groped blindly around until I finally found mine.

"Just remembered an appointment," I said tightly. "I've got to go."

"What about lunch?" Alex asked, turning away from her reflection.

I didn't answer. I was already halfway down the stairs and running for the door.

Twelve

I HAD TO GET away from Alex before I did something crazy, like scream at her for seeing Bradley tonight. Then she'd know exactly how I felt about him; Alex has always been good at reading people. I didn't want her to know. I didn't want *anyone* to know until I figured out how Bradley felt about me. Was I just a friend to him? Or could he fall in love with me all over again, given a chance? Or did he secretly have a crush on Alex now, in which case I'd never have a future with him because I'd always feel like his consolation prize?

I tore down the street, trying to put as much space between me and Alex as possible. Why did being around my sister always do this to me? I was twenty-nine years old, but I felt like I was back in high school again. Alex was on the cover of our city's magazine; she'd be on television tonight, and then she was going out with the guy I liked. She had everything. She'd *always* had everything.

Hot tears blinded my eyes as I took a step into the street. A horn blared, and I jumped back onto the curb as a bus roared by. I'd only walked two blocks, but it had taken me from a residential street to the corner of M Street and Wisconsin Avenue.

I blinked, and a big corner building came into focus. It was Georgetown Park.

I looked down at my plain suit and low-heeled shoes, then I looked back up at the mall.

Suddenly an urge overpowered me. I needed pretty underwear. I craved bright lipstick. I desperately wanted to shed my prim charcoal suit and slip into a new outfit, one that made me feel pretty and sexy and young. One that would let me escape myself and the awful feelings that were bombarding me.

I ran down the escalator leading from the street into the mall. I hurried down the corridor, scanning the names of the stores I passed. Then I saw it: Victoria's Secret.

"We're having a sale on cotton panties," a saleswoman with a silver nose ring told me as I burst inside like someone was chasing me. "Two for one."

"I need something sexy," I told her.

"Are you going on a honeymoon?" the saleswoman asked. I could see her leopard-skin bra strap peeking out from underneath her white tank top. "Because we just got in a gorgeous nightie and matching robe."

A robe? Even the Victoria's Secret saleswoman thought I was prim. She and the other saleswoman, who was lounging against the counter painting her nails dark purple, would probably laugh at me when I was gone.

"At least we unloaded those granny panties on her," Purple Nails would say. "I thought we'd never get rid of them."

I narrowed my eyes.

"What I really need is a garter belt," I said grimly. "My old one's all torn up."

She blinked, then walked over to a display and handed me a garter belt. Black lace, no less.

Twenty minutes later, loaded down with pink bags filled with gel push-up bras, delicate lace thongs, and a red silk teddy, I strode into the next shop over. I walked out a few minutes later wearing tight dark denim jeans, a nude lace camisole, and a dusty pink cropped suede jacket.

This was a start, but I needed more! There was an ache inside of me, a void I felt desperate to fill. I darted into shop after shop like an addict in search of a fix, my eyes ricocheting in all directions. What did I want? A soft leather hobo purse? Bronzing gel? A silky halter top in a shade of eggplant so deep it was almost black?

I twirled around, looking at the tantalizing options displayed on mannequins. The new spring line must've just come in: There were little shrug sweaters and tight T-shirts in sherbet colors. Strappy black heels that crisscrossed their way up the leg. Chunky silver hoop earrings and turquoise cuff bracelets. Off-the-shoulder dresses, flirty little skirts that skimmed the midthigh, gauzy bohemian tops with tulip sleeves. Suddenly I wanted it all: all the makeup I'd never worn, all the cute, sexy clothes I'd turned my sensible nose up at, knowing they would be out of style next season but my well-made classics would last me forever.

I collected an armful of clothes and hurried into a dressing room. I came out with two of the fitted little T-shirts in lime and cherry, a black silk turtleneck with a scoop taken out of the back so the curve of my spine was revealed; an incredibly flattering bustier trimmed in black lace; a fire engine red dress with a deep V-neck, and an off-the-shoulder cream-colored one, too. I looked around, breathing hard. Now I needed some funky earrings, and a new perfume, too. I wasn't done yet; not by a long shot.

The woman behind the MAC counter was staring at me.

"Come here," she said, motioning me over. "We're doing free makeovers today. I'm dying to get my hands on you."

Normally free makeovers scare me. I've seen too many women get up from them looking twenty years older, with thick eyeliner and clown circles on their cheeks. But the MAC woman was young and hip, with a streak of pink in her black hair and a tattoo of a star on her right shoulder. She looked like she understood the concept of blending.

"What the hell," I said. I laid my clothes on the counter and sat down on a stool.

"You've got strong eyes and lips," she said, smoothing something cool and creamy over my face and wiping it off with a cotton pad. "I'd definitely recommend deep colors for you."

"Nothing powder blue or green," I pleaded.

"Relax," she ordered. "Do I look like I'm going to turn you into a Stepford wife?"

I kept my eyes closed while tiny brushes tickled my eyelids and danced across my cheeks and a gentle pencil traced the outline of my lips.

"Where's my plum eye shadow?" she murmured, and my eyes shot open in alarm.

"Keep them closed," she ordered, wielding an evil-looking silver device that I recognized as an eyelash curler—Alex always had them lying around the bathroom.

Alex.

"Stop frowning," the MAC woman ordered me, and I made myself stop thinking about anything at all.

I felt her dot something under my eyes, then draw lines against my upper eyelashes.

"A little gold shimmer would be gorgeous with your olive complexion," she murmured at one point, her fingers moving lightly over my face. "I'm going to dust a touch across your collarbone, too."

A moment later she said, "Do you mind if I do something about those bangs?"

"Be my guest," I said grandly, and she squirted something on them and went to work. I felt her unpin my hair and let it fall around my shoulders, then she began twirling sections of it in her fingers and squirting it with something that smelled deliciously like grapefruit.

Fifteen minutes later I opened my eyes and stared into the mirror. A stranger stared back at me. My eyes seemed bigger, my skin glowed like I'd spent the afternoon on the beach, and my bangs were swept to one side, somehow calling attention to my cheekbones. And my lips . . . oh, my lips!

"You made them bigger," I said, lifting a hand to touch them.

"The trick is to put a dot of concealer just above the bow in your upper lip," she said. "Yours are pretty full, but it fools the eye into thinking your lips are even bigger."

"I'll take it all," I told her. I pulled out my credit card.

"Good," she said. "What I'm going to do is make you a chart explaining exactly how to put everything on so you can do it yourself next time. You need some good brushes, too. Makeup is really all about the brushes. And do us both a favor and let your bangs grow an inch or two longer."

I grabbed the bags and chart she handed me and headed toward the escalator, pausing at every mirror I passed to gape at myself. Shoes. Now I needed shoes. I headed up one level and immediately spotted a pair of caramel-colored leather boots with tiny silver buckles crisscrossing the fronts. The leather was so supple the boots felt like they were practically melting in my hands. I had to have them; it was a physical craving so strong I was helpless in its grasp.

"Do you know the secret of these boots?" a saleswoman sidled over and whispered. "One of the heels is just the tiniest bit shorter than the other."

"Why?" I asked.

"Put them on and walk across the room and you'll see," she instructed, hurrying into the stockroom to bring me back my size.

It was unbelievable. I didn't just have new boots. I had a whole new walk. My hips jutted out like a runway model's, and my rear end swayed ever so slightly from side to side. A guy riding the escalator turned to stare at me and tripped at the end when he forgot to step off.

"They're worth every penny," I told the saleswoman.

It wasn't just the lipstick and the boots that were different. *I* was different, I suddenly realized. My shoulders weren't anxiously hunched forward anymore. My eyes weren't downcast. I was oozing something I couldn't quite put my finger on. Something completely unfamiliar. Something powerful and wonderful and intoxicating.

"Can you give me a pair of those black heels, too? The ones that crisscross up the calves?" I asked, handing the saleswoman my credit card.

"Sure. Size eight, right? You know, Marilyn Monroe used to shave a bit off one of her heels, too," the saleswoman confided, ringing me up. "Your boyfriend's going to love them."

"Boyfriend?" I said, winking. "Don't you mean *boyfriends*?"

"You go, girl!" she said, putting my sensible black pumps and my new strappy sandals into a bag and handing them to me.

I slicked on another layer of my new lipstick and swayed all the way out onto the street. Later I'd assess the damage to my credit card and come to terms with what I'd just done. Later I'd panic and wonder if I should return everything or just shove it into the back of my closet and pretend like this never happened. But right now, all I wanted to do was revel in this absolutely exhilarating feeling.

The outside air was crisp and cool in my face. I lifted up my hand to hail a cab, then let it drop to my side, feeling my euphoria fade. I couldn't sit at home alone while Alex and Bradley had drinks. I knew I'd go crazy, imagining Bradley staring at Alex's photos and telling her how gorgeous she looked while their thighs inched closer together. I felt the dangerous embers of my jealousy heating up again.

Alex and Bradley were going out to a bar? Fine, then I'd go to one, too. I'd have a glass of wine and revel in my new look and recapture some of the joy I'd felt when Ms. Givens had asked me back for another interview. I wouldn't let Alex take that away from me, too.

I started walking downhill, toward the Potomac River. There was a seafood restaurant called Tony & Joe's on the water, just about three blocks away. I strode down the sidewalk, and a couple of guys walking toward me stood back to let me pass. Funny, I was usually the one who stepped aside to let others pass. I'd never noticed it before. I was walking differently, taking up more space and not feeling apologetic about it. My arms swung my packages back and forth, and my strides were longer. A passing motorist whistled at me, and I turned to smile at him instead of ducking my head.

A drink was definitely what I needed. Maybe I'd treat myself to a nice dinner, too.

I was passing through the outdoor parking lot for the seafood restaurant when I heard the voices. A man's low, angry voice and a woman's high, pleading one. Probably just someone squabbling with her boyfriend, I thought, but instinct made me stop walking.

A pickup truck was blocking my view, so I stepped around it and the couple came into view. The man was fortyish, short and skinny, and he wore a suit and tie. I couldn't see his eyes because mirrored sunglasses covered them, even though it was dusk.

"Will you please move and let me get into my car?" the woman was saying. "I can't talk to you when you're like this."

"You're such a bitch," the man shouted. "You can't talk to me? Why the fuck can't you talk to me?"

The guy's fury was clear; he was losing control. Should I call 911, or would that be overreacting? I wondered. He was moving closer to her, and she was backing up, and the expression on his face was one of rage. Neither of them had seen me. Should I yell for help? I glanced around wildly: The only person I could see was a man walking his dog along the water, but he was a hundred yards away. He might not hear me.

Before I could do anything, a sound exploded. Had the man thrown the woman against her car? Without thinking, I dropped my bags and ran toward them.

"Hey!" I yelled. "Get away from her!"

The man was rubbing his knuckles, and the woman was leaning back against the car. When he saw me, he didn't say a word. He just walked away, like he was out for a Sunday afternoon stroll.

"Are you okay?" I asked, running over to the woman.

"I think so," she said. But then her legs gave way and she slid down against the car to the ground. She looked like she was in shock; her face was so pale I was worried she might faint. Her blue eyes were wide and scared.

"Did he hit you?" I asked. I leaned over and scanned her face but couldn't see any marks. "Should I call an ambulance?"

"He hit my car," she said, pointing to a dent in the driver's side door. She blew out her breath in a big whoosh, and I sighed in relief, too.

"But he might've hit me if you hadn't come along," she said. "Thank you."

"I'm just glad I was here," I said. "Do you want me to call the police?"

She shook her head. "That prince of a guy was my ex-husband," she said.

"Wow," I said. I couldn't think of anything else to say.

"Can you guess why I divorced him?" She laughed the kind of laugh that had no humor in it, then shook her head. "I'm such an idiot. I don't know why I agreed to meet him tonight. We had some papers to sign and I should've just left them at his lawyer's office, but I kept thinking about how we were married for seven years. I guess I wanted to honor it or something. I thought we could shake hands and wish each other well. I mean, he wasn't anything like that when I first married him—"

She broke off and stood up.

"I'm sorry," she said. "God, I'm a mess. Here I am telling you my life story. Thank you again."

"Are you sure you're okay to drive?" I asked. She was still pretty pale. "Isn't there someone you want to call?"

"I'll be fine," she said. She reached out and pressed my hand between hers. Her hands were ice-cold. She brushed off her dress, then opened her car door and got in. But she didn't put the key in the ignition.

"If you're sure," I said. I walked a few steps away and picked up my shopping bags, then I looked back. She was still sitting there, staring into space. She looked so sad. Impulsively, I hurried back to her car.

"I was just going to have a glass of wine," I told her, motioning to the restaurant. "Do you want to join me? Maybe if you sit down and rest for a bit you'll feel better."

I don't know what made me do it. Maybe it was the fact that her face was so open and friendly, with deep laugh lines radiating out from her eyes, attesting to the fact that this was a woman who usually smiled. Or maybe it was because I saw in her a kindred soul: Her life had unraveled, too, and now she was trying to put the pieces back together.

"Right now?" She looked up at me. "But aren't you meeting someone?"

"No, I'm alone," I said.

"Really?" she said. "I can't believe someone who looks like you is going out alone."

What could I say to that? That this isn't really me; it's just a costume? That I'm like a kid dressed up for Halloween?

"I'd love to join you, if you honestly don't mind," she said. "A glass of wine sounds like exactly what I need."

She got out of her car, and we walked into Tony & Joe's. It was too late for lunch and too early for happy hour to be in full swing, so we had our choice of seats. We settled into a pair of overstuffed chairs by a glass wall overlooking the water. I should've felt awkward—here I was with a woman I knew nothing about, other than that she had an abusive ex-husband—but something about her put me instantly at ease. Or maybe it was the new me who was at ease. Maybe wearing these clothes and makeup made me feel like I was playing a part, and that it wasn't really me who was directing my own actions.

"I don't even know your name," she said after we'd both ordered glasses of Chardonnay.

"It's Lindsey," I told her.

"I'm May," she said. "And I'm so grateful to you. Would you believe—"

Her cell phone rang, cutting off whatever she'd been planning to say.

"I'm sorry," May said. "It's a work call. Do you mind? I'll make it very quick."

"Not at all," I told her. Funny, May didn't look like the businesswoman type. She reminded me more of the tooth fairy's mother, with her long flowery dress and riot of brown-gray curls. Then again, I probably didn't look like the kind of woman who'd jealously guarded her spot on the dean's list during college, I thought, hiking up my camisole so my boobs didn't pop out.

"Blind Dates," May said into the phone. "Oh, Devlin, how nice to hear from you! But shouldn't you be meeting your date now?"

She frowned while she listened, then shook her head.

"You're just nervous," she said. "It's totally normal. You've only been out on one date in the past fourteen years. It's hard for everyone to get back out there after a divorce."

Hmmm . . . *juicy.*

"Devlin, you're a smart, kind guy. Do you know how many women out there would love to get to know you?" May asked. "Do you want me to go over your list of conversational top-ics?"

Now I'd given up any pretense of looking at the water; I was blatantly staring at May.

"Um-hmm . . . and don't forget your trip to Ireland," May said. "Tell that funny story about the dog sneaking into the pub. And remember the rule about the end of the night. If you're not interested, don't say you'll call her. Just tell her you had a nice time."

May finished the call and dropped her phone into her purse.

"Sorry," she said, taking a big sip of the wine the waitress had delivered while she'd been on the phone. "Ah, that hits the spot. I run a dating service called Blind Dates, and that was one of my clients."

"Really? How long have you been in business?" I asked.

"About eight years," she said. "I love it. I get to know each of my clients personally before I set them up with anyone. That way it really does feel like a blind date to them. And I do back-ground and credit checks, too, just to be safe."

"That's fascinating," I said. "How many clients do you have?"

"About sixty at any given moment," she said. Then she dim-pled up. "I've already had nine weddings!"

"Pretty good success rate," I said. I could see May visibly relax as she talked about her business, but that wasn't the only reason why I was asking questions. I truly was interested.

"But enough about me," she said. "Tell me about you. What do you do when you're not being incredibly kind and rescuing women in parking lots?"

I smiled ruefully. Funny, but I used to love that "What do you do?" question. Now it made my stomach clench up.

"Well, I just moved here from New York," I said.

"That explains it," May said. "I figured there was some reason you weren't meeting a boyfriend tonight. Is there someone special in New York?"

I thought about Bradley, and I could feel my face fall. There *was* someone special, and he was with my twin sister right now.

"I'm sorry," May said. "I'm asking too many questions. But if it makes you feel any better, those guys at the bar have been staring at you ever since you walked in."

I looked over and saw three yuppies at the bar, all wearing dark suits with the ties loosened around their necks. They smiled, and one of them lifted his glass of beer at me in a toast.

I turned back to May. "Really? Since I came in?"

"Come on, honey, you've got to be used to it," she said.

I looked at the guys again, then turned back to May. If only she knew. I had no idea how to act around guys who were flirting with me. What was I supposed to do? Lift my glass back up at the guys? Wander over and say hi? I felt like a foreigner in a strange country, where I didn't know any of the language or customs. And the minute I opened my mouth, everyone would know I didn't belong.

"Tell me more about your company," I said, giving a quick smile to the guys before turning away and getting back on safer ground. "How do you know which people to match up?"

"It's just a feeling," she said, her eyes lighting up. "That's my favorite part of the job. Sometimes I get two people who you'd never think would click on paper, but a sixth sense tells me it's worth setting them up. And would you believe that little whispering voice is right more often than not?"

"Are most of your clients divorced?" I asked.

"Some, but I get all types. College students, widowers, even a former runner-up for Miss Maryland," she said. "She's happily dating a scientist for the National Institutes of Health now. I'm thinking about using the two of them in an ad."

She looked me up and down. "You know, I have one guy I think you'd really get along with. Interested? Of course there wouldn't be any charge."

"Thanks," I said. "But I'm involved with someone. I mean, not really, but I hope to be."

"Ah," May said. "Well, he's a lucky guy."

"Thank you," I said, blushing. Was this what it was like for Alex every day, with compliments being tossed over her like confetti? What a lovely way to live; the only thing that routinely poured down on me was rain.

"But I am interested in one thing," I said. "Tell me about your ad. Are you working with an agency?"

"I went to see an advertising agency, but I don't have the budget for what they want to do. Can you believe they want twenty thousand dollars just to create a few magazine ads? And that doesn't even include the cost of running the ads. I figured I'd just do one myself," May said.

May whispered "twenty thousand dollars" like it was such a shocking sum it shouldn't be spoken aloud. I figured I probably shouldn't tell her that it used to be my annual courier bill.

"I worked in advertising in New York," I said, leaning back in my chair and taking a sip of wine. "Maybe I can give you a tip or two. Why don't you tell me more about your ad?"

"Right now?" May asked.

"Right now," I said.

Suddenly I was itching to help, to dive back into the world I knew so well. May deserved a break, and maybe I could help give her one. Maybe there was a reason May was put in my path today. I could develop a strategy for May practically in my sleep. I could help her business grow. Work had always been my favorite escape. What better way to get my mind off Alex and Bradley and everything else that had happened today than to plunge into it, right here and now?

May's idea for the ad was a disaster. She wanted to use a photograph of a happy couple sitting on a couch and smiling at the camera. There wasn't anything interesting or edgy about it. People would probably flip right past it without caring if it was an ad for toothpaste or one for cut-rate sleeper sofas. It would be completely forgettable, which would be its own death knell.

"I like your idea," I fibbed as she ordered a second glass of wine and I switched to ice water, "but can I give you some thoughts about a different approach?"

"Of course," May said. "You're the expert."

"You need to know what people want in a dating service," I said, leaning toward her and resting my elbows on my knees. "You might think it's obvious—they want to meet someone special—but it's probably a lot more complicated than that. What's keeping a prospective client from picking up the phone and calling you?"

May wrinkled her forehead. "Maybe they're scared?"

"But scared of what?" I asked. "Scared of being set up with a psycho? Scared of being considered desperate for calling a dating service? Until you can pinpoint what's keeping people from calling you, you won't be able to reassure them. And that's what you want your ad to do: reassure them and entice them."

"Wow," May said. "I don't even know how I'd start figuring all that out. How do you do that kind of research?"

"Ever heard of a focus group?" I asked her.

She nodded. "I think so."

"Guess what?" I said, looking around the bar. By now it was jammed full of twenty- and thirty-something men and women, all flirting and laughing and checking each other out.

"We're in the middle of your focus group right now," I told May.

Ten minutes later, I was standing in front of a dozen men and women, all of whom May and I had lured over with the promise of free drinks. My three yuppies were in the group, as was a woman who was out celebrating her divorce with a group of girlfriends. I'd singled them out because her friends had tied a bunch of tin cans to her waist with a string, and they'd taped a sign that said "Just Divorced!" to her rear end. I sensed these women wouldn't be shy about telling me exactly what they wanted in a dating service. The rest of our group was an eclectic mix: a bearded guy who'd been sitting at the bar alone, waiting for a buddy who'd never shown up; a very attractive man and equally pretty woman who'd been friends since college but had never dated each other (the electricity between them was obvious; the first time one of them had one too many lemon drop shooters, they'd be rolling around on the carpet); and a trio of office mates from a law firm.

"Can everyone hear me?" I asked. "Yes? Great. Let's get started. My name is Lindsey, and I'd love to know what you all think about dating services."

"I'd never use one," one of the divorcée's girlfriends instantly piped up.

"Why not?" I asked.

"Too embarrassing," she said, and a few people murmured agreement. "They're for losers."

May was furiously scribbling down notes, just as I'd asked her to.

"What about you?" I asked one of the yuppies.

"I'll join your dating service if you'll go out with me," he said, and his friends laughed and high-fived him.

I hid a smile and quickly turned to the guy who'd been waiting at the bar alone.

"How about you?" I asked.

"I dunno," he said. "Seems kind of weird."

"So dating services are weird and embarrassing," I said.

"Like my ex-husband!" the woman with the sign on her back shouted, and her friends shrieked with laughter. By now a few other people were wandering over, drawn by the noise. I climbed onto a footstool so I could see everyone. Thank God I'd stopped at one glass of wine or I'd probably have toppled over in my lopsided boots.

"I don't think they're so bad," someone said. "Half the people I know use Match.com."

"Yeah, but a friend of mine did it and the guy turned out to be married," a woman shouted from the other side of the crowd. "And fifty pounds heavier than his picture."

"So people misrepresent themselves," I said.

"Like this guy in Cleveland," one of the law firm people said. "He wanted to fly in and meet my friend. And he was like, *sixty*. I Googled him and warned her."

Suddenly half the crowd was nodding assent; they all had a "friend" who'd been burned by computer dating.

"What about blind dates?" I asked.

"Fastest way to ruin a friendship," someone said knowingly. "Set them up and they end up hating each other and they both blame you."

"Once I got set up with this guy my friend worked with, and he was such a dog," one of the divorced woman's friends shouted. She was slurring her words slightly. "I was like, 'So you think *I'm* a dog?' Otherwise why would she have set me up with him?"

"*Bitch*," the woman with the tin cans said sympathetically. "You are so not a dog."

"You're not a dog, either," the first woman said weepily, throwing her arms around her friend's neck. The tin cans clanked as they drunkenly hugged.

"Do you think there are any normal people who use dating services?" I asked. "Anybody who gets married through one?"

"They'd have to lie about it," a yuppie shouted. "They say they met white-water rafting or something."

"Or in prison," a law firm guy hollered, and the crowd cheered.

"So there's no good reason to call a dating service," I said, projecting my voice so it would reach all the way to the back of the crowd and subdue the cheers. My old company had sent me to a media specialist to learn how to do that for speeches. It was one of the reasons I didn't freeze up when talking in front of crowds. But tonight I was even more at ease than usual. My new clothes and makeup gave me an added spark.

"But what about a dating service that does background checks to make sure people aren't married?" I asked. "What if someone checked out your date before you ever met him or her, and snapped a photo of them, too? What if the dating service was selective, so that not just anyone could get in? Would that make a difference?"

"Maybe," tin can woman conceded, and a few people murmured agreement.

"Thank you," I said. "You've all been a huge help."

I stepped down from the footstool and walked over to May.

"You were unbelievable," she said. "The way you took control of that crowd!"

"It was fun," I said, and I realized it really had been.

"I can't believe you're doing all this for me," May said. "It's too much."

"There's only one way you can thank me," I said. "Let me create your ad. I know exactly what I'm going to do."

Thirteen

BY 2:00 A.M., MY eyes were burning, my back was aching, and the taste of stale coffee lingered in my mouth. Dozens of cut-up magazines littered my bedroom floor, and two of my fingers kept sticking together because they were coated with glue.

But my ads for May weren't half-bad.

I looked down at the sheaf of papers spread out over my bed. I'd flipped strategies around midnight, deciding to scrap the idea of a full-page ad. Instead, I'd created four quarter page ads. I'd snipped photos and words from different magazines to create collages of my layouts. I envisioned the ads running on consecutive pages of a magazine, playing off each other like the old Burma-Shave roadside signs.

My first ad featured a cute young woman looking straight into the camera. She was seated at a restaurant table, and opposite her was a gray-haired man with a cane.

"He said he was *twenty-six,*" read the bold red copy above her head.

The second ad showed a guy staring in shock at his credit card bill. This time the red copy read, "I took her out for dinner. *She* took my credit card."

My third ad featured a woman holding up a gold wedding ring. "He asked me to go away with him for the weekend. Then his *wife* called."

My final ad was a simple line of the same bright red copy on a black background: "Blind Dates. Our only surprises are happy ones."

I fell back onto my bed, suddenly exhausted. How long had it been since I'd sat down and created an ad from start to finish, all by myself, without having to research it to death and collaborate with art directors and prima donna fashion photographers all while massaging the ego of a client who routinely demands changes that undercut my best ideas?

Not since grad school, I realized. That was the last time I'd been my own boss. That was the last time I'd had fun at work.

I sat up and tucked my ads in my briefcase. These ads wouldn't win any awards, but they should do the trick for May. And because I'd been working so hard, I'd barely thought about Alex and Bradley tonight. I hadn't thought at all about the new clothes I'd hidden in my closet, still in their bags. I'd just lost myself in the project and pushed my feelings aside, like I always used to do.

This was what my life would be like again if I got the job at Givens & Associates—but minus the creative, satisfying part. Late nights, burning eyes, and ulcers jockeying for space in my stomach. Of course, I quickly reminded myself, there would also be a fat paycheck and stock options and a title high up on the company's masthead.

For some reason Matt's face swam into my mind. I could see his brown eyes and big smile as clearly as if he was sitting next to me on my bed. If he were here now, he'd order us an olive-and-mushroom pizza and nag me about working too hard and stuff tennis balls down his shirt and do his impression of Cheryl. Suddenly, a fierce wave of missing him washed over me.

I reached for my cell phone and started to dial his number,

then I slowly put down my phone. He was probably asleep. With Pammy curled up beside him like a faithful little tabby. No, no, bitchiness wasn't becoming.

I picked up a book, flipped through a few pages, and dropped it back onto my bed. I thought about going into the living room and watching TV, or fixing myself a snack. But I wasn't hungry. And I didn't want to watch TV.

I was lonely.

I couldn't deny it any longer. Without work dominating all my time and thoughts, I realized for the first time just how little else my life held. I'd lost touch with most of my friends from high school and college, other than Bradley. I didn't even have a hobby. I'd signed up for a knitting class last year, thinking it would help my stress, but it backfired when I realized I'd spent more than a hundred dollars and about the same amount of hours creating an ugly sweater with a hole in the middle big enough to throw a baseball through.

What did I have in life, other than those two suitcases of designer clothes and a handful of commercials I'd created?

"Is this what you want?" Matt had asked me the day I was supposed to get the promotion. I hadn't answered him; I'd been too frantic.

Now I thought about how easy it was to get swallowed up by Alex, even as an adult. I thought about my parents' pride in me. I thought about my years of hard work, my carefully mapped out plan for my life. Why, during all those years of planning and scheming, had I never stepped back and thought about what I'd *wanted*? It had just seemed like I was walking down a predetermined path, and there weren't any forks ahead that veered off in other directions. My choices had been so clear, so obvious, that they hadn't required any thought. Until the night I was fired—I reflexively winced, thinking of it—I hadn't missed a single step down that clearly marked path.

But ever since that night, things had gotten so muddled. My flash of fear at Givens & Associates, my shopping frenzy, my unexpected new feelings for Bradley—how had my life gotten so complicated, so fast?

"Is this what you want?" Matt's voice asked again.

I lay there for a minute, thinking about it.

What happened next surprised even me.

"Do I have a choice?" I asked aloud.

Fourteen

THE NEXT MORNING I awoke before seven. As always, it took a few seconds to orient myself, to remember I wasn't in my apartment in New York. The familiar sense of shame draped over me like a heavy comforter: I'd been fired. I'd screwed up my life. And I was lying to everyone. I couldn't stand another bout of introspection—last night's session had been tough enough—so I jumped out of bed, hoping forward movement would banish my thoughts. Even with a half night's sleep, I wasn't tired. I'd trained my body long ago to get accustomed to four or five hours of rest a night.

I hurried into the shower before Dad could lay claim to the bathroom with his crossword puzzle. Literally the second I turned off the water Mom rapped on the door. "Honey?"

"Just a sec," I said, twisting up my hair in a towel turban.

"I just wanted to know if you need anything from IKEA," Mom said.

"No thanks," I said, pulling on my robe.

"I'm going to get some new cushions for the patio furniture," Mom said.

Maybe if I didn't answer her, she'd take the hint; I wasn't a big talker until I'd had my morning coffee.

"They're on sale," Dad shouted through the door.

And maybe not.

"You know you can get breakfast for ninety-nine cents there," Dad continued.

"Don't forget to tell them to hold the lingonberries on your pancakes," Mom reminded Dad. "You know how you hate those."

"Tart little buggers," Dad agreed.

Living alone in my apartment had made me forget the absolute lack of privacy in this house. No one else seemed to crave it. Alex even used to walk in on me when I was in the bathtub and proceed to leisurely put on her makeup, until I got hold of Dad's toolbox and installed a lock on the door.

"What do you think about yellow and white striped cushions?" Mom asked Dad as I smoothed lotion on my legs. They hadn't bothered moving away from the door.

"What's wrong with navy blue?" Dad asked.

"We've had navy blue for years," Mom said. "I want a change."

"You want a change, do you?" Dad growled. "Do you want a change from this, too?"

Holy God! Was that a sexually suggestive tone in his voice?

"Hank!" Mom giggled.

I couldn't bear to think of what was going on in the hallway, so I blasted the hair dryer, suppressing a shudder. Thankfully, by the time I turned it off they'd left, presumably to harass the Swedes.

I dressed quickly, made a pot of coffee, and organized my thoughts along with Mom's junk drawer. (For the love of everything holy, why would anyone cram receipts into little balls like used tissues and hoard nonworking pens instead of throwing them away?) First I'd drop my ads off at May's house, I decided, smoothing out the receipts and sorting them by date before clipping them together. Then I'd hit a cybercafe and get down to work. Next Monday was coming up fast, and I still needed to research Givens & Associates.

I finished wiping down the kitchen counters, then headed to the hallway and scooped up the keys to my parents' spare car. But as I started to lock the door behind me, my hand froze.

Last night I'd looked like a completely different person. What would May think when she saw me now? I glanced into the mirror that hung in my parents' hallway. My hair was twisted up, my earrings were simple pearls, and my clothes were downright somber.

Would May even recognize me?

I thought about the way she'd complimented me last night, and how good it had felt. How crushing it would be to see her do a double take, to watch as her eyes filled with confusion, to imagine her wondering if maybe the lighting had been much darker than she'd thought, or if her wine had been stronger.

Without letting myself think about what I was doing, I walked back into my bedroom. It would take me two minutes to change, another ten to put on a little makeup. This didn't mean anything, I told myself as I pulled off my suit and hung it back up. I'd change back to myself again right after I met with May.

I put on my new black bra and matching panties, then slipped into my Rock & Republic jeans and black turtleneck. The turtleneck looked simple and classic from the front, which made the flash of bare skin in the back all the more unexpected. And my jeans hadn't gotten any looser since yesterday. I squatted and squeezed and shimmied my way into them, working up a light sweat. On the bright side, if I wore them often enough, I wouldn't ever have to go to the gym. (On the not-so-bright side, I might be developing multiple personalities. But hey, at least *one* of my personalities would be skinny!)

The MAC woman had packed my makeup in glossy black bags lined with pink tissue paper, each as beautifully wrapped as a birthday present. I found her chart and began digging through the bags, pulling out concealer and eye shadows and lip glosses and laying everything out on the bathroom sink counter, like a surgeon preparing for a tricky operation.

"Okay," I told my reflection in the bathroom mirror. "Time to get to work."

It wasn't that I'd never worn makeup before. I had a pale pink lipstick I slid over my lips when I thought about it, and sometimes, when my dark circles were especially bad, I dug around in my medicine cabinet and found my crumbly old concealer. But I'd never *played* with makeup. For me, putting on lipstick had always been about as sensual as putting on deodorant. I'd never used the back of my hand to blend together foundation and a shimmery gold powder, considering different proportions until I decided which looked prettiest. I'd never brushed satiny-feeling eye shadow over my lids like an artist filling in the colors of a flower petal. I'd never known makeup could be so malleable and tactile and fluid. I'd never known putting it on could be as much fun as finger painting.

I used my new lip brush to swirl color from two lipsticks and lightly brushed it over my lips. The makeup artist had been right; I did have strong lips, I thought, stepping back from the mirror to examine them. Funny how I'd never really thought about it before. I lined my upper eyelids with a soft gray pencil, then I smudged the line with the tip of my pinkie until it looked smoky, just as the MAC woman had instructed. I put on a coat of mascara, using the end of the wand to prevent clumps, then I slicked on a light layer of clear lip gloss. I studied my face in the mirror, then dusted a tiny bit more of my rosy blush on the apples of my cheeks.

Eye shadow was the trickiest part for me. How was it possible that the MAC lady needed three different shades to make it look like I wasn't wearing any eye makeup? I faithfully followed her chart, putting Wedge in my crease and highlighting with Brulé, and after a bit of blending with a brush shaped like the world's tiniest spatula, my eyes looked unbelievably sultry. If I didn't know better, I'd be shocked by what I was thinking.

I tested it out by trying to remember a recipe for pancakes: Still sultry. I did a few quick multiplication problems in my head and thought about the weather: Still sultry. Makeup was a miraculous thing.

I let down my hair, brushed my bangs to the side, and stepped back from the mirror. Amazing. I barely recognized myself. In the space of a few minutes, I'd been completely transformed. Now I knew how Cinderella felt, carrying around her secret. Was it just the glass slippers and new gown that made her beautiful, or was it something else, something that couldn't be bottled or sold? Because I felt like a completely different person had slipped inside my skin. One who was bolder, and who smiled more often. One whose features looked like mine but whom I didn't even recognize. One whose boobs were a full size bigger (okay, technically that could be bought for $39.99 at the Miracle Bra counter).

I turned away from the mirror and folded my suit and pumps into an empty shopping bag, along with a few tissues and the bottle of makeup remover I'd bought from the MAC lady. Then I picked up my keys again and headed for May's house.

"These are amazing," May said, staring at my ads. They were spread out in front of her on her kitchen table, like a hand of poker.

"If you have any friends or family members who can pose for

you, you won't even have to hire models," I said. "You'll save a ton of money that way."

"I just can't believe you're doing all this for me," May said. "Why are you being so kind?"

"It isn't much," I said. "I love doing this kind of stuff."

The teakettle began to shriek, and May stood up.

"I wish I could do something for you," she said as she moved around her cozy yellow kitchen, fetching clunky earth-colored teacups and a pot of orange blossom honey. "You helped me yesterday, and now you're helping my business. I feel like you're my secret fairy godmother."

She put some chocolate-chip cookies on a plate, and I bit into one while a scruffy little dog stared hopefully up at me. Mmmm. Homemade, with bits of sticky toffee.

"These cookies are my reward," I said. "They're incredible."

"I love to bake," May said. "I used to dream about opening up a bakery."

"Why didn't you?" I asked. I could just picture her in a big white apron, her curly hair tucked under a cap, rolling out piecrusts. She had that nurturing vibe.

"I love to sleep late more," she said, and I laughed.

"I'm not the kind of person who could get up at three A.M. to bake bread. So I load up all my friends with cookies and pies instead," she said.

"What made you get into matchmaking?" I asked.

"I was really lonely in my marriage," she said.

She looked down at her hands, which were wrapped around her mug of tea, then she looked up at me again.

"I could tell you what I tell most people, which is that I saw a good business opportunity," she said. "Or I could tell you my marriage had fallen apart and I wanted to throw myself into something to take my mind off of it, which is part of the truth. But the real truth is, I was deeply unhappy. I desperately needed to believe true love really existed, if not for me, then for other people. Starting this business was an act of hope for me. Every day I'd see people who were coming out of a terrible divorce, people who'd had their hearts broken, people who thought they'd never love again . . . and I *helped* them. I helped them feel better about themselves, and I helped them find hope again, and then I helped them fall in love again. And eventually, when I had enough hope gathered up, I filed for divorce."

"Wow," I said.

Then I burst into tears.

May didn't act all flustered or embarrassed like people usually do when someone cries; she just handed me a napkin and put her hand over mine.

"I'm sorry," I said, wiping my face. "I never cry."

"All the more reason to let it out," May said simply.

"Oh, shit," I said, looking down at the stained napkin, which had a rainbow of colors smeared across it. "I forgot about my makeup."

Then I started laughing as I sat there in the kitchen of a woman I barely knew, me in my too-tight jeans and my collages made from my mother's ancient *Good Housekeeping* magazines— me, who used to wear nothing but Donna Karan and Armani, and oversee teams of art directors and photographers and graphic designers—and I completely lost it. I laughed harder and harder, clutching my sides, with tears streaming down my face, and suddenly May was laughing right along with me.

And when I finally stopped laughing and crying, I told May everything.

"So let me get this straight," May said an hour later.

By now the cookies were gone and I was wondering if I could find a way to discreetly unbutton the top button of my jeans.

"You think Bradley has a crush on Alex," May said. "And you're worried she's flirting with him."

"Not flirting with him, exactly," I said. "Just making him fall in love with her."

"But she's engaged," May pointed out.

"You haven't met Alex," I said. "Guys don't care if she's available. They fall in love with her anyways. Girls, too. In high school, whatever Alex wore to school became what all the other girls wore the next day. Complete strangers come up to her all the time to tell her how beautiful she is. Little woodsy animals and songbirds scamper around her."

May raised one eyebrow at me.

"Well, they would if she ever went into a forest," I said.

"But you're beautiful, too," May said.

"I'm nothing like her," I said. I hated the bitterness that crept into my tone; it made me feel so petty, like I was a jealous three-year-old. "I don't usually wear makeup or anything. I don't even know why I bought all this stuff. It isn't me."

"And fooling around with that guy—Doug, is that right?—that isn't you, either," May said. She reached down to scratch the ears of a black Lab that had wandered into the kitchen. Exactly how many dogs did she have? I wondered absently.

"*So* not me," I said emphatically.

"So what happened?" May asked.

I dropped my head into my hands as her question seemed to echo in the kitchen, bouncing off the walls before coming back to hover in front of me. What *had* happened? Why had I fooled around with some guy I didn't even like? Why had I sabotaged my job in New York? And why, once my life seemed like it might be getting back on track, had I rushed out to go shopping for clothes that had no place in my new life? Then there was that white-hot flash of fear at Givens & Associates, the one that had left me breathless and shaky in the ladies' room.

I'd thought coming home again would ground me. So where were these strange new feelings springing from? Why had I cried myself to sleep last night, when I never, ever cried?

May waited patiently while my thoughts tore through my mind, smashing into each other and creating traffic jams and honking and giving each other the finger. She sat there at her simple wooden kitchen table amid the comfortable clutter of a cookbook opened to a butternut squash soup recipe, stacks of newspapers and magazines, and the chunky teacups she kept refilling with Red Zinger. Everything in her house seemed to fit together as seamlessly as the pieces of a puzzle: her chenille couch and the old Lab who'd wandered over to doze on it; the bunches of dried lavender framing her kitchen doorway; the stacks of soft-edged paperbacks on the coffee table; the racks of spices in tiny stone-colored jars by the stove. This was a woman who liked to cook, liked to be at home, and prized comfort. It was clear who May was, and what she held dear.

I'd been like that just a few weeks ago; I'd been crystal clear in what I wanted out of life. But now, I felt like a wild assortment of loose ends and jagged edges.

"I have no idea what happened," I finally said.

"But your family thinks you're still working for the advertising agency," May said.

I nodded miserably.

"That's a lot of pressure on you," May said. "You don't want to disappoint them."

"It's not just that," I said.

May had been brutally honest with me, and now I owed her the same honesty. Or maybe it was myself I owed it to.

"It's also that I like being the smart daughter. I like it when Mom and Dad ask for my advice about stuff. I like feeling capable and successful. I like"—here my voice dropped—"feeling smarter than Alex."

"Of course," May said gently. "Who wouldn't?"

"And that interview I told you about?" I said. "For some reason every time I think about it I get scared. I think about plunging back into that world, and working all the time, and suddenly . . ."

I had to gulp air; I couldn't even finish the sentence.

I forced myself to continue. "This is the first time in my life I've ever taken a break, and now it's like all these doubts and fears are flooding in. I'm doing stuff I never thought I'd do in a million years. I spent three hundred dollars on makeup yesterday, and I don't wear makeup. Not ever. God, what's wrong with me?"

"I don't think there's anything wrong with you," May said. She got up, refilled our teacups, and sat down again. "But can I tell you what I saw last night?"

I nodded.

"I saw a woman who was confident and smart and kind," May said. "First you scared off my ex-husband. Then you invited me out for a glass of wine because you saw how shaken I was. How many other people would do something like that for a complete stranger? And the way you took control at the bar. You took a group of rowdy people, and you managed to get their attention and make them focus on your questions. You were . . . breathtaking."

I sat there, basking in the glow of that word.

"But it wasn't me," I finally said. "That's the thing. I don't do stuff like that."

May looked at me and smiled.

"Well, whoever she was, I kind of liked her," she said gently.

I stared at her. I was so caught off guard I couldn't respond. I hadn't thought about whether the things I'd done were good or bad—well, other than the near-sex on the conference room table. I was pretty sure that fell into the bad-girl category. I'd only been focusing on the fact that all that stuff I'd been doing wasn't *me*.

May's phone rang.

"Oh, no," she said to me, holding up a finger. "Hold that thought."

"Blind Dates. Yes, we are accepting new clients. Thanks so much for calling," she said. "Can I take down some quick information and phone you right back?"

May reached for a pen and pad of paper by the phone and scribbled down notes while she made sympathetic noises: "Um-hmm. Oh, dear, I'm so sorry to hear that. No, don't worry about a thing. We're going to take care of all that."

I swiped my napkin over my face again, trying to scrub away the last bits of makeup. Would it be really awful if I ate the crumbs on the cookie plate? I wondered. What the hell? My dignity was long gone already.

Sorry," May said as she hung up. "But that just gave me an idea."

I stopped licking my index finger and looked up at her.

"Jane Swenson, age thirty-eight, divorced two years ago," she said, reading from her notes. "She's ready to start dating again. Want to go interview her?"

"Me?" I said.

"Then, if you want, you can set her up with one of our other clients," May said. "We can go through the files together and figure out who would be best for her. And if you like doing it, I'd love to offer you a job."

I stared at her. "Are you serious?"

"I need some extra help," May said. "Especially now that I've got these ads. I have a feeling I'm going to have a lot of new business coming in. And maybe it would help you, too. Maybe you could use a little bit of time to figure out what you really want to do. You can work with me for as long as you want, and if you decide to take that other job, then you can leave whenever you want, too. No pressure."

Work here? With May?

I thought about Ms. Givens sitting in front of her state-of-the-art computer, then I looked at May. She had a smudge of chocolate on her right cheek. She conducted business from her kitchen counter instead of a Hong Kong office. She walked around her house barefoot and thought nothing of having a two-hour talk with me in the middle of a workday. Her life was the opposite of mine. How could I come work for her? How could I stumble off in such a strange, unexpected direction?

May must've sensed my hesitation.

"Think about it," she urged me, "And if you decide not to, I hope we'll still be friends."

May had offered me a job without checking my references. She hadn't even mentioned a salary. Did she have any idea what I'd earned in my last job? There wasn't any way she'd be able to pay me anything approaching what I was used to making. This was all very nice and pleasant, sitting here in her kitchen and sipping honey-sweetened tea and talking, but it wasn't real life. It wasn't *my* life.

I was trying to figure out how to gently turn her down without hurting her feelings when my cell phone vibrated. I looked down and saw an unfamiliar local number.

"Go ahead," May said. "I've been answering my phone since I met you."

"Probably just a telemarketer," I said. "I'll get rid of them."

It wasn't a telemarketer.

My heart started beating a little faster when I heard Bradley's voice.

"Hey," I said.

"Just called the house and your mom gave me this number," he said. "I was wondering if you wanted to go to that movie tonight."

"Sure," I said. God, why couldn't I think of anything witty to say?

"Pick you up around eight?" he asked.

"Great!" I said. Wit *and* charm; Helen of Troy had nothing on me.

"Oops, just got paged by my editor," Bradley said. "Gotta run. See you then."

"Let me guess," May said as I put my phone away. "That was the guy."

"Yeah," I said. I couldn't stop smiling. "I'm seeing him tonight."

"Good for you," May said. "So he's the one, huh?"

"I think he might be," I said.

"I've got only one bit of advice for you," May said. "Don't worry about your sister so much. I think you're pretty spectacular in your own right. And don't forget to think about my offer. Tell you what: if you do the interview and find the client a match, I'll pay you three hundred dollars. Look at it this way: It'll cover the cost of your makeup and you can stop feeling guilty about it."

"Sure," I finally agreed, not wanting to hurt her feelings. "I'll think about it."

I spent the rest of the day working at a coffee shop before finally packing up my laptop around four so I could get ready for my night out with Bradley. I hadn't been able to get much done. Memories of Bradley kept flashing through my mind while I sipped my latte and smiled dreamily into the distance. I probably looked like one of those saps from the General Foods International coffee commercials ("Screw the barking dog and screaming kids and exploding toilet, this is *my* moment"), but I couldn't help it. I was seeing Bradley tonight, and he was all I could think about.

One memory in particular kept coming back to me. It was the summer before we both headed off to college—I to Princeton, Bradley to UConn—and he'd just bought a secondhand Oldsmobile Cutlass Supreme convertible with a hanging-by-a-thread fender and a muffler that didn't muffle. He drove up to my house with the top down and the gas tank full on a sticky August night when we were eighteen and it seemed like anything was possible.

"Love the car!" I said, running out of my house before he had a chance to walk up the steps and ring the doorbell. I'd been watching for him from the living room window.

By now I had dozens of tricks to keep Bradley away from Alex. If she was home, I sometimes pretended I was getting something out of my parents' car when he arrived, so I could intercept him outside before he ever set foot in the house. Other times I met him at the door with my coat on and my purse in my hand, shouting a good-bye over my shoulder and telling Bradley I was worried we'd be late. That excuse didn't always fly when we were heading out, say, to study at the library, but given my anal-retentive neuroses, no one questioned it too much.

Was I being paranoid? Maybe so. But the way Bradley stared at me when he thought I wasn't looking—well, that was the way everyone else stared at Alex all the time. Maybe I should've trusted that Bradley's feelings for me wouldn't evaporate if he saw Alex walking through the house, her hair damp and heavy from the shower, her eyes electric against her summer tan. But by then I'd had enough. That was the year Alex won homecoming queen; the year she appeared on three local television commercials in a single night, causing our excited neighbors to bombard us with calls; the year she flew to New York to shoot a two-page spread for *Seventeen* magazine. (Is it wrong of me to bring up that a deranged art director dressed her as a shepherdess and made her pose with a flock of smelly, gassy sheep?)

It wasn't as if Alex and Bradley never saw each other at school. But at least at school other people acted as buffers between them; Alex was always surrounded by a crowd. They'd shared a class or two, but they'd never spent any time alone, never exchanged words other than a brief hello as they passed in the halls. I wanted to keep it that way.

So I jumped into Bradley's car, and we headed off just before sunset. We were so comfortable together that we barely spoke; we even reached out to change the radio station at the same moment when the song "Louie Louie" came on. We both laughed when our fingers met over the radio dial.

We circled our hometown for a while, stopping at a 7-Eleven and buying cherry Slurpees, before Bradley made his way over to our high school.

Somehow I'd known we'd end up here tonight.

I was aching for my real life to begin—college, then grad school, followed by a fantastic job and a big, strong, hunky 401(k) plan—but on that night, as I stared up at that old red-brick building with the sign in the lawn that said "Congratulations Graduates!" a lump formed in my throat. High school hadn't been the best time of my life, but it hadn't been all bad, either.

"Let's go," Bradley said. He jumped out of the car, hurried over to my side, and grabbed my hand.

"What are we doing?" I asked, letting my hand go limp and slip away from his.

How many times had I done things like that? Bradley never pushed, but he showed me in dozens of ways that he wanted more than friendship from me. He left his arm on the armrest between us at the movies so I could squeeze it during the scary parts. I never did. Whenever we hugged good night, he kept his face turned toward mine, and I knew he was hoping I'd kiss him. But I always pulled away. I adored Bradley, but he felt like a brother to me. If I kissed him, I'd probably burst out laughing, which wouldn't do much for his ego or for our friendship. So I let things drift along, and Bradley, in his gentle way, never pressured me for more.

"See the flat part of the roof?" Bradley asked me, pointing up at our school.

I nodded.

"That's where we're going," he said.

"Up there? Seriously?" I asked. "But won't we get in trouble?"

"What are they going to do?" Bradley asked. "Suspend us?"

"There isn't any way we'll get up there without a ladder," I said. (Actually, I also said something ridiculously geeky like "They could revoke our diplomas!" But it's *my* memory. I'm allowed to edit it as I see fit.)

"You're probably right," Bradley said. "Can we just take a walk around school for old times' sake?"

"Sure," I said, and we headed around the corner, where I almost ran into a big, shiny ladder propped up against the wall.

"Imagine that," Bradley said, gripping its sides and putting his foot on the first rung.

"Bradley!" I hissed, looking around. "Did you bring this by earlier?"

"Who, me?" he said, climbing up another few feet. "It seems sturdy enough. Sure you don't want to join me?"

"You're crazy," I hissed, glancing around again even though the nearest neighbors were a few hundred yards away.

In the grand scheme of things, considering one of our classmates had gotten arrested for hot-wiring cars, one had almost overdosed on LSD in a school restroom, and several others had attended graduation in maternity gowns, it wasn't the most flamboyant act of teenage rebellion ever. Still, up until that point, the only mayhem I'd caused was when I'd gotten a B-plus on a calculus exam. (And, truth be told, the only mayhem that existed was in my own mind. Even Mom had asked me if I wanted one of her Valiums that day.)

"Coming?" Bradley asked as he reached the top of the ladder and climbed onto the roof.

I put a foot on the lowest rung.

"I hate heights," I whined.

"Just don't look down," Bradley urged me.

I put my other foot up on the next step.

"My shoes feel really slippery," I said. "Maybe they're damp from the grass."

"You're not going to slip," Bradley said.

Another step.

"Did you buy this ladder just for tonight?" I asked.

"I stole it," Bradley said.

My mouth dropped open.

"Kidding," he said. "Come on, you're almost there."

"I fell out of a tree when I was six," I said. "I got a concussion. Well, almost."

"Almost fell out of the tree or almost got a concussion?" Bradley asked.

"Both," I said.

"Two more little steps," Bradley cajoled. "Keep your eyes on me."

Then he was reaching out and pulling me into the safety of his thin arms.

"Thanks," I said, stepping away from his embrace, pretending all he was doing was steadying me. I pretended not to see the hurt look flash across his face, either.

"Oh, Bradley," I breathed a moment later, turning around in a circle. I'd never seen our school like this. Stretching out on one side was the giant green rectangle of our football field, flanked by rows and rows of empty bleachers. It seemed majestic, yet somehow sad. Adjacent to the school was the little garage where

Mr. Carey held drivers' ed classes. I spun around to look at a huge oak tree in a corner of the lawn. That had been my favorite place for curling up with a textbook and a brown bag lunch, away from the rowdy table in the middle of the lunchroom where Alex held court. Seeing it all this way made it look like an enormous, sprawling painting.

"Hungry?" Bradley asked, flapping open a red-checked table-cloth and laying it down on the roof. I turned around and saw the picnic basket he must've stashed up here earlier. It was filled with French bread and Brie, strawberries and dark chocolate bars. All of my favorite things.

"Bradley!" I squealed.

He popped open a bottle of sparkling cider and smiled. He'd even remembered to bring along two plastic glasses. He'd thought of everything.

We sat up there for hours, long after the sun had set and the crickets began to sing. I think we both knew it was the last time we'd be together before we left for college. I'd never felt closer to him. As I watched Bradley cut me another slice of Brie, I saw the white scar on his thumb from where he'd fallen off his bike when he was eleven. We joked about the obnoxious football player from our class who'd just gotten a vanity plate that said TGHTEND, and Bradley's eyebrows tilted up in the middle when he laughed, like they always did. We even talked about his mom, who'd died the previous October after a long battle with breast cancer.

"I think about her every day," Bradley said.

He turned his head slightly, but not before I'd seen the tears glistening in his eyes. "I don't think I'll ever stop."

"Remember the time she gave you a half-birthday party?" I said. "She made you half a cake."

"She sang 'Happy half-birthday' to me, too," Bradley remembered, smiling.

"She was such a good mom," I said. We'd spent a lot of time at Bradley's house over the years, and she'd always made me feel welcome. "I miss her, too."

We were quiet for a while, staring out into the night, then Bradley put his arm around me and pulled me close. He'd planned this moment, I suddenly realized: the ladder, the picnic with my favorite foods, the rooftop at dusk. He was wooing me. This was Bradley's equivalent of a Hail Mary throw into the end zone in the final minutes of a game; it was his final, bold stand before we went our separate ways to college.

I closed my eyes right before his lips landed on mine. They were soft and gentle, but I didn't feel anything. No delicious tickling in my belly, no desire to wrap my arms around him and pull him closer. Nothing. I could've been kissing my pillow for all the passion I felt.

After a moment, I pulled away. It seemed kinder to stop this quickly.

"I'm sorry," I said gently. I did love him. But not in the way he wanted.

"I can't—" I began.

"It's fine," Bradley said curtly. His cheeks flushed, and he turned away from me.

Oh, Bradley, I thought, staring at his thin back. I ached to hug him, but I knew that would only make everything worse. After a few minutes of sitting together in the heavy silence, he stood up and offered me a hand. Even though I'd hurt him badly, he was still a gentleman.

"It's getting late," he said. It was barely nine-thirty.

When we left the rooftop of our school, something had inexorably shifted between us, and we both knew it. I was too chatty on the drive home, trying to gloss over what had happened. If we acted normally, maybe we could turn the kiss on the roof into nothing more than a friendly peck between old friends. We could forget it ever happened, and go back to the way we were.

But Bradley wouldn't play along.

"See you later," he said, still not looking at me, when he pulled up in front of my house. I could feel his pain; it was a physical force in the car between us, keeping us apart. Keeping me from reaching over and hugging him, like I usually did at the end of the night.

"I'll call you tomorrow," I said. "Okay?"

"Sure," he said.

I stood in the street staring into the darkness after him long after he'd driven away. Bradley was the best guy I'd ever known.

So why couldn't I love him back?

Fifteen

WHEN I GOT HOME from the coffee shop to get ready for my
night out with Bradley, the worst thing imaginable happened.

Alex was sitting at the kitchen table, flipping through a magazine. And she was wearing my bustier, the insanely flattering
one with the black lace edging.

For one wild moment I panicked, thinking she'd uncov-
ered my secret stash of clothes and makeup in the back of my
closet. But of course, the bustier she was wearing was three
sizes smaller than mine. I looked down at the plain gray suit
and white silk blouse I'd changed into at May's house before
heading to the coffee shop, and inexplicably, a hot shot of anger
fired through me.

"What are you doing here?" I demanded.

Dad, who was foraging through a cabinet, jerked upright and
cracked his head on the edge of the cabinet door.

Perhaps my tone had been a touch shrill.

"Nice to see you, too," Alex said, sounding hurt.

"Sorry," I said. "I was just surprised to see you."

I glanced at my watch. It was almost five-thirty, and Bradley was coming by at eight. If Alex didn't leave soon, I'd call Bradley and suggest we meet at a restaurant instead.

"I just wanted to see everyone," Alex said. "And you ran out on me so quickly yesterday. What was up with that?"

"Forgot about a meeting," I said, opening the refrigerator and burying my head inside. I didn't want her to see my face. She'd know I was lying.

"Are you girls hungry?" Mom asked, coming into the kitchen. "I can make us some dinner."

"No," Alex and I shouted in unison.

"I was thinking I'd treat everyone to takeout," Alex said. "Chinese or Indian sound good?"

I looked at her in surprise. A cozy night at home with her parents and sister? Was Alex really that hard up for entertainment? The last time the four of us had spent a quiet night together at home was . . . I wrinkled my nose, thinking back, and came up blank. Maybe Christmas two years ago, before we realized Mom had forgotten to turn on the oven when she'd put in the turkey and we ended up going out for pizza at a joint with a neon sign in the window and a sullen teenager who monopolized the pinball machine in the corner. Our holiday meal was punctuated by his shouted curses whenever a ball dropped into the gutter. He wasn't very good, and he seemed to have an endless supply of quarters. All in all, it wasn't the holiest way of celebrating the baby Jesus' birth.

"That sounds lovely," Mom said. "The whole family together for a nice dinner."

"Where's Gary tonight?" I asked.

"He's taking the red-eye back from L.A.," Alex said. "I'm picking him up at the airport tomorrow morning."

"Don't park next to any vans with dark windows," Dad warned.

"He watched *Dr. Phil* today," Mom confided. "It was about a woman who was kidnapped in a parking lot twelve years ago."

Her voice dropped to an ominous whisper: "Disappeared without a trace."

"I didn't *watch* it," Dad objected, but everyone ignored him.

"So Chinese or Indian?" Alex asked.

"Chinese," Mom said, at the exact moment Dad said, "Indian."

Tonight I could wear my new jeans and Marilyn boots with one of my classic sweaters—the white cashmere turtleneck would look nice, and its demureness would offset the fuck-me factor of my painted-on jeans—and maybe I'd even put on lipstick. I wanted to look pretty. I wanted Bradley to stare at me the way he used to.

"What are you thinking about?" Alex demanded. "Your special friend in New York?"

"You've got a special friend in New York?" Mom squealed.

"No, I do not," I said, shooting Alex a death glare.

"Is something in your eye?" she asked me innocently. "It's all squinty."

"I'll get some drops," Dad said, rocketing off toward the bathroom. "Don't touch it! Eyes are very susceptible to infection!"

I couldn't help laughing, and Alex laughed along with me.

Then she leaned closer to me. "Did you pluck your eyebrows since the last time I saw you?"

"Just a little," I admitted.

"They look good," she said.

I think it may have been the first heartfelt compliment Alex had ever paid me. It felt odd. She must've realized it, too, because she immediately said, "The guys from *The Sopranos* were getting jealous."

"Nice," I told her. "Have your boobs gotten smaller?"

There, that felt better.

"Now, girls," Mom said.

"We're just kidding around," Alex said. "Right, Linds?"

"Right," I said. And in the same spirit of playfulness and fun, would it be wrong to hope that she dripped some moo shu sauce down the front of the bustier she'd all but stolen from me?

"Oh, Lindsey, I almost forgot," Mom said. "Mrs. Williams wants to know if you'll talk to her son about the SATs."

"Talk about what?" I asked.

"Just tips on how to take the test," Mom said vaguely. "I told her how you scored a nine hundred on the math part of the test, and she was really impressed."

"Mom," I said, "the test only goes up to eight hundred."

Mom flapped her hand, as though physically squashing my point. "Will you be home for dinner tomorrow, honey?" she asked me. "I could ask them to come by after that."

"Fine." I sighed.

"Perfect," Mom said. "I'll bake cookies."

Alex winked at me, and I couldn't help smiling. I'd have to remember to pick up some cookies, just in case.

"I'm going to pick up dinner," Alex said. "Want to come get it with me, Sis?"

I looked at her sprawled in the kitchen chair, one long leg hooked over the armrest. Sunlight was streaming in from the window behind her, turning her hair into a wild riot of reds and golds. As always, the gentle planes and graceful curves of her face were expertly made up to look completely natural and flawless. Or maybe she wasn't wearing any makeup at all—it was hard to tell.

"Sure," I said after a moment.

But I couldn't help wondering why she'd asked. Alex had never been eager to spend time with me before. Even when I'd lived in New York, she'd only called when she happened to be passing through. Sometimes we grabbed a quick drink or a cup of coffee, but more often than not I was out of town or too busy to see her. If either of us had made an effort—if she'd called me in advance, or if I'd rescheduled my meetings—we could've spent more time together. But neither of us had bothered.

So why was Alex trying now, when the space between us had grown so vast that it seemed almost impossible to traverse?

"Ready?" she asked, jingling her keys in her hand.

"I'll meet you in your car," I said. I glanced at my watch. I'd better call Bradley and suggest we meet somewhere near the theater, just in case. "I have to make a quick call."

We were finishing up dinner (Chinese; by the time Mom was through with him, Dad was certain that it had been his preference all along and that she was doing him a favor) when the doorbell chimed.

"I'll get it," Alex said, hopping up.

I looked at my watch: almost seven-thirty. I was itching to get ready for my night out with Bradley. I'd left him a message saying I'd meet him at the coffee shop next to the theater at eight, which meant I'd need to pack up my clothes and go find a gas station where I could change. I didn't want Alex to see me in my new clothes. I knew she'd circle me like a shark, then she'd make some crack, maybe something snide about me finally shopping in the twenty-first century. I'd feel silly under her scrutiny, and the magic of my new look would disappear.

Alex came back to the table just as I stood up, and I realized the worst thing imaginable hadn't happened yet. It was happening now.

Bradley was two steps behind Alex.

"Oops," Mom said, looking at me.

"Hey, everyone," Bradley said.

I looked back at Mom.

"I forgot to tell you Bradley called while you and Alex were out getting dinner," Mom said.

"No big deal," Bradley told me. "I can hang out and wait if you're not ready. I just happened to be doing a shoot nearby, so I came straight here after work."

"No, this is great," I said, forcing a smile as I looked down at my suit. This wasn't how tonight was supposed to start. Bradley was supposed to open his door and see me in my new boots and jeans, with my hair loose and pretty. The smile was supposed to slide away from his face, like it had all those years ago.

"Want a beer?" Alex offered.

"No, I'm good," Bradley said.

If I took down my hair or put on lipstick now, everyone would notice. Worse, it would look like I was making an effort for Bradley. Besides, I couldn't take the time to change. I had to get out of here, fast, before Bradley and Alex started talking. They'd already gotten to know each other plenty well enough.

"Ready to go?" I asked, just as Alex said, "Hey, Bradley, how about some Chinese?"

Suddenly, she was filling a plate with egg rolls and garlic chicken and Mom was fetching him a glass of water and Bradley was sitting down at the table.

"You won't believe how great Bradley's photos are," Alex said, sitting down next to him. Why not just climb in his lap? I thought bitterly. No, no, not bitterly. *Bitterly* conjures up images of a pursed-lip maiden aunt. *Sassily,* that was the word I was striving for.

"I'll drop off some copies for you next week," Bradley told my parents. "Alex finished picking out the ones she liked best last night."

I felt like I was in a boat that had become unmoored and was drifting out to sea. I had to regain control. I quickly pulled over a chair and sat on the other side of Bradley.

"Remember that picture you took for the school yearbook?" I asked him. "The one where you climbed up into the rafters to get shots of the school play?"

I'd helped Bradley develop those photos; I wanted him to think about us spending those hours together in the darkroom.

"That was when I knew I wanted to be a photographer," Bradley told me, smiling.

"More rice?" Alex asked him, and he turned to look at her.

"More water?" I asked him, and his head jerked back.

"I'm good," he said, looking a little startled. And possibly whiplashed.

"So Bradley, tell me what else you're up to these days," Mom said. "How's your dad?"

"He's doing great," Bradley said. "Still working at the law firm, but he cut down his hours a few years ago."

"And what else is going on with you?" Mom asked. "Are you dating anyone?"

Oh, Christ. Why? Why? Mom even gave me a little wink. Once again, the bar for the worst imaginable thing was raised. It was like playing limbo in reverse.

"Not right now," Bradley said. "Actually, my girlfriend and I broke up a few months ago."

"Which movie do you want to see?" I asked. Not the best segue ever, but Mom had to be stopped at all costs.

"Oh, are you guys going to the movies?" Alex asked, and I realized I'd walked into a trap. But I had no one to blame; I'd laid it for myself.

"Yeah, the new one with Orlando Bloom," Bradley said. "Want to join us?"

Of course Bradley would say that. He was a nice guy; what

else could he say when Alex left her question hanging there and stared at us with puppy-dog eyes?

"Love to," Alex said. "Sure you guys don't mind?"

She looked directly at me, and I choked out, "Of course not."

What else could I do? Leap across the table and throttle her? Yank her hair? Kick her in the shins? Put Nair in her shampoo bottle? Make her—

"What time do we need to go?" Alex asked, rudely interrupting my thoughts just as they were getting creative.

Bradley looked at his watch. "We should probably head out," he said. "Parking is always a pain in Bethesda."

"Should we drive separately?" I suggested helpfully. Strategic planning has always been my forte. "I mean so you won't have to come back here afterward to pick up your car, Alex."

"No, I'll just squeeze in with you guys," Alex said cheerfully.

I dashed upstairs, ripped off my suit but left on my silk shirt, and threw on some tan pants and flat shoes. I forced myself not to think of my new, pretty outfit in the trunk of my car. I made it downstairs just in time for the tail end of Bradley's tussle with Mom over whether he could put his dishes in the sink. Then Alex and I headed out for my dream date with Bradley.

"Don't keep my daughters out too late!" Dad yelled after us, chortling and slapping his knee.

Oh, Christ.

When you can't give your full attention to Orlando Bloom's bare buttocks, you know there's a problem. I sat in my seat, fuming. Bad enough that Alex was tagging along tonight. Bad enough that the guy at the concession stand had flirted outrageously with her and even given her free popcorn while he mixed up my order—and the only thing I'd ordered was a bottle of water.

But now, despite the fact that I'd planned our seating arrangement with more zeal than any Bridezilla, everything had gone wrong.

I'd run plays through my head like a football coach as we bought our tickets. If Bradley walked down the theater aisle first, followed by me and then Alex, then he'd naturally take the innermost seat in the row. I'd sit next to him, and Alex would be on the outside. Perfect. So all I had to do was get Bradley to go down the aisle first.

But what if Bradley went first, then stood aside to let me and Alex file into the row of seats first? Then Alex would be in the middle, and I'd be forced to kill her if she gripped his arm during the scary parts. Especially since we were seeing a romantic comedy.

"Bradley? Want butter?" Alex asked, accepting the free jumbo tub of popcorn from the concession guy. I reached into my pocket and pulled out one of the little plastic packets of honey I'd pilfered from a coffeehouse. Bradley's eyes met mine, and we both smiled.

"No thanks," Bradley said, and the tightness in my chest eased the slightest bit.

Luck seemed to be with me for once when we went into the theater. The place was packed, but we found seats in the very last row, and I ended up between Alex and Bradley with no scuffling necessary. Perfect. Well, as perfect as things could be, considering I was out on a date with a guy who didn't know it was a date and my sister was leaning over me to grab a handful of the popcorn from the bucket he was gripping between his manly thighs.

Should I let my knee accidentally brush against Bradley's when the movie started, or would that be too obvious? Maybe I should whisper something to him during the credits instead. I felt around in my purse for a breath mint.

Was this how Bradley had felt all those years ago, wanting desperately to touch me but not knowing how I'd respond? I felt a pang of sympathy for that skinny, sensitive, teenage Bradley. I wished so much I'd returned his feelings back then. But then again, how many high school romances survive into adulthood? It was better this way, better that I was discovering Bradley later in life, when our relationship would have a real chance.

I sat back in my seat and tried to think of something funny to whisper to Bradley. Maybe I could casually put my hand on his arm when I leaned over, too. Just to emphasize my point.

A preview for a movie about a mass murderer came on. Probably best if I didn't crack a joke about it; not everyone saw the slapstick humor in cannibalism. The next preview rolled. Ah, here we go: This one was about a wedding where everything went wrong. Excellent. I was testing out punch lines in my head when the door to the theater opened and two women came in. One had a broken leg and was using crutches. They waited in the aisle next to Alex's seat, blinking as their eyes adjusted to the change in the light.

"Here, do you want my seat? Then you'll have two together," Alex offered, gesturing to the empty aisle seat next to her. "I can move over."

"That's so kind of you," the younger woman said.

"No problem," Alex said, flashing them a smile. She hopped up and slipped past me, into the empty seat on the other side of Bradley.

And just like that, my night was officially ruined. But little did I know the bar was about to be lowered again.

"I'm never eating popcorn with butter again," Alex said as we exited the theater. "The honey's worth the sticky fingers."

She sucked her index finger, and a guy walking toward us nearly smashed into a tree.

"Need a wet wipe?" I asked sweetly, handing her one.

She looked at me, then threw back her head and laughed. "Always prepared, aren't you? Hey, do you guys want to grab a drink? There's a place right across the street."

"I've got a big day tomorrow," I said quickly. I wanted nothing more than to go home, to try to forget the memory of Alex leaning over to whisper to Bradley during the movie. To erase the sounds of their low laughter.

During one part of the movie, when Orlando was reading a letter from his ex-girlfriend, Alex had even put her hand on Bradley's knee. "What does it say?" she'd whispered, like she couldn't read the giant letters on the screen. I'd barely held back a snort.

"C'mon, Lindsey," Alex said now. "Live a little."

"Just one drink?" Bradley suggested. "We'll make it a quick one."

"Sure," I finally agreed. What else could I say?

The bar was full; a DJ even held court in a corner, and a few people had ventured onto the dance floor. We stood near a booth where a couple was sitting with an empty beer pitcher in front of them, pouncing when they left a few minutes later. Bradley and I slipped into one side, and Alex sat across from us. I took a bit of comfort in the fact that he'd chosen to sit next to me. But just a bit. After all, he was looking across at Alex.

"I'll get the drinks," Alex said. "Sam Adams all around?"

"Sure," Bradley said, handing her a twenty. "But it's on me."

"I'll just have water," I said.

"Three Sam Adams coming up," Alex said, heading for the bar.

I rolled my eyes at her, then twisted around so I could look at Bradley. He was wearing jeans and a polo shirt with the sleeves pushed up. He looked casual and relaxed and—and *great*.

"So," I said.

"So," he said, smiling.

I tried to quash my nervousness; this was *Bradley*.

"What were you working on today?" I asked. Bradley's passion for photography was contagious; he was one of the few people I knew who adored his job.

"A portrait of this artist who lives in Takoma Park," Bradley said. "He's an amazing guy. Paralyzed in a car accident ten years ago. He paints by holding the brush between his teeth."

"That's incredible," I said.

"I know. I couldn't believe it when I walked in his house," Bradley said. "The entire place is filled with paintings. They're stacked three deep against the walls. He told me painting saved his life. The funny thing is, he'd never picked up a brush before his accident."

"How'd you shoot him?" I asked.

"It was tough. I wanted to emphasize his work, not his wheelchair, but it's so big that it was hard to keep it out of the frame. I also wanted people to get a sense of what he feels like when he's painting—his emotions. I finally stacked a few of his paintings in the background of the shot, then I centered him in front of a fresh canvas," Bradley said. "He's got the paintbrush gripped in his teeth, and he's just putting on the first stroke of color."

"So it's like anything is possible," I said. "His imagination can take him anywhere."

"Exactly," Bradley said, smiling at me.

Alex came back to the table, carrying the beers by their necks. She tossed the twenty back at Bradley.

"I wanted to treat," he protested.

"They were free," Alex said. "The bartender recognized me from my show."

"Nice," Bradley said. "Remind me to take you to bars and buy you drinks more often."

I laughed merrily. Like hell.

"So where's Gary tonight?" Bradley asked. *Excellent* question, I silently commended him. Let's continue with that train of thought.

"In L.A.," Alex said. "His company's developing an apartment building out there."

"Does he travel a lot?" Bradley asked.

"Mmm, a few nights a week," Alex said. "Usually L.A. or New York."

"Do you ever go with him?" Bradley asked.

"Sometimes. I did at first. But it got a little old," Alex said, grinning. "You've raided one minibar . . ."

Out of the corner of my eye, I could see two guys talking and sneaking looks at Alex. Maybe one of them would come over and ask her to dance. Maybe one of them would happen to spill a sticky drink all over Alex, and she'd have to run home to shower. And if the drink just happened to be radioactive . . . I tuned Alex out as she prattled on. I wanted another five minutes of this fantasy, my consolation prize for letting my sister take away Bradley. Well, technically not *take away*. It wasn't like Bradley was forcibly yanked away from me as he belted out "And I Am Telling You I'm Not Going" like Jennifer Hudson.

". . . New York?" Bradley was asking.

"Sorry," I said. "Didn't hear you over the music."

"I was just saying, do you miss New York at all?"

Yes, I thought suddenly, surprising myself. I missed my friend Matt. I missed my apartment. I missed the sense I had of waking up every morning and knowing exactly where I was supposed to be and what I was supposed to be doing. But . . . I didn't miss my job. Not even a little bit.

"Sometimes," I said honestly. I took a sip of beer and looked at Bradley. "But it's good to be home, too."

Just then Fergie's celebration of her lady lumps came to an

end and the DJ spoke into his microphone: "All right, now we've got a dedication going out. This one is for the lady in black. From a secret admirer."

Bradley and I both looked at Alex, sitting there in her black bustier, her thick hair loose and wavy around her shoulders, as James Blunt began to croon "You're Beautiful."

Oh, Jesus, it was like something from a sappy movie. Was the guy going to come over next with a red rose and a Phantom of the Opera mask and ask Alex to slow-dance?

"Looks like you've got a fan," Bradley said. Funny, there must've been a half dozen women wearing black at the bar. But we both knew exactly who the DJ was talking about.

I should've been used to this stuff by now. I *was* used to it. So why did I feel like I was physically shrinking against the back of the booth, fading into invisibility, while Alex grew brighter and brighter? Why did I feel like Alex was sucking all the attention from the room, leaving me more diminished than ever?

What Alex did next shocked me more completely than if she'd stripped off her bustier and thrown it to her admirer. Maybe even more; Alex has always been a bit of an exhibitionist.

"So, Linds, tell me about work," she said.

I stared at her in surprise, waiting for her to scream "Gotcha!" I'd never had Alex turn the conversation to me before. What was going on? Did she sense I had a crush on Bradley? Or could she possibly be trying to be kind by sharing the spotlight with me?

"It's going well," I said. "Really well."

"When do you think the D.C. office will open?" Alex asked.

"Um, not for a while," I said.

"It's amazing how well you've done," Bradley said.

I took a gulp of beer to hide my discomfort. If he only knew.

"Thanks," I said.

"No, seriously," Bradley said. "I mean, the campaigns you've created. I see the one for Dell all the time. It always makes me laugh."

"Thanks," I said again, this time meaning it. That had been a bitch of a campaign; I'd had to rewrite my storyboard thirty-eight times while the client agonized over whether he wanted the ad set inside a computer store or inside a twenty-something customer's home. Finally, he'd settled on my very first story-board—which was set inside a cybercafe.

Bradley's praise took some of the sting off the DJ's dedication; I sat up a little straighter.

"Cheers," Alex said, raising her beer. "To my sister, brilliant creator of the Dell campaign, and to Bradley, brilliant inventor of honey on popcorn. How'd you come up with that anyway?"

Bradley shook his head. "It was at the end of senior year in high school. Dad and I were on our own then, and we'd never cooked much. One night we were watching TV and the only things we had in the house were popcorn and take-out menus."

"I've heard take-out menus aren't bad if you deep-fry them," Alex said.

Bradley laughed and took another sip of Sam Adams. "I was so sick of pizza by then. I made the popcorn, but we didn't have any butter. It was either honey or Tabasco sauce—that's all we had in the house."

"I think you made the right call," Alex said. She leaned forward in the booth and began teasing the label off her bottle of beer. "You know, there's something I've never told you," she said.

I mentally wrote her next line: *I'm struggling with flatulence. And losing the battle.*

"Your mom helped me out once."

"Really?" Bradley said. "What happened?"

"There was this guy I was seeing sophomore year in high school," Alex began. "God, it was so long ago, but it seemed so important then."

"David?" I asked.

"No, someone else," Alex said.

"Jon? Steve?" I asked, before stopping myself. It might be quicker if I eliminated the names of guys she *hadn't* dated.

"You never met him," Alex said. She pulled the label off and plastered it against the scarred wooden table, smoothing out its edges as carefully as if she was ironing it. "He was a sophomore, too. But in college. Dad would've freaked. Anyway, he came to pick me up one day at school—I was cutting class to meet him—and the jerk broke up with me, right there, with me standing on the street corner. He didn't even bother to get out of his car. We'd only been dating for a month or two, but it was a complete shock."

I'll bet, I thought sarcastically. Probably the first time anyone had ever broken up with Alex.

"He drove away, and I didn't know what in the hell to do," Alex said. "I couldn't sneak back into school because I couldn't stop crying."

She shook her head and looked down at her beer, as though needing a moment to compose herself, even after all these years. "You're beautiful, it's true," warbled James Blunt consolingly.

Alex, crying over some guy? Now that shocked me. She had a million guys panting after her in high school. Why would she get so upset over one measly breakup?

Suddenly, a long-ago memory snapped into place: That was *the* guy. I'd been searching Alex's purse for some of my babysitting money that had gone missing. At first I'd thought the packet of pills was a new kind of vitamin; then I'd realized what I was holding. I'd dropped the clamshell packet back in her purse, shocked by how little I knew about my sister's life, how different we'd become. I'd only kissed a few guys by that point (fine, technically one, if you don't count passing the peace in church). Who were the pills for? I'd wondered back then.

Now I wondered if the guy had dumped her after she slept with him.

I looked at her and felt a twinge of sympathy. Alex and I weren't close, but she was my *sister.* I didn't want her to be hurt, especially not in that way. I just hadn't ever considered before that she could be hurt. Alex was the one who broke hearts, not the one who stood on street corners, crying as a guy sped away from her.

"So I start walking home, and it's freezing out, and I'd left my coat at school because I'd snuck out," Alex said. "Then all of a sudden I see your mom coming down the street. She'd just finished showing a house to some clients and she was heading for her car. She recognized me and she stopped."

Alex looked off into the distance, remembering. "She was wearing these great black leather boots. I remember thinking how much cooler she looked than any other mom I knew. I made up some excuse for why I wasn't in school, but I didn't fool her. She knew something was wrong."

"Did she take you back to school?" I asked.

Alex shook her head. "No. She took me home." She looked at Bradley. "To your house. Your dad was still at work, so it was just the two of us. She poured me a Coke and we sat in the kitchen and she talked to me. Really talked to me. And then, when it would've been time for school to let out, I walked home."

"She never said a word," Bradley said.

"She promised me she wouldn't," Alex said. "I trusted her. I told her everything about the guy. Stuff I didn't even tell my friends. She was . . . amazing."

Bradley nodded, his eyes sad. "Yeah."

I wanted to say something—to agree that Bradley's mom had

been wonderful, which was the truth—but I couldn't. Their conversation had its own intimate rhythm; whatever I said would jar it and draw even more attention to the fact that, right now, I was the outsider.

"It sucks that you lost her," Alex said.

Bradley nodded again, his eyes wistful. "Yeah."

We all sat there for a moment, then Alex said, "Can I make another confession?"

"Sure," Bradley said.

Alex took a deep breath and whispered, "I really hate this song."

Bradley looked at her for a second, then he started laughing, a true, rich belly laugh.

And in that moment, I *knew*. The thing I'd feared most was happening. Bradley was falling under Alex's spell.

The worst part was, I couldn't even blame him.

Sixteen

I HAD ABSOLUTELY NO idea why I was doing this.

Maybe it was because I had to do something, *anything,* to get my mind off my night with Alex and Bradley. I'd been reliving it for two days now, and the memories hadn't gotten less painful with time. Or maybe it was because there was another image still clinging to a corner of my mind, despite my best effort to shoo it away: May with a smudge of chocolate on her cheek, telling me, "Maybe it would help you, too . . . Maybe you could use a little bit of time to figure out what you really want to do."

I stepped out of my car and double-checked the address I'd written down on the top of my yellow legal pad. This was the right house. It was a small bungalow with a grassy lawn that held a tricycle, a miniature plastic slide, and a couple of big plastic balls in bright colors. I climbed the front steps and rang the bell, and a tiny person opened the door and peered at me through the screen door.

"Is your mommy home?" I asked, kneeling down to look her in the eye and giving her my friendliest smile. I've got a way with kids, if I do say so myself.

"Stranger!" the kid bellowed.

"No, no, honey—" I protested.

"Stranger! Stranger! Stranger!"

I never knew kids that small could be so loud; she was like a miniature DEFCOM siren.

"Katie, what have I told you about opening the door?" a woman said, walking up behind her. She scooped her daughter up in one arm and opened the screen door with the other.

"You must be Lindsey," she said. "Come on in."

Jane looked like she was barely twenty-eight, but May had told me she was a decade older. Her bright red hair was swept up into a careless ponytail, and she wasn't wearing any makeup. A sprinkling of freckles danced across her small, upturned nose, and her smile was genuine. I liked her on sight.

"Don't mind the mess." Jane laughed, kicking a plastic wheelbarrow out of my path as she led me to the living room. "I swear I cleaned up before you came over, but I've got two miniature tornadoes living here."

"You've got a great house," I said, and it was true. Even though it was obvious Jane didn't have much money, the warmth of her personality had infused her home. A blue crocheted afghan was draped across the sofa, and kids' artwork decorated the walls. A small wooden bookshelf was stuffed with books, and next to it was a battered, oversize chair with cozy-looking pillows. The yummy scent of baked apples and cinnamon lingered in the air.

"Thanks," Jane said. "We love it here."

She looked around the room. "Chris, where are you?"

She peered under the afghan, and I could see her kids had covered the sofa with tic-tac-toe games written in permanent marker. Bright red marker.

"Uh-oh," she said. "He's hiding again. Could you do me a favor? He always hides when we have visitors. If you could make a production out of searching for him, you'd make his day."

I cleared my throat. "Don't worry, Jane, I'm the best little-boy finder in all of Maryland. I even have a trophy from the mayor. I'll find Chris."

I walked through the house, past a chair that had two little-boy legs sticking out from under it, and began talking loudly: "Where could Chris be? He's not in the living room, he's not in the trash can, he's not in his bedroom . . . This kid is the best hider in the world!"

The legs quivered, and I pretended to trip over them.

"Oops! That chair tripped me, Jane. Now that chair is giggling! You've got a crazy giggling chair!"

"It's me!" Chris erupted from underneath the chair, his face flushed. "Am I really the best hider?"

"The best I've ever seen," I promised him.

"I think the world's best hider and his sister deserve a treat," Jane said. "You guys can pick one show to watch."

The kids took off upstairs like they'd been shot out of a cannon, and Jane gestured for me to sit down.

"Can I get you some coffee or tea? We're guaranteed a half hour of peace," she said. "They don't get to watch TV very often."

"I'm fine, thanks. And they're great kids," I said, pulling out my notebook.

"Thank you," Jane said, looking pleased. "I think so, too. When my husband and I split up, I vowed I'd do everything I could to make their lives happy."

"What happened between you and your husband?" I asked. I had to dive right in if we only had half an hour. May had told me to get as many details as I could; that way, if Jane had broken up with her husband because he was a workaholic, we'd know not to set her up with another one.

Jane sighed. "Oh, you don't want to know. Have you ever met a walking cliché?" She couldn't quite pull off the lighthearted tone she was aiming for, in part because her lower lip was trembling. "I'd love to be able to say that we grew apart, but the truth is I messed up," she continued. "I married the wrong man."

I nodded sympathetically. Ouch. What an awful realization, especially when there were kids involved.

"One day I went to his office to surprise him," Jane said. "It was his birthday and he had to work late, so I decided to bring him a piece of the white chocolate cheesecake I'd baked for him. That was his favorite."

She took a deep breath. "That's how I found out he was having an affair."

"I'm sorry," I said.

"I didn't walk in on him or anything," she said. "But his secretary told me he'd left early. It didn't take long to figure it out, once I'd waited up for him and he'd come home pretending he'd had a long day at work. Anyway, I've gotten over it for myself, but it kills me that the kids will be affected by this for the rest of their lives. So I only say good things about Daddy to my kids. But between you and me, I burned all our wedding pictures."

She shook her head. "I didn't mean to lay all that on you. You're a good listener."

"I'm glad you told me," I said. "I need to know all about you if I'm going to pick the right man for you."

"My husband—I mean my ex-husband—is getting remarried next month," Jane said, so softly it was almost as though she was speaking to herself. "For some reason I couldn't resist treating myself to something special. It doesn't make any sense, and God knows I can't afford it—I'm a schoolteacher, and you know how well that pays—but I'd love to meet someone. I'd love just one more chance to pick the right guy."

I looked around at her cozy house. Three aprons—one big and two miniature—were hanging in the kitchen, next to a tray of what looked like homemade muffins. A giant stuffed giraffe with chewed-on ears and a plastic doll were sitting at the dining room table, the remnants of a happy little tea party on the table before them.

"I'm sure May told you about our sliding scale," I said briskly, holding up my notebook so she couldn't see the page I was staring at was blank. "I see here we can offer you a rate of twelve hundred dollars instead of our usual fifteen hundred."

"Really?" Jane said, her eyes widening. "But that's wonderful!"

So I'd have to give up my commission to help Jane. If a single-mom schoolteacher with a cheating ex didn't deserve happiness, who did?

"Tell me about your ex-husband," I said. "Then I'll know what kind of guy not to set you up with.

Jane wrinkled her adorable little nose. "How can I sum up Kyle? Let me put it this way. I spent a semester in college abroad, and I remember the French had a saying that went something like this: There's always one who kisses the cheek, and one who lifts their cheek to be kissed."

She grinned wryly. "My husband was the cheek lifter."

"Got it," I said. "So we need to find someone to kiss your cheek."

"That would be wonderful," she said. "And he has to love kids. They come first."

She looked down at herself. "There's peanut butter on my knee. I drive an old minivan. And my dress-up clothes are overalls. Do you seriously think you're going to find a guy who wants a schoolteacher with lunch smeared across her leg?"

I looked at Jane sitting there with worry in her eyes, and a wave of protectiveness washed over me. How dare her ex-husband make her feel undeserving? How dare he take away the hope in her eyes? What a jerk he must have been.

"Hey, Jane?" I said.

She looked up from trying to scrape the dried peanut butter off her overalls.

"Who said anything about just one guy?" I asked.

Jane stared at me for a moment, then broke into a grin so huge that her eyes nearly disappeared.

"You're a matchmaker?" Matt asked. "Seriously?"

"Sort of," I mumbled, cradling the phone against my shoulder and pouring myself some Red Zinger. The stuff was addictive.

"You went to this woman's house, signed her up for a dating service, and then you picked a guy to go out with her?" Matt said. "When do we get to the 'sort of' part?"

"Well, when you put it *that* way," I said, carrying the tea to my room.

"I've always been a stickler for logic," Matt said. "Oh, wait, no—that's you."

"Stop picking on me," I said. "I'm going through a midlife crisis."

"What about the ad agency?" Matt asked. "Are you still going back for the interview?"

"Of course," I said.

"Then you're not having a midlife crisis," Matt said. "If you were having a midlife crisis, you'd chuck it all and become a matchmaker and take up bungee jumping."

"You know I hate heights," I said.

"That's the point of a midlife crisis," Matt said. "You do stuff that's completely out of character. If a midlife crisis just made you eat more fiber and read Tolstoy, who would bother having one?"

"Did I tell you I'm babysitting for the woman I set up?" I said. "She never goes out, so she doesn't have anyone to leave the kids with. I think I'm more nervous than she is about her date."

"Who'd you set her up with?" he asked.

"At first I was thinking another teacher—you know, someone who loves kids and shares the same interests. But then I found a file for this guy named Toby. He'd filled out a questionnaire, and it was kind of dry. He's a doctor. Podiatrist, actually," I said, curling my legs up under me on the bed and taking a sip of tea. "I know, I know, fallen arches aren't sexy, and Jane's so energetic that I wasn't sure about him at first. I was going to put his questionnaire back in the pile, but then I turned the page. And I saw that he'd doodled these little intertwined hearts all along the margin of the second page. It was so sweet."

"Interesting," Matt said.

"It's a gamble, but I just have this sense about him," I said. "He seems really kind. Jane needs kindness. So I called him, and we talked for an hour. He's a great guy. If it doesn't work out, I'll find someone else for her. And him, too."

"What's May like?" Matt asked.

"She's wonderful," I said. "The stuff she's been through with her ex-husband—I mean, what a jerk. But she's so positive. She makes you feel good just by being around her."

"Um-hmn," Matt said.

"I mean, can you imagine me working with her? She sets her own hours and she interviews clients with a dog on her lap and when I went by to tell her about my meeting with Jane, she was just waking up from a nap," I said. "Ridiculous. It's a completely insane way to run a company."

"Um-hmn," Matt said.

"We'd drive each other crazy," I said. "Who doesn't use computers? She actually has her clients fill out forms by hand.

They've all got ring marks from her teacups. Oh, and sometimes when she laughs really hard, she snorts."

"Um-hmn," Matt said.

"Don't make your shrink noises at me," I said.

"Mnmh," he said, then swallowed. "I'm eating."

"Anything good?" I asked.

"Butterball turkey," he said. "The client sent us a freezer full.
First I had to look at turkeys for a month, now I'm eating them.
I'm going to boycott Thanksgiving."

"Matt?" I said. "I don't think I'm going back to Givens for my
second interview."

"Yeah," he said. "I thought so."

"What do you mean?" I shouted. "I just said that. I didn't really mean it!"

"Lindsey," he said gently but urgently. *"Jump."*

"I don't want to," I said, squeezing my eyes shut.

"You can do it," he said. "You just spent zero seconds talking
about the ad agency and an hour telling me about May."

"You're wildly exaggerating," I said. "Bordering on pathologi-
cal lying. You should really see someone about that."

"Stop changing the subject," he said. "You can always go back
to an agency later. Consider this a sabbatical."

"When am I going to get another opportunity like this?" I
wailed. "Givens will never want to see me again if I blow her off.
And if I keep flaking out like this, I'll have to move every three
weeks. I'll run out of cities and have to start applying for jobs in
Europe. And I hate kippers."

"Don't forget escargot," Matt said. "They're nasty, too."

"What am I doing?" I asked. I fell back onto my bed and put
my hand over my forehead. "I'm not sure how, but I know this
is all your fault."

"You're scared. But it's going to be okay," he said. "Lindsey? I
don't mean this to come across wrong, but I'm proud of you."

Then me—me, who never, ever used to cry—lay there with tears streaming down my cheeks, feeling like something inside of me that had hardened into rock long ago was breaking up into little pieces and being washed away.

"It's going to be okay," Matt soothed me as I clung to the phone like it was a lifeline. "Everything's going to be fine."

Seventeen

WHEN A CUSTOMER BANGED on the convenience store's bathroom door, I nearly stabbed myself in the eye with my mascara wand.

"Just a minute!" I called, swiping on my final coat. I still hadn't gotten up the nerve to let my family see me in my new clothes, so I'd found another place to change. This restroom was clean and the lighting was good, plus there was a hook for my clothes. All that and an endless supply of Hershey's bars and Laffy Taffy—I could practically live here.

"She's usually in there awhile," I heard the cashier say.

"How often does she come in here?" the woman asked incredulously.

"Every day for the past two weeks," the cashier said. "It's the darndest thing. It's like one girl goes in and another comes out."

"Well, I have to *go*," the customer said. "I've given birth to five children! When you've had that many children, you can't hang around waiting for a bathroom. Do you catch my drift?"

"No, ma'am," said the teenage clerk meekly.

"Unless you have a mop, you'd better let me in there!" the customer threatened, banging on the door again.

I quickly gathered up my makeup, shoved my navy blue suit into a garment bag, and opened the door.

"Sorry," I said as she rushed by, shooting me a dirty look.

"I like that shirt almost as much as the red dress," the cashier said, eyeing my light green halter top with approval. I'd paired it with my skinny jeans and new chunky Marni heels with the buckles on the fronts, and I'd used a straightening iron to make my hair fall in gleaming sheets to my shoulders.

"Thanks!" I said, darting out the door and jumping into my parents' old station wagon. I was going to be late to meet Jacob Weinstein, thirty-four, who'd moved to town a few months ago and was ready to start dating.

For the past two weeks, ever since I'd officially been hired by Blind Dates, I'd gotten a whole new kind of education, one that didn't have anything to do with product differentiation or target demographics or branding. I'd learned about people, I'd learned about their fears and desires. I'd learned the secrets they held close, hidden from colleagues and acquaintances and family members.

I'd also learned that looking into the files of a dating service can break your heart. What people yearn for, more than anything else, is a connection with each other. They want someone to raise a family with. They want someone to hold hands with. They want someone to take care of them when they're sick, and to still love them when they're old and wrinkly. Incidentally, if these services can be performed by a person who looks like Heidi Klum or has the bank account of Donald Trump, so much the better.

I'd spent hours curled up on May's couch, reading through the stacks of files. What I'd discovered is that during every wedding and baby shower and birthday party—every life event, really, both major and minor—there are people clustered on the sidelines, in the shadows just beyond the spotlight, outwardly celebrating but inwardly wondering what they've done wrong, why they've ended up alone while the rest of the world seems to have paired off, and if they're always going to be this lonely.

May was good at drawing people out. I read about a widower who told May he bought cans of tuna fish for his lunch one at time, just so he could go into the grocery store every day and experience human contact during his brief chat with the cashier at checkout. I glimpsed the secret of a woman who'd been obese as a teenager and still saw herself as fat and unlovable in the mirror, even though she exercised every day and was now a healthy size. I learned about the anguish a man suffered when his fiancée literally left him at the altar. The maid of honor had come up and whispered the news in his ear while he stood there in his tuxedo, waiting for his bride to walk down the aisle.

Had there always been this many lonely people in the world? I wondered, marveling at the stacks of folders surrounding me.

"We do more than just fix people up," May had told me on my second day. "We listen to them; in fact, listening is probably the most important skill you'll bring to this job. We find out what went wrong in their past relationships, and we work with them to make sure they get out of any bad patterns they may be in. We help people discover what kind of partner they really want. We're more than matchmakers; we're therapists and best friends and sometimes even drill sergeants."

"Really?" I'd said.

"Sure, for people who have totally unrealistic expectations," May had replied. "If a fifty-year-old guy comes in here wanting to be set up with a nineteen-year-old Playboy bunny, we have to do a little ass kicking, find out what's really going on with him and why he's having such a crisis of confidence that he needs arm candy to prove to the world that he's important and desirable. And if that doesn't work, we tell him to go find a mail-order bride and we show him the door. There aren't a lot of clients we turn down, but you'll have to be prepared to do it now and then. We have an informal no-jerks-allowed policy."

I'd nodded, loving the way May was already using the word *we,* like I was her full partner.

"On the flip side, a lot of the clients we see are facing a crisis of confidence," May said. "So build them up a bit. Give them a compliment or two, but only if it's sincere."

Now, as I walked into a restaurant-bar called Parker's and looked around for my client, I remembered what May had told me—that listening was the most important part of my job. "Everyone has a story," she'd said. It was time to find out what Jacob's was.

He was sitting in a booth against the far wall. He was a nice-looking, dark-haired guy who was on the short side. The sleeves of his shirt were pushed up to reveal strong-looking forearms. His file told me he was a mortgage banker who enjoyed skiing, traveling, and cooking ethnic food.

"I've never done anything like this before," Jacob confessed right after we'd introduced ourselves. His shoe was drumming a rat-a-tat-tat against the floor.

"Relax," I told him as I sat down across from him. "We're just going to have a conversation, then I'm going to find a really lucky woman who gets to go out with you."

He smiled, revealing an endearingly crooked front tooth, and I knew I'd said the right thing. Funny, but there was no sign of the shyness that usually plagued me in social situations. Maybe it was because the voices in my head, the ones that told me I'd never be as pretty and desirable as Alex, had lost some of their power now that I knew how many other people had harsh voices inside their heads, too. Maybe my new clothes and makeup helped as well; I was still playing a part, still acting outside of myself, in some ways.

"Anything to drink, hon?" the waitress asked, motioning to the drink menu.

"What are you having?" I asked Jacob.

"A martini," he said. "Mine's plain, but I heard they make good chocolate ones here."

"Perfect," I said.

The waitress walked away, and Jacob leaned back against the cushioned padding of the booth.

"I'm kind of embarrassed," he said. "I still can't believe I'm doing this."

"I know," I said. "It's horrifying. I mean, having a plain martini when there's chocolate available."

Jacob smiled, a bigger smile this time.

"Listen, I think you're brave," I told him. "You're going after what you want."

"I guess you could look at it that way," he said.

"So tell me about you. You cook and you love to travel?" I said, crossing my legs and leaning closer to him. "Clearly you'd be the perfect man, if it weren't for that plain martini flaw."

Was I flirting with my client? But Jacob seemed to need it; he was so anxious.

"Maybe I could change, for the right woman," he said, smiling again. His foot had stopped tapping, I noticed.

"Tell me who would be the right woman for you," I said. "What qualities are important to you?"

"I love good food, so she can't be the kind of woman who picks at a salad and says she's full, then sneaks home and wolfs down a bag of Chips Ahoy!" Jacob said.

I laughed, and he seemed emboldened. "And I love to travel, so agoraphobics are out, too."

Jacob was cute, funny, and nice. My chocolate martini was perfection. And I was getting paid for this?

"What else?" I said lightly. "Tell me about your last girl-friend."

"Sue?" Jacob said. "Mmm . . . how should I put this?"

"As bluntly as possible," I joked. "I need to know all the details if I'm going to pick the right woman for you."

Jacob sighed. He started to say something, stopped, then blurted out, "Everything made her cry. And I mean *everything*. At first it was one of the things that made me fall in love with her. I thought she was so sensitive. I brought her a rose on our first date, and she cried. One of her friends announced she was pregnant with twins, and Sue cried. Then I realized she never stopped crying."

"Sappy commercials?" I asked. Jacob nodded.

"Sunsets and sad movies, too . . . Then one day her parents came to visit and we picked them up at the airport. And I somehow ended up crushed between Sue and her mom, and the two of them were wailing away—I mean, *wailing*—and I looked over at the dad, and he was just pulling tissues out of his pockets with this resigned expression. And I started to laugh. I couldn't help it; the harder they cried, the more I laughed. And of course her mom thought I was laughing at *her*, and, well . . . things just went downhill from there."

"What happened when you broke up?" I asked.

"Sue didn't shed a single tear," Jacob said.

I looked at him, and we both burst into laughter.

"So no criers," I said, pretending to scribble it down. "Check. What else?"

"And, um, it would be kind of nice if the woman you picked . . ." Jacob's voice trailed off.

I stayed quiet; May had said that letting silence linger could be a powerful tool in getting clients to open up.

"If she just . . ." Jacob cleared his throat.

I knew Jacob was too good to be true. Here's the part where

he'd say he wanted someone who would let him wear her false eyelashes, or go to *Star Trek* conventions every weekend.

"If she looked like you," he said.

I floated home with Jacob's compliment ringing in my ears. But his words came to a screeching halt, like a needle being yanked across a record, when I pulled into the driveway. Alex's shiny black Lexus—the one Gary had given her for her twenty-ninth birthday—was there. It was a Thursday night. What was Alex doing here?

"Back so soon?" she called from the living room as I opened the front door as quietly as I could. I'd been hoping to sneak past my parents and change and wipe off my makeup before creeping back outside through my bedroom window and making a pretend entrance. My parents wouldn't have noticed a thing; Alex, a champion nocturnal escape artist, would be harder to fool.

"Be right there," I said, darting into the hallway and heading for my room. I made it four steps before my heels tripped me up and I sprawled on the carpet. Crap! Now they'd all come running and see me!

"What was that?" Mom said.

"Sounded like someone dropped a vacuum cleaner," Dad observed.

"Probably Lindsey fell down," Alex said, and they all said, "Ah!" and turned back to watching their *Wheel of Fortune* rerun.

"I'm fine!" I shouted. "Just in case you were wondering!"

No one answered me, so I got up and kept walking, slightly disappointed that I didn't need to use the G.I. Joe crawl I'd been mentally rehearsing to maneuver into my room. I slipped into slacks and a blue button-up blouse, creamed off my makeup, and brushed my teeth before heading back into the TV room.

"How was your date?" Alex asked.

"Date?" I said. "What date?"

"Oops," Mom said again. "Maybe I shouldn't have said anything. But I was walking by your room when you were making plans to meet him."

"Who?" I asked.

"Jacob, silly," Mom said.

"How long did it take you to walk by?" I demanded.

"Details," Alex ordered.

"We, um, just went for a walk and talked," I said.

Alex tore her eyes away from Pat Sajak. "You went for a walk?"

"That sounds nice, honey," Mom said.

"Your date sounds nice to your mother," Alex said. "Do you realize how many things are wrong with that sentence? Why didn't the guy at least buy you a drink? Is he cheap?"

"I don't need to drink to have fun on a date," I said, stifling a hiccup. That second martini had been strong. "And why aren't you out tonight?"

Alex didn't move, but something in her face changed, grew almost sorrowful. "I was tired," she said.

"So let me get this straight," I said. "You're hassling me for going out on a boring date, but you stayed home with your parents?"

"Hey," Dad said, wounded.

"We're still hip," Mom reassured him, patting his hand.

"I didn't feel well," Alex said.

I knew instantly that she was lying. I can't say how; maybe because I'd watched her lie so many times to my parents I'd become an expert in detecting a subtle change in her tone, or a slight flicker of her eyes. I knew with a rush of certainty she was here for another reason. Were she and Gary having problems? A stab of fear tore through me. Please don't let it be that. I couldn't help imagining Bradley consoling Alex, the two of them sharing another bottle of wine, him putting an arm around her and—I squeezed my eyes shut. No. *No.*

"So what did you and your young man talk about on your walk?" Mom asked me.

"Mom," Alex and I groaned in unison.

"Well, he is a young man, isn't he?" Mom asked in her best annoyingly reasonable tone.

"We talked about work, mostly," I said. "He's, um, a mortgage banker."

"Sexy," Alex commented.

"It was fun!" I protested.

"Did he show you his jumbo loans?" Alex said, making it sound dirty. "Does he have a . . . *position* on reverse mortgages?"

"Jacob's a great guy," I said hotly. "Maybe he likes me for my mind. Maybe he actually likes talking to me."

"Blank in the blank blank blank," Dad said, staring at the puzzle on the screen. "It's a phrase."

"Now Alex," Mom said. "Stop teasing. The only reason why Lindsey got her big promotion is because she works so hard."

I smiled, vindicated. Well, sort of.

"Something in the way she moves," Alex told Dad.

"Who?" Dad asked.

"It's the answer to the puzzle," Alex said.

I looked at the screen. Only four letters were showing, but it fit.

"You've been watching this show way too often," I said. "You're scaring me."

"Oh, Lindsey, before I forget," Mom said. She rummaged through a pile of papers on the coffee table and unearthed a crumpled envelope. "We got this in the mail today. Something about our house assessment. It went way up and our taxes are going up now, if you can believe it."

"I'll take care of it," I said. "You can usually appeal these things and get a reduction if you know how to navigate through the bureaucracy."

"Thanks, honey," Mom said as I took the envelope from her. I stood up at the next commercial and went to my bedroom to change for what seemed like the umpteenth time today, this time into my sweats. Alex followed me and flopped on my bed.

"I was going to ask you if you remembered to bring along a condom tonight," she said. "But that blouse is protection enough."

I picked up a pillow and threw it at her, but I couldn't hide my smile. I sat on the edge of the bed, pulling off the blue flats I'd just put on ten minutes ago and making a show of massaging my toes.

"Remember when our biggest worry was what to wear to school?" Alex asked. Her eyes were closed, and she had faint purplish smudges underneath them. I frowned; was something keeping Alex up at night? I didn't want to think about what it could be.

"Calvin Klein or Jordache jeans," Alex mumbled. "I agonized for hours."

"That was never my biggest worry," I said.

"It should've been," Alex said. She'd tried for a teasing tone, but her voice was so weary that it fell flat.

I glanced at her. Her eyes were still closed. And did she look even thinner?

I got off the bed and hung up my clothes, then neatly lined up the black cowboy boots Alex had kicked off when she came into the room. I kept my back to her as I finally asked the question that was begging to be asked.

"Is everything okay? I mean, with Gary?"

She didn't answer, and when I turned around, I saw that she was curled up into a ball, sound asleep. Her hands were clasped under her chin, and for a moment, I was struck by the thought that she looked like a little child making a wish. A blond, angelic child with perfectly waxed eyebrows and a lavender thong you could practically floss your teeth with.

I watched her sleep as a complicated, familiar mix of feelings fell over me like a densely woven tapestry: rivalry, loyalty, jealousy, love—all the threads mixed so tightly together it was impossible to tell where one ended and the others began. Then I turned off the light, pulled my comforter over her, and left the room, moving quietly across the floor.

The next morning when I awoke on the couch, with a crick in my neck and the unfamiliar taste of a mild hangover in my mouth, I found a message in Alex's handwriting on the pillow next to me: "Jacob called."

My heart skipped a beat until I saw the next line: "He wants to know if you can help him reseed his lawn on your second date."

I laughed and crumpled up the note in my hand. When I went into my bedroom, Alex was already gone. She must've awoken early, which was odd, because Alex never woke up early. Odder still, she'd actually made my bed.

Eighteen

"I'VE GOT THE PERFECT girl for you," I told Jacob when I phoned him three days later.

"So you're going to go out with me?" he asked.

I smiled, feeling more pleased than was professionally appropriate.

I'd picked the manager of a women's clothing boutique for him—a pretty, half-Spanish, thirty-one-year-old named Jimena who loved to go bike riding on weekends. When I'd been combing through our files, her picture had jumped out at me. She looked fit and happy and together, and after the crier, I suspected Jacob might be ready for someone with positive karma.

"Don't drink too much coffee before your date," I warned Jacob, remembering how anxious he'd been when I'd first met him. A few jolts of caffeine, and he'd levitate through the roof. "And wear a blue shirt again. It looks great with your eyes."

"I just feel so out of the dating world." He sighed. "I mean, Sue and I were together for almost two years."

"Can I give you a little tip?" I said, skimming over the fact that I'd already given him two unsolicited ones. "Don't bring up Sue. Not until the third date. Keep the focus on your date, not on your ex."

"You're right," Jacob said. "What else?"

"Other than that, you're perfect," I teased. "Definitely mention what a good cook you are. Women can't resist that."

"You know, you could save me a lot of time if you'd just go out with me," he said.

"Stop tempting me." I was glad he couldn't see me blushing.

"Lindsey?" he asked. "Did you mean that? About looking good in a blue shirt?"

I thought about Jacob's strong arms, and his endearing shyness.

"You'd look good in anything," I said. "But blue is definitely your color."

Was flirting really this easy?

May winked at me when I hung up.

"Ego boost?" she asked. It took me a second to realize she was talking about *Jacob's* ego.

"Yeah," I said. "He's a good guy, but his confidence is a little low. It seems to be recovering nicely, though."

As was mine, I thought, feeling my cheeks grow warm again as I remembered the way Jacob's eyes had widened when he saw me walking into the martini bar to first meet him.

For the rest of the week, I buried myself in work, studying May's files and phoning her clients to introduce myself and get to know them. Of course, burying myself in work had a slightly different definition these days. Instead of staying at my desk and gnawing on cold pizza crusts at 3:00 A.M., I was routinely kicked out the door by May at six o'clock sharp.

"Go have fun!" she'd admonish me. "It's a beautiful night."

"I live with my parents," I'd remind her. "A big night for us is leftovers and a Lifetime move. Last night we saw one called *My Lover, My Hostage*. It was about a woman who tied up her boyfriend when he tried to break up with her. I can't believe I didn't learn that trick long ago."

"Shoo!" May said, snatching away the files I was trying to sneak out and making sweeping motions with her arms. "You're too young and pretty to work your life away. Go to a bookstore or a movie."

Sometimes I did, and sometimes I went shopping. My old wardrobe wasn't much use to me these days because there wasn't any comfortable way to curl up on May's couch while wearing an eight-hundred-dollar suit, plus there was always the chance I'd have to race out and meet a client on a moment's notice, and I didn't want them to think they were about to be audited. So my suits got pushed to the back of my closet, and the front began filling up with my new jeans and skirts and tops. But my parents never saw those clothes. I made sure I was covered up in a jacket or wrap whenever I left the house. Maybe it was because I was gearing up to tell my parents I'd lost my job at the advertising agency, and there was only so much shock they could take. Or maybe it was because, in front of my family, I knew I'd feel like the emperor in *his* new clothes. Just like that little boy in the crowd, they'd be able to see right through me. Alex was the one who brought home bags of sexy clothes; I brought home glass jars from the Container Store to organize the dry goods in my parents' pantry. So I kept my makeup case hidden away in my parents' spare car, and I applied mascara and lipstick at stoplights, and I ignored the little voice that told me this had gone on way too long.

Maybe I felt that, by not telling my parents, I was still playing at this new life, dipping in my toes without making a real commitment to it. Telling them would make it real—make it irrevocable—and I wasn't ready for that. I wasn't ready to give up my identity as the overachieving, successful daughter.

But little by little, I was settling into my split life and learning how to straddle the distance between my two worlds. At my parents' house, I knocked out their taxes in an hour and reminded Mom to have the oil changed in her car. At work, I woke up from a catnap with files scattered all around me and a scruffy little mutt snoring on my chest. At home, I balanced my parents' checkbook and helped them set up a reverse mortgage before I changed into a sky-blue slip dress and sky-high heels and headed out to a singles' bar to sign up potential clients (and, somehow, ended up getting pulled onto the stage and singing background during karaoke night).

Sometimes I couldn't believe I was getting paid to work for May. One morning I signed up two clients at once—a pair of lifelong best friends in their early seventies. One was recently separated, one never married, and they'd dared each other to join Blind Dates. I'd interviewed them at a hole-in-the-wall-diner over perfectly cooked omelets and fresh biscuits that practically melted in my mouth. When I'd asked them what they wanted in a man, they'd looked at each other and giggled like teenagers.

"One with all his own teeth?" the never-married one suggested.

"I'd settle for consciousness," the newly separated one said.

"You've got pretty high standards," I said, mock sternly. I wanted to be these women when I grew up.

"Maybe we should save the money and hire us a Chippendales dancer for a few hours," the never-married one said, a gleam coming into her eyes. "One of those young, nubile ones who can do the splits and peel an orange with his tongue."

This is my *job,* I reminded myself as I cracked up. Somehow, that thought was feeling less scary these days.

Nineteen

IT WAS JUST A simple phone call. Nothing more, nothing less. Thousands of people made them every day. I flipped open my cell phone, punched in a few digits, and promptly hung up. For the third time.

It was just that so much was riding on this. If Alex and Gary were having problems, and if those problems were even remotely connected to Bradley . . . well, then I'd feel like a complete fool if I made this call.

Rationally, I knew Alex could be stressed about her wedding. Or something could be happening at her job. There could be a hundred explanations for why she'd been drawing closer to our family lately, and for why Gary hadn't been in the picture much. But every time I remembered Alex and Bradley together—the photographs he'd taken when they thought they were alone; the way he'd looked at her when she talked about his mother— terror galloped through me.

But Alex was *engaged,* I reminded myself. Maybe she and Bradley had had a few nice conversations and a shared bottle of wine at a Thai restaurant. So they were becoming friends. I could learn to handle that.

Jump, Matt had said.

If I were going to screw up my life, why stop at halfway? Why not go down in a giant, screaming fireball? After all, I'd always been an overachiever. I picked up the phone and dialed.

"Hey," I said when he answered. It was our old high school greeting; we'd never needed to identify ourselves on the phone. I hoped Bradley would still recognize my voice; if not, there was always the innovation of caller ID to soothe my ego.

"I was just going to call you," he said, and the tight knot of worry in my stomach loosened.

"So I've got a plan," I said, glad he couldn't see the goofy smile spreading across my face.

"Tell me," he said.

"Nope," I said. "But I'll pick you up next Saturday at six."

"Saturday?" He paused and the knot tightened again. The pause seemed to stretch forever.

"Just checking my schedule," he said. "I'm working that night. Is next Sunday okay?"

"Perfect," I said.

"Sure you can't give me a hint?" Bradley said.

"Mmm," I said. "Bring an appetite. I'll take care of everything else."

I hung up the phone and leaned back against my car's seat. I shut my eyes and pumped my fist into the air. I'd finally done it.

After a moment, I stepped out of the car and walked up the front steps to Jane's house. I'd driven here before making the call because I hadn't wanted to risk making it from home. With my luck, Dad would pick up the other phone and punch in numbers and start bellowing his Chinese food order at me while Mom stood in the hallway, pressing her ear to a glass she was holding against my bedroom door.

I didn't want my family to know anything about next Sunday

night. It was just for Bradley and me. It was finally time for me to find out where I stood with him.

I rang Jane's bell at seven o'clock on the nose; I was right on time.

"Katie, can you get the door?" I heard Jane call.

Katie said something I couldn't make out.

"No, it's okay if Mommy asks you to," Jane said. "You're not allowed to open it unless I say so, though."

Katie's high little voice asked another question.

"Yes, I'm asking you to open it," Jane said. "It's not a stranger. It's Lindsey."

Another squeaky question.

"I know it's Lindsey because I can see her out the window! Can you just— You know what, never mind. Mommy will get the door."

A second later the door was flung open, and Jane stood there in a bathrobe and red high-heeled shoes. "Don't say a word," she warned me, then burst into tears.

"They're not that bad," I told her, opening the screen door and letting myself in.

"They're awful," Jane said through a half sob, half laugh. "What was I thinking?"

I peered at her bangs. If you could call them bangs; they were so short they were more like a mini-Mohawk.

"I was just going to trim them a little," Jane said, wiping her eyes. "Then the left side looked shorter than the right, so I trimmed the left side. But then the right side was shorter so I tried to—"

"Even them up again?" I ventured.

"Then again," she moaned. "And again. It was like a seesaw. Oh, Lord, I'm a nightmare. Look at me!"

I mentally reviewed the tips May had given me, but I was

pretty sure she hadn't covered a haircut by Edward Scissor-hands.

"I never should've done this," Jane said, her lower lip trembling. "The guy's going to take one look at me and run away screaming."

I had to take control, fast. "Come on," I said, grabbing her hand and dragging her into the kitchen. "The first thing we need is a glass of wine."

"Is there some kind of trick for fixing hair with wine?" Jane asked eagerly, sloshing some Chardonnay into a plastic cup with a cartoon character on the side, the kind they give out to kids at restaurants.

"No," I said. "Take a big gulp. No, that was a sip. I want you to take a gulp. Feel better?"

"A little," Jane said.

"Now about those bangs," I said. "Let me take a closer look."

I peered at them and ran my fingers through them, murmuring like a doctor: "Mmm-hmm. Mmm-hmm."

"Don't move a muscle," I said. I hurried out to the car, opened the trunk, and grabbed the makeup kit I'd been keeping hidden near the spare tire. I made Jane sit down in the living room, where the light was good, and I opened my case.

"Close your eyes," I instructed, and I swept her bangs back and to the side, anchoring them into place with a big squirt of my grapefruit-scented hair spray.

"That's better already," I said, tapping my lower lip with my index finger. "But we need something else."

I looked around the living room but didn't see anything I could use.

"Can I check your closet?" I asked.

"Please," Jane said. "Maybe you can find me something to

wear while you're there. I just put on some pants and discovered a muddy little handprint on the butt. What was I thinking? I'm not ready for dating yet. I'm a disaster."

I left her babbling there and dashed upstairs. I whipped through Jane's closet, finally settling on a dress with a loose, silky sash. The dress was hopelessly out of date, but I had plans for the sash. I liberated it from the belt loops and raced back downstairs.

"Let me tie back your hair," I said, wrapping the sash around her head, close to the hairline so it covered up her bangs. "Let the ends trail over your shoulders like this, so it looks like a long scarf. You look like a chic Frenchwoman. Perfect!"

Jane stood up and checked a mirror.

"It looks good!" she said. "Can you come over and do this every morning for the next month?"

With her mangled bangs swept off her face, Jane still looked young and fresh-faced, but somehow she seemed elegant, too.

When the doorbell rang five minutes later, Jane was ready. She was wearing a black skirt and a simple plum-colored sweater that we'd rolled with Scotch tape to get off the guinea pig hair, and a dash of my lipstick.

Jane looked at me and grinned. "It's him!"

"I know," I whispered.

"I'm really nervous," Jane said.

"It'll be okay," I promised. "Just breathe."

She inhaled deeply. "I feel a little better now."

"*Open the door,*" I mouthed to her. What was it with this family?

"Oh, right," she said.

She pulled open the door, and standing there was the podiatrist I'd picked for her. He was in his mid-forties, never married, and he was on the shy side. But his smile was kind, and so were his blue eyes.

"I'm Toby," he said, clearing his throat.

"I'm Jane," she said. "It's a pleasure to meet you. Do you want to come in?"

"Sure," Toby said, stepping into the living room. He was extremely tall, and his shirtsleeves weren't long enough to cover his wrists, but he was holding a bouquet of daffodils. I felt like a fairy godmother, watching the two of them smile nervously at each other.

"I'm Lindsey," I told him. "Nice to meet you in person."

"And these," Jane said as Katie and Chris raced into the room, "are my twins."

Toby looked down at them. "Hi."

"You're big," Katie informed him somberly.

"I know," Toby said agreeably.

"Why are your feet so big?" asked Chris.

"Because my arms are so long," Toby said. "Want to see a trick?"

Both kids nodded, so he pushed up his sleeves and took off one of his shoes. He sat down on the floor and bent over, so his right forearm was on the floor against his right foot.

"See how they're the same size? Every grown-up is built the same way. Their feet and their lower arms are the same length," Toby said.

"Really?" Jane asked. "That's amazing."

I liked the way Toby explained things simply to her kids, without talking down to them.

"Oh," Toby said. "These are for you." He put on his shoe, but not before I noticed he had a little hole in the heel of his brown sock. He stood up and handed the daffodils to Jane.

"Thank you," she said, her smile growing wider. "I'll just put these in some water."

She hurried off to the kitchen as Toby stood there, rocking back and forth on his heels. He was definitely nervous now that he wasn't imparting an anatomy lesson to the kids; I could feel anxiety coming off him in waves.

I stood on my tiptoes and whispered into his ear, "I think she likes you."

He looked taken aback for a second, then hopeful. "Really?"

"Definitely," I whispered, smiling up at him and trying to will him some confidence. "You're going to have a great time tonight. She's a lucky woman."

"You look, um, really nice," he said when Jane came back into the room.

Go, Toby, I cheered him silently.

There was a brief bit of confusion at the door, as Jane went to open it at the same moment as Toby tried to hold it open for her and Katie let out a wail upon realizing her mom was leaving, but Jane managed to sort everything out with a quick whispered bribe of ice cream.

"Have fun," I called after them, closing the door with satisfaction; then I turned to the twins.

"Ice cream," Katie demanded, her hands on her tiny hips. Something about the way she was standing reminded me of Alex as a kid.

"Find me!" Chris ordered, racing upstairs.

I sensed I wasn't going to get a moment to bask in my matchmaking success. "Here's the plan," I told Katie. "I'll find your brother, then I'll get you some ice cream."

"Ice cream first," she said, canny as a New York City lawyer at the settlement table.

"Wouldn't it be nice if we all had ice cream together?" I asked her in the fake-bright tone I've noticed parents using when they're trying to convince their kids to do something the kids are hell-bent on not doing. I remembered too late that the fake-bright tone only seems to piss kids off more.

"Ice cream!" Katie hollered. I promptly caved (tough love,

that's my philosophy) and gave her a scoop, then went upstairs to find her brother.

"He's not in the bathtub!" I said merrily. "Not in the closet! Not under the bed!"

Where the hell was that kid? Ten minutes later I was panicked. I'd lost a kid. This was definitely a fireable offense, worse even than throwing down a colleague on a conference room table.

Just then my cell phone rang: *Jacob.*

"Hey, you," I said, trying to sound relaxed and in control.

"I'm heading out on my date now," he said.

"That's great," I said, huffing as I ran back downstairs. "Hang on a second."

I pressed the phone to my side to muffle my voice.

"Chris? If you come out I'll give you a surprise!" I yelled.

I raised the phone to my ear again. "Jacob?"

"I'm still here," he said. "I'm about to go into the restaurant. I just . . . I guess I just wanted to hear your voice."

"Are you nervous?" I asked as I threw aside the sofa cushions and peeked under the dining room table again.

"A little," Jacob said. "And . . . well, I like talking to you."

I pushed the button to mute my phone, bellowed, "Chris!" and unmuted it.

"I like talking to you, too," I said.

"Is this a bad time?" Jacob asked. "You sound kind of busy."

"No!" I said, wiping my sweaty brow with the back of my hand. "Everything's great."

"Anyway, I had a huge favor to ask," he said. "I need some new clothes, if I'm going to be dating again. Will you go shopping with me? I hate shopping, and I always end up grabbing a black sweater to appease the salespeople and get out of the store. I probably have nine of them, and none of them fit right."

Where the hell was that kid?

"Sure," I said as I yanked open the stove and peered inside. "I can definitely help you break your black sweater addiction. It's a specialty of mine."

"Thanks," Jacob said.

"And have fun with Jimena tonight," I said before I hung up, feeling a little twinge of . . . could it be envy? I imagined sitting across from Jacob in a cozy little booth, maybe leaning in to taste his drink while holding his eyes with my own.

"More ice cream?" Katie asked, appearing at my side.

Oh, God. *Chris!*

Suddenly I had visions of Chris being trapped in an old refrigerator—not that there was an old refrigerator around, but it was the sort of thing my father warned us about incessantly when we were growing up. (He also warned us about standing fans and seemed to take a perverse pleasure in showing us how the rotating blades could snap pencils in two. "That's what'll happen to your fingers if you put them in there," he'd say to us, solemnly holding up a stump of a pencil, and he'd leave it on the dining room table as an ominous warning. We were terrified of the fan for about a week, then Alex decided to see what else it could snap. She made it through a ruler, a wooden mixing spoon, and a chicken bone before breaking it on the handle of Dad's tennis racket. Which wasn't a great loss, since he'd given up on the game after whacking himself in the eye while learning to serve.)

There weren't any standing fans around Jane's house, were there? Or sharp-edged tables that could take out an eye, flammable clothing, open bottles of Drāno, or men in raincoats? (Dad had a lot of safety concerns.)

"I'll give you the best surprise in the world," I promised desperately as I raced upstairs again. "Just come out!"

A second later the cabinet door underneath the bathroom sink opened, and a tiny rumpled head poked out. How had he managed to squeeze in there? He was like a miniature Chinese contortionist.

"I want your trophy," Chris said. "That's my surprise."

"What trophy?" I asked, sinking onto the edge of the bathtub in exhaustion.

"For being the best kid finder," he said. "You said you got it from the mayor."

A crash came from downstairs, and I shot upright again. "Katie!"

I ran down the stairs and found her in the middle of the kitchen, her bowl in pieces on the tile floor beside her. A chocolate puddle was forming on the floor, and she look like she'd grown a brown beard.

"My ice cream broke," she said helpfully. "More."

An hour later I'd stuffed both kids with ice cream, soaked them in the tub, and cleaned up the tsunami of water they'd splashed on the bathroom floor. I tucked them into bed and darted around the room, collecting the various stuffed animals they demanded. I fetched cups of water, took them to the bathroom again, rearranged their stuffed animals twice, answered several unsettling questions ("Do boogers have vitamins?" "Why is your bottom bigger than Mommy's?"), and picked out bedtime stories. But first we underwent fierce negotiations:

Katie: "Three books!"

Me: "Just one!"

Chris: "Three!"

Me: "Oh, hell."

Katie: "Oh, hell."

Me: "No, no, I said, 'Oh, bells!'"

Katie and Chris: Suspicious looks.

Before I'd gotten to the end of the second book, all three of us were asleep. That's how Jane found me a few hours later when she came home from her date—curled up on an animal-print rug in a kinder version of nature in which tigers and zebras frolicked together joyfully.

"They weren't any trouble, were they?" she asked.

"None at all," I lied brightly, rubbing my eyes and staggering downstairs. "How was the date?"

"Fun," Jane said. "He was a little shy at first, but he opened up after a while. We've got a lot in common. We were both born in Delaware. Isn't that interesting?"

I could tell she liked him; it wasn't *that* interesting.

"So do you want me to set you up with more guys, or do you want to see how this one plays out?" I asked.

Jane thought for a minute.

"I don't really have time to juggle a lot of dates," she said.

"I understand," I said.

"And I can't be going out all the time," she said, frowning.

"Definitely," I agreed.

"It wouldn't be fair to the twins if I were gone every night," she said.

"True," I said.

"What do you think?" she asked.

"Maybe we should see what happens with Toby," I said. "If it doesn't work out, we can go to Plan B."

"Well, if you're sure," Jane said doubtfully.

She tried to give me some money for babysitting, but I batted it away.

"At least let me treat you to dinner or something," Jane said.

"Tell you what," I said. "If things work out with you and Toby, I get invited to the wedding."

Jane smiled shyly. "Deal."

We headed downstairs, and she collapsed onto the sofa. I glanced at my watch and idly wondered if Jacob was home from his date, too.

"My feet are killing me," she said, wincing as she took off her shoes and rubbed her toes against the carpet. "This is the first time I've worn heels in a year. Do you want a glass of wine?"

"No, I'd better go, but don't get up," I said. "I'll let myself out."

I gave her a hug good-bye and walked toward the door. As I gathered my purse and cell phone, I paused for a moment to listen to the unexpected sound I could hear coming from the living room. Then a smile spread across my face as I realized what it was.

Jane was humming.

Twenty

MAY AND I WERE spending a peaceful morning on the phones, checking in with clients and updating files. At around eleven or so, I poured myself a cup of tea and snuck one of May's chocolate-chip-and-toffee cookies. (The scrambled eggs I'd had for breakfast had been on the skimpy side. And so had both of my pieces of toast.) I'd just settled down to consider possibilities for my new clients when the phone rang. I was the closest so I grabbed it.

"Blind Dates," I said. I kicked off my shoes and wiggled my newly pedicured toes. I'd had them painted bright red last night when May had forced me to leave early. Aside from the fact that I was so ticklish I'd almost kicked the pedicurist in the face (good reflexes, that one; she'd reared back like a young pony), the experience had been fabulous.

"Is May there?" an unfamiliar voice asked.

"May I tell her who's calling?" I asked.

"Who is this?" the guy said angrily. "Is this her secretary? You got to be kidding me. She has a secretary now?"

May saw the expression on my face and reached for the phone.

"This is May," she said. "Oh, it's you."

Her face fell as the guy launched into a diatribe. I couldn't make out his words, but I could hear him shouting.

"I'm asking you to please not call me again," May said. "We've signed all the divorce papers. There's nothing more to discuss."

Ah, the charming ex-husband. Should I leave the room and give May privacy? I sat there in an agony of indecision, pretending to be absorbed in reading a file, while he raged awhile longer. May's voice stayed calm, but her fingers grew white as she clenched the phone.

"I think it's best if we communicate through our lawyers from now on," she said at one point. Finally she rolled her eyes and hung up.

"Told you he was a prince," May said. She tried for a smile, but she couldn't pull it off.

"Sorry," I said. "That must've been a tough conversation."

May nodded and turned back to her papers. Clearly she didn't want to talk about it. I tried to get back to work, too, but my concentration was shot. The peaceful vibe we'd been enjoying was shattered. After a bit, I stood up, gathered our teacups, and washed them out in the sink. I looked at the clock and saw it was almost noon.

"Why don't I run out and get us some sandwiches?" I suggested. "I'll bring you back anything you want."

"You know what I want?" May said, putting down the paper she was reading and rubbing her eyes. "I want to get out of the house for a little while and take my mind off what just happened. I've read this page five times in a row, and I still don't have any idea what it says."

"Then let's go," I said, grabbing my purse. We climbed into May's yellow VW Bug, and she started up the engine. I reached to turn on the radio so she wouldn't feel pressured to talk. But my hand stopped in midair when she began to speak.

"Do you know I used to be a completely different person?" May said. She half-smiled, the kind of smile that has no joy in it, and reached into her wallet.

"I keep this here so I won't ever forget what I used to be like."

She reached into her purse and handed me a photograph that was worn around the edges from being handled so often. The woman in the picture was rail-thin and wore a knee-length, pleated skirt and a tight smile. Her lipstick was Barbie pink, and her straight blond hair was pulled back by a flowered headband, so tightly it gave me a headache just looking at it.

"That's you?" I asked incredulously, looking at May's unruly curls, her Birkenstock sandals, her unpolished fingernails.

"My husband was a state senator," May said, smiling wryly, as she started up the car and headed down the street. "And I was the perfect society wife. I was secretary of the Junior League. I gave teas like you wouldn't believe. I can still make a killer watercress sandwich with the crusts cut off at ninety-degree angles. I've got a black belt in flower arranging."

I took another look at the photo. The eyes were the same, but that was the only resemblance. I knew May was telling the truth, but it seemed impossible to believe.

"I thought I had everything I wanted," May said. "But then, I never thought about what other options were available to me. I never had time to think about what else might be out there; I was too busy starching my husband's shirts."

I sensed May had kept this bottled up for a long time, and she needed to get it out of her system. I stayed quiet and kept my eyes fixed on her.

"I'd probably still be living that way, except that my husband lost one of his reelections," she said. "That's when he went from being arrogant to being truly mean. The more he drank, the more it became my fault that he'd lost the election. I didn't smile up at him enough during debates, or I hadn't dressed in patriotic colors. And he said it was my fault we hadn't been able to have kids—if he'd had a baby to hold up for photo ops, voters would've liked him more. Can you believe that?" Her voice changed; grew rougher. "He turned my infertility, the most painful thing in my life, into a political flaw."

May paused for a moment, lost in the sad memories.

I reached over and put my hand on hers and squeezed. "That must have been so awful," I said softly.

"I knew I had to leave, then and there, or my life would be over," she said. "And it did end, in a way. In the best possible way. My old existence was over. And now it's seven years later, and we've only just finished hashing out the divorce agreement. Can you believe it? He thought a divorce would be a political liability, so he fought it as long as he could."

"I'm sorry," I said, feeling like the words were inadequate.

"Me too," May said. "Sorry I wasted twelve years on that guy."

Then she laughed, but there wasn't any bitterness in it.

"Most of the time I don't let it bother me," she said. "It took me years of therapy to not let it bother me. But when he calls, I get flashbacks to that time—that sad waste of a life—and I can't help but feel down."

"Was it hard to change?" I asked. "From the person you were then, to the person you are now?"

May chewed on her lower lip while she thought about it. "Yes and no," she finally said. "When I was nine, I was terrified of the high diving board at my pool. One day I got to the pool right when it opened. I was the only one there except for a couple of lifeguards, who were flirting with each other and not paying me any attention. I still remember how it felt when my toes gripped those cold metal stairs as I climbed that ladder. I must've stood there for fifteen minutes, just staring down at the water that seemed impossibly far away. And then I took one step forward. One tiny step into the air."

"Was it scary?" I asked her.

"It was the easiest thing in the world," May said. "All I had to do was let gravity take over. Nature knew exactly what to do, once I got out of its way and let things unfold as they were meant to. The fear was almost impossible to bear, but actually doing it was easy."

"So you reinvented yourself," I said. "That's incredible. To think that you changed everything."

"But I don't think it's extraordinary," she said. She leaned her head back against her seat's headrest and smiled. "I think we're all constantly reinventing ourselves. First we change from babies into little kids, and then teenagers, which are a whole separate species that probably belong in a zoo. We barely have a chance to try out being young adults before there's pressure on us to find a partner and a new identity as a couple, and then most of us turn into parents. The next thing you know time is moving faster and faster and middle age is upon us. Those of us who have kids are dropping them off at college, and the rest of us are looking at strangers in the mirror with crow's-feet and gray hair, and wondering how we've managed to morph overnight into our parents. But I think if we don't fight it too hard—if we don't cling to the person we used to be and instead let go of the paralyzing fear and turn into who we're meant to be next—it's easier."

The light changed, and May turned left, onto a street lined with restaurants and shops. A red muscle car squealed past us; in the driver's seat was a man with an award-winning comb-over.

"See?" May said. "Clinging isn't attractive."

I smiled but didn't say anything; I was too busy thinking about the wisdom in May's words.

"Do you have any sisters?" I asked.

"I'm an only child," she said.

"Sometimes I wonder if I'm the person I am because of my sister," I said, forcing the words out. My throat felt tight. I'd never talked about this to anyone before. "It's like Alex is in the beautiful role, and I'm in the smart one. And I wonder if my family will ever let me change into someone else. They're so invested in me being smart and successful. That's my identity in the family. I don't know if they'll ever be able to see me any other way."

May nodded. "Families are like that," she said. "If you change, it means everyone else has to shift to make room for the new you. And change can be scary."

"How did you do it?" I asked. "When you changed?"

"It was easier for me," she said. "I left it all behind and moved away from Annapolis. Geography can help give you a fresh start. But when I go up to New Jersey to see my parents every year, I swear I get sucked into the same old patterns I've been fighting my entire life. My mother always finds a way to criticize what I'm wearing. That's a real talent, considering I've gone from Talbots to tie-dye in the last decade."

"So how do you deal with it?" I asked, grinning.

"I run back to Maryland with my tail between my legs as fast as I can." May snorted. "Can you imagine a fifty-year-old woman cowering on the train while her eighty-year-old mother hobbles alongside it with a walker and shouts through the open window not to eat the train food because God knows it'll make you sick?"

"I thought it was just my crazy family." I giggled.

"Ha," May said. "You know the definition of a dysfunctional family, don't you? It's any family with more than one member in it."

May pulled into a parking spot and turned off the ignition, but neither of us reached for the door handles.

"I have to tell my parents about my job," I said. I could feel the smile fade away from my face. "I've been putting it off for too long. But I don't think I can tell them I was fired."

"Why not?" May asked. "Why would it be so awful for them to know you're human?"

"Being successful is all I have," I said. "And now I've lost that." I cringed, thinking of how that sounded. "I don't mean working for you isn't something to be proud of—" I started.

"But it's not jetting to Tokyo and overseeing photo shoots and doing all that other stuff you told me about," May said understandingly.

"I'm living with my parents," I said. "My mom buttered my toast this morning, for God's sakes. I feel like I'm trapped in a bad sitcom or something. Maybe it wouldn't be so awful if everyone hadn't expected great things of me. I thought I'd be running a company someday. I thought I'd be able to send my parents on fabulous trips, and fly everyone out to my place in the Hamptons for the holidays." I gave a half laugh. "The irony is that *Alex* is getting all that. She's getting everything I wanted by marrying a rich guy. She doesn't have to work for anything. It all comes so easily to her."

"That doesn't mean she doesn't have problems, too," May said.

"Yeah." I snorted. "I'm sure it's real tough figuring out if she should see her manicurist first or go to the tanning bed."

"You don't think there's anything that worries Alex?" May said. "Anything that causes her pain?"

I thought about my sense that things with her and Gary weren't as perfect as they looked on the surface. She never mentioned him. She hadn't brought up the wedding lately, either.

"Have you ever talked to Alex?" May asked. "I mean *really* talked."

"Sure," I said. "Back when we were six. We don't have anything in common, other than our parents. It's like a genetic joke that we're twins, but the joke's on me."

"Why do you put yourself down like that?" May asked. "You're beautiful."

I shook my head.

"Yes, you are," May insisted. "That night we met, you were dazzling in that bar. You had this glow about you. But when you talk about your sister, your whole essence changes. It's like the light goes out of you."

I looked down at my hands. "I guess I feel like no one looks at me when she's around," I said softly. "Like I don't matter."

"What would happen if you tried to get past all that stuff and talk to your sister?" May asked. "What if you told her you'd been fired?"

I shook my head. "She'd be the last person I'd confide in."

"Because you're so competitive with her?" May asked.

That one stung a bit, even though May's tone was gentle.

"She's competitive with me, too," I said. "God, listen to me. I sound like I'm two. I should have someone buttering my toast for me."

"I'm just saying she might surprise you," May said. "And if she doesn't, what's the worst thing that could happen? You're still smart. You're still capable. You're still *you*."

"Okay," I said. I knew I didn't sound convinced. "Maybe."

"And now that's enough of that," May said. "You sat through my lecture, so you get a reward. Pie or ice cream?"

"You mean I have to choose?" I asked as we got out of the car.

"That's my girl," May said, linking her arm through mine.

Part Three

Jump

Twenty-one

IT SEEMED LIKE SUNDAY night would never arrive. Bradley's face kept floating into my mind at the oddest moments: during my morning shower, while I was waiting in line at the dry cleaner's, while I munched on an afternoon snack. (Since I'm not a Freudian, there's no significance to my selection of snack food and any associated imagery. Besides, bananas are high in potassium.) I considered different plans for Sunday night, rejecting and tweaking and refining, until finally, every last detail was just right.

I pulled up to his house at a few minutes before six, after circling the neighborhood for fifteen minutes. I would've been fashionably late, but a woman who was out power walking kept shooting me suspicious looks as I passed by in my parents' old rattletrap of a car. I was probably one more loop away from being Maced, which wouldn't get tonight off to a rip-roaring romantic start.

Bradley lived in the Woodley Park neighborhood, right behind the National Zoo. His block was filled with older but well-maintained homes. I could see lots of front porches with Adirondack chairs and folded-up baby strollers, and a shaggy golden retriever gnawing on a tennis ball on his front lawn, and kids playing tag in the soft evening light as a dad kept one eye on them and one on the newspaper in his hands.

It was just the kind of neighborhood I'd pick for Bradley. He wouldn't fit in to the glitz of Georgetown or the hyperimportant bustle of Capitol Hill. This was a neighborhood where people held block parties and knocked on each other's doors when they ran out of sugar. It had real homes, and real people inside of them.

"Hi," I said simply when Bradley came to the door. He looked so good it made me ache. He wore faded jeans and a black pull-over, and his hair was kind of rumpled. I could still see traces of the teenage Bradley in the way his eyebrows tilted up when he smiled at me, and the way his Adam's apple still stuck out the tiniest bit. Time had softened his sharp teenage edges, but Bradley hadn't changed all that much. It was me who saw him through new eyes now.

"Lindsey?" Bradley sounded incredulous. I just stood there, letting his eyes rove over me. Just like Bradley had long ago, I'd gone for the Hail Mary tonight.

I'd worn my new jeans and Marilyn boots and my tight, nude lace camisole and dusty pink suede jacket. My hair was loose and wavy, and I'd spent half an hour on my makeup. Bradley was the first person who'd known the old me to see me this way. I pleaded with him with my eyes to like me.

"You look beautiful!" he said, opening the door so I could come inside.

"Thanks," I said.

"Did you do something with your hair?" he said.

"I probably need a haircut." I laughed. "I've just been so busy."

"I like it like this," he said.

"Yeah?" I asked. His compliment felt loaded with significance. He liked it. He liked *me*.

"Yeah," he said, giving me the once-over again. His look warmed me like sunshine as it traveled over me. A giddy happiness welled up inside me. "Definitely."

We smiled at each other, then Bradley said, "Let me give you the five-second tour."

"I believe I paid for the ten-second tour," I mock-complained.

"Okay, then we'll walk through the place twice," he said. "Living room, obviously, and back there is the eat-in kitchen—"

"Oh, Bradley," I said, cutting him off as I walked into his living room. It was filled with photographs, dozens and dozens of photographs. My eyes flitted around the room, soaking in the beauty of Bradley's work. There was a picture of an old man clutching his metal lunch box at the bus stop, his face a weary road map of wrinkles and lines but his posture straight and proud. There was a little girl chasing a firefly through a field, her eyes big and smile bigger as she came close to capturing magic in her hands. There was a black-and-white photo of a pair of entwined hands—a man's and a woman's, and I knew instantly that they'd been married for decades, and that they were still in love. Bradley's photographs were more than fleeting snapshots of moments in time. They told entire stories.

There was also a picture of me.

I was about sixteen, and I was studying at Bradley's parents' kitchen table. I'd been puzzling over an English essay, chewing the end of a pencil. Squares of sunlight filtered in from the paned window behind me and fell on my dark hair.

"I don't even remember you taking this one," I said. I couldn't help smiling; Bradley had a picture of me in his living room. He'd kept it for all these years.

Bradley came up and stood behind me.

"God, we were so young," I said, turning around to look at him.

"I know," he said. "Sometimes I feel like so much has changed, but other times it seems like everything's the same."

"I know exactly what you mean," I said. I kept my eyes on his for an extra beat, hoping he'd know what had stayed the same for me and what had changed. My feelings for him had done both.

Bradley was the first to break the moment.

"Let me show you the upstairs," he said, leading the way. The old wooden stairs creaked comfortably as we stepped on them.

"Bedroom—whoops, forgot to make the bed—bathroom, guest room, he said.

"It's perfect," I said, and it was. On one wall, instead of paintings, Bradley had hung a trio of antique cameras. His old guitar was propped in a corner. Dark wood bookshelves lined the walls of his bedroom, and they were filled with history books and biographies. I saw a pair of ten-pound hand weights in a corner and hid my smile, remembering Bradley's single-minded devotion to Wheaties.

"How long have you been living here?" I asked.

"I bought it last year," Bradley said. "I love the neighborhood. There was a ton of work to do on it at first, but it's getting there. And it's only twenty minutes to Dad's, so we get together once a week or so."

"I'd love to see him again," I said.

"I'll call you next time I go over," he said. "He's dating this new woman, and I think it's getting pretty serious. She's an environmental lawyer."

"Do you like her?" I asked.

"I do," he said. "She's perfect for Dad; you'll see when you meet her."

I clung to that promise: He wanted me to meet the woman his father was dating. Our lives were weaving together again.

"So am I dressed okay for wherever we're going? Or should I change into something nicer?" Bradley asked.

"You look perfect," I said. I cleared my throat and looked away; I hadn't meant to sound quite so fervent.

I led the way to my vehicle of seduction—the battered old station wagon with Dad's bifocals and Tums littering the front seat—and headed north, toward Maryland.

"You're not even going to give me a hint?" Bradley said, flicking on the radio and leaning back in his seat. Bruce Springsteen started singing about girls in summer clothes, and I rolled down the window. Summer would be here soon, just like Springsteen was promising; the air was warm and moist and filled with promise. What would it be like to spend the summer with Bradley? To drive down to the beach for the weekend on a whim, or to spend the evening on his front porch, leaning over to give him a kiss as we shared a cold beer?

"No hints," I said. I'd been so nervous about tonight, but now I felt nothing but exhilaration. Bradley was sneaking little looks at me, as if he couldn't quite believe his eyes. It was a gorgeous night. Everything was perfect.

As I pulled up at a stoplight, my phone rang inside my purse. Unbelievable; it was Alex calling. Did she have some sort of home wrecker's ESP?

"Aren't you going to answer that?" Bradley said.

"It's not important," I said, pushing the button to turn it off and dropping it back into my purse as I smiled at Bradley. Alex wasn't going to intrude again. Not tonight.

"Hey, I recognize this place," Bradley said as I pulled into the parking lot and turned off the ignition.

Our old high school hadn't changed a bit. I'd called the front office earlier in the week to make sure there weren't any events at the school tonight; with my luck, they'd have been staging a production of *Oklahoma!* and I'd've had to woo Bradley over the high-pitched strains of "The Surrey with the Fringe on Top." But the place was deserted.

"Come on," I said. "Let's take a walk around for old times' sake."

We got out of the car, and I led the way to the back of the school. The ladder I'd put there an hour ago was still in place.

"No way," Bradley said, starting to laugh. Then his voice dropped to a whisper: "They could revoke our diplomas."

"I did not say that!" I protested, punching him lightly on the arm.

"Ready to climb?" he said. "Want me to go first?"

"I'll go first this time," I said, clutching the edges of the ladder. I exhaled and climbed up, forcing myself not to look down as Bradley shouted encouragement from below. It was easier this time; of course, I'd had a lot of practice earlier tonight.

When I reached the top, I quickly looked around. Everything was still there. Everything was perfect.

"Whoa," Bradley said when he reached the top of the ladder. He stayed there, on the final rung of the ladder, as he looked around.

The red-checked tablecloth and picnic basket I'd brought by earlier were laid out in the center of the roof. I'd added a few flourishes of my own—a little bunch of blue irises, a few chunky candles in hurricane vases—but other than that, everything was exactly as it had been eleven years ago. It was only the ending that I wanted to rewrite.

"Lindsey—" Bradley started to say. Then he stopped. He seemed too stunned to talk.

"Hope you don't mind that I substituted wine for sparkling cider," I said, holding up a bottle. I'd peeled off the price tag so Bradley wouldn't know how much I'd spent on it.

"No, this is—" He swept his hand around, encompassing it all. "Wow."

I walked over to one of the cushions I'd laid out next to the tablecloth and stood there, waiting for Bradley to join me. But he was still perched on the top rung of that ladder. A cold twinge of unease worked its way up my spine.

"Coming?" I asked.

"Oh, sorry," he said. "I was just—"

Once again, he didn't finish his sentence. He walked over and sat down on the cushion next to me. Maybe he needed a little time to absorb what was happening. I'd had months to get used to the fact that my feelings for Bradley had changed; this must all have been coming at him like a fastball. And I'd hurt Bradley badly before; naturally he'd be careful about opening his heart to me again.

I'd take things slowly. I should've thought of that.

"I'm thinking of opening a restaurant here," I said lightly. "Picnics 'R' Us."

"Great idea," Bradley said. He took a sip of wine and looked down into the glass. Why wasn't he looking at me? Why couldn't he seem to meet my eyes?

"Of course, I'll have to give the customers a fitness test first," I said. "Make sure they can climb the ladder."

"Won't that scare some of them away?" Bradley said.

"Yeah, but that's probably a good thing," I said. "I've only got one picnic basket."

Bradley laughed.

"Cheese and crackers?" I offered enticingly. I've always been a seductress like that. "I've got summer sausage, too."

"Sure," Bradley said, accepting the plate I handed him. In-

stead of Brie, I'd bought sharp Cheddar, which I knew he preferred. I wanted him to notice; I wanted him to feel like I'd put
a lot of care into tonight.

"Cheers," I said, clinking my glass to his.

Bradley took a little sip of wine. "I can't believe you did all
this."

"It wasn't such a big deal," I said. "And you did it for me long
ago."

Bradley took a bite of cheese and cracker.

"Lindsey," he said after he'd swallowed. "I'm really glad we've
stayed friends."

"Me too," I said. His tone was so caring, and so were his
words. That had to be a good thing, didn't it?

"So how long are you going to stay in town?" he asked. "I
know you're scoping out opening a new office here, but will
you stay and run it, or are you going back to New York?"

"Here's the thing," I said. I felt like May must've all those
years ago, staring down into that impossibly faraway pool of
water, knowing I had only one way to get there.

"I haven't told my family yet, but I'm thinking about changing jobs," I blurted out. I needed Bradley to know this; I needed
him to know everything about me, all the confusing, jagged,
tumultuous bits. If I wanted a relationship with him, I had to
be honest with him.

"I got this offer the other day from a dating service, believe
it or not."

"Seriously?" Bradley said. "But I thought you loved your
job."

"Not so much," I said slowly. "I mean, there are things about
it that I love, but the stress was getting to me. Slowing down
sounds kind of nice. My old job didn't leave me a lot of time for
anything but work. And there's more to life than advertising."

Bradley nodded. "Good for you."

"Really?" I said. "Because it's one of the scariest things I've ever done. Almost as bad as climbing that ladder."

Bradley grinned. He seemed more relaxed now. He was meeting my eyes again. I hadn't realized I'd been clenching my wineglass so tightly; I loosened my grip and felt the blood flow back into my fingers.

"You'll be successful at whatever you do," he said. "So tell me about the job."

"I'm a matchmaker," I said. "Can you believe it?"

Bradley threw back his head and laughed. "That's fantastic. I never would've guessed."

"It kind of happened by accident," I said. "But I met this great woman, and we got to talking, and she offered me a job. And I really like it."

"That's all that matters," Bradley said. "I'm really happy for you."

"I haven't told anyone else yet," I said.

I swear I didn't plan to say my next sentence. It just escaped from me, and the minute I said the words, I wanted to snatch them back. "I wanted you to know first."

A shadow passed over Bradley's face, and he looked down. Oh, God, I'd made a mistake; I had to cover it up, quickly.

"Do you want some more wine?" I offered.

"No, I'm good," he said. He'd barely touched his glass.

"Sure?" I said. "I'm driving. You can go crazy."

"I'm good. But thanks."

"More cheese?" I asked. Now I was losing it; my voice was high and anxious. I was desperately trying to sound lighthearted, but it was backfiring.

"No, this is perfect," Bradley said. He'd barely touched his food, either. His body language was all wrong; his arms were crossed, and he sat up rigidly, as if he was perched on a pile of stones instead of the soft cushion I'd chosen at Pier 1 earlier today.

"And save room for dessert," I babbled. "I brought your favorite."

"Lindsey," Bradley said. Just that one word, said ever so gently. How could my name hurt so much?

I looked down at my little vase of blue flowers and felt tears prick my eyes.

"You know how much I care about you," Bradley said. "I always have."

Not this. Please, not this. Bradley was letting me down gently. He was giving me the same speech I'd tried to give him the last time we were on this roof. The twinge in my spine turned into something sharp that reached around and jabbed at my guts. Pain radiated through my entire body.

"Is there someone else?" I asked.

Bradley looked down at his plate. I knew he wouldn't lie to me; Bradley was too honorable for that.

He lifted his eyes and said, "Yes." That's all he said, just that single, shattering word.

Once, when I was about twelve years old, I'd tripped and fallen down while carrying a heavy bowl of spaghetti to the dinner table. My stomach hit the floor first as I held up the spaghetti with both hands, trying to keep the bowl from breaking. The blow was so powerful and unexpected that I couldn't breathe or speak or move; the wind was knocked completely out of me. That was exactly how I felt now.

I wanted to ask who it was, but I couldn't. I knew if I opened my mouth again I'd start to cry, and I couldn't do that. Besides, I knew it was Alex. It was always Alex.

I inhaled a deep, shuddering breath, fighting to push it into my lungs.

"You used to be in love with me," I said. I knew I was making things worse, but I was powerless to stop.

"I did," he said. His eyes were so kind; they were killing me. "But that was a long time ago."

"When did you stop?" I asked. My voice was no longer high and squeaky; now it had dropped to the opposite end of the scale. It was a rusty croak, as though it was being forced through a shredder. I knew I'd hate myself for this later, but I couldn't stop.

"Oh, Lindsey, I had to move on," he said. "You did, didn't you?"

I nodded. He was right; it wasn't fair to expect him to keep pining for me for all these years. It had just been so lovely to imagine he had.

"I guess our timing is a bit off," I said, pushing away my tears with the backs of my hands. I never used to cry, and now look at me, I thought bitterly: I was turning into Jacob's old girlfriend, Sue.

I'd wanted to be pretty for Bradley tonight; I'd wanted him to love me. I'd told him everything and let him see the secret bits of me no one knew about. But it didn't matter. He didn't want me. He knew everything about me, and he still didn't love me.

He handed me one of the blue napkins I'd bought to match the color of the irises. I'd tried to anticipate every last detail, but I'd missed one. The only one that mattered: Bradley's true feelings. How could I have been so wrong, so stupid, so utterly clueless?

"Things are confusing right now," he said. "For you and for me. I think we should just step back and talk again tomorrow."

"Sure," I said, then I gave a bitter laugh. I couldn't stop. I was like a wrecking ball that had gone mad and was turning back and destroying its own controller.

"It's my sister, isn't it?" I said. "Look, she does this to people.

Guys. She makes them fall in love with her. It happens all the time. It doesn't mean anything to her, you know."

"Have you talked to Alex lately?" Bradley said.

"Why?" I asked.

"Lindsey, I—" Bradley started to say, then something shrilled. It was his cell phone. He'd taken it out of his pocket and put it on my red-checked tablecloth when we'd sat down.

We both stared down at it. We both knew exactly who it was.

"It's her, isn't it?" I asked. I hated the way I sounded, but I couldn't stop. All the anger and resentment I'd harbored toward Alex for years was bubbling out of me, like a poisonous venom. "She's *engaged*, you know. Some people consider that a pretty serious commitment, but I guess she doesn't."

"Lindsey, have you talked to Alex lately?" Bradley repeated.

I shook my head. What did that matter?

The phone beeped with a new message, and Bradley looked down at it again. I think I would've died if he'd picked it up, but he left it lying there.

"We should go," I said. Suddenly I had to escape from here, from Bradley and the pity and discomfort I saw on his face. I stood up and began repacking the basket, shoving in plates with food still on them. I tossed the water out of the vase and blew out the candles and threw them on top of the plates of food, my movements fast and jerky. Everything would be ruined, but what did that matter? I'd been an idiot to think Bradley would take one look at my pathetic little picnic and sweep me into his arms. Things like that only happened in the movies. They didn't happen to me.

"Can I carry that for you?" Bradley offered.

I shook my head and started down the ladder. Bradley's phone rang again.

"Go ahead," I said. "Answer it."

"Not now," Bradley said. He climbed down the ladder after

me and hurried to catch up as I strode across our old school's lawn. "Look, I know you're upset."

"It's fine," I said. "I'll be fine."

"Do you want to go somewhere and talk?" he asked.

I want you to hold me, I thought desperately. I want you to tell me you love *me*.

"It's getting late," I said, just like he'd said to me that night long ago on this same roof. I tried to smile, but I felt my lips form a grimace. "I should go. Early day tomorrow."

We climbed into the car, and I started down the road toward Bradley's house, driving too fast. I'd done everything wrong tonight. I hadn't rewritten the ending; all I'd done was flip the characters' lines. How could I have miscalculated so spectacularly?

Would he tell Alex? I wondered, feeling a fresh wave of tears of hurt and rage building behind my eyes at the thought. Would the two of them talk about how sorry they felt for me?

Bradley's phone chirped; someone had left him a text message. He glanced down at it, and I blinked, hard. He couldn't even ignore Alex's message for another ten minutes. That's how strong her hold on him was.

So what was going to happen next? Was she going to break up with Gary for Bradley, or was this just another flirtation for her? I honestly didn't know which would be worse: seeing them together as a couple, or watching Bradley's heart break and knowing that any chance we might've had was ruined because Alex had just wanted a bit of fun.

"Lindsey?" Bradley said. He put a hand on my arm. "You need to turn around."

For a second I was completely bewildered. Turn around? Go back to the school?

"What is it?" I asked. I looked at him. His jaw was tight and his face was pale.

"It's Alex," he said. "She's been in an accident."

Twenty-two

"HE CAME OUT OF nowhere," Alex said.

She was sitting up on a gurney in a private cubicle in the ER, looking like an actress playing the part of an accident victim. Only on Alex would a hospital gown slip so fetchingly off one shoulder. Only Alex would come out of a car crash with her mascara unsmudged. Considering the fact that she'd been cut out of her Lexus by a team of firemen and that the guy in the other car had a shattered thighbone, it bordered on a miracle. Alex's luck.

"Look, I wasn't using my cell phone or changing the radio or anything," Alex was saying as we entered her room. A police officer sat in the corner, taking notes on a little spiral notebook, and a doctor was checking Alex's blood pressure.

"He said you stopped at the stop sign, then pulled out right in front of him," the officer said, flipping back a few pages in his notebook.

"I didn't see him. He must've been flying, because he wasn't there one second, and the next he was slamming into the side of my— Whoa!" Alex gaped at me. "Nice outfit, Sis!" She craned her neck toward me. "Are you wearing *makeup*?"

I'd almost forgotten. Trust Alex to call attention to the only thing that could make me feel worse: a reminder to me and Bradley of just how much effort I'd put into tonight.

"Yeah," I said flatly, avoiding her questioning eyes. Why did we have to rush here if Alex was fine? And why—this was the question I knew I'd turn over and over in my mind all during the darkest hours of tonight, knowing there couldn't be any good answer—had Alex called *Bradley*?

I looked down at the floor, but not before I saw Alex glance back and forth from me to Bradley. She didn't say a word, but she could do the math. It was nighttime, the two of us were together, and I was wearing sexy clothes and makeup. The air was so heavy with unspoken thoughts and dawning realizations that I felt like I was drowning.

"We'd like to do a blood alcohol test," the doctor said, pulling the Velcro cuff off Alex's biceps. It was like someone had fired a shot into the room; Bradley, Alex, and I all started.

"Are you kidding me?" Alex asked. "I haven't had a thing to drink tonight. Well, maybe one glass of wine—*half* a glass; it was really crappy wine—but that's all. And that was a couple of hours ago."

"So you don't have any objections?" the police officer said.

Alex rolled her eyes. "Fine. But you'd better do one on the other driver, too. He was the one who came blasting through that intersection."

So far Bradley and Alex had barely looked at each other. It was more deliberate and obvious than if Bradley had swept her up for a big kiss. The energy it took them not to acknowledge each other practically electrified the room. I wanted to shrink away to nothing, to disappear and never see either of them again. Or better yet, to make both of *them* disappear.

"There's something you should know," Bradley said suddenly. His usually gentle voice was so authoritative that everyone in the room stopped what they were doing and turned to look at him.

"She's been having trouble with her vision for a couple of weeks," Bradley said.

"Bradley," Alex whispered, like she was pleading with him.

How did he know? The question screamed inside my head. How often had they seen each other over the past few weeks?

Bradley reached over and put his hand on the hospital sheet next to Alex's hand. That's when I saw it: Alex's ring finger was bare. I fumbled for the wall behind me as my vision started to swim. I stared at their hands, suddenly remembering Bradley's photo in his living room of the entwined hands of a long-married couple.

Please, not this.

"She has to enlarge the font of her emails to read them," Bradley said. He looked back and gave me an apologetic look. I turned my head away, I couldn't bear to meet his eyes.

"I was tired," Alex said, sounding angry now, almost belligerent. "God, I mean, I'd been going through a hundred emails. That's all it was. My eyes were tired."

The doctor pulled a small light out of the breast pocket of her white coat.

"Look up," she said, aiming the light into Alex's eyes. "Now left. Right. Into the light."

She kept the light on Alex's eyes for another minute. "Do you have any other symptoms?"

"No," Alex said, at the exact same moment that Bradley said, "Headaches."

I squeezed my eyes shut. How could I have been so stupid? How could I have not known what was happening between my own sister and the guy I loved?

"How often?" the doctor said.

"A couple times a week," Alex said. "It's stress. I have a lot going on. Look, I'm not drunk, and I'm not going blind. Go pick on the other guy, okay? This was his fault."

"I'm going to order an MRI," the doctor said. "Just as a pre-caution."

Alex sighed. "Come on, do you really think it's necessary? Look, maybe I wasn't paying attention. Maybe I glanced down for a second or something."

"We just want to be extra safe," the doctor said.

"Alex," Bradley said. He kept his eyes on her. It was as though I wasn't in the room, as though he'd already forgotten about me. She stared up at him, and something passed between them. It was like they had a whole conversation without saying a word.

"Okay," she finally said. "Okay."

"We'll send you up to Imaging now," the doctor said. "You might have to wait a bit, but they'll squeeze you in."

"Now?" Alex said, her voice suddenly tight.

"You might as well get it over with while you're here," the doctor said, putting a hand on Alex's shoulder. Her expression was kind, much kinder than it had been earlier. My God, she couldn't think there was something seriously wrong with Alex's eyes, could she? The room tilted and spun again. Too much was happening too quickly.

"It'll be easier than coming back next week," the doctor said.

Alex wrapped her arms around herself and nodded.

"Is there any way I could have a blanket?" she asked.

"I'll have a nurse bring one in," the doctor said. She squeezed Alex's shoulder and left the cubicle. The police officer followed her without a word.

"Here," Bradley said. He yanked off his pullover and tucked it around Alex. This time he didn't look apologetically at me; the only expression on his face was concern. For Alex. A knot that felt as big and hard as a golf ball formed inside my throat, making it hard to swallow.

"These hospital gowns suck," Alex said.

"Yeah," I said. It was practically the first thing I'd said since I'd gotten there. I was so shocked I felt numb. Too much was happening, and I was shutting down.

The movie, I suddenly remembered. I'd thought Alex was flirting with Bradley. My God; she really couldn't see the words on-screen.

"Linds?" Alex asked. "Come with me for the MRI?"

I nodded. "Sure." What else could I say?

"Look, this isn't the time, but there's stuff I need to talk to you about," she said. "I've been trying to catch you."

"Yeah," I said. "I've just been really busy."

"I know, I know," she said. "Work, right?"

I glanced fearfully at Bradley, but he didn't betray me.

"Yeah, the usual," I said.

The nurse bustled into the room with a blanket and draped it over Alex.

"Ooh, it's heated," she said.

"Nothing but the best," the nurse said. "I'm a fan. Love your show. I watch it all the time. Is your cohost really as cute in person?"

"Promise you won't tell?" Alex said. I could see her slipping into celebrity mode; she tossed back her hair and smiled her bright TV smile. How could she do it? I wondered. Was that what so many years in front of the camera did to you? Did it teach you to shut off your true feelings as easily as if you were flipping a switch?

Because right about now, that was a skill I'd kill to have.

The nurse nodded eagerly.

"He has a hair transplant," Alex stage-whispered. "You can see the little lines of seedlings on his scalp when you're up close."

"Oh, man, you just ruined my fantasy." The nurse laughed.

"Sorry," Alex said, winking. "You'll have to go back to Brad Pitt like everyone else."

An orderly entered the room with a wheelchair.

"He's going to wheel you up for your MRI," the nurse said. "It'll be a snap. Ready to get in the chair?"

Alex pushed aside her covers and swung her legs over the side of the bed. Her toenails were painted hot pink, and her legs were smooth and lightly tanned. Even here, even under these circumstances, Alex moved as gracefully as a dancer.

No wonder Bradley had chosen her, I thought dully. Who wouldn't?

"Bradley? Wait for us here?" Alex said.

He nodded. "Whatever you want."

I walked alongside as the orderly wheeled us to the elevator and took us down to the basement. He left us in a little room after conferring with the nurse at the front desk.

"This is a crazy time to tell you this," Alex said. "But I'm not engaged anymore. Gary and I broke up a few days ago. I wanted to tell you, but—"

"But you couldn't reach me," I said. Alex had called twice in the past two days, but I hadn't returned her calls. "Have you told Mom and Dad?"

"I was on my way over there when that asshole hit me," Alex said. She shook her head. "I know they're going to be upset. They love Gary. God, I keep thinking about that engagement party. There are so many people we have to tell."

I bit back the question hovering on my lips—"What happened?"—because I didn't want to know. Or maybe because I already knew. Alex and Bradley were together. If they weren't already, it was only a matter of time.

I'd thought it would be just as bad if Alex had been playing with Bradley, but I'd been wrong. This was worse. So much worse.

Alex was looking at me, waiting for me to say something.

"Things seemed so good between you and Gary," I finally said. "You looked so great together."

"Do you know how many people told me that?" The words exploded out of Alex so fiercely I almost recoiled. "How great we looked together? It's like everyone thought we should be together because we looked the part. I think . . ." Alex's voice softened, as though what she wanted to say next was the hardest part. "Oh, shit, I think maybe that was part of why Gary loved me, too."

She ran a hand over her eyes, then began massaging her temples.

"We looked like we should fit," she whispered. "But we didn't. We never did, no matter how much I tried to make us."

I stared at her. This wasn't the Alex I knew. No quips or sharpness; she was telling me her real feelings, opening up, just like May had advised me to do. If it had been anyone but Bradley, this moment might've been a turning point for us. We might've even become sisters in every sense of the word. But the dark, ugly seed of my jealousy had grown into something hard and gnarled, something that pushed up between me and Alex.

"I loved Gary," Alex said. "I thought I did, at least. But something was missing. We never *talked*. We did stuff together all the time and we always had fun, but when we were alone, we didn't have much to say. Not like with—" She cut herself off.

"With Bradley," I said flatly.

Alex looked down. "I know you guys have been friends forever. I never thought of him as anything but your friend. But then when he was taking photos at my engagement party, we kind of connected."

At your engagement party, I thought bitterly. Nice timing.

"I kept wanting to tell you about it," Alex said. "But it

wasn't ever the right time. And nothing's really happened between us."

Yet, I thought. God, why did Alex always do this to me? Why couldn't things ever be simple between us? Here we were, waiting for an MRI to tell us if there was something wrong with her eyes, and I was filled with so much jealousy and anger and shame that I felt like I was about to explode. How could I despise my sister when she was at her most vulnerable?

"I know it's kind of weird, because you and Bradley were so close," she said. "But he said nothing ever happened between you two."

I felt her eyes rove over my tight camisole, my loose hair, my face. "You really look amazing, you know." Her voice grew questioning. "Anyway, you've got that guy in New York. Don't you?"

I squeezed my eyes shut. Oh, my God. So many misunderstandings. So many crossed signals. The story of Alex's and my relationship.

If I said no—if I said I didn't have anyone in New York, and that it was Bradley I loved, would you leave him alone? I wondered. Or would you decide your happiness was worth more than my misery, like when those seniors wanted to stuff me in that locker?

"Lindsey?"

I nodded. Just once—it was more like a head bob—but it was enough for Alex. What else could I do? Bradley didn't want me. It was bad enough that my heart was broken; at least I could try to salvage the shredded remnants of my pride.

"I knew it!" she said, grinning and looking relieved. "I knew you were just being secretive. So are you ever going to tell me about him?"

The nurse saved me.

"Alexandra Rose?" she called.

I stood up and wheeled Alex over.

"Follow me," the nurse said. She led us through another door, into a sterile-looking room with a white machine that was shaped like a giant donut in the middle. "You're going to lie on this table. It'll take about half an hour. Any problems with claustrophobia?"

"If I say yes, will you go instead of me?" Alex joked. The nurse didn't even crack a smile.

The technician, a young Latino guy, came into the room and pressed a few buttons. He barely even glanced at Alex and me.

"Cheerful bunch," Alex said, rolling her eyes at me and grinning broadly. "Do you all moonlight at a funeral home?"

She was trying to joke, but something was off. Her voice and gestures were almost manic, her jokes forced. She must be terrified, I realized with a jolt. I'd been so locked in my own misery I hadn't seen it. Of course she was terrified; who wouldn't be?

"Remove all your credit cards from your wallet and leave them outside," the technician instructed us. "Otherwise they'll be demagnetized."

I fumbled for my wallet as Alex did the same thing. I collected our credit cards and put them in a little plastic tray just outside the MRI room.

"Please stay still, miss," the technician said. "We're going to center you on the table and hold your head in place with this mask. Are you comfortable?"

"About as comfortable as Hannibal Lecter," Alex said as the technician fitted her head into a gray plastic mask attached to the table. "You don't have any fava beans handy, do you?"

The technician looked at her strangely, then he made a few adjustments to the mask covering Alex's forehead, pinning her head into place. Could this really be happening? I wondered. Could the doctors actually think something was wrong inside Alex's brain?

"Lindsey?" Alex asked. Her voice sounded far away and shaky. "Can you do something for me?"

"Sure," I said, feeling awful that my immediate thought was, *Please don't ask me to go get Bradley for you.* Alex paused, then asked, "Will you hold on to my foot?"

I hesitated for a second, surprised, then I reached for her left foot, the one closest to me. It was ice-cold. After a moment I automatically began rubbing it, trying to get some warmth into it. When was the last time I'd touched Alex? I wondered, staring down at her foot. Had it been a year? Two? Hard to imagine we'd spent the first nine months of our lives doing slow somersaults around each other as we grew toes and eyebrows and fingernails.

"Very still now," the technician said. He looked at me. "Miss, you'll need to step back."

"It's okay, Alex," I said. I let go of her foot and moved a few feet away. "You're doing great."

The machine made a surprisingly loud noise—like someone hitting a pipe with a hammer—as the table slid into the center of the giant donut and Alex disappeared from view. We stayed like that for what seemed like forever as the machine took endless cross-section pictures of Alex's brain.

"Okay, you can get up now," the technician finally said. "Wait until the machine slides back."

"I'm free to go?" Alex asked as she sat up. "So everything's okay?"

"Back to the ER," he said. He was busy at a computer now, printing out the scans of Alex's brain. "I'll send these to your doctor so she can review them."

"Can I at least ditch the chair?" Alex asked.

"Hospital policy," the technician said. Alex sighed and hopped in the chair. I wheeled her to the door, and we started down the hall. But when we were halfway to the elevator, something made me glance back over my shoulder. The technician was standing in the doorway, looking at Alex. Funny, but I hadn't noticed how soft and long-lashed his brown eyes were. They were like a deer's eyes.

As he stared at Alex, his right hand began moving—to his forehead and then down to his heart, to the right side of his chest and then the left side.

"Why'd you stop moving?" Alex asked. "Pop a wheelie and let's roll."

I couldn't answer; I couldn't speak.

The technician was making the sign of the cross. He was sending Alex a silent prayer.

Twenty-three

I DON'T KNOW HOW any of us managed to sleep that night. After the ER doctor urged Alex to come in the next morning for a consultation with a neurosurgeon, after Alex stared at her and demanded to know exactly what she saw in the MRI, and after the doctor weaseled out of our barrage of questions by repeating, "I'm not qualified to make a diagnosis," we finally left the hospital.

We drove Bradley home first, and I waited in the car while Alex walked him inside. She wasn't gone for more than five minutes. It seemed like an eternity. I leaned back against the driver's seat headrest, trying to escape my relentless vision of the two of them standing in Bradley's living room, holding each other.

When Alex came back to the car, I asked, "Should I take you back home?" I frowned. God, the entire world had careened upside down tonight. *Was* that even her home anymore?

Alex shook her head. "Can I stay with you at Mom and Dad's? I don't want to be alone. Gary's out of town, and I haven't moved out yet."

"Of course," I said, even though I desperately did want to be alone. But in the hierarchy of emotions, my pain over Alex and Bradley couldn't compete with Alex's terror. Even I knew that. Bradley did, too; I'd seen the conflict play over his face when she'd jumped out of the car after him to walk him inside his house. He hadn't wanted to hurt me, but how could he push away Alex? Somehow I'd managed to give him a brief nod, to let him know I understood what he needed to do.

"I don't want Mom and Dad to know anything," Alex said now. She took a deep breath. "Not until we know."

We'd been at the hospital for hours, and now it was close to midnight. The roads were empty and slick from the light rain that had fallen while we were in the ER. Everything felt surreal, as though we were on a deserted movie set where the houses were nothing but pieces of painted cardboard and the trees were made of papier-mâché. We drove through the darkness, watching our headlights flash against the streets.

"Think that's Dad's raccoon?" Alex asked, breaking the silence. She pointed to an animal scurrying by on the side of the road.

Dad had been waging an all-out assault against a raccoon that had a fondness for his trash. He had set up motion-sensitive lights, invested in two different kinds of trash cans, and was talking about building a fence before I finally bought him a three-dollar bungee cord and secured the trash can's lid.

"I swear that man was one step away from buying a shotgun," Alex said. "What are the odds that he'd shoot off his own toe?"

"About even," I said. "But in a few years, the story would've been that the rabid raccoon wrestled the gun away and shot Dad before they fought to the death."

Alex tried to smile, but she couldn't pull it off. I tried to think of something else to say, but I came up empty. She turned to stare out the window. We drove the rest of the way in silence, each of us locked in our own thoughts.

"I'll make up some excuse for why we have to leave tomorrow morning," I said as we crept inside quietly so we wouldn't wake our parents. I handed Alex one of my T-shirts to sleep in.

"Thanks," she said.

"Can I get you anything?" I asked. "Some tea?"

"I think I'm just going to sleep," she said. "I'm exhausted."

"Take my bed," I offered. Dad had inexplicably taken over Alex's bedroom as an "office" on the day he retired, so there weren't many sleeping options. I grabbed a pillow off my bed to take to the couch.

"Linds?" Alex hesitated. I paused, my hand on the doorknob, and turned back to her.

"Stay with me?" she finally asked. "The bed's big enough for both of us." She gave a half smile. "I swear I don't snore."

What could I say?

"Sure," I replied.

I lifted up one side of the covers and climbed in, and Alex got in on the other side. She fell asleep so quickly it was like she'd been picked up and dropped into it, but I lay awake for hours as images tormented me: Bradley's face when he told me he was involved with someone else; Alex's and Bradley's hands side by side on the white hospital sheet; the technician's fingers moving across his chest as he looked at Alex.

On my last night in New York, Matt had accused me of pushing away my emotions. Well, he should see me now, I thought as I rolled over, trying to find a comfortable position. I'd ping-ponged wildly back and forth from exhilarated to devastated to enraged to terrified in the space of a few hours. I felt sorry for my sister for the first time in my life—and I was more jealous of her than ever. I hated Bradley, but I still loved him.

Emotional enough for you, Matt? I wondered, staring up at the ceiling. Because right about now, those sixteen-hour days at the ad agency looked pretty damn good.

I sighed and flipped over again. In a few hours we'd meet a neurosurgeon and we'd find out what the scans had revealed. Maybe it would all be a mistake. Maybe the technician was a religious whacko who blessed everyone who crossed his path. Maybe the doctor would say Alex had an eye infection or a pinched nerve. He'd probably hand her a prescription for a bottle of drops and tell her to scram so he could get to the patients who really needed his help.

I looked over at Alex, the curves of her face peaceful and relaxed in sleep.

I knew the neurosurgeon wouldn't say any of those things.

The next morning I gulped three straight cups of black coffee, hoping to chase away the lingering haze from the eerie dreams that had plagued me during the hour or two I'd actually slept. I deliberately waited until my mouth was full before I mumbled an excuse to Mom and Dad about Alex and me going shopping together.

"*Shopping?*" A furrow appeared between Mom's brows, and she stopped spooning Equal into her coffee. "Don't you have to work?"

I probably should've come up with something more believable, like a tractor pull. Alex and I had never, ever gone shopping together.

"Actually, yes," I said. "I have to, um, check out some ads in the mall to make sure they're displayed correctly."

"You're going to the mall?" Dad asked, peering out from over the top of the sports page. "What I would do is take the Beltway. Normally you should avoid it at all costs—too many morons on the road—but at this time of day it should be safe."

"Are all the morons at work?" Alex asked innocently.

She had almost pulled it off. Her jokes, the way she'd casually hoisted herself up to sit on the kitchen counter—to a casual observer, she seemed utterly carefree, a girl with nothing on her mind but finding the perfect sundress for summer.

Then she got down from the counter and walked over to Dad.

"I love you," she said. She wrapped him in a giant hug that lingered a few beats too long. Then she hurried out of the kitchen, but not before I'd seen silent tears streaking down her face.

"Lindsey?" Mom called as I started to follow Alex.

I froze.

"I'm glad you girls are going shopping together," Mom said. She hadn't seen Alex's face after all, I realized with a rush of relief. The frown was gone from Mom's face. She believed my story. "It's just so . . . *nice.*"

I left my parents like that—sharing the paper, refilling their coffee mugs from the fresh pot I'd brewed, kvetching over the forecast on the Weather Channel—glad that they could have one more ordinary day.

An hour later, we were sitting in the office of a neurosurgeon whose silvery hair and deep, authoritative voice seemed straight out of central casting. Even his name, Dr. Steven Grayson, seemed like it was created by a Hollywood agent with an eye for the marquee.

First we'd stopped at Alex's so she could change clothes, then we'd swung by to pick up Bradley on the way to the hospital. I kept my eyes straight ahead when he got into the car and somehow managed to say hi in a normal-sounding voice. The three of us were ushered into the neurosurgeon's office at exactly our appointed time. That made me nervous; weren't doctors supposed to run late? Was it a bad sign that he *hadn't* kept us waiting?

Alex had barely said a word since we'd left Mom and Dad's, as if she'd used up all her energy trying to act normal at breakfast. Now she looked like a fearful flier listening to the captain of the plane announce that severe turbulence lay ahead. Her face was ashen, and her hands turned into claws as they gripped the armrests of her chair.

"There's good news and bad news," Dr. Grayson began.

"Just tell me quickly," Alex said. I could see her chest rising and falling rapidly under her thin T-shirt.

"The scans show a tumor pressing on the optic nerve," the doctor said. "That's what's causing problems with your peripheral vision."

Everything shrank down around those five letters. *Tumor.*

"We don't think it's malignant," Dr. Grayson said. His voice was reassuring and calm, like he did this every day. He *did* do this every day, I realized with a jolt. How could someone do this every day? How could he deliver this kind of news again and again with the bland authority of a weather forecaster?

"The medical term is *adenoma*," Dr. Grayson said. "It's located under the optic nerve and pushing up against it, which is typically how these tumors present. That's why you were having vision problems."

"It's not cancerous?" Alex asked.

"We won't know for sure until we get in there," Dr. Grayson said, steepling his fingers. "But I'm fairly certain it's benign. Pituitary tumors usually are. Typically we like to access them through the nose. But because of the size of the mass and its location, we need to do a craniotomy."

"A craniotomy," I said. This was all happening so fast; my

mind was churning to keep up. "You mean you're going to have to open . . ." My voice trailed off.

"We'll need to access the mass by opening the skull," the doctor said.

It was as if by using impersonal language—"the mass" instead of "your tumor"—the doctor was trying to soften the news. But all it did was take it a second or two longer for the meaning to hit, like the brief delay between a foreign speaker's words and his translator's interpretation.

"When?" Alex whispered, like getting out that single word took everything she had.

"As soon as possible," Dr. Grayson said. "We can schedule surgery for Thursday. You should know that there's a chance I might not be able to get out the entire tumor. If it would risk damaging the optic nerve, I may have to leave a tiny bit behind, in which case, we may need to follow up surgery with a course of radiation. But I'm hopeful radiation won't be required."

"You want to operate in three days?" Bradley said. "That's so soon."

"Why so soon?" I asked, looking up from the blue spiral notebook I'd been using to frantically scribble down the unfamiliar terms. "You said it's not fatal—an adenoma, right? So why do you have to operate in three days?"

"This type of tumor presents a lot of secondary complications when it presses against the optic chiasm," the doctor said, looking directly at Alex. "Your vision may be permanently impaired if we wait. As the mass grows larger, your vision will get worse and worse, and it will be harder to salvage. Right now, the tumor is the size of a walnut. In another few weeks, things will become more . . . complicated."

I saw Bradley reach for Alex's hand, and I hated myself for noting it, for feeling a white-hot pang in the center of my chest. I averted my eyes and looked behind the doctor, to his wall of pride. University of Pennsylvania medical school. Yale for undergrad. Board certifications and professional awards and commendations. I took notes on all of it so I could check him out.

"Am I going to go blind?" Alex asked.

"It's highly unlikely," he said. "I can't say for sure until we get in there and see what we're dealing with. But most patients recover most of their sight, if not all."

"But some go blind," Alex said.

"Few," the doctor acknowledged. "I don't expect that to happen to you. Worst case, your vision may be compromised."

"So what's going to happen?" Alex said. "You're going to take out the tumor and then everything will go back to normal?"

"Eventually, yes, that's the goal," the doctor said. "As I said, you may need radiation following surgery. And I'm going to prescribe steroids to hold down inflammation."

"Okay." Alex exhaled loudly. She lifted her chin. "Let's do it. Get this thing out of me. I want you to do it as soon as you can."

"I'll need some more scans and blood tests," Dr. Grayson said. "I'll want you to see an endocrinologist this week, too. And I want you to come to the hospital immediately if your vision worsens or if you have any other symptoms. Vomiting, loss of balance, that sort of thing."

"Hey, can you tell that to the cop who wanted to test me for DUI?" Alex said. She was smiling, a big, happy trademark-Alex smile; how could she possibly be joking around now?

"Pituitary tumors are the next it thing in Hollywood," Alex said in her TV voice. "Whenever Paris Hilton or Lindsay Lohan drives over some paparazzi or falls down in a nightclub, they can just pull out their MRI scans and they've got a get-out-of-jail-free card. Hey, I'm starting a *trend*."

Dr. Grayson and I just gaped at her. Was Alex making fun of this? I didn't know what to do. But Bradley did.

"*Alex.*" He stood up and reached for her, and she collapsed into his arms. Bradley stroked her back and whispered something into her ear, something only she could hear, as Alex wrapped her slim arms around his neck and sobbed.

Twenty-four

"LINDSEY?"

"Mmm?"

"Remember my Magic Eight Ball?" Alex asked.

I smiled. Alex had gotten the ball for her twelfth birthday, and that little black sphere had ruled her life like a squatty, enigmatic dictator.

"Should I wear my Gloria Vanderbilt jeans today?" Alex would ask earnestly, shaking the ball. "All signs say yes," the Magic 8 Ball would decree, and Alex would breathe a huge sigh of relief and slip them on.

"You realize that means nothing," I used to admonish her. By then, I was already dismissive of things like Ouiji boards and the fortune-teller who had come to a friend's birthday party and treated everyone to palm readings. Underneath the fortune-teller's gray wig I'd spotted brown hair, and her breath smelled like McDonald's. I'd known instantly she was a fraud; a real fortune-teller drank bubbling potions and brews, not McFlurries.

"Look, there are only a few answers," I told Alex one day, ripping it out of her hand after she'd agonized over whether or not some stupid guy liked her.

"I'll ask it the same question twice and it'll give me two different answers," I said, shaking the ball. "Will I pass my spelling test today?"

"Cannot predict now," Magic 8 announced.

"Will I pass the spelling test today?" I shook up the ball and held it up triumphantly: "Cannot predict now."

"Stupid ball," I said. "I'll shake it up again and it'll come up with a different answer."

"Don't!" Alex yelled, snatching it out of my hand. "Sharon Derrigan's cousin's sister did that and the ball got mad at her for not trusting it and it put a hex on her!"

"That's silly," I said as I stared at the ball out of the corner of my eye. The murky blue-black fluid inside did look a little witchlike.

"Anyway, I've got to run," I said, hurrying toward the door. "I have a spelling test."

It was pure coincidence that my teacher lost all the spelling tests that day. I'd never told Alex about it, but from then on I couldn't sleep unless the Magic 8 Ball was tucked safely in a drawer, where it couldn't stare at me with its unblinking blue-black eyeball.

"What made you think of that?" I asked now as I turned out the light and climbed into bed beside Alex. She hadn't wanted to sleep alone tonight. I couldn't blame her.

"That ball had all the answers," she said. "Anything I wanted to know. I never had to wonder about anything. I wish I still had it."

We were quiet for a moment.

"You're going to wake up tomorrow after surgery and the doctor's going to tell you the operation was a perfect success," I said firmly.

I sounded good. Believable. Thank God the bedroom was dark and Alex couldn't see my face. Then she'd know what I knew: That even if the surgery went perfectly, her life wouldn't be the same afterward.

"I just wish tomorrow afternoon was here," Alex said. "I want this over."

"I know you're scared," I said. "I wish I could do something."

Actually, I had done something, but Alex didn't know about it. During the past few days, Alex had disappeared for long hours with Bradley. He must've taken the week off work, like I had. Sometimes he picked her up outside my parents' house, and sometimes she disappeared after the phone rang. I knew he was trying to protect my feelings by not coming into the house so I wouldn't see him with Alex, but I wasn't fooled for a second. I recognized his tricks. They were the same ones I'd used to keep Alex and Bradley apart back in high school.

"Bradley?" Mom had said once after answering the phone. "How are you, honey? Good, good. Yes, she's right— I'm sorry, did you say Alex?"

And Mom had handed over the phone to Alex and looked at me with a question in her eyes. I know Mom had always secretly hoped Bradley and I would end up together. Or not so secretly, given that once, in a bakery, she'd loudly pointed out that the plastic bride and groom on top of a wedding cake looked *exactly* like Bradley and me.

"It's okay," I'd said. I'd looked at Mom and mustered up all the conviction I could. "I'm happy for Alex and Bradley."

At any other time, that would've unleashed a barrage of questions. But Mom and Dad were already reeling from the news Alex had laid on them—the tumor, her broken engagement— so all Mom did was nod with a kind of exhausted resignation. I don't think she could've taken another intense conversation. I know I couldn't have.

Every time Alex left, I launched into a cleaning frenzy, orga-

nizing the kitchen cabinets and sorting the piles of papers in
Dad's office into neat, color-tabbed files. And while I scrubbed
the bathroom, if a few tears splashed into the tub along with
the running water, no one was around to see. By the time
Alex came home from being with Bradley, my smile was back
in place and Visine had banished the redness from my eyes.
I'd chat with Alex while I studied her face, wondering if this
was the day Bradley had decided to tell her everything. But
the moment I feared never came, and gradually I realized it
never would. Bradley was keeping it a secret, saving me that
crushing embarrassment. Somehow, knowing him, I wasn't
surprised.

I only wished it didn't make me love him more.

"It's strange," Alex said now. She rolled over in bed to face
me. "I kept telling myself I needed to change my prescription
for my contacts," she said. "But I think I knew it was more than
that. I just couldn't face it."

"You were probably scared," I said. "Anyone would have
been."

She didn't say anything for a moment, then I heard the sound
of her start to quietly weep.

"I'm still scared," she said, her voice choked. "I've never been
so scared. They're going to cut open my brain. What if something happens? What if I don't wake up?"

"Oh, Alex," I said. I reached over and grabbed her hand. I
held it as tightly as I could.

"I don't want to be kept alive as a vegetable," Alex said
fiercely. "Don't let them do that to me, okay? You've got to
take charge, Lindsey. Mom and Dad won't be able to. I need
you to promise me."

"It's not going to happen," I said. "You're going to wake up.
I promise you."

"What if I don't?" she said.

I opened my mouth to speak, to reassure her, but suddenly a wave of regret and sadness washed over me, taking my breath away. Alex had tried since I'd come home—the invitation to lunch, the phone calls I hadn't returned, the way she'd flipped the conversation back to me that night in the bar—but it was *me* who'd pushed her away. I'd told myself that she hadn't changed, but she had. I was the one who hadn't.

My jealousy had kept us apart. What if Alex *didn't* wake up? What if I never got a chance to know my sister?

"Alex, I promise you it's going to be okay," I said. I wanted to believe it so fiercely I felt like I could make it happen by sheer willpower alone.

"In a way that dumb accident saved me," Alex said, her voice thick with tears. "What if I'd waited until my vision was really bad? What if it was too late?"

"I think it's normal to be in denial," I said. "I would've been."

"You?" Alex said. "Uh-uh. You take things head-on. You always have."

"About that," I said. Suddenly I knew how I could distract Alex from her fear, if I had the courage.

"Are you finally going to tell me about the guy in New York?" Alex asked. Her voice was still shaky, but she'd stopped crying. She reached for a tissue on the nightstand and blew her nose. "You've been saving it because you knew I'd need a distraction the night before the operation. Very Florence Nightingale of you."

I swallowed hard.

"I was fired."

The words hung there a moment, as boldly as the blazing sun on a cloudless summer afternoon.

"Shut up," Alex said after a pause.

"Swear to God," I said.

"What happened?" Alex asked.

"I didn't get a promotion and I kind of freaked out," I said. "I did some stuff—messed up a little—and everyone agreed it would be better if I left."

"*You* were fired," Alex said.

"Let's not dwell on it," I suggested.

"Fired," Alex said. "You."

"Or we could dwell on it."

"What happened?" Alex asked.

"I already told you," I said.

"Right, right," she said. "It's just . . . it's so . . . *unlike* you."

"Yeah," I said. "So I've heard."

"Wait a second!" Alex shrieked. She sat bolt upright in bed. "The whole time you've been saying you've been going to work? The whole thing about scouting out a new D.C. branch of the agency?"

"Lies," I said. "I'm a fired liar."

"And a poet, too," Alex breathed. "Awesome."

"You admire this?"

"My God, you're like the—the—statue of David of lying," she said. "You're perfection as a liar!"

"Wouldn't I be more like the Michelangelo?" I suggested. "He's the one who created David."

"Or so he *said*," Alex said.

I laughed. I was surprised by how good it felt to get that off my chest. I hadn't been aware of how those lies had bogged me down, like little sharp fishhooks digging into my skin.

"Did someone scream?" Dad flung open the bedroom door.

"Sorry," Alex said meekly. "I thought I stepped on a bug. But it was just Lindsey."

Dad nodded. "Do you need anything?" he asked. "Cocoa?"

"No thanks, Dad," Alex said.

"Love you," he said and closed the door again.

"What the hell was that?" I said.

"It was the best I could come up with," she said. "I'm not the liar in the family."

"Look, I haven't told Mom and Dad yet," I said. "So don't tell anyone, okay?" *Don't tell Bradley,* I thought. He probably pitied me enough.

"I'll keep it a secret. Probably best to spread out our Dr. Phil moments," Alex agreed. "We've had enough of them this week, don't you think? But at least they recovered from the shock of my broken engagement when I told them about the tumor. Maybe you could come up with something like that: 'Mom and Dad, I was fired, and guess what? I have herpes!'"

"Nice," I said.

"Which brings us back to your guy in New York," Alex said.

"How, exactly, does that bring us back?" I demanded.

"What's he like?" Alex asked.

"Look, there isn't really anyone in New York," I said. I thought about the night my eyes had met Matt's and I'd felt an undertow of something deep and unfamiliar, and how I'd run away from him. Funny how long ago that seemed, like it was in another lifetime. "Maybe there could've been," I said slowly, "but things just got . . . complicated."

"I thought it was that guy from work," Alex said. "The one with curly hair. Remember I met him when I came by your office?"

Matt. He'd known I had a fraternal twin sister, but he didn't know what Alex looked like until the day she'd popped by my office. Matt had stuck out his hand and introduced himself, then he'd turned away from Alex and reminded me that I'd promised to grab coffee with him before I left for Europe the next afternoon. He hadn't tried to prolong his conversation with Alex. He hadn't snuck looks at her over his shoulder as he walked down the hallway to his office. He'd just smiled at her and turned his attention back to me. I'd forgotten how good that had made me feel.

"We're friends," I said. "Good friends."

"I still can't believe you were fired," Alex said.

"Let's dwell on it," I said. "I was fired. Fired, fired, fired."

"Reverse psychology didn't work on me when Mom told me I wasn't allowed to eat any vegetables," Alex said. "And I was two then."

"Mom did that?" I asked. "Really?"

"Sure," Alex said. "She sat there eating peas and carrots and told me I couldn't have any. So I got cake for dinner. I remember because it was some of our leftover birthday cake. Yellow cake with white icing and pink roses."

"You'd just turned two?" I asked incredulously. "And you remember all that?"

"Can we get back to the juicy stuff?" Alex asked. "So you're unemployed?"

"That's another story," I said.

"We've got all night," Alex said. "Lucky for you."

I owed Alex the truth. She'd been brutally honest with me, and I owed it to her to do the same.

"Okay," I said. "Let me just figure out where to start."

Three hours later, Alex's breathing was deep and even. We'd talked tonight, really talked, for the first time in a long time. Maybe even ever. I was surprised by how easily the words flowed between us, with no gaps or awkward silences. In the darkness of our bedroom, with the rest of the house still, it was almost like we were strangers cocooned together on a train, opening our hearts because we knew we'd never see each other again. I told Alex about May and my new job, and I learned Gary wasn't as perfect as he looked. He lost his temper over stupid things like misplaced keys, and he was vain enough to have had a nose job in his twenties. "The thing is, I think his nose looked better *before*," Alex said, and we both laughed. Was this what it could've been like for us all along, if only we'd been different people? I wondered. Was this what normal sisters did—stay up late together, giggling and talking and conspiring?

After a while, Alex fell asleep, but I remained wide awake. If only she were with anyone but Bradley, I thought. Why did it have to be Bradley? A dark, wormy thought started to burrow into my brain—*But isn't that precisely the point? Maybe Alex is drawn to Bradley because she knows how much he means to you*—but I forced it away. Alex hadn't sought Bradley out; they'd gotten stuck in an elevator together by pure chance. The wedding section of our newspaper was filled with love stories that were jump-started by coincidence: seatmates on an airplane discovering they were reading the same novel; grocery shoppers bumping into each other and chasing down runaway cans of soup together; childhood playmates unexpectedly meeting in a conference room decades later. It happened all the time.

I'd just never thought it would happen to Alex and Bradley.

Plus, Alex hadn't known about my feelings for Bradley, I reminded myself. This wasn't a competition for her. Accepting that didn't make my pain go away, but it did help ease my anger.

Alex and Bradley. Bradley and Alex. Even imagining their names linked together hurt. What would it be like to see them as a couple? Would I ever be able to go to Bradley's house and see a photograph of Alex where there had once been one of me? Could I choke down dinner at Antonio's while Mom and Dad bickered and Bradley and Alex smiled over their wineglasses, the kinds of intimate smiles meant only for each other? Could I give a toast at their wedding and make everyone believe I meant every word?

It would get easier, wouldn't it? After a few months or years or decades? Wouldn't it have to get easier?

I curled up in a ball and hugged a pillow to my stomach, hoping it would absorb some of my pain. It seemed like everyone in the world had a partner. Even Matt had Pammy now. While everyone else was pairing off, I'd spent my twenties killing myself for a job I no longer had. I'd made so many mistakes. I'd never get back that time, those lost opportunities.

I wasn't the only one who felt this way.

The words were as clear and vivid as if someone had entered my bedroom and spoken them aloud. Right now, just a few miles away, lived a widower who made up excuses to go into the grocery store every day just so he could talk to someone. How lonely was his bed at 3:00 A.M.? And what of the man whose fiancée had left him to explain to a church full of their family and friends that there wouldn't be a wedding after all? Then there was Jane, who'd baked her husband a white chocolate cheesecake for his birthday and sat staring at it while she waited for him to come home from his night with another woman.

People hurt each other all the time, both wittingly and unwittingly. And some made the choice to keep moving on, through the pain and uncertainty, and others barricaded the walls of their worlds and stayed safely inside those narrow confines. Some people tried to find hope again, and others . . . well, others flew to Hong Kong for forty-eight hours and substituted dinners with clients for a social life.

Was this what Matt had been trying to tell me all along?

Alex flung one arm outside of the covers and muttered something. "No," she whimpered. "No." She kicked off her covers, like she was trying to escape from something.

"It's okay," I whispered. I rubbed her back until she stopped thrashing. Her shoulder blades felt as delicate as wings beneath my hand. I pulled the covers back up over her so she wouldn't get chilled.

She used to have nightmares, I suddenly remembered.

Why hadn't I ever remembered that before? When Alex was four or five, she used to sneak into my bed in the middle of the night. I'd never wake up, but in the morning, I'd be all toasty warm and she'd be curled against my back like a baby koala bear.

I looked down at Alex's long, slender fingers. Earlier today I'd noticed her ring finger still bore an imprint from the engagement ring she'd taken off. A few days ago, I'd gone with Alex to Gary's house and we'd filled up three of her suitcases and brought them back to my parents' house. While Alex was sorting through her jeans and underpants and makeup, I'd looked around and realized something. Alex was walking away from French-country-inspired interior decorators and country-club memberships and jewelry boxes pulled out of breast pockets for no reason, so she could walk toward a middle-class photographer with a giant heart.

I thought I'd known my sister, but I hadn't. She'd been as much a stranger to me as I'd been to her. I hadn't known *Alex,* the person I'd spent every waking second with for the first few years of our lives. We'd learned to crawl on the very same day. Mom still had a photo on the mantel of me with a bowl of spaghetti dumped over my head, and Alex laughing in the next high chair over.

In my old baby book with the pink cover, Mom had recorded the first word I'd ever spoken: my sister's name.

Right here, right now, I had a second chance to have a relationship with my sister. I could choose to move on through the pain and hurt. I could hope I'd reach the other side instead of drowning. Maybe Alex and I would never be close—maybe we'd always be too different for that—but at least I could give it a chance. Give Alex a chance.

When I finally fell asleep, my cheeks were wet, but my hand was over my sister's.

Twenty-five

I COULDN'T BEAR TO wait in the hospital while the neuro-surgeon opened my sister's skull and cut into her brain.

I left my parents sitting hunched together on a couch in the waiting room with Bradley by their side. They'd aged ten years in a week. For once, Dad wasn't complaining about the lack of a nougat-based candy like Mars in the vending machine or the fact that the parking garage charged by the full hour even if you left your car there for ten stinking minutes. He was just staring into space, his thin shoulders slumped. Somehow that made me sadder than anything else.

There was only one thing Alex wanted, one thing she'd said would comfort her. It was crazy, but I wanted desperately to get it for her, right now. I couldn't stand to sit there, staring at my watch. If I hurried, I'd have time to get it and come back to the hospital before she woke up.

"I'll be back in a few minutes," I told my parents, hugging them tightly. "Everything's going to be fine, okay? I researched this doctor, remember? He's one of the best."

It was as though they hadn't even heard me.

"Take care of them," I said to Bradley. "I have to get something for Alex."

He nodded, his eyes dull and worried.

I raced to the elevator and jumped inside, impatiently jabbing the button for the parking garage even though I knew it wouldn't get me there any faster. I leapt into my parents' car and rushed to their house, barely tapping the car brakes at stop signs. I tore inside and yanked down the pull stairs leading to the attic. It had to be up there; it was the only place I could think to look.

I climbed the creaky steps and began searching through the mounds of boxes Mom stored up here, pushing aside baby shoes and containers of Christmas tree ornaments and the piles of photos Mom had never gotten around to putting into albums.

Mom couldn't have thrown it away; she never threw anything away.

I was going to find Alex's Magic 8 Ball and get someone to remove the little answer pyramid inside. I'd have them replace it with a new pyramid, one with only good answers. It was an insane plan—where was I going to find a Magic 8 Ball restorer?—but I couldn't stop my frenzy. I had to do something; I'd go crazy sitting in the waiting room, staring at my watch reluctantly dragging around its hands.

The day of Alex's diagnosis, I'd spent hours on the computer. I'd researched her illness as thoroughly as I could. What I'd learned took my breath away. First, Alex would lose her hair when the neurosurgeon shaved her skull. Then the steroids designed to reduce inflammation in her brain would have the side effect of bloating her body. One woman on a website I'd found said she gained thirty pounds in a month from steroids. If it turned out that Alex needed radiation, it would sap her strength and might leave bald patches after her hair grew back.

How many times had I wished my sister would fade away, that she'd stop drawing admiring glances? Soon she'd be unrecognizable; her beauty stripped away. In a week, my sister would be a completely different person.

It wasn't my fault; *of course* it wasn't my fault. But the guilt was consuming me.

You wanted this, a cold voice whispered. *She took Bradley and you wanted her to pay.*

"I didn't," I said aloud, fighting the shame that threatened to engulf me. "I didn't want *this.*"

I ignored the tears flowing down my cheeks and tore through another box, tossing aside old report cards and scribbled childhood drawings and the smiling teddy bear Dad had won us at Hersheypark one summer. Alex and I had fought so bitterly over who got to hold the bear that Dad spent thirty dollars winning another one, I suddenly remembered. Next I picked up a photograph of our family vacationing in Ocean City when Alex and I were babies. Our diapers stuck out from underneath our bathing suits, I was chewing on a plastic shovel while Alex sucked her thumb, and we were both squinting into the sun and looking extremely annoyed. I put the photo aside; I'd frame it later.

Suddenly I found it in a shoe box along with some yellowing old papers. I yanked out the Magic 8 Ball, and an envelope that was stuck to its side with some unidentifiable sticky substance came with it.

I'd take the Magic 8 Ball with me back to the hospital, I decided as I pulled off the envelope and automatically glanced down at it. It was a legal-size one, bearing an official county seal.

I paused, staring down at the envelope in my hands.

The normal thing to do would have been to shove the envelope back into the shoe box and race to the hospital, where, right about now, the surgeon's gloved hand was poised to cut into Alex's naked skull and the anesthesiologist was monitoring her steady, deep breathing, and machines beeped and hissed while nurses stood by over trays of savage-looking instruments.

That would've been the natural thing to do. So why didn't I do it?

Why did I open that envelope? What compelled me to look inside it while the Magic 8 Ball's murky eyeball stared up at me?

Words jumped out as I scanned the first page: ". . . official results . . . Stanford-Benet . . . intelligence quotient . . ."

My God, these were the results of the IQ tests Alex and I had taken in the fourth grade. I glanced down at Alex's score; then I flipped the page, to my score. I read it once, blinked hard, read it again. The room swirled around me, spinning faster and faster as I stared down at the papers in my hand. How could this be? There had to be a glitch somewhere, some flaw in the system. It must be a computer error.

I double-checked the names at the tops of the pages again. But nothing had changed. Alex and I had different Social Security numbers, and different fourth-grade teachers. All of that information was correct, so the scores had to be, too.

How could this be?

I was smart. Garden-variety, run-of-the-mill bright. Your average clever kid, the kind that can be found in every classroom all across the country.

But Alex was a genius.

Part Four

Trading Places

Twenty-six

AT OUR OLD ELEMENTARY school, there were two boys with faces full of freckles and round blue eyes and curls that looked spring-loaded. Their names were Johnny and Tommy, and they were identical twins, the only pair in the school. They were cute enough to star in a commercial for breakfast cereal, or to be the world's most cherubic-looking altar boys.

But looks were more than just deceiving in this case; looks were shifty-eyed snake-oil salesmen who took your money and skedaddled to the next town in the dead of night before you woke up and realized you'd been suckered.

Because angel-faced Tommy and Johnny were total hellions.

Tommy—or it could've been Johnny—once leaned over his desk, a pair of scissors in hand, and snipped off the long, shiny braid of the girl sitting ahead of him. Johnny—or maybe Tommy—snuck a garden snake into school under his shirt and threw it in the teachers' lounge before closing the door and holding it shut with all of his ten-year-old might. They tied sheets together and rappelled down the side of their house (one broken leg—Johnny); they bribed the neighborhood girls to show them their private parts (two victories; two apoplectic fathers); and they stole a life-

guard's bullhorn and snuck up behind unsuspecting adults, bellowing, "Fire!" (one near heart attack—old Mrs. Mullens). They
were constantly being hauled into the principal's office, where their
harried mother would come, a baby on one hip and a runny-nosed
toddler trailing behind her, throwing around apologies like confetti
as she dragged one or both of the twins home.

But no one was ever sure if the right kid was being punished.
Because Tommy and Johnny also loved to switch identities.

"Tommy!" our teacher would bellow after he'd belched the
alphabet in the lunchroom.

The kid—whoever it was—would invariably shout, "It wasn't
me! I'm Johnny!"

"No he isn't!" an outraged voice would shriek. "*I'm* Johnny!"

What would it be like to slip into another person's skin like
that? I wondered once as I watched the giggling boys swap jackets before heading home. How would it feel to shed your own
identity and try on someone else's? Would it be like wiggling
into tights that were three sizes too small, or would it feel deliciously liberating?

Who would I change into, if I could be anyone at all? I wondered as I loaded my backpack with gifted and talented math
notebooks and Great Books reading assignments while Alex flitted past in the hallways, a gaggle of girls trailing behind her like
ladies-in-waiting.

Would I become the president? A princess? A superhero with
the ability to fly and see through walls?

If anything were possible, who would I be?

Who was I?

I stared down at the papers clutched in my hands as the
words on them finally stopped churning and twisting around
and slowly settled back onto the page. My entire life was a mis-

take. I was never supposed to be a National Merit semifinalist, or make the dean's list, or win a scholarship to grad school. *Alex* was supposed to do all that.

Everything I'd thought about myself had been flipped upside down. My very identity was wrong, all the way down to its core. I wasn't the smart sister. I never had been.

Alex had unusually early childhood memories.

Most geniuses did; I'd learned that in a psych class in college.

I dragged a hand down my face. How many other clues had I ignored because they didn't fit in with what I thought I knew?

The Wheel of Fortune *puzzle.* She'd solved it with almost no letters showing. I'd made a joke about it, then I'd reached over Alex to grab Mom's house assessment letter to decipher.

Mom had asked the wrong sister for help. *Alex* was the smart one. I could barely wrap my mind around it. How had such a staggering truth been buried for so long? How could I suddenly feel like a stranger in my own skin?

I lifted my hand to massage my forehead again and caught sight of my watch. It jarred me back to the present. I had to go right now; I had to get back to the hospital immediately, before Alex woke up. I dropped the IQ tests to the floor and ran down the stairs.

I left the attic a complete mess, with papers scattered everywhere and half-empty boxes turned on their sides and the Magic 8 Ball sitting there in the center of it all. It wasn't like me to leave things a mess, but then again, I wasn't quite sure who me was anymore.

A few hours later, Alex's eyes slowly opened.

"Hey," I whispered, gently patting her shoulder and being careful to avoid bumping the tubes snaking in and out of her body. She was in the ICU, a place devoid of color. Everything was starkly white—the walls, the glistening tile floors, the nurses' rubber-soled shoes. No one spoke above a whisper so as not to disturb the patients, who were tucked into private rooms with futuristic-looking machines surrounding them. The machines went about their business efficiently, dripping fluids into Alex's veins and displaying dancing EKG lines and monitoring her vital signs with metronomic beeping. Alex's room smelled like bleach and vinegar and something else, something musty and unfamiliar and unsettling.

Alex looked at me like she didn't recognize me. I concentrated on not doing the same thing to her.

"You're at Georgetown Hospital," I whispered. "Your surgery went great. The tumor wasn't malignant, Alex. It wasn't malignant."

Alex gave a tiny nod. Her once-delicate face was puffy, and her head was swathed in a giant white bandage. Underneath it, I knew, was a shiny, bald skull with an angry-looking incision where her hairline used to be. A tube snaked up Alex's nose, and more disappeared beneath her sheets.

"Honey?" Mom stepped up next to me and reached for Alex's hand. "We're here. You can go back to sleep if you need to."

"We'll watch over you," Dad promised as he took Alex's other hand. I felt tears come to my eyes as I watched my parents stand guard. In spite of their bifocals and arthritis and cholesterol medication, they'd protect Alex with a ferocity that would scare away anyone or anything that tried to harm her.

I stepped out of the room and into the hallway, where Bradley waited.

Impossible to believe it had been less than a week since I'd been breathlessly anticipating my date with him. Everything had changed; it was like we were inhabiting a whole different world now. I didn't even feel uncomfortable around him anymore. I knew he wasn't thinking of me sobbing on the rooftop while he tried to tell me, as kindly as he could, that he didn't love me anymore.

The only thing Bradley was thinking about right now was Alex.

"She woke up," I said. I watched relief pour into Bradley's eyes and smooth the furrow between his eyebrows. "I think she's going back to sleep, but the nurses will wake her up every hour to make sure she's recovering."

"Thank God," Bradley said. "She's not in any pain?"

"No," I said. "And she's going to have a morphine drip, so she'll be able to control it if she does. The nurse said you can see her after a few hours. They're only allowing family in now, but once she stabilizes you can go in. I know she'll want to see you."

Bradley nodded. "Thanks." He searched my eyes for a moment. "Are you okay?"

"I'm good," I said. "The important thing right now is Alex."

Bradley took a deep breath and exhaled with a soft whooshing sound. I knew his question was loaded with meaning, and I'd given him the answer he wanted. We weren't going to talk about us—or the lack of us—now. That conversation could wait.

"If she's asleep, I might go grab a cup of coffee," Bradley said. "Can I get you one?"

"No, thanks," I said.

He smiled at me and headed toward the elevator.

"Bradley?"

He turned around, his finger poised over the call button, and raised his eyebrows questioningly. How could I say this? "I think the recovery might be tougher than Alex expects. I just want her . . . to be prepared."

"She's pretty strong," Bradley said.

"Physically, I mean," I said. "The steroids come with side effects."

"We'll get through it," Bradley said simply. "Whatever it is."

He loved her, I realized. It was as simple as that. He might as well have shouted it so the words echoed off the walls of the long hallway: He loved her and he wanted to be by her side. He was making a vow right here and now to be with her through sickness and health, good times and bad. And for just a moment, my pain and confusion lifted and I felt nothing but pure gladness. Bradley would take care of Alex. He wouldn't care if they looked perfect together, if everyone stood back and admired them.

Because Bradley had always found beauty in the unexpected.

I left the hospital around seven o'clock that night to drive my parents home. By then Alex was conscious and even responding to questions. Mom and Dad had wanted to stay, but we'd all convinced them it would better if they had a hot meal and a good night's rest before coming back tomorrow. I think the only reason they let themselves be talked into it was because Bradley was staying with Alex all night long. He refused to leave her side.

When I left, his chair was pulled close to her bedside, and he was leaning over to talk to her in a low voice, even though her eyes were closed and she seemed to be asleep. I quietly pulled the door shut behind me and went to bring the car around for my parents. I'd pick up dinner at Antonio's and open a bottle of Merlot, I decided. My parents would go to bed early, the stress of the day and the wine combining to make them drowsy. They needed the rest.

Then I'd climb the rickety stairs into the attic—into my past—to dig through boxes of old report cards and school papers and standardized tests that Mom had never thrown away. To piece together my life's story, and Alex's.

Twenty-seven

I USED TO LOVE to draw. How could I have forgotten?

Stacked in a pile beside me was irrefutable proof: dozens—no, hundreds—of my pencil sketches of winged fairies and horses and flowers, doodled in the margins of my childhood books and on the pages of my three-ring notebooks. Some weren't bad, especially for a five-year-old.

Why had I stopped drawing? I wondered as I yanked open another box, sending decades of dust swirling into the musty air.

"Lindsey is a happy little dreamer," my kindergarten teacher had written in big, looping cursive on my midyear evaluation. "Sometimes she doesn't pay attention in class because whatever is going on in her own mind is much more interesting to her!"

I carefully placed that evaluation on top of my pile. Next to my pile was one for Alex, filled with her old notebooks and homework assignments and report cards.

"Fantastic imagination!" an enthusiastic teacher had written on one of her stories. "Great job!" blared the faded red ink atop another perfect first-grade spelling test. "Above-grade reading and math skills," gushed Alex's kindergarten teacher.

I dug for hours, like a detective seeking clues in a missing persons case. By the time the sky was growing light outside, my fingertips were black from rubbing against old ink and my two piles were as big as sofa cushions. And any lingering doubts I might have had about the IQ test scores being switched were gone.

Alex was the smart one. She always had been.

So why had I achieved a 3.96 grade point average in high school while she floated around in the vicinity of a B? Why had I gone to a top college before rocking a career in New York while Alex dabbled in courses at community college and never ended up finishing her degree?

The switch must've happened gradually, I realized as I pulled out a photograph of Alex's third-grade class. I leaned over, ignoring the crick in my neck that had come from hunching for so long. In the photo, Alex was positioned in the middle of the first row. The other kids were cute—a little boy wearing a lopsided bow tie, a beaming girl in a red and white striped sailor dress—but there was no question who the star was. There was a reason the photographer had positioned her in the prime spot. Already, Alex was being rewarded for her looks.

As time passed, the message must've been pounded home more and more strongly. If you heard often enough that your beauty was what made you special, would those words eventually overpower your other natural gifts? Would those constant compliments be like soft, relentless water gradually imposing its will on the rocks it flowed over, shaping and smoothing them into the image it chose?

I unearthed a photograph of Alex at a friend's birthday party. The theme was a Hawaiian luau, and the girls were given leis and grass skirts to wear. Even in that one photograph, you could see the boys watching while Alex's hips were captured in midsway as she mimicked a Hawaiian dance. How old was she then? Thirteen, maybe?

Even back then, Alex's crowd was composed of the best athletes, the prettiest cheerleaders, the genetic cream of our school's crop. They adhered to the adolescent adage that had been passed down through the ages, the one that decreed it wasn't cool to be smart. The cool kids called the guys on the debate team Screeches, and tripped them in the halls and laughed when their glasses broke. They met on weekend nights to drink a case of beer bought by someone hip enough to have a fake ID. They hit the mall after school and hung out in packs, appraising each other's strengths and weaknesses like hungry predators. Alex was the undisputed queen of that crowd, reigning over it with her high cheekbones and blue-green eyes and flawless skin.

Had Alex even studied in high school? I frowned, trying to remember. We hadn't spent a lot of time together, but I was pretty sure she only cracked open her books the night before a test. She coasted by on her natural intelligence, racking up Bs without any real effort. Meanwhile, I was stationed in the library, poring over my textbooks until my head throbbed, quietly amassing knowledge and perfecting my Latin. I'd killed myself to get a near-perfect average. To be noticed. To be set apart from Alex.

And in the process, I'd reshaped myself, too, as determinedly as running water.

I looked down at the IQ test results again. Had my parents just cast the letter aside and forgotten about it? Maybe they'd never even read it all that carefully. It was possible.

Or—my eyes squeezed shut as the thought hit me—could they have deliberately kept the results secret because they understood how desperately I needed to believe I was the smart sister? Maybe my parents saw me more clearly than I'd ever realized.

All these years I'd prided myself on being the one who took care of my parents. Could they have been secretly protecting me all along?

I sat up straighter and rubbed my weary eyes. The dust on my fingertips made a sneeze tickle my nose. I'd been up here so long I didn't even know if it was night or morning.

Did Alex have any idea how brilliant she was? I wondered. During her whole life, the only thing everyone focused on was her looks. Her beauty was how she earned a living. It was what defined her. What set *her* apart.

Until now.

I flashed back to Alex in her hospital bed, her face puffy, her hair gone. She'd lost something today. We both had.

Suddenly a bone-deep exhaustion crashed over me, making my mind feel fuzzy and numb. I pulled the string on the overhead light, plunging the attic into darkness. I climbed down the stairs, then accordioned them back up into the ceiling and staggered into my bedroom. I slipped off my shoes and crawled onto my bed without even bothering to get under the covers, and within seconds, I was sound asleep.

"I'm just saying the sideburns don't match!" Dad was bellowing when I woke up.

Ah, right on schedule. The 9:00 A.M. debate over whether Regis Philbin dyes his hair. More reliable than any alarm clock. Soon they'd move on to whether Kelly was getting too skinny, and from there, none of the women of *The View* would be safe. An ill-considered perm, a flash of more-robust-than-usual cleavage, a jarring shade of orange lipstick—it would all be picked apart, scrutinized and dissected with the kind of concentration usually reserved for the insides of laboratory frogs.

"Hi, honey," Mom said as I stumbled into the kitchen and beelined for the coffeepot, lured by its rich, earthy scent. "Bradley called an hour ago. He said Alex had a good night."

"Let me just hop in the shower and we can go see her," I said as I guzzled my coffee. I leaned against the counter, wishing it would decide to follow me around today and help hold me upright.

"Someone needs to take that girl to an all-you-can-eat buffet," Dad opined, watching Kelly do the salsa with the latest winner of *Dancing with the Stars*.

Everything was back to normal, except that nothing ever would be again.

I took a quick shower and was just toweling my hair when I heard the phone ring. A moment later, Mom burst into the bathroom without knocking. I was gearing up to holler, "Privacy!" when I saw her wide, frightened eyes.

"That was Bradley calling," she said. "Something's wrong."

I could hear Alex crying as I tore down the hallway. Bradley stood outside her door, still wearing his clothes from yesterday, though by now only one of the tails of his plaid shirt was tucked in; the other was hanging out of his jeans. His hair was more rumpled than usual, and his face looked drawn and tired.

"She won't see me," he said, sounding stunned. "She won't let me in anymore."

"What happened?" I asked.

"She asked me to hand her her purse, and she pulled out a mirror," Bradley said. He took off his glasses and rubbed the little indentations they had left on the bridge of his nose. "I hesitated for a second. But what could I do? Of course she looks different. She had brain surgery, for God's sakes. But she just started crying."

"She saw herself?" Mom asked as she hurried up beside us.

Bradley nodded and put his glasses back on. "The thing is, she's doing so *well*. The doctor couldn't believe how alert she was this morning, and her peripheral vision is already better.

That's why they moved her out of intensive care. She's doing better than anyone expected. I keep trying to talk to her, to tell her that, but it only makes her more hysterical whenever she hears my voice."

"I'll go in," Mom said.

I put a hand on her arm to stop her.

"Let me try?" I asked, and she nodded and stepped back.

I knocked on the door and eased it open. "Alex? It's me."

Alex was in a new room now, one filled with the flowers that weren't allowed into intensive care. Yellow daffodils in wicker baskets and bunches of spring tulips and sweet-smelling roses crowded every available surface. In the middle of it all was Alex, curled into a wretched ball, tubes still snaking all around her. She looked so sick and sad that it broke my heart.

"Hey," I said. I tried to keep my face from revealing my surprise.

Alex was like a stranger. Her skin was blotchy, and angry-looking bruises snaked around her arms from the repeated needle sticks. Her eyes were red-rimmed, and her cheekbones—her beautiful cheekbones—had sunk underneath her puffy flesh.

I eased into the chair next to her bed, the one Bradley had slept in. Alex just lay there, tears steadily rolling down her cheeks.

"I know you're upset," I began stupidly. God, talk about stating the screamingly obvious. Why couldn't I be one of those people who always knew what to say?

I tried again.

"Alex, the swelling is going to fade. It's just temporary," I said. "And your hair is going to grow back."

It was as though she didn't hear me. "I'm so ugly," she said, her voice raw and guttural. Her vocal cords must have been worn out from crying.

"You had brain surgery," I said gently. Was it possible Alex had blocked any thoughts about how she'd look after surgery, just like she'd denied anything was wrong when the headaches and fuzzy vision first struck?

"It's going to take time to recover," I said. This was coming out all wrong; I sounded like Dr. Grayson trying to skate over the severity of the situation by using bland, innocuous words.

"How long?" Alex asked.

"A little while," I hedged.

Alex pinned me down with a stare. "I know you've researched everything," she said. "That's what you do. So tell me. How long?"

Maybe I should've lied to her. But I guess I thought that would make things even worse. Alex would've known I was lying; it has always been impossible to slip anything by her. From the time she was a little girl, Mom would complain that Alex always knew when Mom was trying to trick her into going to bed early, or was secretly taking her to the dentist to get a cavity filled.

Another missed clue, I thought. *Another sign we all overlooked.*

Alex was waiting for my answer. If she caught me in a lie, I'd lose her trust, on top of everything else. "Your face is going to be swollen for a while," I said. "The steroids will make you puffy." She closed her eyes. "But you only have to take them for a couple of months," I said quickly.

"A couple of months," she said. "How many?"

"Two," I said. "Maybe less." *Maybe more,* I thought, *if you need radiation.*

Alex's red-rimmed eyes opened again. "I just started taking the steroids," she began slowly. I knew what was coming, but I was powerless to dodge the question.

"It's going to get worse, isn't it?" she said. Her voice was almost matter-of-fact. This time I was planning to muster up a lie and pray Alex wouldn't see through me, but I didn't have a chance. Her quick mind had jumped ahead to the inevitable conclusion; all the protective barriers her brain had put into place before her surgery were crashing down.

"It's temporary," I said feebly.

Alex looked around the room, and I followed her gaze. I could see a cluster of bright balloons in a corner, its dangling tag imprinted with the NBC logo.

"Do you think they're going to put me on the air looking like this?" she said. "Do you think anyone's going to hire me for a shoot? Like I'm going to model bathing suits when I look like a fucking linebacker?"

"It's temporary," I said again, wishing I could think of something, *anything* else to say.

"It's not just going to be for two months," Alex said. "It'll take me forever to lose the weight afterward. It'll take my hair two years to grow back."

Alex turned to me, and something in her face changed. For the first time, she seemed to see me. "Look at you," she said in her hoarse, unfamiliar voice. Surprise seemed to cut through her misery—surprise and something else.

I hadn't thought about it; I'd just grabbed the clothes in the front of my closet and yanked them on after Bradley's call. Now I glanced down at my new jeans and boots and fitted top. I couldn't see my hair, but it was much longer than usual, and I knew it had probably dried in its natural loose waves in the car.

"You look . . . pretty," Alex said. She tried to smile, but her lower lip wobbled and a fresh wave of tears rolled down her cheeks.

I knew how she felt. I *knew* it; I felt the truth of it all the way to my core. Alex was jealous of me. Of my looks. In the space of a day, Alex and I had switched identities, just like those two little boys in our old elementary school. But we wouldn't be able to trade jackets or backpacks to turn back into ourselves. Nothing would be that simple, not ever again.

"Alex, I . . . ," I started to say, but I didn't know how to continue. What could I say? Maybe *I've been there? I know what it's like to be so jealous of your sister's looks that you can barely breathe?*

But don't worry, you'll get used to it—even if you'll never completely get over it?

"I'm tired," Alex said, and she closed her eyes once more. But this time she didn't open them again.

"Mom and Dad want to come in," I said.

"Later," Alex said.

"Bradley wants to see you, too," I said.

"No," Alex said. And the way she said it—the finality in her tone—was like she'd shut a door and slammed home the dead bolt.

I left the door cracked open as I eased out of the room, feeling like I'd made everything worse. When Bradley approached in the hallway, I just shook my head. His face sagged, and he stopped walking toward me.

"How is she?" Mom asked.

"It's going to take a little time," I said, somehow managing to give my parents a reassuring smile. "It's all kind of a shock to her. Her face is still pretty swollen."

"Maybe we should get her something from the gift shop," Dad said. His forehead wrinkled, and I knew how helpless he felt. "Do you think she'd like a box of chocolates?"

"That sounds good," I said, patting Dad's arm. "Let's let her rest for a while, then you and Mom can visit her."

"Can I go in now?" Bradley asked in a low voice as my parents headed for the elevator.

I shook my head.

"Doesn't she know?" Bradley asked in an anguished voice. "I don't *care* how she looks!"

It was the truth, and the irony was almost unbearable. My sister, the most beautiful girl I knew, had fallen for the only guy in the world who didn't care about her looks. And now that she'd lost her looks, she was pushing away the only guy in the world who still found her beautiful.

"Give her time," I said to Bradley, echoing those vague, useless words I'd used to try to comfort my parents. God, how had the world become so complicated that I was comforting the guy who'd broken my heart? How was it possible that I was counseling him on his relationship with my twin sister?

"She just needs a little time," I said again, because I didn't know what else to say.

But time only made things worse.

Days turned into weeks, and Alex left the hospital and moved into her old room, after Dad and I hastily carried out his desk and files and books. Mom went shopping at Macy's the day before Alex came home and bought her a new comforter, a pretty one decorated with sprigs of lavender, and a new nightstand and lamp. I scrubbed the walls and sprinkled fresh-smelling baking soda into the carpet before vacuuming it back up. I made sure a good selection of books was on her nightstand, and I put a pretty pitcher and glass for holding ice water there, too. But Alex didn't even seem to notice the changes. She just crawled into bed and lay staring into space. When I left for work every morning, Alex was still in bed. When I came home in the evenings, she'd only have ventured as far as the backyard, carrying a wide-brimmed hat and a book. She refused to leave the house other than to take long, aimless drives once the doctor cleared her to do so. But Alex only went out at night, when she could hide in the shadows.

"All those years of dieting," she said one evening. She looked down at the tray I'd brought into her room when she hadn't come out for dinner. She picked up a fork and flicked at the baked sweet potato I'd piled next to a grilled chicken breast and buttered rolls.

"I was hungry for ten years," she said. She lifted up a big

forkful of potato and swallowed, but she didn't seem to take any pleasure in the taste. "I had this game I played. If I was really good—if I limited myself to thirteen hundred calories a day—I let myself eat four bites of dessert once a week. I could make a forkful of cake last five minutes." She began methodically eating the rest of the potato. "Four fucking bites," I heard her whisper.

"She sounds clinically depressed," Matt said one night when I phoned him.

"Maybe," I said, speaking softly so Alex couldn't hear me, on the off chance that she'd ventured out of her bedroom. "But isn't it normal for her to be depressed after what she went through?"

"Sure," Matt said. His voice was low and reassuring. I felt it wrap around me like a soft blanket as I leaned back on my bed and pressed the receiver to my ear. "It's probably scary as hell for her," Matt continued. "She had a brush with mortality, and now she probably feels like she lost everything. Her career, her looks, her boyfriend."

"So what should I do?" I whispered.

"Just be there for her, I guess," Matt said. "And if it doesn't get better, try to get her to see someone. Maybe she needs medication."

"I doubt she'd leave the house to see a shrink," I said.

"Is it really that bad?" he asked.

I flashed back to the sight of Alex. When I'd gotten home from work, she was sitting on the couch, wearing a pair of navy blue sweats she'd bought online at Old Navy. None of her old clothes fit anymore. She'd been alternating those sweats with a pair of almost-identical black ones. Her fingers were so puffy she could no longer wear rings, and her face still looked swollen. When she took off her scarf, I could see her hair was starting to grow back, but it was just a bit of peach fuzz. But worst of all was the lifeless expression in her eyes as she stared at hour after hour of television.

"It's pretty bad," I said. "I was thinking of calling her doctor. But I'm worried she'll be mad if she finds out."

"Call," Matt said without hesitating.

I heard Pammy in the background asking something about a bottle of wine. They were probably about to share one. I'd wanted to tell Matt about the IQ tests and Bradley and everything else, but suddenly I felt self-conscious. It was a Friday night, and he was with his girlfriend. He probably wanted to get off the phone.

"I should let you go," I said.

"It's okay," Matt said.

"No, really," I said. "Besides, *Jeopardy!* is on. It's kind of a big deal around here."

Matt laughed. "Call me after you talk to the doctor, okay?"

I hung up and lay there, staring at my ceiling. A few minutes later, a text message arrived via my cell phone:

Cheryl arrested for indecent exposure; implants quarreling over defense strategy. Right implant threatening to defect and join Pamela Anderson's body.

I laughed and snapped shut my phone, finally feeling a little bit better.

The next morning I laced up some old sneakers—not the wildly expensive leather pumps I used to wear in New York, and not the flirty heels I'd been wearing recently—and I put on old jeans, too, a soft, faded pair I'd owned since grad school. It was a bit chilly for April, so I topped a plain white T-shirt with Dad's navy fleece jacket. When I finished dressing and pulling my hair back into a ponytail, I looked into the mirror. Today I wasn't the brainy workaholic, or the pretty matchmaker who liked to shop and laugh and fix up strangers. It was as though I'd called a temporary truce between my warring identities by dressing neutrally. Today I was . . . just Lindsey.

I headed for one of my favorite places on Earth: the wooded Capital Crescent Trail that links downtown Bethesda with Georgetown. Just a few blocks away, cars whizzed by and buses belched gray clouds of exhaust as they lurched down the busy streets, but here on the trail, it was like being in a shady, tree-lined oasis cutting through the middle of the city. I walked for hours as bikers flew past me on the path, shouting, "On your left!" and dogs with their tongues lolling out trotted by, dragging their owners behind them. I passed women pushing kids in brightly colored jogging strollers, and couples holding hands as they sauntered along. It was easy to lose yourself on this woodsy trail, to blend in with dozens of other people in sneakers and fleece jackets out for some fresh air on a Saturday.

After a while I began to search the faces of the women who passed me, at least the ones who looked around my age. What about those two friends power walking together, their arms pumping in unison? Were they happily married? Or was one of them secretly pining for the old boyfriend she believed she should've ended up with? And that tired-looking woman with the tiny baby strapped to her chest—was she happy? Had she given up her career to stay home with her child, or was she guilt-ridden but anxious to go back to work? Had she made the right choice? And how about the gorgeous dark-haired woman in the biking shorts who was arguing with the guy walking next to her? Had she moved to Bethesda to be with him, and was now regretting it?

How did you know which life was the right one for you when there were so many to choose from? I wondered. How did you know if you were in the right place, or whether there was some-where else entirely you were supposed to be?

I'd thought my destiny was to run a top ad agency in New York. I thought I'd work seventy-hour weeks and command a staff of a hundred from a corner office with a private granite bathroom. Then, when I came home, I suddenly decided that I was supposed to end up with Bradley.

Now I had to rethink everything I once knew about myself. I wasn't supersmart. I wasn't successful, at least by my old standards. I wasn't destined for greatness. Six months ago, that would've devastated me. Now it just felt strange, and a little scary. I felt hollow and sore inside, as though some vital part of me had been surgically removed and I was feeling its phantom pain.

I wasn't the girl Bradley loved anymore, either. I had to keep telling myself that as often as possible and hope the pain would dim. Maybe if that elevator hadn't broken, or if Alex's engagement photographer hadn't canceled at the last minute, or if a million other little factors hadn't fallen into place just so, I would've ended up with Bradley after all. Maybe.

A troublesome thought squirmed into my brain. I'd tried to push it away before, but it kept returning: I hadn't thought about Bradley much while I was living in New York. So what had finally sparked my interest in him? Could it have been knowing that Alex liked him?

I rolled the thought around in my mind, testing it out, but I already knew the answer: No. That wasn't the only reason I wanted Bradley, I realized with a rush of certainty. He wasn't some prize in a competition; he was too good for that. My feelings were real and complicated and deep—but maybe, just maybe, they'd been ignited because of Alex's interest. I had to concede that possibility.

But in the end, what did it matter? A life with Bradley wasn't the one that was waiting for me, either.

So how did I find the right life? I wondered, watching a white-haired couple pass by, the man throwing a stick for his golden retriever, and his wife watching and smiling. How did I know which way to move from here? How did *anyone*?

I loved my job with May, but if I were being brutally honest, deep down it still made me feel like a bit of a failure. I made less than a quarter of my old salary. My title wouldn't impress anyone. Was the happiness I felt enough to compensate for losing all that? Or a few years from now, would I have regrets? Not knowing what to do was one of the hardest things I'd ever faced. I'd always known what to do, how to fix problems, which way to go. And I'd liked that part of myself, the part that was always certain of what to do next.

The day was beginning to warm up. I pulled off my fleece and tied it around my waist, then I resumed walking. Ahead of me the path curved. Even though I couldn't see beyond another hundred yards or so, I knew that if I kept moving, I'd reach my favorite point on the whole trail, an old covered wooden bridge. I'd turn around there, I decided. Then I'd walk back along the shady path until it abruptly ended and spilled into the heart of Bethesda, where the sun shone brightly over the coffee shops and bookstores and galleries that crowded every inch of street-front. Where people milled around, eating ice cream cones and clutching green plastic bags from Barnes & Noble and nursing glasses of wine under the awnings of sidewalk cafés.

Funny how you could be in one place and, a split second later, be in another place entirely, I thought, pushing my hands deeper into my pockets as I picked up my pace.

Twenty-eight

"SO NOW YOU'RE THE pretty one, and Alex is the smart one?" May asked. She was sitting across from me in her favorite overstuffed chair, and she'd put on a new Andrea Bocelli CD for us to listen to as we worked. Normally this was my favorite time of day: The sun streamed in through the big picture window behind us, the dogs were curled up by our feet, and I had a cup of warm, sweet-smelling tea in my hand. But for one of the few times in my life, I hadn't been able to keep my mind on work. Whenever I tried to read through a client's file, I saw the words on those IQ tests flash by instead.

"I don't know what to think anymore," I said. I sighed and looked away from the file I was resting on my knees. "Alex is going to be beautiful again, but she might not be able to lose all the weight. Some people don't. Her hair might come in looking different. I feel like she's not going to be happy until she looks exactly the same, but that might not happen. Ever."

"That would be hard for anyone," May said. "But especially someone like Alex."

"And I can't help feeling like I was duped," I said. "It's not as bad for me, but I kind of know how Alex feels. Only you can't see what I lost. My whole life was a fraud. Everyone kept telling me how smart I was. My parents, my teachers—they kept talking about my *potential* like it was this amazing thing without any limits. But I'm just kind of ordinary."

"You're a very smart woman," May said loyally.

"But nothing"—I paused—"special."

"I'd disagree with that," May said. She got up, sliced the loaf of banana bread she'd taken out of the oven a few minutes ago, and brought a generous piece over to me. I breathed in deeply; there isn't anything that smells better in this world than fresh-baked banana bread.

"Mmm," I mumbled through a greedy mouthful. "If you're trying to distract me, you should know I'm not that cheap. I require at least two pieces."

May smiled at me. "Have you told Alex about the IQ tests?"

"Not yet," I said. I swallowed my mouthful. "I was going to, but now I think I should wait until she feels a little better. She's dealing with so much already right now."

May nodded, then her forehead wrinkled in thought.

"There's another way to look at all this," she said slowly.

"Tell me," I said. "My brain is exhausted from everything that's happened. Of course, my brain is a lot smaller than it was rumored to be."

May shook her head at me. "What I was going to say is, you could believe that you have unlimited potential, even more now than you had before. Look at where you got in life based on sheer hard work and willpower. What else could you do with your gifts? Where else could you go?"

I looked at her in surprise. I had never thought about it that way.

"Reinvent yourself again if you want to," May said. "I think you can do anything you set your mind to."

"My parents still don't know I was fired," I said after a moment. "Can you believe that? I probably would've told them by now, but with everything going on with Alex . . ." My voice trailed off.

"I don't think you need to tell them," May said. "Just tell them you were offered a job as a full partner in one of D.C.'s top dating services."

"Yeah, but . . . ," I started. Then I stopped speaking and looked at May. "Full partner?"

"Do you have any idea how badly I want to go to India?" she asked. She wrapped her arms around herself and gave herself a squeeze as her eyes grew dreamy. "I've been fantasizing about it for years. I want to see the Taj Mahal, and sleep in a tent under the stars. It'd be so nice to know the agency is in your hands while I'm gone. Besides, you deserve it. Do you know business is up more than thirty percent since you started working here?"

"I don't know what to say," I said. To buy myself some time, I started picking crumbs of banana bread off the couch, which made Bonnie, the black Lab, who was trying frantically to lap them up, stare at me with wounded eyes. Suddenly panic engulfed me. I couldn't look at May. If I did this—if I accepted the partnership—my life wouldn't be the same, not ever. There would be no turning back; I'd be officially tossing my dreams into a bonfire. I'd never have a house in Aspen. I'd never have a car and driver, or an unlimited expense account. I'd be trading all that for a lifetime of dog hairs on my jeans, of laughing with clients in old diners, of babysitting and fixing chopped-off bangs. Of skipping out of work early on warm summer evenings. Of helping hope spring into people's eyes.

Jump, Matt's voice said again.

Matt's voice was getting kind of bossy.

"Lindsey? Are you okay?" May asked, pressing a tissue into my hand.

"I'm . . ." I searched for the word and finally found it. "Happy," I said. "I'm happy." I put my arms around May and hugged her, and felt her solid, comforting warmth. *"Thank you,"* I whispered as I wiped the tears from my eyes. And I realized I'd spoken the truth. Mixed in with everything else—the confusion and worry and panic—there was happiness, too, growing up as straight and true as a flower.

"What can I do?" Bradley ran both hands through his hair and paced his living room. "She won't read my letters. She won't answer the phone. She won't see me. What can I *do*?"

He'd called my cell phone that morning while I'd been at work. For just a second, before I remembered, my heart had leapt up when I saw his name flash on my caller ID. But that only meant my heart had further to crash back down. It'll get easier, I reminded myself for the hundredth time, and I answered the phone.

I'd never seen Bradley like this. He looked like he'd lost ten pounds overnight, and his face was seamed with worry.

"It isn't just you," I told him. "Alex doesn't want to see anyone."

"I just wish I could make her understand," Bradley said. He sank down onto the couch beside me. "The way I feel about her has nothing to do with how she looks. Why can't she understand that?"

"I know," I said. "I'm going to talk to her. I've been worried about upsetting her even more, but this has gone on long enough."

"Thanks," Bradley said. He sighed and turned to me and seemed to truly focus on me for the first time since I'd been there. "God, is it weird that I called you? I just didn't know who else to talk to." He swallowed and looked away. "And I know we never finished talking—"

"Bradley." I cut him off firmly. "There isn't anything to talk about. Everything's fine."

"You mean it?" His face grew hopeful. Bradley hated to see anyone hurt, I remembered. It was one of the things I'd loved about him.

"Of course," I said. "Look, I was kind of confused when I moved back home and switched jobs and everything got muddled. You're right; we're much better off as friends."

Alex was right; I'd become a really good liar.

Bradley let out a breath. "I'm so glad," he said. "*Good* friends." He reached over and hugged me. He still hugged the same way; tightly, and with both arms. I'd always loved the way he hugged, too. When would I stop counting the things about him I loved? I blinked hard and pushed away the thought.

"Alex is going to need you," I said briskly, pulling back. Pulling away from him. If he kept his arms around me for another second, I'd burst into tears. I clenched my hands behind my back, where Bradley couldn't see, and dug my nails into my palms.

"I'm going to talk to her," I promised. "I'll do everything I can. And if she still won't see you . . . then we'll figure something out. I promise."

Bradley nodded, and I saw tears glistening in his eyes.

"Thank you," he said. In his face I could see gratitude and something more. Maybe even love. Just not the kind of love I'd wished for so desperately.

But it would have to be enough. I'd forget about the longing I'd felt when his arms had closed around me and I'd inhaled his faintly woodsy smell and had to force away the sob welling up in my throat. He'd chosen my sister. This would have to be enough.

Twenty-nine

WHEN I GOT HOME that night, Alex was waiting for me.

"I need a favor," she said.

I was so surprised to see her up and alert that I just nodded. "Of course," I said. "Anything."

"I lost my driver's license," she said. "It was probably that night when I pulled out my credit cards before the MRI. I haven't been able to find it since. And I got pulled over last night. Dad's left headlight was out. The cop let me go, but if they catch me again I'm in trouble. So can you take me to the MVA?"

"Right now?" I asked.

She hesitated. "If I can't get out of the house at night I don't know what I'll do," she said. Her tone was soft, but desperation rang through it.

"Then let's go," I said.

"It closes in an hour," she said. "I thought if we got there close to closing time. . . ." Her voice trailed off, but I knew what she was thinking. If we got there close to closing time, there wouldn't be as many people around.

"Sure," I said. Maybe her getting pulled over was a blessing, I thought as I took my keys back out of my purse. Maybe it would force Alex to reenter the world, one baby step at a time. Today we'd go to the MVA, and maybe later this week Alex would let me take her out for coffee. Maybe this would finally give her the push she so desperately needed.

TAKE A NUMBER, the big sign above the MVA counter graciously instructed me. I grabbed one from the dispenser and rejoined Alex in the row of hard orange seats in the waiting area.

"Shouldn't be long," I said. "They're on eighty-one and we're eighty-six."

"Which means it'll be three hours," Alex said. She sighed. "I can't believe I'm going to have this damn picture on my license for the next ten years." She finished filling out the clipboard full of paperwork and put it down on the empty seat beside her. Alex wasn't wearing her wig after all, even though she'd started out wearing it in the car. The itching drove her crazy, especially around her incision, so she'd put on a big floppy hat with the sides pulled down low to disguise her lack of hair. I recognized the hat; Alex had been holding it in one hand on the cover of *The Washingtonian,* the one in which she'd worn the blue bikini. Now I wondered if the art director had instructed Alex to take off the hat during the shoot, so that it didn't cover up her glorious hair.

"Maybe you can come back and retake the picture later," I said. I knew better than to bullshit Alex, to tell her that she still looked beautiful.

For the first time I could remember, no one was staring at my sister. I hadn't realized how accustomed I'd become to it: the furtive glances from men, the blatant double takes and whispers from people who recognized her, the constant cheesy come-ons from guys like the one who'd come up to Alex in a bar with a smarmy grin and said, "I have amnesia. Do I come here often?"

What surprised me was how sad it made me. If Alex noticed—and she had to have noticed—she didn't say a word.

When Alex's number was called, I walked with her over to the photo area. The woman operating the machine looked so bored she was practically in a trance. I didn't blame her. The sum total of her job involved telling people to stare at a little red light, then pushing a button.

"Stand on the blue line," the woman instructed in a mono-tone.

Alex started to comply, then she paused. "Just one second?"

She pulled a compact out of her purse and looked into it as she dabbed on some shiny pink lip gloss. A year ago, I'd have been rolling my eyes at her vanity. But now I felt like crying. That little spark, that bit of pride—it was a glimpse of the old Alex. It was like she was slowly surfacing, through the scars and steroids and puffiness.

"Okay, I'm ready," Alex told the woman.

"You need to lose the hat," the woman said.

"Sorry?" Alex asked.

"Take off the hat," the woman said. She wasn't even looking at Alex; she was fiddling with something on the machine.

"But I have to wear it," Alex said. She grabbed it with both hands, like she was scared the woman was going to jump over the counter and tear it away.

"No hats in the photos," the woman said, sounding like she was rattling off MVA rule thirteen, subsection B, line four—the one right before line five, which decreed that no flattering pictures were allowed.

"I have to have my hat!" Alex said. Her voice was panicked.

What I should have done—what I didn't think about doing until much later—was quietly step up to the woman and explain why Alex needed a hat. I should've figured out a way to fix it for Alex. But instead, I just stood there helplessly.

"No hat or no picture," the woman said. "You choose."

Alex stared at her, fear transforming into anger across her face.

"We can come back later," I said, starting to approach Alex. "Or let me talk to a manager." I glared at the photo woman. "What's the name of your supervisor?"

"No," Alex said. She closed her eyes and seemed to gather herself.

"Alex, we can go home," I said gently. "Come on."

But it was as though Alex didn't even hear me. "No," she whispered again, almost to herself. She hesitated for a moment, then she reached up and ripped off her hat.

It was as though the MVA was suddenly transformed into a theater, and the curtain had come up to reveal Alex standing alone under a spotlight at center stage. A hush fell over the room. Everyone sitting in the rows of hard orange chairs— the middle-aged Hispanic woman bouncing a baby girl on her knee, the guy in camouflage pants, the giggling pack of young girls getting their learners' permits—they all collectively froze as they stared at Alex.

Alex stood in the middle of the cavernous room, letting everyone take a good, long look. A faint layer of reddish gold fuzz covered her scalp, but the area around her incision was still naked. Her angry-looking scar shone under the bright industrial lights.

The woman operating the camera gaped at her. "You can put the hat back on," she finally said in a subdued voice.

Alex's voice broke as she said, "Just take the damn picture."

Then Alex turned to face the camera, which was adorned with a little yellow happy-face sticker instructing her to "Say Cheese!" While everyone stared at her, Alex lifted her chin high and, as she'd done for so many years, posed while the camera clicked.

* * *

"I was losing my looks anyway," Alex said.

I turned to her in surprise. It was the first thing she'd said since we left the MVA twenty minutes earlier. She'd been sitting in the passenger's seat of the car, staring straight ahead, cutting short my attempts at conversation. No, she didn't want anything to eat, even from a drive-through. No, she didn't need me to pick up anything for her. No, she wasn't too hot. Or too cold, either.

I'd wanted to keep her talking, to try to sort through what had just happened. Maybe it was her rock bottom, the worst thing she could imagine happening. Maybe now that she'd hit it, she'd slowly start coming back up, if only because there was no other way to go. When Alex had pulled off her hat and stared defiantly at the MVA woman, it seemed like she was finally ready to fight back, to reenter the world. But after we collected her new license and got into the car, as the long minutes passed and Alex kept staring out the window, I began to worry that maybe the opposite would happen instead. Maybe now Alex would never want to come out of her room again.

That's why I was so surprised when her voice suddenly cut through the darkness.

"I got called for this modeling job a few months ago," Alex said. She drummed her fingers against her knee. She was wearing the hat again now, even though it was dark out and no one could see what she looked like inside the car. "My agent told me they needed a young woman and her mother. We were doing a catalog for Chevy Chase Pavilion. And when I got to the studio, I saw this gorgeous kid—she was probably thirteen, and I swear she was all legs—sitting in the makeup chair. Suddenly it hit me: *I* was the mother."

She shook her head. "This is the part that kills me. That kid couldn't smile with her teeth showing because she had braces. She kept doing this Mona Lisa smile all day."

"Little twerp," I said. "I bet she came down with a violent case of acne the next day."

Alex smiled. At least I'd gotten a smile out of her. It felt like a minor victory.

"The jobs were going to dry up anyway," she said. "It just happened a little faster."

"Alex, come on," I said. "You're only twenty-nine."

"That's ancient in my business," she said. "The only reason I'm still working is because we're in D.C. In New York it would've been over five years ago. Do you know what I've been doing the past few years at shoots? I put Preparation H under my eyes before I get in the makeup chair. It makes those little lines disappear. I was going to start Botox next year, too."

I cringed, thinking of the times I'd written off as pure vanity Alex's facials and sessions with a personal trainer. She'd worked as hard as I did, even though she knew her career had already peaked. Maybe that knowledge had made her work even harder.

"Did you ever think about doing anything besides modeling?" I asked her.

Alex shrugged. "I like the TV stuff," she said. "I always wondered if I could parlay it into something bigger, maybe show my reel around New York or L.A."

"You can still do that," I said. "A few months from now . . ."

"I guess," Alex said, but she didn't sound convinced. "Do you know how fierce the competition is for TV jobs? If you're not young and gorgeous, producers won't even look at you. And I'm not either. . . . Not anymore."

I pulled into our driveway and flicked off the headlights.

"There's something I want to show you," I said.

"Unless it's a carton of Chunky Monkey, I'll take a rain check," Alex said. "I'm tired."

"Come on," I pleaded. "It'll only take a minute."

Alex sighed, but she didn't protest any more. I unlocked the front door, and we went inside. It was eerily quiet—it took me a moment to realize that was because of the absence of blaring televisions—and I found a note taped to the hall mirror that said, "We're picking up pizza for dinner! Back soon!"

"Thank God they left a note," Alex said. "I was about to turn on *COPS* to see if they were on the lam."

The little jokes, that fleeting smile . . . it was like seeing pieces of the old Alex. I'd missed her humor, I realized. I missed talking to her, too. Funny, but I'd seen my sister more these past few weeks than I had in the past decade. So why was it only now that I was missing her?

"Follow me," I said. What I was about to do was a gamble, but something told me the timing was right. I pulled down the attic stairs and started climbing. I'd left the two piles I'd sorted out undisturbed up there.

"What's all this crap?" Alex said, climbing the stairs after me. "God, I'm surprised the ceiling hasn't collapsed and killed us all. Hey, my old Barbie mobile. How much do you think I could get for that thing on eBay?"

"I want to read you something," I said. I rummaged through one of the piles until I found what I was looking for. I cleared my throat and began. "'This student shows an unusual strength in spatial awareness'—Alex, stop taking the pants off that Ken doll and listen—'and her capacity to reason is outstanding.'"

I lowered the paper and Alex raised an eyebrow. "So?"

"Let me read you one more," I said. I turned the page: "This student is three standard deviations above the norm in terms of general intellect. She falls into the profoundly gifted category."

Alex yawned.

"It's you," I said. I tossed the IQ results at her, and she automatically caught them. She looked down at the papers, then up at me.

"You're the smart one," I said.

"Shut up," Alex said, frowning. "Are you joking? They were talking about you."

"Take a look around," I said, indicating the pile behind me. "Trust me, you're the smart sister. You always have been."

Alex lifted up a paper from the top of her pile—I recognized it as a report card from second grade—and she started to read. After a moment, she moved the card closer to her face.

"You don't have to be a model, unless that's what you really want to do," I said. "You can start a whole new career. You can do anything."

Alex was silent, but after a moment, her hand slowly reached out and grabbed another piece of paper from her pile.

"I guess it's a good thing Mom never threw anything away," I said.

"Just give me a few minutes, okay?" Alex said. She put down the paper and grabbed a few more, a big handful this time.

"Take all the time you need," I said. "Want me to bring you some pizza?"

"Sure," Alex said distractedly.

Before I went to bed a few hours later, I poked my head into the attic. She was still there, utterly absorbed in her own history.

Thirty

"HAVE TIME FOR A drink?" Jacob asked. "I know a place where they make great chocolate martinis."

I hesitated. I'd been putting Jacob off for weeks, but we'd finally gone shopping together today. I'd been surprised by how much fun we'd had, and how easy it was to be with him.

"Step away from the black sweaters," I'd instructed when we first entered Banana Republic.

"How about gray?" he'd asked, holding one up against his chest. "I'm not sure I can make a clean break that quickly."

"Try this on," I'd said, tossing him a cream-colored crewneck that felt incredibly soft. "We've got to do this cold turkey."

"Your girlfriend has great taste," a salesman—probably sucking up for commission—had said as he'd wandered over.

Neither of us had bothered to correct him.

Now Jacob was looking at me with those dark-lashed blue eyes, and I knew the implications of his invitation. He'd liked Jimena, but they hadn't completely hit it off. I'd set him up with another woman, but he hadn't called her yet. I knew Jacob was hoping I'd change my mind.

It would be easy to slip into this, I reflected. So easy to flirt and sip martinis and revel in the feeling of his eyes on me. I could see the night stretching out before us: Jacob would walk me to my car in the velvety air, and I'd turn toward him instead of unlocking my door and getting inside. He'd lean in, and I'd reach up to feel his slightly rough cheek, with its hint of five o'clock shadow. Then I'd close my eyes—

But no. It didn't feel right. Jacob was ready for a serious relationship. He deserved someone who adored him, not someone who'd barely thought of him while she'd been dreaming of life with another man.

"I'd love to grab a drink with you," I finally said, and there was real regret in my voice. "But I have more errands to run."

"Can't blame a guy for trying," Jacob said. He leaned in for a hug and lingered there for a moment.

"I really am going to find you the perfect woman," I promised.

Jacob winked at me, and I turned around and walked toward Nordstrom. When I looked back, Jacob had already disappeared into the crowd of shoppers.

The phone rang once, and then someone picked it up. But they didn't say a word.

"Jane?" I asked. "It's Lindsey, from Blind Dates. Hello?"

Ominous silence.

"Is everything okay?" I asked as my father's voice began narrating possible disasters: She'd had a stroke; she'd been tied up and gagged by a robber and had managed to knock the phone off the receiver with her big toe; she'd hit her head and had soap-opera amnesia.

"Jane, can you hear me?" I asked. "Make a noise if you can."

The heavy breathing intensified, then this solemn proclamation: "Elmo's red."

"Hi, Katie, it's Lindsey! Remember me? I gave you all that ice cream?" I said. "Can you do me a favor and get your mommy?"

"Okeydokey," Katie said cheerfully, then dropped the phone. Two minutes later, I was still waiting. I could hear Jane in the background asking Katie if she wanted some water, and Katie negotiating hard for an upgrade to lemonade, then they walked out of the room and I couldn't hear any more. I hung up and tried again, but the phone was still off the hook so the line was busy.

I gave up and checked in with the septuagenarian best friends, who'd had fun on their recent double date but wanted a bit more "bang for their buck," as they'd put it. "Get us someone who can stay out past midnight!" the never-married one giggled.

"And no guys with small hands!" her friend hollered in the background.

"Big hands!" I noted dutifully, trying to hold back my laughter. "Ladies, I'm on it."

This was my job, I reminded myself. This was what my new life looked like. In three weeks, May was leaving for India and I'd be in charge of the company. We'd decided that I'd stay at her house and take care of the dogs while she was gone, and after that . . . well, after that was what I was going to investigate this afternoon.

"Do you mind if I duck out early?" I asked May, closing the folder on my lap.

"It's four-thirty," she said. "It's not early."

I grinned and took my teacup to the dishwasher, then tossed the dogs a few treats and headed outside, to the driveway, where my newest splurge was waiting for me. Last night I'd gone to a Volkswagen dealership and driven out in a light blue Cabriolet convertible.

I'd put down the top and felt the wind lift my hair as I'd

stepped on the gas. It felt like a movie moment, the kind where the music swells and the heroine throws back her head and laughs as she roars down an empty highway. Except for the fact that I wasn't speeding (I always go five miles under the limit, just to be safe). And that at home, my parents were peering out the window, fretting about whether I'd be late for dinner. Plus technically, my car wasn't exactly an impulse buy, given that I'd spent four solid days comparing safety ratings from *Consumer Reports* and looking up model numbers so I could be aware of exactly how much the dealer had paid for the car before I made an offer.

But hey, at least I'd turned up the music as I headed home. Was it my fault that the only station not playing a commercial was airing a Lionel Richie–a-thon, which didn't exactly lend itself to swelling?

Tonight I'd gotten wiser. I'd loaded some CDs into my car and I picked Coldplay for my drive. Even though rush hour hadn't officially begun, I knew the Beltway would be clogged, so I took back roads and wound my way east until I reached Takoma Park. I'd always loved this area. It was a funky mix of artsy small-town shops and coffeehouses, but it was big and busy enough to qualify as a city.

The real estate agent was waiting for me outside the house.

"Lindsey?" he said, coming toward my car as I got out and offering his hand with a warm smile. "I'm Jim."

Jim had a great voice, deep and calm and sexy. When we'd been talking on the phone, I'd idly wondered if he might just happen to be a square-jawed, newly single real estate tycoon who would serve as a lovely distraction from Bradley. But since this is my life, he was just a portly middle-aged guy in a velour sweat suit with a bald spot shaped like a yarmulke.

Lionel Richie and velour sweat suits. I could see it now: Jennifer Garner and Anne Hathaway would duke it out over the rights to my life story. ("Don't skimp on the Krispy Kremes," the director would instruct the movie's caterers. "We need to plump up my actress.")

"So this is it?" I asked, looking up at the house.

"This is it," Jim said, spreading out his hands.

I'd known real estate agents had a reputation for stretching the truth. But when Jim had called this a fixer-upper, I'd assumed there would be at least equal amounts of fixer and upper. My eyes traveled past the yard—technically weeds and bare spots—to the front walkway, which was missing half of its stones. An upstairs window was broken, and bits of jagged glass clung to its frame, making it look like an angry mouth. Jim headed across the front porch, and when I followed him, the boards creaked ominously. If Jim were a serial killer, this is where he'd lure his victims, I thought, reminding myself to use the ballpoint pen in my purse as a weapon if he attacked. ("Go for the eyes!" I could hear my father coaching.)

"It's a little dusty," Jim said apologetically as he opened the creaking door, oblivious to the fact that, in my murderous fantasy, he was on the ground writhing in pain while I liberated his young female hostages.

When I looked in the front door, I saw that dust was the least of this house's worries. Random holes were hacked into a wall, the living room floorboards buckled in the middle, and a pile of what looked like mouse droppings decorated a corner. Then I looked up, and I noticed beautiful exposed oak beams lining the high ceiling.

"This house needs a little TLC," Jim said in possibly the biggest understatement in the robust history of real estate fibs. "The owners were elderly and they couldn't keep up with it. They died about ten years ago and their son never bothered to check on the house. He lives in Seattle in some sort of commune."

Jim's voice dropped to a conspiratorial whisper: "Drugs."

I stepped into the kitchen and opened a cabinet. The wood was faded and worn, and the linoleum on the countertops was a color that Benjamin Moore would call Solitary Confinement Gray.

But if you stripped and refinished the cabinets, and tore up the linoleum, and knocked down the wall between the kitchen and living room . . . I blinked and saw yellow tiles on the countertops, cherrywood cabinets, and a cozy little breakfast bar separating the living room from the dining room.

"Nice stove," I said, lifting a burner on the big, old-fashioned range. It broke off under my touch.

"Want to see upstairs?" Jim suggested brightly after a bit of an awkward pause.

The upstairs was even worse than I'd feared. Underneath a thick layer of cobwebs I could see two bedrooms with big windows and a bathroom with an old-fashioned claw-footed tub that may once have been white. The bedrooms had the feel of a haunted house, with sheets draped over a few pieces of furniture and dust motes swirling in the meager light that came in through dirty windows.

Jim whipped a sheet off the bed, revealing a stained, saggy mattress, then covered his mouth with his handkerchief and suffered a coughing spasm.

"The furniture conveys!" he announced grandly when he could breathe again. "If you're interested, I'm sure we could work out a deal."

I wandered over to open a window, letting fresh air stream into the room for the first time in far too long. The windows were old-fashioned, floor-to-ceiling ones that spread open like arms to embrace a beautiful view of the crepe myrtle and apple trees lining the street below. I wandered back across the room and peeled off a strip of old-lady flowered wallpaper over the bed. What would this room look like bathed in a coat of warm, rose-colored paint? I wondered. With snow falling outside those huge windows, and a wood fire burning in the little brick fireplace tucked into one corner?

I walked to the fireplace and looked at it more closely. Someone had painted the bricks dirt brown, I thought indignantly, scraping at one of them with my fingernail. Underneath the layers of drab paint were old bricks in rust tones. What would they look like cleaned and polished?

"Sometimes people don't see the beauty in something when it doesn't hit you right in the face," Jim said. He was leaning against the doorframe, his hands in his pockets, probably because he didn't dare sit down anywhere. "This house could be beautiful, if someone took the time to appreciate it. But a lot of people just walk right by it, not ever knowing how special it is."

I did a quick bit of mental math. My savings account could cover a healthy down payment, with enough left over to fix the house up, especially if I did some of the work myself. Despite my frequent shopping sprees, my account still had a nice balance. After all, I'd spent seven years building it up. Seven years of never taking a risk. Of watching the world pass by beneath the glass windows of my office.

I'd only done the math as a formality. I'd made my decision as soon as I walked inside this house.

I turned to Jim and smiled.

"I want it," I said. I'd never felt as sure of anything in my life.

I was just drifting off to sleep, my mind filled with images of exposed ceiling beams and window boxes overflowing with gerbera daisies, when Alex knocked on my half-opened door.

We'd barely talked since I'd shown her the old IQ tests. Once or twice she'd come out of her room to join me and our parents in front of the television, but she hadn't engaged anyone in real conversation.

"Are you okay?" I'd asked once when we passed each other in the hallway, me on my way to the bathroom and Alex on her way from it.

She'd nodded. "I just need a little time to think. There's a lot to process, you know?"

"Yeah," I said. I was still processing it myself.

"Come in," I said now, pushing myself up on one elbow. "I'm awake."

Alex opened the door and entered my room. She was wearing her black sweat pants again today, but earlier in the hallway, I'd noticed she'd painted her fingernails for the first time since the surgery.

"Are you okay?" I asked.

Alex didn't answer my question. Instead she sat down on the corner of my bed and tucked her knees up to her chest.

"I saw you when you were leaving for work this morning," she said. The moonlight filtering in from my window played across her face, and for a moment, at that angle, I caught a glimpse of the old Alex. Then she turned her head and the mirage disappeared. "You looked good," she said softly. "Really good."

I'd met with a new client at lunch, and I'd worn a blue skirt and gauzy white shirt with a deep V-neck. But I'd waited until I was at May's before putting on my makeup. Somehow I'd felt guilty, as if by letting Alex see me trying to look pretty, I'd be betraying her.

"I always used to wonder why you wore your hair up all the time," Alex said. She hugged her knees tighter. "And you never dressed to show off your body, either."

"Why would I want to show it off?" I joked, then I wanted to knock myself in the forehead. Right now Alex probably had ten pounds on me. How could I joke about being overweight?

"Are you serious?" Alex frowned at me. "Being curvy suits you. Do you honestly think you're fat?"

"I guess I always felt chunky around you," I said. I swallowed hard and continued. "And I felt like it wasn't worth the effort to put on makeup. Or do anything with my hair."

"Because?" Alex prodded.

"Because no one noticed me next to you," I said softly. It almost physically hurt to say those words, like ripping a scab off an old wound that hadn't fully healed. I thought back to high school, when I'd cowered before the cool senior guys while Alex made them all fall in love with her. I thought about the old woman who'd grabbed my hair with a hand that looked like a claw and announced it was a shame I didn't look like my sister. I thought of a thousand painful slights, big and small: the times waiters rushed to fill Alex's water glass and left mine empty; the times guys gaped at her after their eyes flicked past me; the times people said *"Your sister?"* in a tone of voice that didn't bother to conceal their shock.

I didn't hold those moments against Alex anymore, because I finally understood they weren't her fault. But that didn't mean those memories no longer hurt.

"Look, Alex," I said. "You're going to go back to being gorgeous soon. And I'm glad, I honestly am. But I guess I always felt like I faded into the background when you were around. It's not your fault, of course," I added quickly.

"I didn't know," Alex said, and I realized it was true. Alex hadn't known how I'd felt, but of course, neither of us had known much about the other. She shook her head. "I thought you didn't care about clothes and stuff."

"Apparently I do," I said. "I've been shopping like crazy lately."

"I was a little jealous of you, too," Alex said.

"You?" I said. "Seriously?"

"Of your job," Alex said. "The way you flew around the world and dreamed up all those commercials. It always sounded so cool."

I stared at her for a moment, stunned. Alex had been jealous of *me*?

"I was jealous of Gary," I blurted. "He seemed like the perfect guy. And he adored you."

"I was jealous of your independence," she said. "I've lived in this town my whole life. You went away to college and grad school and you lived in New York. You had this great little apartment and you knew the city like you'd lived there forever."

She'd been jealous of *me*. I still couldn't fathom it. All this time, I'd had no idea.

"You know, I thought I had a little crush on Bradley when I first came home," I said casually.

"You did?" Alex was truly surprised; I knew her well enough to know she wasn't faking. So Bradley had never said anything after all.

"Crazy, huh?" I said. "I was kind of mixed up for a while there."

I forced a laugh, to show how inconsequential my crush had been, but Alex didn't join in.

"Do you still—" She paused and her forehead creased in worry.

"God, *no*," I said.

"Because I thought you had that guy in New York," she said. "And then you were going out with Jacob."

"Alex," I said, putting my hand over hers. I had to make light of this, but maybe someday I'd tell her the whole story—and maybe I'd be able to really laugh about it by then. "Bradley and I were only ever meant to be friends. I was just trying to work up a crush on him so I didn't have to deal with the fact that I was fired. And there's one other thing I have to confess," I said, making my voice grow somber.

"I'm not sure if I can take it," Alex said. "It's like Jerry Springer around here."

"I was also insanely jealous," I said slowly, "of your . . . toe-nails."

"My toenails," Alex said slowly.

"They always look perfect. Who the hell has pretty toe-nails?"

"Well, it's official," she said. "You need more therapy than me."

I looked at Alex, and we both smiled.

"Look, I know this sucks," I said. "But your hair is already growing back. You'll be off steroids soon. It's going to be okay."

Alex nodded, but she didn't seem convinced. Maybe it wouldn't be the same, I realized. Maybe once you'd lost your beauty overnight, you'd realize how fleeting a thing it was, and it would always seem like a mixed blessing.

"So about those test scores," Alex said.

"Weird, huh?" I said. "Not that I'm jealous or anything."

Alex smacked me in the arm. "I was thinking maybe I'd stop modeling. I want to keep doing the TV stuff, but by the time my hair grows back and I lose the weight . . . I don't know, it just seems easier to stop now than to let it drag out. Quit while you're at the bottom, right?"

"Are you going to pursue something more in TV?" I asked.

"Don't laugh," Alex said.

"I won't," I promised.

"I was thinking," Alex said slowly, "about going back to college."

"Do it," I said instantly.

"Really?" she said. "Don't you think I'd feel weird, going to college at twenty-nine?"

"Nope," I said. "What classes are you going to take?"

She lifted a shoulder and gave a half shrug. "Business, maybe."

"Just do it," I said again.

"Thanks, Nike," Alex said. "I figure by the fall, things will be back to normal. Maybe I could start then."

"Sounds perfect," I said.

She nodded and leaned back, lost in thought about an unexpected future. Just like I'd been moments before.

"I was just wondering," I said casually, "if you'd thought about calling Bradley."

The dreamy look dropped away from Alex's face. "Not yet," she said in a guarded voice.

"Alex, he wants to see you," I said.

Alex unfolded her legs and stood up.

"Don't push me," she said.

"C'mon," I said. "Just call the guy. Put him out of his misery."

But Alex was already walking through the doorway, as though she was desperate to put space between herself and any mention of Bradley.

"Good night," she said, and she gently closed my door.

Thirty-one

"ALEXANDRA ROSE?" THE RECEPTIONIST called.

As Alex and I stood up and crossed the threshold into the inner office, a terrible sense of déjà vu crashed over me. The last time we'd been here, the doctor had delivered the news about Alex's tumor.

Dr. Grayson rose from his seat behind his desk to shake our hands. His expression was perfectly bland, the facial equivalent of tapioca pudding. I could see Alex's new scans on his desk, spread out like a hand of poker. Yesterday, a different technician, a young mother of three who'd chatted about her kids during much of the procedure, had taken those scans while Alex lay inside the MRI tube. Afterward I'd searched the woman's eyes, but she didn't reveal a clue about the results.

Although during surgery Dr. Grayson had removed most of Alex's tumor, a tiny slice—the shape of a thin crescent moon— was resting on the optic nerve, and he hadn't been able to risk cutting away that part. If the tumor had grown, even a little bit, he'd have to bombard it with radiation to wipe it out before Alex's vision was permanently damaged.

Right now, *radiation* was the scariest word I could imagine.

It meant Alex's recovery would be delayed. It meant months of steroids, of daily visits to the hospital, of lethargy and nausea and a dozen other potential side effects. It meant the old Alex would stay hidden away where no one could see her.

I looked down again at the scans on Dr. Grayson's desk. Suddenly I remembered that, in poker, you never laid down your hand until you were finished gambling and the game was over.

"I'm sorry," Dr. Grayson said, looking at Alex.

Just those two little words. How could such small words be powerful enough to almost knock me down? I reached for Alex's hand. It was ice-cold, like her foot had been the night she'd disappeared inside the MRI tube, the night this had all started.

"Are you sure?" I blurted out.

He nodded. "It grew several millimeters. Not much, but in such a short time it's enough to send us a warning. We need radiation to kill all the cells that are producing the mass."

Alex nodded, like it made perfect sense. "When do I start?" she asked. Her voice was as calm as if she were asking when her favorite television program would begin, or when an airline flight would be taking off.

"I'm hoping we can schedule you to start Monday," the doctor said. His voice was grave, his expression reassuring yet concerned. Did they teach that in medical school? Did they have a course in how to look sorrowful yet optimistic? Suddenly I wanted to leap up and grab his shoulders and violently shake him. This was all his fault; he hadn't gotten out the whole tumor. Suddenly I hated this doctor with his steepled fingers and fancy diplomas. What good were all those degrees if he hadn't been able to help Alex, damn it?

"I'd like a six-week course of radiation," Dr. Grayson said, oblivious to my raging thoughts. "The treatment itself will be relatively straightforward. You won't experience any pain, if you're concerned about that."

"I've read all about it," Alex said. "I know what to expect."

Something was terribly wrong. She should be yelling and screaming about the unfairness of this all, of being forced to battle a brain tumor at the age of twenty-nine. She should be crying and fighting. Why was Alex so calm?

She was slipping away, I realized as fear gripped my stomach. She was going back to the place of endless television and dull eyes. Alex was disappearing again, maybe so far that this time I wouldn't ever be able to reach her.

"Radiology will need to mold a mask for you, so that the beams hit only the mass and the rest of your brain is protected," the doctor said.

"I see," Alex said, as unemotionally as if he'd just offered her a glass of water.

"It's going to be okay," I said inanely, squeezing her hand. *Stay with me,* I pleaded silently. But Alex's hand lay limply in my own.

"Do you have any other questions?" the doctor asked. "I know this isn't what you wanted to hear today, but the good news is I'm confident we'll be able to knock this out with radiation."

"I thought you were going to say the tumor hadn't grown," Alex said. "My vision is still good, so I was hoping that meant . . ." She swallowed and continued. "That nothing had changed."

"The change is small," the doctor said. "But there is a change."

Alex nodded. "Then let's get on with it," she said simply.

The last time we'd been in this room, she'd gripped her armrests until her fingertips turned white, then she'd cracked jokes and burst into tears. Now she was completely numb. I almost wanted her to make a joke, to do something to show that she wasn't going to spend the next three months sitting on the living room couch, staring into space.

The doctor rose from his desk. "You can call me with any

questions," he said. "If you want to wait outside, I'll see if they can squeeze you in for the fitting today."

A few months ago, Alex was being fitted for clothes she'd model on the pages of magazines. Now she was being fitted for a plastic face mask that would cover her skull and protect her brain from the devastating radiation rays. It was so terribly unfair.

"I'm so sorry, Alex," I said, squeezing her hand again as we walked into the waiting room. I'd never felt more helpless.

"Do you really want to do this today?" I whispered as Alex and I sat down on a cracked brown leather couch. "We can wait if you're not ready."

"It's fine," Alex said. She picked up a dog-eared golfing magazine and flipped through it so quickly I knew she wasn't reading a word.

"Talk to me," I begged. "Please."

She shook her head, her blue-green eyes—the one feature her tumor hadn't changed—averted from mine. "Just let me get through this and go home."

I lowered my head, wondering what I could say to help Alex. I was supposed to be the problem solver in the family. So why couldn't I fix this? Why couldn't I find a way to reach her?

When I looked back up, a boy who appeared to be no older than ten was entering the waiting room with his parents. He was on the skinny side, with a sprinkling of freckles across his nose. His head was swathed in a fresh white bandage, and his face bore the same telltale puffiness as Alex's.

". . . coach said next season for sure," the mother was saying as they entered the room.

"Yeah," the boy said listlessly. His big brown eyes were echoes of his mother's. But her eyes looked pinched and worried, and contradicted the bright tone of her voice.

"We can shoot free throws this afternoon," the dad said, patting the boy on the shoulder. His hand lingered there. "If you're up to it."

"Okay," the boy said, again without any enthusiasm.

They all sat down on a couch opposite ours, with each parent claiming a spot on either side of their son. Something about that spoke volumes: It was as though even here, in the safety of the waiting room, they wanted to sandwich their boy between them so they could protect him.

I was looking at the fresh Spider-Man Band-Aid near the inside of the boy's left elbow and realizing he must've just had some blood work done when someone spoke up. It took me a second to realize who the voice belonged to.

It was Alex's.

"Are you a Wizards fan?" Alex asked, motioning to a hardcover book the kid was holding on his lap. I looked over at my sister in surprise. She'd dropped her magazine, and she was looking at the boy, really looking at him. The vacant expression was gone from her face.

"Yeah," the boy said, looking down at the book. Its cover featured a color photograph of a guy dunking.

"I met him once, you know," Alex said, gesturing to the star center on the cover of the book.

"Yeah?" the kid asked, but now, for the first time, the dullness in his tone was replaced by a spark of interest. "You really met him?"

"He told me he had a clubfoot when he was born," Alex said. "He had to have three operations when he was a kid. And now look at him. He's one of the best athletes around. What did he shoot last season? Eighty-nine percent in free throws?"

"For real?" the boy said, wrinkling his little forehead. "He had three operations?"

"He spent a lot of time in hospitals," Alex said. "He hated it, but it made him better."

"Do you have a tumor?" the boy asked Alex. I'd forgotten how kids did that; they always cut to the heart of a sensitive matter without the dancing around and delicate words adults used. Somehow it was a relief.

"Yep," Alex said. She took off her hat. By now her hair was a bit longer; a spiky crew cut. She ran a hand over it and grimaced. "It sucks, doesn't it?"

The boy nodded, but he didn't say anything.

"At first I was really scared," Alex said. "Then I got mad."

"Me too," the boy said. "I can't play basketball this year."

"Wow," Alex said. "That does suck. What position do you play?"

"Center," the boy said proudly.

"Just like him," Alex said, pointing to the book.

"Excuse me, but aren't you—" the mother said. "I mean, I think I've seen you somewhere before. And your voice is so familiar."

"I'm Alex," Alex said. She didn't say anything else—she didn't slip into her public persona, or smile her bright TV smile, or acknowledge that yes, the woman had seen her before, probably twice a week on her television screen.

"What else did he say?" the boy asked Alex.

She smiled. "Guess what he ate for lunch when I was talking to him?"

"What?" the boy asked.

"French fries with mustard and hot sauce," Alex said.

The boy wrinkled his nose, then looked at his mom. "Can I try that?"

"Sure, honey," she said, squeezing his knee.

I sat there in wonder, staring at my sister as she kept chatting to the boy and comforted him so subtly he didn't realize that was what she was trying to do.

Alex doesn't need me to fix this for her, I suddenly thought. She's going to figure out a way to fight through it herself.

"Center, huh?" Alex said. She was smiling at the boy again. "You must be pretty good."

"I am," the boy said proudly. His thin legs were too short for his feet to touch the floor, and they began to swing back and forth.

"Can you take your dad in free throws?" Alex asked. "He looks pretty tall."

"I beat him last week," the boy said. One of his front teeth was missing, and that made me ache for him all the more. Here he was, trapped in the hospital, while the joys and milestones of childhood passed him by. How many birthdays and Halloweens and basketball games would he have to miss?

"But I bet you won't beat me today," his dad said. "I'm feeling good today."

"I'll still beat you," the boy said, grinning.

I saw the boy's father reach into his pocket for a handkerchief and pretend to cough while surreptitiously wiping his eyes. *Thank you,* he mouthed to Alex.

I didn't care what those scans said, I thought fiercely. Because the scans were wrong. Alex was going to be just fine.

Thirty-two

"STOP MOVING," I INSTRUCTED Alex.

"You've gotten bossier lately," she said. "And I feel compelled to tell you it's not completely becoming."

"Sssh," I said. I traced my dove gray eyeliner along her upper lash line and used my pinkie to smudge it. "Just a little more," I murmured, almost to myself. "Damn, you have perfect eyebrows."

"I'd say something modestly charming, but I'm not allowed to talk," Alex said.

I grinned and stepped back, then reached into my makeup kit again.

"Where'd you get all this stuff?" Alex asked. "I thought you hated makeup."

"A little more blush," I decided. "Suck in your cheeks."

"I *am* sucking in," Alex said. "Fucking steroids. I'm like a chipmunk hoarding nuts for the winter."

"Sorry," I said. But after a second, she burst into laughter, and so did I. Would I have the courage to laugh at myself if I was facing my first radiation treatment tomorrow? I wondered. I was learning more about my sister every day. Learning more, and liking her more, too. Of course, some of the things she did drove me crazy. She never rinsed out the sink after she'd finished using it. And she left her shoes everywhere, instead of stacking them on the pretty little shelf I'd bought and put by the front door.

"Slob," I'd mutter, lining them up.

"Anal," she'd shoot back. "Mom, you know you potty-trained Lindsey too early, right? And now we're all paying the price."

But we were talking every night now, really talking late into the night, making up for all those years of silence. We weren't strangers anymore.

Now I studied her face in the bathroom light and reached for my gold shimmery highlighter.

"Remind me why I'm doing this for you?" Alex asked as I stroked it over her brow bone.

"Because I need the practice," I lied. "I have to make up one of my clients for a big date and I need a guinea pig."

"Nice," Alex said. "Calling Steroid Girl a pig."

I grinned. "Keep your lips still," I ordered her.

I found my rose-colored liner, and I traced the outline of her lips. Her upper lip was a little fuller than her lower one, which gave her mouth a slightly exotic look. I had similar lips, I realized, only mine were a tiny bit bigger. Why had I never noticed that before? Alex and I actually had something in common physically. When you saw us side by side, you'd never know we were related, but if you isolated that single feature, you could just barely see the resemblance.

"Almost done," I said. I reached into the shopping bag I'd put next to my makeup case and pulled out a scarf. It was a bold Pucci print in swirling pinks and blues and creams. When I'd seen it in Nordstrom, tied around the waist of a mannequin, it had made me think of summer. I'd picked out a half dozen scarves for Alex, but this one was the prettiest.

"Is your client bald, too?" Alex asked drily as I tied the scarf around her head and adjusted the ends so they trailed down her back.

I still wasn't sure if I was doing the right thing or if this would all backfire. But sometimes, like Matt says, you just have to jump.

"You look great," I said, tossing her another bag. "Here are some jeans and a new shirt. Go change."

"What's going on?" Alex asked. She looked down at the Nordstrom bag suspiciously.

Just then, the doorbell rang. Perfect timing.

"Do you want to answer it or change first?" I asked. "It's for you."

"I want you to tell me what's going on," Alex demanded. She seemed panicked.

"Just open the door," I said. "Come on."

"I'm not ready to see him yet," Alex said. Her voice rose to a shriek. She wrapped her arms around herself, like she was trying to hide her body. "Why are you pushing me, damn it?"

When the doorbell rang a second time, Alex ran into her room and slammed the door so loudly the sound reverberated through the house.

I sighed and slowly walked to the front door. There he was, standing on the doorstep, his eyes full of hope.

"I'm sorry," I said. "I tried, but . . ." I didn't have to finish my sentence. I'd called Bradley today and told him that Alex was emerging from her self-imposed exile, that something had changed when she'd comforted the little boy with a tumor. I'd told him I thought she was ready to finally see him.

The hurt spreading across Bradley's face was a terrible thing to see.

"Can I come in?" he asked. I saw then he had his guitar case with him.

"Sure," I said. "Of course."

"Where is she?" he asked. I led him down the hall to her closed door. "You can knock if you want," I said. "I think she knows it's you. But don't be upset if she doesn't answer . . . I'm sorry, Bradley."

He nodded and opened his guitar case. The guitar inside wasn't an expensive one; in fact, I was pretty sure it was the same old battered one he had been lugging around since high school. He pulled it out and strummed a few chords. Suddenly I remembered something: Last year, Gary had taken Alex to a private party—a charity gala where tickets cost five thousand dollars a pop—and Sting had appeared and sung three of his classic songs. Alex had even gotten her photo taken with him. ("I could barely look at him without thinking of the Tantric sex," she'd told me. "He's tiny, but holy God, what a stallion!") And now here was Bradley, with nothing but his battered old guitar, sitting cross-legged on the worn carpet in front of Alex's room.

He cleared his throat and finished tuning his guitar, and then he began to sing. It was an old Beatles song, I realized after a moment.

Oh, Bradley, I thought. So what if his voice wasn't all that good? What girl wouldn't choose him over Gary with his private fund-raisers and celebrities and three-hundred-dollar bottles of wine? Who wouldn't rather be with Bradley?

"Here, there, and everywhere," Bradley sang, his voice gaining strength. ". . . watching her eyes and hoping I'm always there . . ."

Bradley was strumming louder now, putting his heart into his song. His voice cracked once, but he kept on singing. He kept trying to reach Alex.

Open the door, I willed her. Don't do this to him. He doesn't deserve to be shut out.

Bradley just kept singing. Somehow I suspected he'd stay there all night if he had to. But after just a few minutes, I saw it: The doorknob turned ever so slightly. It stopped moving for a second, then it turned the rest of the way and the door opened. Not all the way open. But just enough for Bradley to stand up and slip inside.

"Okay," I whispered. I blinked back tears—tears of happiness for Alex, and maybe some of sadness for me. Because that door opening meant the one between Bradley and me would stay forever closed.

"Okay," I said again. I pushed away my tears with the palms of my hands and stood there, wondering what to do next. This would be the last time I'd ever cry about this, I vowed. One final cry, and then I'd move on for good.

I put a few tissues in my pocket, then I grabbed the car keys and went out for a long drive.

Thirty-three

IT WAS DARK OUT, and I could hear the summer's first crickets singing as I stood on the broken walkway, shining my flashlight up over the house. I'd thought it might look spooky at night, with all the cobwebs and the jagged mouth of a window in the upstairs bedroom, but as I stared at it, I realized it just looked lonely. I made my way up the creaky porch steps and fitted my new key into the lock.

A few hours ago, I'd sat in the office of a title company and flipped through dozens of papers, signing my name at the bottom of each one. As of 3:00 P.M. today, after weeks of negotiating with the druggie son in the commune, I owned this house. It still seemed surreal.

I shifted my purse higher up onto my shoulder and played my flashlight over the walls of the living room. In the semi-darkness, the inside of the house didn't look so bad. The shadows hid the cracks in the plaster and the buckling floorboards. I carefully climbed the stairs and peered into the master bedroom, my eyes roving over the huge, arched windows, the fireplace with its wrought-iron screen, the delicate crown molding around the ceiling. This house had no idea what was in store for it. It was going to be so beautiful when I was finished with it.

I walked over to the bedroom window and unlatched it and let it swing open. I leaned out and breathed in the heavy, damp air and closed my eyes.

Something had happened to me, something I couldn't explain or even fully understand. It was as though a rupture had formed deep inside of me the day I'd gotten fired, splitting everything that was familiar to me into jagged shapes. These past months had been strange and sometimes frightening, but I'd felt more alive than I had in a long time. Maybe ever. Accepting May's offer and buying this house meant I'd made a decision: I was embracing the unexpected new contours of my life rather than piecing the safe old ones back together. I was moving down a new path, one with twists and turns that camouflaged what lay ahead, and I had no idea where I would end up

Earlier today, as I'd poured May a fresh cup of tea, I'd broached something I'd been turning over in my mind. "Maybe down the line, we could think about opening up another branch," I'd said.

May had taken a sip, then nodded thoughtfully. "We could."

"I'm not saying we'd have to," I'd said. "It was just an idea."

"I've thought about it before, too," May had said, stretching out her legs. "We could try to take our company into New York and Baltimore and Philly. We could even go national. Of course, it would change the nature of our work. We'd have to make sure that's what we really wanted to do."

It would mean more travel, and longer hours, I'd realized. And more money and prestige. Someday we might decide to look into it. Right now, though, I was content with not knowing exactly what the future held.

For the first time in my life, uncertainty didn't terrify me.

I wasn't the only one whose life had split apart, of course.

When I'd climbed into the attic the other day to finally sort and put away all the old papers I'd pulled out of boxes, I'd seen something: Alex's modeling portfolio. It was lying beside a stack of papers, as though she'd just dropped it there and walked away without looking back. I sat down and opened the black leather book and stared at the glossy photos and tear sheets from magazines: Alex kneeling on the beach in a gauzy white shirt that hit her at midthigh, looking sleepily sexy; Alex in a long red dress and diamond necklace, her hair upswept and elegant; Alex in a tiny bikini, her head thrown back and her stomach muscles glistening with oil. Funny how I saw those photos differently now. They weren't evidence that Alex had won the genetic lottery, leaving me with the doggie bag of leftovers; they were beautiful illusions she'd worked impossibly hard to create. Four bites of dessert a week, I thought, shuddering, as I closed the portfolio. Looking back over your shoulder at the thirteen-year-olds chasing you. What a way to live.

Funny how Alex and I had both been so wrapped up in our identities, never suspecting that things could change in a heartbeat. But Alex was already moving on. She was spending every possible second with Bradley, and they seemed incredibly happy, despite the fact that Alex was enduring nausea because of her daily radiation treatments. Bradley was the one who took her to the hospital most days, and he paced outside the room until she was finished.

These days when he came to pick her up, he didn't wait in his car for her. He came inside, and sometimes, if Alex wasn't ready yet, we chatted casually.

When Bradley had to work, I drove Alex to treatment, and afterward we went out for the plain bagels and ginger ale that helped settle her stomach. Sometimes we talked, and other times we shared the newspaper and sat in companionable silence. And a few nights ago, I'd walked into her bedroom and

discovered her reading a catalog from the University of Maryland.

"Anything interesting?" I'd asked.

"Maybe." She'd shrugged a shoulder. "There are a few classes
this fall that look pretty good."

I smiled now, thinking of it. Alex the businesswoman. And
me with my old, falling-apart house and closet full of sexy
clothes and low-stress job.

No one who'd known me in New York would've believed it.

No one except Matt, who'd cheered me on every step of
the way of my transformation, and had consoled me when I'd
phoned and told him the whole tangled story about me and
Alex and Bradley. Ever since then, Matt and I had grown even
closer, talking and texting nearly every day. This morning, when
I'd gotten cold feet about writing the check for my house, he
was the one I'd called for reassurance.

"It's me," I'd said when he'd answered the phone.

"Hey, you," he'd said in his familiar voice, and I'd instantly
felt better.

"Can you talk?" I'd asked.

"God, yes. Would you believe I'm on the Hormel account?"
he'd said. "If I have to look at any more photos of pork products, I'm going to start oinking. I'm trying to decide which is
Spam's best side."

"Definitely the right side," I'd said. "I think Spam's agent put
a clause in its contract saying that it can only be photographed
from the right."

Matt had laughed. I'd pictured him leaning back, his feet
up on his desk, holding a mug of the mocha-flavored coffee he
loved so much.

"So it's the same old thing there, huh?" I'd asked.

"Actually, no. I've got a little news for you," he'd said, and I'd
heard the smile in his voice.

"Let me guess," I'd said. "Cheryl got bigger implants."

"Even better. Cheryl got dumped."

"Are you kidding?"

"She was dying to become Mrs. Fenstermaker the fourth, but Fenstermaker is dating one of the Gloss models now. And Cheryl has to stare at the model's face every time she works on the account. I have a feeling Fenstermaker might yank his business any day now. Cheryl's campaign isn't doing too well."

"You have no idea how happy that makes me," I'd sighed.

"Someone may have typed up a sign that says 'Karma is a bitch' and taped it to Cheryl's computer."

"Someone?"

"Some mysterious guy. A kind of superhero-like figure, really."

"I always thought you'd look good in a cape," I'd said.

"But not the superhero underwear and tights," Matt had said. "That undercuts the whole macho thing."

We'd talked for an hour.

Now I unlocked my front door and stepped inside. I looked around at my cobwebby walls and sheet-shrouded furniture, then I reached into my purse and pulled out a brown paper bag. Inside was a miniature bottle of Moët. It was time to replace my bad associations with champagne with good ones.

I popped the cork and watched the vapor rise like a ghost from the mouth of the bottle. I sat down on the floor of my living room and took a sip, then I splashed a few drops into the air, so my house could celebrate along with me.

"Cheers," I said, lifting the bottle in a toast.

The doorbell rang.

The doorbell? I almost laughed out loud; something in my house actually worked. Probably someone collecting for the Sierra Club. I stood up and brushed the dust off my jeans.

"Who is it?" I called through the door.

"Pizza guy."

"I didn't order a pizza," I shouted.

Though maybe I shouldn't be so quick to send him away; I'd skipped lunch.

"Says here one extra large black olive and mushroom."

"But I—" Then it hit me and I yanked open the door. "It's you!"

"It's me," Matt agreed.

"But you were in New York," I babbled.

"This morning I was," he said. "But there's this new invention called a train."

"You took a train?" I still couldn't believe it. Matt was *here*. He was the first person to see my house. Suddenly it made me so glad.

"First things first," Matt said, stepping inside and looking around for a place to put the pizza box before setting it down on the floor. "Tammy and I broke up."

"I'm sorry," I said. And I truly was, if it meant Matt was hurting.

"It was a long time coming," he said.

"What happened?"

He paused for a long moment. "She didn't make me laugh."

"Oh," I said. My heart pounded faster. My palms grew moist. It was just *Matt*, I told myself. Matt, the best friend I'd ever had. Matt, who made me laugh and took care of me. Matt, who had the warmest brown eyes I'd ever seen.

My Matt.

"That's not the only reason we broke up," Matt said. "Remember when you told me a while ago about that guy you and your sister both liked? Something weird happened."

"What?" I whispered.

"I got jealous."

I looked into his eyes and remembered him in his red fleece jacket, standing on the platform as my train pulled away, his face so sad without his big smile. I thought about the night we'd watched *Casablanca* and how I'd caught him staring at me instead of the movie, even though it was his all-time favorite. I saw his hand reaching out between us on the table at Ruby Foo's.

"I kept telling you to jump," he said. "Now it's my turn."

I felt something unfurling inside of me, something that had been closed up like a fist.

"What I can't figure out is if this is a recent thing, or if I've loved you all along," Matt said. "Maybe it took you leaving to make me realize it."

"You love me?" I whispered.

"I love everything about you," he said. "I love the way you skip dinner when you're dieting and then eat a pint of ice cream later because you get so hungry. I love the way you line up your pencils at right angles to your stapler. I love how you're looking at me so seriously right now with this big smudge of dust on your nose."

He stepped closer to me and gently rubbed it off with the pad of his thumb.

Everything seemed to swirl around me as I stood there, inside my new life, the one rich with so many possibilities. Inside my new house. And inside Matt's arms.

It was exactly where I wanted to be.

Acknowledgments

MY FIRST READER IS always my father, John Pekkanen, and he's the best editor and writer I know. Dad, I've got a proposal: I'll forget about the surprise in your voice when you said, "Hey, you might actually be able to get this thing published!" and you forget about that little incident involving me and the nocturnal break-in at the neighborhood swimming pool. Deal?

Lynn Pekkanen, my mother, is a fine editor in her own right—and the most supportive one I could wish for. Thanks for believing, Mom. And thanks to my brothers Robert and Ben, both excellent writers themselves, who encouraged and harassed me along the way.

I'm lucky to have three sisters-in-law who read early chapters and gave me good critiques: Saadia Pekkanen, Tammi Lee Hogan, and Carolyn Reynolds Mandell. And other readers improved this book in countless ways: Rachel Baker, Anita Cheng, Lindsay Maines, Janet Mednick, and the gang in Hildie Block's class at the Writer's Center, especially Rick. And my gratitude to Susan Coll, for inspiration and guidance over sushi.

Chandra Greer generously taught me about the world of advertising, and Mike Langley and Karl Wenzel also helped fill in the gaps. The book *Adventures of an Advertising Woman* by Jane Maas provided both a rollicking good read and some valuable background. I hope in creating Lindsey's fictional agency I didn't stretch the facts too much—but if I did, please feel free to blame Mike.

I've been so touched by the warm welcome I've gotten from book bloggers, who have generously mentioned *The Opposite of Me* on their websites and let me post guest blogs. Thank you all for championing books, and for supporting not just me but so many other authors.

My agent, Victoria Sanders, is as smart and kind as they come—and her dedication is unmatched. Here's proof: She once emailed me from the dentist's chair. Victoria, I hope I'm lucky enough to work with you for many, many years. Victoria's editorial director, Benee Knauer, pored over this manuscript and helped shape it from page one. Benee, thank you, thank you, thank you. My appreciation also to Chris Kepner in Victoria's office.

Chandler Crawford helped this book see the world—my deep gratitude to her and to my publishers in foreign countries.

When it came time for my agent to submit this book, the name of one editor was at the top of my dream list. Greer Hendricks, you are my literary Harvard! I knew your reputation as being the best in the business. What I didn't know was how kind and warm you would be—and how good you are at coming up with book titles. Thanks also to Greer's assistant, Sarah Walsh, for helping in innumerable ways during this process, and to the entire team at Atria, including Judith Curr, Kathleen Schmidt, Jessica Purcell, Carole Schwindeller, Sarah Cantin, Anna Dorfman, and the amazing sales team. I can't imagine a better home for a novelist. And my deep appreciation to Jennifer Weiner, for her support and suggestions.

I've been fortunate to learn about writing from some wonderful newspaper and magazine editors, starting with Jack Limpert at *The Washingtonian*, who gave me my first job in the business, possibly against his better judgment. Thanks to Leland Schwartz for hiring me at the late, great States News Service and to David Grann, Marty Tolchin, and Al Eisele at *The Hill*. My gratitude also to Jeff Stinson and Judy Austin at Gannett. The day John Carroll gave me a job at *The Baltimore Sun* will always stand out in my memory. Thank you, John, for fighting the good fight for storytelling, and for allowing me to work with Jan Winburn, who showed me how it's done. Steve Hull of *Bethesda Magazine* is the kind of editor every writer should have—supportive, enthusiastic, and whip-smart. Finally, to my friend Bill Marimow, now at the helm of *The Philadelphia Inquirer*. Bill is that rare individual who seems happiest when he is helping others succeed. Thanks for everything, Bill. Our next round of beers is on me.

An extra biscuit to Bella for warming my feet while I wrote.

And to my husband, Glenn Reynolds, and our sons, Jack, Will, and Dylan. You all make me so happy, every day.

The

Opposite

of
Me

SARAH PEKKANEN

A Readers Club Guide

QUESTIONS AND TOPICS FOR DISCUSSION

1. When you first encounter Lindsey Rose, what is your reaction to her workaholic attitude? Do you see it as justifiable in her profession?

2. Lindsey's nemesis in the office is Cheryl, and Lindsey is upset by how Cheryl uses her sexuality to advance her job. What do you think of Cheryl's tactics? Is Lindsey right to be so opposed to them?

3. What is your opinion of Alex, Lindsey's sister? Lindsey views Alex's life as flawless—do you agree with that characterization? Are there any clues you noticed that showed her life may be less than wonderful?

4. How would you describe the dynamic between Alex and Lindsey? How does being twins affect their relationship as adults, especially since Alex received so much attention growing up?

5. What did you think of the sisters' parents? Do you see their bumbling, funny personalities as having a balancing effect on their daughters?

6. When Lindsey hides in the bathroom and overhears how much Cynthia Givens's employees dislike their boss, why does it have such a big effect on her?

7. After Lindsey's shopping spree, how did her personality change? Was this just a superficial adjustment for her, or did it have a deeper effect? And why did she hide it from her parents and Alex?

8. Why do you think Lindsey didn't want to be with Bradley when they were younger? Did something else come into play besides the fact that Lindsey wasn't ready for a "real" relationship?

9. Describe the relationship between May and Lindsey. In what ways were their previous lives—Lindsey as an executive, May as a political wife—similar? In what ways did May rub off on Lindsey, and vice versa?

10. How does Alex's medical condition affect the relationship between the sisters? Was such a major event the only way they could start over, or do you think they would have eventually formed a better relationship anyway?

11. Do you think it's common for people to be assigned certain roles in their family—like the "pretty" sister or the "smart" one—and do you think those labels are fair? Were they fair to Lindsey and Alex? Do you feel like you have a certain label in your own family? Do you think it fits you?

12. How did Alex's flirtation with Bradley affect Lindsey's feelings for him? Do you believe Lindsey would've fallen for Bradley if he and Alex hadn't connected first? Do you think Lindsey would have been happy with Bradley if they'd ended up together?

13. How do you feel about the relationship that suddenly develops between Matt and Lindsey? Do you think it will last? Do you see Lindsey being happy staying in Maryland? Or do you think she will return to New York City?

14. Lindsey's mantra throughout the later part of the story was to "jump." How did she eventually learn to do this? How has she changed since the story began?

A CONVERSATION WITH SARAH PEKKANEN

What was the inspiration for your book? Is it based on any real events in your life?

Nope, it's pure fiction. I'm lucky to have two brothers I adore, but I've always wondered what it would be like to have a sister. I'm fascinated by the rich, complex relationships my friends have with their sisters. So when it came time to write *The Opposite of Me,* I made the relationship between Lindsey and Alex as messy and loving and complicated and competitive as possible.

I'm also intrigued by the way people get assigned certain labels in their families, like the "smart" one, the "pretty sister," the "drama queen," or the "peacemaker." What if those labels don't fit how we feel inside? What if they're all wrong for who we are really meant to be?

What do you think the term "chick lit" means today? Is it what you would consider this story?

I think "chick lit" refers to fun, smart books about women

who are figuring out their choices in life. As in every other genre, there is a wide range of books—some better than others. I'm not sure if *The Opposite of Me* will be classified as chick lit. I'm just hoping people will think of it as a good book!

Have you had bosses like the ones in the story? Or were you that type of driven employee yourself?

Luckily, I've never had the kind of bosses Lindsey had in New York (though I've had several bosses who turned into friends, like May did with Lindsey). I'm not especially driven—I watch far too much reality TV and I have a love affair with Sunday afternoon naps—but I am passionate about writing. I can't imagine my life without it. It's what I've wanted to do ever since I was a child, when I used to get in trouble in school for not paying attention and wandering into the wrong classroom ten minutes after the bell rang. I was busy creating stories in my mind—and I still do it today, which means I often miss my exit on the highway and don't realize it until half an hour later. By the way, my husband just *loves* this quality in me.

You are from Maryland yourself; did you find it easier to write about an area you knew?

Definitely. I knew it would be fun to write about my hometown and give cameos to my favorite spots and restaurants. But someday I'd love to stretch my imagination and create a fictional town as a setting, too. Can you imagine the sense of power as you create tall buildings and lakes and highways while you sip your morning cup of coffee?

Why did you decide to make Lindsey and Alex twins? Do you think it creates a special bond or competition between them?

I've always heard that twins do have a special connection,

and some even create their own language as babies, or have a physical reaction at the precise moment something bad happens to the other one miles away. But when I sat down to write, I wondered what would happen if Lindsey and Alex were complete opposites. What if they had absolutely nothing in common, yet were constantly compared because they were twins? How would that shape their relationship?

The parents are such lovable, fun characters. Are they based on your own parents, or were you just hoping to add a light-hearted touch to the story?

Thank you! They're completely fictional, although my parents read *The Opposite of Me* and expressed suspicion about a few similarities (My parents adore Ikea's low-priced breakfasts, lingonberries and all.) I love books that make me laugh, so I wanted Lindsey and Alex's parents to provide some comic relief. I grew really fond of the parents, and hope readers will, too.

Have you ever gone on a blind date? Why was it a field you decided to throw Lindsey into?

I've never been on a real blind date—I can only imagine the angst and phone calls to my friends and quantity of hair care products involved!—but I thought a dating service would provide such great material for a novel that I couldn't resist making it Lindsey's new workplace. It was interesting to dream up all the reasons why someone would seek out a dating service, and I tried to give Lindsey an eclectic mix of clients.

I'm sure everyone is curious: Is honey on popcorn actually good?

Ooh, it's so good. One of my sons' babysitters made it that way once, and I loved it. As Alex says, it's "worth the sticky fingers." Try it!

Finally, what projects are you working on now?

I'm diving into the next book, which isn't a sequel and doesn't have a title yet. (I'm terrible at coming up with titles; my editor dreamed up *The Opposite of Me* after I suggested a few clunkers.) And I'm gearing up to meet with lots of groups and book clubs who want to discuss *The Opposite of Me*—please contact me via my website at www.sarahpekkanen.com if you'd like me to visit or phone in to chat with your group!